PEBBLE
& DOVE

Also by Amy Jones

Every Little Piece of Me (2019)

We're All in This Together (2016)

What Boys Like (2009)

PEBBLE & DOVE

Amy Jones

McCLELLAND & STEWART

McClelland & Stewart and colophon are registered trademarks of
Penguin Random House Canada Limited.

Library and Archives Canada Cataloguing in Publication data
is available upon request.

ISBN: 978-0-7710-9931-1
ebook ISBN: 978-0-7710-9932-8

The epigraph is from the song "Rock and Bird," by Michael Edward
Timmins, performed by Cowboy Junkies. Lyrics © Paz Junk Music Inc,
Peermusic Publishing. Reprinted with permission.

This is a work of fiction. Names, characters, places, and incidents either are the
product of the author's imagination or are used fictitiously. Any resemblance
to actual persons, living or dead, events, or locales is entirely coincidental.

Text and cover design by Kelly Hill
Cover images: (jungle) L Feddes / Getty Images; (manatee) Morphart
Creation / Shutterstock Images; (beach ball) HSNKRT / Adobe Stock;
(background) Zerbor / Adobe Stock

Typeset in Adobe Caslon Pro by M&S, Toronto
Printed in Canada

McClelland & Stewart,
a division of Penguin Random House Canada Limited,
a Penguin Random House Company
www.penguinrandomhouse.ca

1 2 3 4 5   27 26 25 24 23

Penguin
Random House
McCLELLAND & STEWART

For my parents, Richard Jones and Shelagh Hagen

And in memory of Snooty, a.k.a Baby Snoots (1948–2017)

And rock became her anchor, and bird became her dream.

Cowboy Junkies, "Rock and Bird"

PEBBLE
& DOVE

Ray

Once there was a ship that contained the ocean.

I know this ship as well as I know myself. As well as I know you, Rayna. As well as I know the contours of your jaw, the delicate skin behind your knees, the arrhythmic beating of your faulty heart, *beat-squish, beat-squish*. Better, even, than I ever knew your mind, which to me has always been like one of those hedgerow mazes—a dozen different turns you could take, but only the one way that will lead you to the centre.

You know this ship too, although I'm sure there have been many times you wished you didn't. But you asked me for a story, Rayna, and this is where it has to begin—the same place I always begin, all the other times I tried and failed to tell you this story before.

The ship was called the *Prins Viggo*. One of the last great behemoths of the sailing ship era, she was a four-masted Danish barquentine navy training vessel, and built for war at a time when war was over—at least temporarily, as war is never really over. She served as a blockade runner for the Germans before being sold to an American trading company and used to transport coconuts to Florida from the Caribbean. Even now, the lower decks hold the nutty-sweet scent of the milk spilled from cracked shells, and occasionally I come across a long, fibrous tentacle of husk lodged in the floorboards.

On what was to be the *Prins Viggo*'s final sailing, her captain, drunk on bootlegged rum, misjudged the radius as he piloted out of the turning bay of Sunset Harbour, and raked the hull against the pilings of the dock. The ship capsized, snapping the foremast in two and blocking off traffic to the inner harbour for over a week before she could be righted. By the time the *Prins Viggo* was finally towed to shore, her captain and crew had already fled, and the company that owned the ship quietly sold it to a fellow named Harry Sharples, an entrepreneur and self-professed "man of adventure" who planned to keep the ship docked at the Flamingo Key Marina and turn her into a floating hotel. This was during the great Florida land boom of the 1920s, after they began to drain the Everglades and money seemed to be falling from the sky. Sharples's team worked on the ship for over two years, but even with all the repairs, state officials deemed her unsafe for habitation, famously saying that "the only beings fit to stay here are the creatures that live in the water below it."

Sharples, ever the opportunist, took this as a sign. Within a year, he had the *Prins Viggo* encased in a steel bulkhead at the Flamingo Key Marina, and procured an assortment of over 2,500 fish and aquatic mammals—some from other aquariums, but most, as the state officials had foretold, from the water below it. And thus, in the spring of 1932, the Flamingo Key Aquarium and Tackle was established. Instead of wealthy men and women from around the world, now the *Prins Viggo* housed clownfish and piranha, otter and sea turtle, seahorse and hermit crab, octopus and manta ray—all enclosed behind glass built into the walls of the cabin.

The crowning glory of this floating aquarium was a West Indian manatee that Sharples himself had harpooned thirty-five miles up the coast. In those days, no one thought about man's dominance over the animal kingdom; manatees would not be put on the endangered species list until 1967, and even though hunting them was illegal, no one batted an eye when Sharples hooked her through the tail and dragged her back to Sunset behind his boat. It took twenty men and a series of winches to hoist the manatee up to the deck and into the concrete tub Sharples had built for her at the stern of the ship, tucked under a white-and-green-striped canvas tent and encircled by a wooden viewing platform with bleachers for guests. He didn't know the manatee was pregnant. The next year, she died in that same tank while giving birth. But her calf lived, becoming the first manatee born in captivity, and one of the few never to be released into the wild.

For decades, the aquarium was a truly magnificent place to visit. People came from far and wide to gaze in wonder at the mysterious creatures from the depths of the ocean, to applaud the feisty sea otters tumbling together over the plastic rock-slide, and to marvel at the gators staring out, unblinking, from their man-made pond. Sharples would throw glamorous parties onboard—the broken mast and the canvas tent adorned with a thousand twinkling lights, as men and women dressed in their finest evening wear drank martinis and listened to a jazz band amid the coral reefs and the eternally undulating jellyfish. But the star of the show was always the manatee, raised in a tank and nurtured by handlers. A manatee who had no natural fear of humans, and would happily perform for the hundreds of people who crowded into the pavilion to watch her swim through hoops, slide up onto the platform to give kisses, or roll over onto her back for belly rubs. She was something exotic and ethereal, seemingly from another time, with her twitching snout and mammoth body, her pectoral flippers reaching out for toys, food, even people, her eyes like tiny beads tucked into the folds of her elephantine hide. The people of Sunset couldn't get enough of her.

I wish I'd seen the aquarium in those early days, in all its Old Florida glory. But of course, I wasn't there for any of it. Not the coconuts or the mast cracking in two when the ship went over, nor when Sharples allegedly pushed the state official over the gunwale and into the Gulf when he rejected the permit application for the hotel. I wasn't there when he harpooned the manatee, or when the manatee calf was born, although sometimes, when I gaze into her eyes, I feel as though I was.

But I'm getting ahead of myself. It's so hard these days to think about time being linear. All the moments of our life together, big and small, seem to be stacked on top of one another, rather than spread out in front of me in a way that I can make sense of, that I can piece together into something resembling a story. The story you asked for, and the one you deserve to hear. It's a story that, until I met Imogen, I didn't understand I needed to tell you. A story that, until I met Dove, I didn't know I was ready to.

Lauren

It's late in the evening when Lauren and Dove finally reach Swaying Palms, south of Sunset, Florida, and just off the Tamiami Trail, that stretch of highway beginning in Tampa that hugs the Gulf Coast before veering off across the Everglades to Miami. Lauren nearly misses the turn—the faded sign is almost entirely obscured by a trio of dogwoods heavy with blooms, the streetlight above flickering like a strobe.

Beside Lauren, her daughter rests her head against the window, feet tucked beneath her. Dove has barely said a word since they left Lennox Heights sixteen hours ago, other than to ask how much further they have to go. But her curiosity gets the better of her as the car slows. She lifts her head, takes out her earbuds, and peers into the dark as they make their way through the eerily quiet grid of identical white trailers and neatly manicured squares of lawn. They creep down smooth, asphalt roads lined with streetlights and palm trees that do, in fact, sway in the evening breeze, casting shadows onto signs that say things like WELCOME TO PARADISE or I'M ON VACATION TIME. The inhabitants of

5

Swaying Palms are mostly retirees from the Midwest or Canada; most of them don't even stay for the entire year, packing up and driving back to Michigan or Ontario as soon as the temperature rises above eighty-five. But now, in mid-February, there is a sensible, just-washed sedan tucked into every driveway, the light of a television flickering behind each drawn blind.

The trailer belonging to Lauren's mother is lonely and unadorned in the midst of all this ordered chaos—windows shuttered, garden fallow. It's been uninhabited since Imogen died almost three months ago, and it certainly looks it. As she pulls into the driveway, Lauren notices someone has been tending to the landscaping—the lawn is freshly mown, and the palmettos have been trimmed back, away from the eavestrough. Even the driveway appears to have been recently power-washed. Thank god for small miracles.

"Well," she says, cutting the engine. "We're here."

Neither of them moves. Outside, the cicadas are singing at a frequency that works its way under Lauren's skin like an itch. Her body buzzes with forward momentum, but there is nowhere else to go. Suddenly, it's as if the weight of everything she's been trying not to think about has settled on her chest, like a heavy lead ball. She closes her eyes and tries to visualize rolling the ball off a cliff into a deep, bottomless chasm, but all she can picture is it rolling back over her.

"Is Dad coming?" Dove asks.

The sound of her voice startles Lauren's eyes open. "Daddy's in Peru, I told you," she says, her hands clenching involuntarily in her lap.

Dove rolls her eyes. She hasn't called Jason "Daddy" in years. "He's coming home in a few days."

"I know." Lauren's nails dig into her palms. It hadn't occurred to her until now that the text she got from Jason might not have been the only one he sent. "We'll see. Depends on how long we're going to be here."

How long are *we going to be here?* Dove's unspoken question hangs in the air, but Lauren is fluent in Dove's silences. She wishes she had an answer for her—to this, and to all the other questions that float between them.

Lauren opens the car door and steps outside. The humidity hits her like a damp towel, her hair immediately beginning to frizz above her ears. Around her, the darkness hums with life, the air thick with night-bloom and something else, a subtle rot beneath the surface.

"This is going to be really awesome," she says. "You'll see. A little vacation, just you and me." She turns around and peers back into the car. But Dove is already gone.

Inside the trailer, Lauren flips the light switch and is surprised when a dim bulb in the middle of the room flickers to life. In the dusty glow, she gazes around the main room, which contains the kitchen with a rickety card table, and a living room with a pullout couch, a wicker rocking chair, a shelf with a few books on it, and a television. To the right is the bedroom and the bathroom, and to the left is the sunroom. The kitchen appliances are a dingy off-white, and the floor is covered in pale yellow linoleum, bulging from the humidity and littered with insect carcasses. A tall lamp has toppled over. When she picks it up, a gecko springs out from under the shade and scurries across the room.

Lauren puts her duffle bag down on the table. *So this is it*, she thinks. *This is where my mother spent her final days.* She was expecting at least a quick whiff of Imogen's American Spirits, or a low-ball glass with her signature wine-coloured lipstick on the rim. But nothing about this place feels like Imogen, and she doesn't know if this is because there really isn't anything of Imogen left here, or because she wouldn't recognize it if there was.

She pushes open the door to the bedroom. The last time she was here, the room was off limits—her grandmother's domain. Lauren slept on the pullout with Imogen, their bodies as far apart as possible on the thin, uneven mattress, but the feeling of the sheet rising and falling with her mother's breathing was so uncomfortably intimate that Lauren was barely able to sleep. A queen-sized bed takes up most of the space now; it's meticulously made up, and she wonders if Imogen left it that way. Did she get out of bed on her last morning thinking she would return to it at the end of the day? Or did she suspect she wouldn't be sleeping in it ever again, and made sure her bedroom was presentable for whoever found it later? Lauren realizes she doesn't even know where her mother died. Was it here? In a hospital? Or god forbid she was out in public, on the bus or in the middle of a grocery store, the indignity of a stranger's hands doing chest compressions, their unfamiliar mouth against hers.

"Is this the only bedroom?" Dove asks, appearing behind her.

"Yup." Lauren folds her arms across her chest, an unexpected chill moving through her body. "You can have it, if you want." She wonders if she should leave the room as it is or strip the bed, wash the sheets, flip the mattress, maybe perform an exorcism before letting her daughter sleep in it.

Dove tentatively presses her hand against the mattress. "Where will you sleep?"

"The couch is a pullout." Lauren doesn't want to sleep there either, but she doesn't have any other options. She really should have thought this through. "Let's open a window," she says, reaching for the blind cord and brushing away the cobwebs. When Lauren turns back around, Dove has already crawled under the sheets and kicked the comforter off the end of the bed. No exorcism tonight, then.

What must Dove think of this place? When Lauren woke

her daughter at five this morning and told her they were going to Florida for a vacation, Dove didn't ask any questions. But Lauren could see the surprise on her face just now when they pulled into the trailer park. This place must seem so wrong to her, the opposite of the picture she has in her head of her mysterious grandmother, who she met only once, and who Lauren never talks about. But when you're related to Imogen Starr, internationally famous portrait photographer and notorious libertine, it's hard not to envision a life of glamour and excess. Lauren would know. While Imogen travelled to exotic locales to photograph movie stars and party with the world's elite, Lauren spent her childhood imagining the life her mother was having without her.

This place isn't Imogen, Lauren wants to say, although she doesn't know if that's true. How did her mother end up here? What happened to her in the past ten years that left her broke and living in a trailer in Florida, that took her from designer gowns and Michelin-starred restaurants to caftans and canned tuna? Suddenly, she regrets never having told Dove anything about Imogen. Imogen might have been a terrible mother, but she was *Lauren's* terrible mother.

"You know, your grandmother . . ." Lauren stops. Where does she even start?

"What?" Dove mumbles, pulling the sheet up toward her face.

"She brought me here once. When I was your age."

Dove lifts her eyebrows. With the bottom half of her face covered by the sheet she looks exactly like Jason—same wide forehead, brown eyes, long lashes—and in spite of her anger toward him, Lauren's heart squeezes in her chest.

"Is that what this is?" Dove asks. "Some Starr woman rite of passage?"

"I guess. Yeah. That's what we'll call it. Tomorrow, the ritual cleansing of the sacred feminine in the Swaying Palms pool."

"Gross." Dove flips over, her phone lighting up in her hand.

When Lauren doesn't leave right away, Dove glares over her shoulder at her. And Lauren remembers why she's never told her anything about Imogen. She gets about four minutes of Dove's attention at any given time, and she doesn't want to waste it talking about her mother.

Dove

All Dove wanted was to get revenge on Chelsea and Madison. She thought about it during math class, watching Chelsea two seats ahead of her, her French-manicured fingernails fiddling with the small gold hoop in her ear, her equally golden hair cascading down her back. She thought about it walking to school in the morning, when Madison swooped by her in the brand-new turquoise vw bug she'd gotten for her sixteenth birthday, singing along to Ariana Grande and puffing on a vape pen. She dreamed about it at night, falling asleep with her Kazu app open to Chelsea and Madison's joint profile, where they posted videos of their "band," The Laura Lauras, playing terrible stripped-down covers of RuPaul songs on expensive acoustic guitars.

The idea came to her after she remembered something her mother, of all people, had said. And the plan came together easily once she made the decision. All she had to do was convince Yuri, the head of the Worley Academy Apiary Club, to lend her some bees for the afternoon. "I'll have them back to you by lunch," she told him, even though she wasn't sure how she was going to make that happen. And even though she didn't tell him what they were for, she knew that he knew. He hated Chelsea and Madison just as much as she did, ever since that time he got an erection in English class while giving a presentation on *Hamlet* and Chelsea said really loudly, "To jerk off or not to jerk off, that is the question." Dove took his willingness to participate as tacit approval.

Dove picked up the bees at noon, Yuri handing them off in a crate with a handle and wheels, like a rolling suitcase. She took the back hall that no one ever used to the girls' washroom by the art room, which Chelsea and Madison and their minions commandeered every lunch hour to do their makeup or practise giving blow jobs on cucumbers or whatever it was they did when they were together. Without giving herself time for second thoughts, Dove raised her phone, pressed record, and swung open the door.

Four perfectly made-up faces turned toward her with four perfectly matching expressions of scorn. "Oh look, it's Lurch," Madison said.

Chelsea laughed. "Where'd you get that outfit? The dumpster behind Goodwill?" She turned back to the mirror, applying a swipe of lip gloss. "Get the fuck out, freak."

Dove didn't respond. She just stared at Chelsea, held her phone up higher, and opened the top of the crate.

In retrospect, she's not sure what she thought was going to happen; maybe the bees would fly around or sting them once or twice before returning to the hive. Instead, all the bees went straight for Chelsea. The minions ran away, pushing past Dove as she continued filming from the doorway, Chelsea and Madison screaming as the bees congregated on Chelsea's head until she was wearing a living, humming, bee wig. Even now, after everything that happened, Dove can't help but laugh when she thinks about it: Chelsea screeching, her hand clamped on to Madison's arm. Madison trying to get free. The bees not giving a shit about any of it.

Chelsea and Madison had to stay in the washroom for over an hour, waiting for professional beekeepers to get the swarm back into the hive. Dove missed that part, having fled the scene as soon as she got enough footage, but later, Yuri texted that there was something about Chelsea's hairspray that made the bees want to protect her, like she smelled like a queen bee or something.

That's too on the nose, Yuri, Dove texted.

A couple of them landed there too, he replied.

If it had just been the bees, Dove might not have gotten into so much trouble. She dug her own grave by posting the video on Kazu. But she had to—otherwise what was the point of even doing it? The real revenge part was the humiliation of everyone seeing it. And even *that* might not have been too bad, except that the video went viral, and not viral like her other Kazu posts, the ones that might get shared 5,000 times—this one was everywhere. By the afternoon it was on Facebook and Instagram, on Reddit, on sketchy clickbait media outlets, probably on the bulletin board at the old folks' home. So of course Principal Matharu saw it. He called Dove into his office and told her that she had to take down the video and apologize to Chelsea and Madison in front of the whole school.

"But what about what *they* did?" Dove asked. Although she wouldn't normally talk back to a teacher, she wasn't a doormat. The bees and the video had been justified, and she wasn't responsible for what people did with it after she'd posted it. She shifted forward in the chair, but the slippery wood made it impossible for her to keep from sliding backward. "Why don't *they* have to apologize?"

Principal Matharu folded his hands in front of him on the desk, his moustache twitching. "They have been spoken to about that. But really, there is no comparing the two events, Ms. Sandoval. What you did to Ms. O'Keefe and Ms. Sawyer was potentially life-threatening. What they did was a harmless joke."

A sound between a squeal and a growl escaped from Dove's mouth before she could stop it. *A harmless fucking joke?* Did he not understand one single thing about teenage girls? Was she just supposed to stay quiet and take all the shit that was dumped on her and her friends, because they weren't rich or popular? Because they should just be grateful to be at Worley Academy at all? *Fuck grateful.* Before she had time to think about it, she grabbed Principal Matharu's coffee mug off his desk and dumped it in his lap. He leapt up, screaming, dark brown liquid running down the front of his khaki pants.

Dove opened Kazu and held up her phone, clicking record. "Let's see how you like it."

"Ms. Sandoval, give me your phone," he shrieked.

"Uh-oh, looks like Principal Matharu had a little accident," Dove said loudly.

He shoved back his chair and charged around the desk toward her. "Turn that off!"

Clicking the record button off, she tucked her phone back in her pocket. "What?" she asked sweetly. "It's just a harmless joke."

They stared at each other a moment. Then, without breaking eye contact, he picked up his phone and pressed a button. "Cheryl," he said, his voice flat. "Can you call Maria in the guidance office? And you'd better call Gerald Eddy, too." Dove stiffened. Principal Matharu calling in Vice Principal Eddy was like your mother telling you to *wait till your father gets home.* "And can you please come in and escort Ms. Sandoval to the waiting area?"

When they called her back in after what seemed like hours,

Principal Matharu was wearing a different pair of pants and Vice Principal Eddy was holding an envelope with her name on it. Dove knew immediately what it was.

"We just can't overlook this," Vice Principal Eddy said. "What you've done is an egregious violation of the school's anti-bullying bylaws. We could have let it go with a warning if you hadn't escalated it, but here we are."

Dove snatched the envelope out of his hand, her face growing hot with indignation and embarrassment. "Will Chelsea and Madison be expelled, too? Or did they not bully me hard enough?" No one responded. "Oh, right, they're not scholarship students, never mind." She could finally see Worley Academy for the fake, pretentious place it really was, and she didn't want to be a part of it anymore. At least, that was what she told herself as she was escorted to her locker to get her things.

Ten minutes later, Dove walked out the main doors of Worley Academy with a letter of expulsion in her hand. Dex and Kait were waiting for her on the front steps, crowded around Kait's phone.

"You didn't have to wait for me," Dove said.

"Are you kidding?" Dex said.

"We had to find out what happened after this," Kait added. They held up their phone, where the video Dove had taken of Principal Matharu was playing. "You're such a badass!"

"I'm not."

Dove took the expulsion letter out of the envelope so they could both read it. After a minute, Dex's eyes flicked up to meet hers. "Holy shit," he said.

Kait threw their arms around Dove. "What's your mom going to do?" they asked.

Dove pulled away and shrugged. "I have no idea," she said, crumpling the letter up and throwing it in the garbage can next to the entrance. *Whatever makes her come out looking the best, probably.*

For the rest of the afternoon, the three of them hung out in Dex's basement and played *Legends of Everrain* on their laptops and ate chocolate-covered espresso beans, not talking about what had happened or what was going to happen. Dove's phone was turned off the whole time, but it was like she could feel her Kazu notifications coming in, a constant gentle tapping like water dripping from a faucet reverberating through her body. Worse, she knew there must be a million voicemails from her mom or dad, or both—her mom already filling out applications for an even more pretentious private school with even nastier rich kids; her dad telling her to "keep vibin', kiddo" and how they could have a "rap sesh" when he got home. Then Dex's moms came home and Kait had to go for dinner, so Dove just walked around until after seven, when she knew her mom would be out at her bougie candle party.

All evening Dove sat on the couch in front of the television, watching the comments on the bee video stack up and bracing for a text or a call from her parents. But there was nothing. They were probably on the phone with each other right now. Maybe they'd seen the video and were proud of her for standing up for herself. Maybe her dad would even come home early, so they could figure out what to do, together. She waited, and waited, but no messages came. Finally, she fell asleep on the couch, the television playing softly, her phone still in her hand.

Hours later, as the sun was coming up, her mother shook her awake. Dove hadn't even heard her come home.

"Babes," she said. "Come on, wake up. You need to get packed."

"Where are we going?" Dove mumbled, rubbing the sleep from her eyes.

"Florida."

"For school?" she asked, confused.

"What? No. No school today. We're just going on a little trip."

"Where's Dad?"

"In Peru, babes. You know this."

Dove squinted at her mother. She was dishevelled and pale and reeking of Buddha's Fart or whatever those candles were supposed to smell like, and her yoga pants were on inside out. Had she been up all night, making plans to cart Dove off to some military school, or maybe a camp for juvenile delinquents where they'd have to live in the forest and grow their own food? How would she even know what to pack for that?

It wasn't until they reached North Carolina, when her mother said something about asking Dex to keep her apprised of homework, that it began to dawn on Dove that her mother didn't know she'd been kicked out of school. A few minutes later they pulled off the highway at a combination gas station/White Castle, and while her mother pumped gas, Dove snuck around the side of the building to call Dex.

"Why are you calling me? Who actually calls anyone anymore?"

"Because it might be an emergency?" Dove walked past the drive-thru, watching the White Castle girl pass bag after bag to a shirtless guy in a pickup truck. "I think my mom is kidnapping me."

"Your mom can't kidnap you. She's your mom."

"She can so. Haven't you learned anything from watching *Crime Files* with me?"

"I guess not. Where are you?"

"I don't know, a gas station somewhere off the I-95? We're driving to Florida. I mean, I'm being kidnapped to Florida."

She could almost hear Dex rolling his eyes through the phone. "Do you really think you're being kidnapped? Like, doesn't your grandmother live in Florida?"

"Yes, but she's not there right now; she's off travelling somewhere. And I'm worried that my mom is going to feed me to the alligators or something."

"What did she say about you getting expelled?"

"Nothing. Like, really nothing." Dove rounded the back of the building, startling two gas station employees on their smoke break. Giving them a little wave, she walked out further into the scrubby field, where a flock of seagulls were ripping apart a bag of garbage that had fallen out of a dumpster. Beyond, a rusty barbed-wire fence made a taut line between the seagulls and the cars whizzing by on the interstate. "I don't even know if she knows."

"How could she not know?"

"I mean, she's so spaced out! She has no idea what's going on anywhere anymore!" Dove sighed. "Fine, she's probably not going to feed me to the alligators. I just wanted to tell someone where I was, just in case."

"Fair." Dex yawned, and she pictured him lying on his couch, scrolling through all his gaming forums, which he treated like a full-time job. She wished so hard that she was there, stretched out across from him, reading a comic book and not worrying about anything except whether one of his moms would drive her home later.

"So, what's going on there?" Dove asked.

"Not much. We had that test today on the quadratic equation, the one you were freaking out about last week? It wasn't so bad."

"Not so bad for *you*. You're a math genius." She wanted him to keep talking, to tell her about everything that was happening at Worley. But suddenly the scrubby field she was standing in felt so far away. "I've gotta go," she said. "I'll keep you posted about the alligators."

"I'll watch for you on *Crime Files*," Dex said, before hanging up.

When Dove got back to the car, her mother was sitting in the driver's seat. The car wasn't on, there was no music playing, and she wasn't on her phone. She was just sitting there, blankly staring straight ahead. Dove watched her through the window for a moment, wondering if maybe she was having a stroke. But when Dove opened the door, Lauren smiled that weird smile she'd developed over the past few months, like she was an alien who'd learned how to mimic human facial expressions from watching movies. "There's some Combos and mini Skors in the back seat if you want some later," she said, starting the car.

"Thanks," Dove mumbled.

She spent the rest of the drive staring out the window and worrying about the buzzing in her stomach, as though in some kind of karmic justice her body was now filled with bees. And even though she knew it was impossible, her mind filled with images of bees floating through her lymphatic system, building hives in her internal organs, her veins and arteries dripping with honey. Even her favourite true crime podcast couldn't distract her—it just reminded her of how the world was full of bad people.

And she couldn't shake the feeling that maybe now she was one of them.

Lying in her grandmother's bed, staring at the water-stained ceiling, Dove picks up her phone. *Not dead yet*, she texts Dex. She waits for a response, but none comes. *Guess the alligators will go hungry for another day*, she adds. Still nothing. She tries to think of something else to say before realizing it's after midnight on a school night, and Dex is probably fast asleep, visions of quadratic equations dancing in his head.

She opens Kazu. She deleted the video of Principal Matharu almost immediately, but the video of Chelsea and Madison is still there. Forty thousand likes and counting. *Maybe I should delete that, too*, she thinks. But wouldn't that be letting them off the hook too easily? Shouldn't she wait for them to post an apology, or at least do something to show they've learned a lesson? Isn't that the whole point of all this? Or maybe leaving the video up is turning *her* into the bully. Wouldn't the easiest thing be to just take it down? But then she remembers something Nana once told her: *The right thing isn't always the easy thing.* She *wants* to do the right thing, but she's not sure what that is anymore, and she has no one to tell her. And there's a part of her that's worried that this is how it's going to be from now on—just her fumbling around, trying to figure shit out on her own and getting it wrong half the time. Is this what it's like to be an adult? How can you even live like that?

Above her, she hears a scratching noise, then a scrabbling over the metal roof. She wishes Nana were here. There was a brief moment in the car, between turning into Swaying Palms and driving up to the trailer, when she thought maybe this was an elaborate plan to surprise her—that her grandmother was actually still here, and they were finally going to meet, and maybe they had found a really cool private arts high school for Dove in Sunset, and on the weekends Nana would take her shell-collecting and they could go to that city nearby with all the Scientologists and eat that popcorn-flavoured ice cream she liked at Yummy's. But now she has no idea what is going on. If they're not here to see Nana, and they're not here for some kind of epic punishment, then why *are* they here?

The buzzing in her stomach redoubling, she opens her email app and begins to type.

Dear Nana,

I know you said you were off on your big grand adventure and wouldn't have access to email, but on the off chance you see this, could you write me back? It's kind of an emergency. I think there's something wrong with Mom.

She stares at the words. *Is* it an emergency? Or is she just overreacting? What right does she have to bother Nana, wherever she is, just because she's being a drama queen? Mashing her finger against the backspace, she deletes the email, then flings her phone across the bed. Curling up on her side, she listens to the sounds of the roof-creature until she finally falls asleep.

Lauren

Sitting on the toilet in her mother's trailer, Lauren stares at a photo of a man standing on a bridge. The photo is tacked to the bathroom wall, along with dozens of others, most of them ripped from magazines or printed on cheap photo paper, edges curled from the humidity. After spending much of her adult life trying to avoid her mother's work, Lauren hadn't expected to be confronted with a retrospective during her morning pee.

She carefully removes the tack and takes down the photo of the man on the bridge, drawn into the image against her will. Even the poor quality of the faded magazine page can't disguise the depth of Imogen's gaze. Imogen was renowned for photographing her subjects—mostly famous, mostly artists, mostly men—in whimsical, fantasy-like settings that revealed their inner vulnerability. Even though Lauren knows the photographs are good, brilliant even, they have always made her feel uneasy. Looking at the world through Imogen's eyes is not something she's ever been keen to do.

The text of the article surrounding the photo is in another

language—Italian maybe, or Portuguese—and the only words that Lauren recognizes are names. Imogen Starr. Zamir Khouri, the man her mother referred to as "Zed." Lauren remembers him, and that bridge. More importantly, she remembers her mother, camera hanging around her neck, holding a small plastic wand that produced a steady stream of bubbles floating away on the wind. Lauren doesn't recall what city they were in, but she knows the wind was warm, and the bubbles her mother blew were not for her but for the man standing on the bridge's cement wall, arms out as the bubbles drifted around him. Imogen snapped photo after photo, a lit cigarette dangling from her lips, the wind blowing tendrils of hair around her face. At one point, she stopped to change her lens and put the wand back into the bottle, which was enticingly blue and purple. As Imogen bent over her camera case, Lauren remembers reaching out a pudgy hand for the wand and sticking it in her mouth. But it didn't taste like candy; it tasted like soap, and she backed away, knocking over the bottle. Her mother looked up, took in the spilled bubbles, and sighed deeply, gesturing for her sister, Joy, to take Lauren away. Lauren couldn't have been more than four years old.

She asked her mother once if that man was her father. Imogen stared off into the middle distance in a way that made Lauren think she had retreated into a sepia-toned memory of a great love, her present self engaged in some monumental internal struggle. Then she turned her attention back to Lauren. "No. Zed was in Morocco when I got pregnant with you. There's no way it could have been him." There was no inner turmoil. Imogen was just doing the math.

That city with the bridge might have been the last work trip Lauren took with Imogen, who abandoned her with Auntie Joy as soon as she was old enough to go to school. Although of course that's not how Imogen would have put it—she probably talked about "stability" or "consistency" or how it was for Lauren's "own good." All Lauren remembers, when she lets herself think back on that frightening, confusing time, was that her mother was gone, and Lauren didn't understand where she was, or why she had left. But Imogen was a genius; she couldn't be burdened with something as ordinary as family obligations. And back then Lauren still adored her. When she would come to visit, she was like a queen from a far-off kingdom, aloof and beautiful in her designer jeans and white linen blouses, her feet bare in the backyard while Lauren excitedly played her favourite songs on the ukulele or showed her the pollinator garden Auntie Joy had let her plant herself. One time Lauren made her mother a necklace out of polymer clay, a swirling disc of colour attached to a leather cord, both their names etched into the back.

"That's lovely," Imogen said, running her hand over Lauren's hair as she pocketed the necklace. Lauren beamed with pride. But after Imogen left, Lauren found the necklace on the kitchen counter, amid a pile of receipts her mother had clearly meant to throw out.

As the years went by, Lauren saw less and less of her mother. Imogen would still come to Lennox Heights every now and then, and they would spend an occasional weekend together in Chicago, but that was it. Imogen went on with her life as if she didn't even have a daughter. It was heartbreaking for Lauren then, but now that she has a daughter of her own, she finds it nearly incomprehensible. She would be with Dove 24/7, if Dove would let her.

Lauren runs her finger along the edge of the page, feeling the thinness of the paper, how easily she could just crumple it in her hand. An ache grows inside her, like a balloon inflating, threatening to burst. *This is all there is*, she thinks. This depressing little bathroom shrine in a Florida trailer is all the world has left of Imogen Starr. *Was it worth it, Mom?*

"Mom!" Dove yells, knocking loudly on the bathroom door, which bounces vigorously against the large rock Lauren has wedged against it. She found the rock in the shower and assumed that was what it was for, since the door refused to stay closed, and it was just like Imogen to come up with that kind of half-assed stop-gap.

"One sec!" Lauren calls back. She tacks the photo back up on the wall and flushes the toilet, then pushes the rock out of the way with her foot. "Come on in."

The door swings open and Dove enters, in just her underwear and a black T-shirt that says *Death Magnet* on it. Immediately, her eyes go to the pictures on the wall. "What are those?"

Lauren wishes she had torn them all down. She has no idea whether Dove has seen her grandmother's work before, or if she even knows how famous she was. But there's no hiding it now. "Some of your grandmother's photographs."

Dove wrinkles her nose. "Why are they in the bathroom?"

"I have no idea." Dove touches a photo of an actor best known for playing James Bond, posing shirtless against a booth for one of those carnival games where you shoot water into a clown's mouth. "You probably don't even know who any of these people are," Lauren says, gently nudging Dove away from the wall.

"Yes, I do," Dove shoots back. "I'm not *culturally illiterate*."

"Oh, well, in *that* case."

Dove's eyes flash briefly heavenward. "Sorry, do you need me to use smaller words?"

Lauren ignores her, ushering her toward the door. "Come on, let's get some breakfast."

"No thanks. I'm going back to bed."

"Come on!" Lauren elbows her. "You can't sleep this beautiful day away!"

But Dove only glares at her. "Can I pee now?"

Lauren sighs and steps out of the bathroom. "Be my guest."

Wordlessly, Dove closes the door, and the rock scrapes across the floor as she wedges it firmly in place, locking Lauren out.

After Dove finishes in the bathroom and retreats into the bedroom, Lauren gets into the shower, which she has to turn on with a rusty wrench that seems to be permanently attached to the knob. The pressure is weak and the water smells of sulphur, but at least it's hot. She doesn't even wash anything—there isn't so much as a bar of soap in the bathroom, and she didn't bring any—just lets the water trickle over her head, the steam a buffer between herself and the stuffy, barely air-conditioned air inside the trailer. When the water runs cold, she turns the wrench again and steps out onto the bath mat. It squelches under her feet and she realizes it is soaking wet—the shower door has been leaking the whole time.

In the kitchen, she sets some water to boil for instant coffee. While she waits, she pokes around, searching for remnants of Imogen. Beneath the sink, she finds a plastic Publix bag stuffed with other plastic Publix bags, and she hungrily digs through them for receipts, as if she might understand what happened to her mother by figuring out what she ate. When she finally finds one, it's so mundane she could cry. Bread. Concentrated OJ. Microwave popcorn. Tin foil. Frozen pasta dinners. Is this the same woman who smuggled black truffles out of Italy in the lining of her bra, so she could recreate a meal she ate at a secret restaurant run by a celebrity chef in a castle in Tuscany? Or who travelled to a tiny town in Japan to eat a rare type of sushi made from fermented goldfish? Lauren smooths out the receipt and stares at the fading ink. The date at the top reads November 23, 2018. The day before she died. Did Imogen really leave this world with nothing but boxed wine and a Michelina's frozen lasagna for one in her stomach?

When the coffee is ready, Lauren brings it with her outside.

She hadn't thought the rickety air conditioner in the trailer was doing much, but the heat of the sun is like a blast from an open oven door. Her T-shirt immediately adheres to her skin as she drags a rusty lawn chair into the shade of a lemon tree and sits down. Shielding her eyes from the sun, she gazes at the trailer. From the outside, it isn't that different from those around it—a little more dated, perhaps, and with a lot less character, but nothing that would belie the disaster inside: the dead potted plants, stacks of old newspapers and magazines, boxes of empty tin cans and old light bulbs, kitchen cupboards crammed with dollar-store tableware, novelty bottle openers, acrylic gas-station slurpee cups smeared with grease. But outside, the windows have been washed, the eaves cleared, the trees trimmed. There's even a fresh coat of paint on the step.

Lauren chugs half her coffee before turning on her phone, bracing herself. She hasn't checked it since before they left Lennox Heights. The first thing she sees are notifications of several missed calls from Dove's school. Below them, a text from Hayley, dated yesterday.

Hey girl! What happened last night? Hope you're okay.
Debra was pretty pissed you skipped out on her, but I told
her you had a family emergency. Don't forget quarterly
sales are due at the end of the month! You'd better get on it
or you're gonna own a lot of candles lol.

Ignoring the text, she scrolls through the rest of her notifications. Group texts from her book club, an evite to a baby shower, minutes from the PTA meeting two nights ago, an email from Joy forwarding a coupon for a vegan restaurant in Lennox Heights— all remnants of a life that now seems so far away. There is nothing from Jason. It's been over forty-eight hours since she last heard

from him, and still no text, no email, no phone call. Lauren briefly
wonders where he is, although in the back of her brain she knows
he's somewhere near the border between Peru and Ecuador, pilot-
ing a plane en route from Lima to Quito, where he will stay for
his mandatory twenty-four hours off before heading back to the
States. She has always had a Jason clock steadily running in the
back of her mind, although this time it feels less like a countdown
and more like a timer on a bomb. She opens his Instagram, but
his last post is still from a week ago: the nose of a plane hovering
over fluffy white clouds, no caption or hashtags, 101 likes.

She thinks about texting him, but she can't bring herself to
open their message thread, to see his last text still hanging there.
If she never looks at it again, maybe she can convince herself she
imagined the whole thing in an early-morning dream state, that
Jason is at this very moment thinking about going to the market
when he lands in Quito to buy her those dried chilis she likes.

A sudden stinging thwack against her arm startles her out of
the reverie. "What the hell?" she mutters, rubbing her arm. On
the ground in front of her is a plastic tube, about two inches long,
with a yellow sponge protruding from one end. As she bends over
to examine it, another projectile hits her in the back of her neck.
"Ow!" She straightens up, and a third projectile whizzes past her
ear. A fourth bounces off the lattice trim around the carport. She
turns around to see a tiny white-haired woman in a long, striped
nightshirt and bare feet, standing on the steps of the neighbouring
trailer with a toy dart gun in her hand, her face twisted into a frown.

"You're trespassing!" she says, firing off another dart.

Lauren ducks, and the dart flies past her head and hits a tree.
"Wait," she says, holding up her hands in surrender. "I'm not
trespassing. I'm Imogen's daughter."

"I don't care who you are, get off my lawn!" The woman clicks
the trigger on the toy gun again, but she is out of ammo.

"This is *my* lawn! I mean, it was my mother's lawn. She left it to me."

The woman sighs and gestures to Lauren's feet with the toy gun. "My lawn." She swings the gun and points to the patch of mostly bare ground beside Imogen's driveway. "Your lawn."

"Oh." Lauren stands up, holding her hands near her face to ward off any sneak attacks. "Sorry." She picks up a sponge dart from the ground, holding it out to the woman as a peace offering. "I'm Lauren Sandoval. I'm here with my daughter, Dove. We'll probably be seeing a lot of each other." She smiles. "Any rules I should know about?"

"Rule number one, don't trespass on other people's property," the woman snaps, snatching the dart from Lauren's hand.

"Got it," Lauren says. "It won't happen again, I promise."

They stare at each other for a moment. "Are you stupid or something? *You are still trespassing!*" the woman yells, poking the dart gun against Lauren's shoulder.

"God! Okay." Lauren takes a step back, raising her hands. "Nice to meet you, too."

"And make sure you keep your trash out of my garbage cans!" the woman shouts as Lauren drags her chair away. "Your mother just loved to try to hide hers in there."

Lauren slams the chair into a tiny patch of shade on her side of the lawn and plops down into it. The woman next door goes back into her trailer, but Lauren sees her peeking through her blinds, watching her. Lauren sticks her tongue out. The blinds immediately snap closed.

Jason is going to laugh his ass off when I tell him about this, Lauren thinks before she can stop herself, before the memory of his text comes rushing back. She picks up the lawn chair, feeling the woman's eyes on her back as she retreats into the trailer.

Lauren

They say bad things always happen in threes, but for Lauren it's always twos. You'd think that would be better, but when you secretly believe in superstitions the way she does, it means you spend all your time waiting for that other shoe to drop.

Monday morning, like every morning, Lauren awoke and immediately checked her phone for messages from her husband. Jason was away for three weeks in Central and South America— Bogotá, Quito, Lima. When he had first started flying for the airline, three years after they were married, they were in almost constant contact while he was away, whispering into the phone late at night from their beds in different hemispheres. *I miss your toes. I miss your eyebrows. I miss your pie de manzana. I miss the way you talk about food in Spanish. I miss. I miss. I miss.*

She still missed him, of course, but it wasn't sustainable to miss someone with that kind of intensity, like a knot in your chest pulling tighter and tighter every time you were apart. Eventually, it became too exhausting, and they both had to let go. As the knot began to loosen, their conversations while they were apart started to drift into the realm of taxes, doctor's appointments, dinner parties, their daughter—the tedious chatter that makes up the never-ending backing track of a marriage. And so *I miss* became *I have to, I need to, I will.* And yet, even now she got a twinge of excitement when his name flashed across her phone screen. Like this morning's notification, nestled below an email from her yoga studio and a string of texts from her book club group chat.

She pressed her finger against the notification, smiling into the pillow, peeking at her phone with one eye still closed. The text was only one line, glowing white letters against a blue background. At first, her eyes settled on the typo: *wnt.*

That's so unlike him, she thought, pressing her face deeper into the pillow as her stomach twisted around itself. *Wnt.* She focused on those three letters, not even a word, her eyes refusing to travel any further along the sentence. She knew what was waiting for her there, at the end, could sense the word on the screen. But as long as she concentrated on that missing *a*, she could stay suspended in that moment, in that strange space between *a* and no *a.*

Lauren, I wnt

Lauren, I wnt

Lauren, I wnt

She swiped the message away and threw her phone on the bed, just out of arm's reach. Rolled over onto her back and stared up at the ceiling. Inhaled, exhaled. The room breathed with her, contracting and expanding with her lungs, and she wondered if she was having a panic attack. Anxiety and panic disorders were common in high-heeled shoe types, according to Dr. Constance Lightfoot, author of *Putting Your Best Foot Forward*, the latest self-help book Lauren has been reading. Dr. Lightfoot was a fashion-designer-turned-psychologist who believed that all people could be categorized into types of shoes. Lauren was an open-toe canvas cork-soled wedge, although she was striving to be more of a black leather low-heel pump.

"Dove!" she yelled, rising from the bed with a lightness in her body that surprised her. Her vision sparkled as the blood rushed from her head, weighing her back down to earth. "Are you up? We're late!"

When she opened her bedroom door, Dove was standing in the hallway, her toothbrush handle protruding from her mouth, her eyes quizzical. "I'm up," she said, her words muffled. A trickle of saliva laced with toothpaste dribbled from the corner of her mouth and onto the Cookie Monster T-shirt she had slept in, and Lauren flashed back to Dove as a baby in her arms, her eyes drooping after a feed, droplets of foamy milk still wobbling on her bottom lip.

"Okay." Lauren swiped the drool from Dove's chin with a finger, and Dove's body involuntarily tensed at her touch. It was something she had always done. It normally didn't bother Lauren, but now she wished they could have one interaction that didn't end with her daughter recoiling from her. She wiped the toothpaste on her own pajama bottoms and forced a smile. "Let's hustle, though. I have a busy day."

"Mmmph," said Dove, retreating into the bathroom.

Lauren went through her morning routine—shower, dress, coffee, school lunch—with the precision of a factory robot. She even cut the crusts off Dove's sandwich, something she hadn't done since Dove was in elementary school. She was pretty sure Dove didn't eat the sandwiches she made her anymore, but she couldn't bring herself to stop making them. She found it reassuring, how the Tupperware containers fit together inside the insulated lunch bag, sandwiches and apple slices and yogurt neatly compartmentalized and stacked. Even if it all ended up in the garbage, at least Dove would know she had done that for her.

After Lauren dropped Dove off at school, she went to the post office, she went to the bank, she stopped in at the pharmacy to renew Jason's prescription for heartburn medication. In yoga class, the teacher instructed them to "breathe from the backs of your knees," and Lauren pictured little mouths puckering at the tops of her calves, making her laugh so hard she had to leave the room. At the grocery store, she pushed her cart a little too fast down the quiet aisles, forgoing her list and grabbing things at random, things she would never usually buy: white bread, Chips Ahoy!, Froot Loops. She loaded up her car and drove away, not realizing until she was on the highway that she hadn't paid for any of it—she'd just walked out of the store with a full cart, and no one had batted an eye.

She dropped the groceries home and then headed across town to her storage unit, where she kept all her Gordon Lake inventory. She was supposed to give a party that evening at the apartment of her dental hygienist, who had reluctantly agreed to host after Lauren promised to buy a teeth-whitening session from her. Lauren had been recruited into Gordon Lake three months ago by a woman from her Mindful Barrelates class. Hayley had such perfect highlights in her blonde, beachy waves that Lauren would have said yes to anything she'd asked. Gordon Lake wasn't a multi-level marketing scheme, Hayley had insisted—it was a *business opportunity* in the high-end home fragrance industry, an untapped market in smaller cities like Lennox Heights that were just beginning to understand the importance of aromatherapy. The brochures made it seem so friendly, so wholesome, so suburban: lush family rooms with sparkling clean floors, cheese plates, white wine spritzers, athleisure wear, fresh cut flowers on the kitchen island. If she could sell Gordon Lake products to these women, those pictures promised, then maybe she could *be* one of those women.

"Besides," Hayley had said, leaning over her skinny pepper-mint mocha at Starbucks, those perfect beachy waves tumbling over her shoulders. "Haven't you been working your whole life to make your family happy? Haven't you done everything for *them*? Don't you want something just for *you*?"

In the end, of course, it turned out Gordon Lake *was* a multi-level marketing scheme, and selling candles and oil warmers to middle-class suburban housewives, which might have been easy for Hayley, was more of a challenge for someone not quite as young and beautiful and enthusiastic as she was. After a couple of lacklustre parties, Lauren watched her future full of *Live Laugh Love* throw pillows and kale smoothies receding into a cedar-and sage-scented mist. She now had a storage unit full of product and was quickly running out of friends and relatives to sell it to, and she owed Hayley an embarrassing amount of money that she couldn't bring herself to tell Jason about. Every surface in her own home was cluttered with diffusers, candles, warmers, and spray bottles. Dove claimed it smelled like "someone ate a bath bomb and threw it up in the compost."

As Lauren drove, she called the dental hygienist and got her voicemail. "Hi Debra!" she chirped. "Just calling to check in about tonight! I'm going to see if I can round up some more guests to come by. The bigger the crowd, the more people are willing to buy! I'll see you around seven!" She hung up, feeling the weight of her phone in her hand like a brick, something she could throw through a window if she wanted.

She was just pulling into the lot outside the storage unit when her phone rang. She answered it without looking, assuming it was Debra.

"Hi Lauren." Her Auntie Joy's voice filled the car.

"Oh, hi Joy." The last person she wanted to talk to right now was Joy, who knew her better than she knew herself; who could probably tell from five hundred miles away that her shoulders were tensing.

"Are you okay?" Joy asked. "Are your shoulders tensing?"

"Nope!" Lauren replied brightly. "All good here! Just picking up some Gordon Lake stock for my party tonight."

"Oh, lovely! That sounds like so much fun. I wish I could come to one sometime."

Lauren slid into a spot by the door and put the car in park. "Well, maybe next summer, if you come up for a visit." Several years ago, Joy—widowed young and with no children of her own—had sold the house Lauren grew up in and moved to Palm Desert to live with three other widowed girlfriends, *Golden Girls*–style. When Lauren was young, she had been embarrassed by Joy, who taught at her high school. Even though Lauren hadn't been in any of her classes, she heard the stories the other kids told about Mrs. Perez the crazy biology teacher catching her sweater on the corner of her desk or becoming so enthralled by a documentary about butterflies that she cried in front of the class. Back then, Lauren had lived in fear of seeing Joy in the hallways, having her wave excitedly, the millions of bracelets on her arm jangling jubilantly. Now, though, she missed her fiercely, and often drove by her old house just to catch a glimpse of the rhododendron bushes she had planted in the front garden, wishing she could see Joy there one last time, in her gardening hat and thrift-store Backstreet Boys T-shirt, reaching up to prune a branch. "Dove misses you. Maybe we could take a day trip to Marty's Cove for clams."

"I'd love that." Joy paused. "Sweetie, I'm calling about your mother's estate."

"Oh, finally." Lauren began rummaging through her purse for her key card. "So you found her secret stashes of money?"

"Well, that's the thing. Her will's a mess, but as far as we can tell there were no secret stashes of money."

Lauren stilled, her wallet in one hand and a bottle of hand lotion in the other. "How is that possible? Mom had *millions* of dollars. You said so yourself. She must have hidden it in a Swiss bank account or something."

"I thought she did. We even hired a forensic accountant, but all he found was an empty bank account."

"Well, that's just ridiculous." Lauren tucked her wallet back in her purse and uncapped the bottle of hand lotion, squeezing some into her palm. She'd known about her mother's archives and royalties, which had all been donated when she retired. But there were supposed to be *assets*. "What about the house? The condo?"

"All gone," Joy said sadly.

"Gone *where*?"

"Does it really matter?"

The lotion bottle sputtered as she squeezed it harder, trying not to think about the dozens of unpaid Gordon Lake purchase orders stuffed in her glove compartment. "So, she didn't leave us anything at all?"

"Oh yes!" Joy said brightly. "That's the good news. There is something. The trailer."

"The *what*?"

"Your granny's old trailer, in Florida. In that retirement community. I told you Imogen had been living there for the past few years."

If Joy had told her that, Lauren hadn't been listening. Lauren had been Dove's age when she visited that trailer, and all she remembered was the smell of the place, musty and fetid, and the heat, which pushed in on you from every angle. Why any normal person would want to live there was beyond her, but her mother? Imogen Starr—darling of the art world, consort to rock stars and film directors and even royalty—in a trailer park in Florida? It sounded like a performance art piece.

"I'm really sorry, Lauren," Joy said. "I know you were counting on that money."

"No, I wasn't," Lauren said quickly. *I never counted on Mom
for anything.* "I mean, it would have been nice, but Jase and
I . . ." Her hand clenched around the lotion bottle. "I'm fine. Of
course I'm fine."

"Well, you can take some time to figure out what you want to
do with the trailer. The key's under a shell in the carport, apparently, if you want to go check it out."

"Thanks." Lauren looked down at her hand and realized she
had squirted almost the entire bottle of lotion into her palm.

"It's going to be fine, sweetie. Just breathe, okay?"

As if I have a choice, Lauren thought.

When she slid open the door to her storage unit, the smell
knocked her back. Holding the sleeve of her parka over her nose,
she stepped inside and was met with a sea of boxes. *How did this
happen?* But she knew the answer. It had started out with just
one box, then two, then increased exponentially in relation to
how much she tried to push it all out of her mind. In the three
months since she'd started, she'd sold about 10 per cent of her
inventory. Every week she quietly and secretly transferred her
unsold product from her bedroom closet to her car to the storage unit, opening the door just high enough to shove the box
through without having to see inside.

She crouched down next to a box labelled ENLIGHTENED
VANILLA ESSENTIAL OIL, peeled back the tape, and pulled out a
bottle. *What the hell is enlightened vanilla, anyway? Vanilla that's
been blessed by a Buddhist monk?* She sniffed it and gagged. It
smelled like someone had left a can of Betty Crocker frosting out
in the sun. *Who would want their house to smell like this?*

It wasn't like she had been counting on her mother's money.
But it had always been there, like the tire barrier lining a go-kart

course, cushioning her as she ricocheted around the track. Even though it had been years since she and her mother had spoken, for Imogen to just squander away her inheritance, *Dove's* inheritance, was unthinkable. She knew her mother had liked nice things, but she had never been completely irresponsible, at least when it came to her finances. Maybe she hadn't been paying taxes? Maybe her accountant had been stealing from her? Maybe she had fallen for one of those Nigerian prince scams? There had to be something other than it just being *gone*.

Or maybe she had given it to someone else, so Lauren couldn't have it, the way she had with her life's work. The thought buzzed around in her head, making her dizzy. Could Imogen really have done that to her? Jason made good money as a pilot, but they still had a mortgage, and Dove's education to save for, not to mention her mounting Gordon Lake debt. And she'd hoped one day Jason would retire, and they would buy a place on the beach and spend more than a few days together at a time. They had talked about it so often—granite countertops, a porch swing, chilled white wine and lobster tails.

Although apparently Jason didn't even want that anymore.

A scream erupted from somewhere deep within her, and she hurled the bottle against the wall of the storage unit. It smashed on impact, its contents splattering over the concrete like grease on a stovetop. She picked up another and threw it, and then another, and another, until she had smashed all twelve bottles of Enlightened Vanilla Essential Oil, the ground in front of her slick and glittering with broken glass. Then she turned and, with a roar, pushed over the tower of boxes behind her, the air exploding with the scents of Cedar Serenity and Ocean Tranquility, reverberating with the sound of shattering bottles.

Breathe, she commanded herself. She took a deep breath in, her lungs filling with enlightenment and serenity and tranquility, and promptly threw up.

It took her four hours to clean everything up, but she couldn't just leave it that way. Her phone vibrated in the corner by her purse as she worked, with calls from Debra, then Hayley, then Hayley's boss, Ron, as well as several calls from Dove's school, who had been trying to get in touch with her for days about the final payment for a class trip to Williamsburg that she didn't have the money for. She ignored them. After all, what did it matter? Even the things she hadn't destroyed were ruined—candles and warmers and melts all covered in oil so slick she could barely hold them in her hands, the plastic wrap slipping through her fingers as she tried vainly to wipe them off with paper towels she stole from the public washroom at the storage facility. Worryingly, she had stopped being able to smell anything, although she knew the scent was on her clothes, in her hair, seeping from her pores. She imagined herself, months from now, catching a whiff of a Gordon Lake candle at someone else's house and immediately vomiting on the floor.

It was close to 10 p.m. by the time she got home. Dove was asleep on the couch, one of her true crime shows on television, a blanket pulled up to her chin. For a moment Lauren stood by the door and watched her, bathed in the television glow, an open can of store-brand soda water wedged between the couch cushions beside her. Lauren put her keys down on the hall table as quietly as she could and tiptoed to the bedroom. *No point in waking her now*, she thought, although really she just didn't have the energy to talk to Dove, to put on the face she'd need to hide the fact that everything was falling apart.

Later, Lauren lay on her side in bed, staring at Jason's pillow. Even when he was away, she still slept on her side of the bed, which suddenly struck her as ridiculous. Why had she never spread out, put her pillows in the middle, sprawled across the mattress beneath the 800-thread-count Egyptian cotton sheets she had insisted they buy, *insisted*, because they were adults, and they needed an adult bed, one of the many things they had talked about over email while Jason was in Santiago, or Panama City, or some other place she had never seen? Why did she continue to curl up on the edge, taking up as little room as she could, even though she was alone in the bed more often than not?

Jason was her oldest friend. From the moment his family moved in next door when they were both ten, they had spent all their time together. Their first kiss had been in a classmate's basement during a party in ninth grade, the first time either of them had been drunk. They danced together, crazily in the beginning, their arms and legs everywhere, laughing as the alcohol softened their corners and blurred their edges, the joy of being free and young like tiny tender bubbles bursting against their skin. And, when they couldn't handle it anymore, moving closer and closer, their lips coming together in a sour mash of warm beer and Doritos while "Kiss from a Rose" played on the stereo, just needing contact, a place to put all their energy, needing someone—anyone—to give themselves to.

What a great story this will be, she'd thought then. *Our children will love it.*

She wiggled a couple of inches toward the middle of the bed. But she couldn't bring herself to go any further.

They say bad things always happen in threes. But this time, she wasn't waiting for the other shoe to drop. The money was one thing. But the text. There was nothing that could hurt her more than that. When she finally closed her eyes, it was all she could see—the words burned into the backs of her eyelids—so she opened them again and stared at the ceiling until the first light started to creep through her bedroom window, a plan forming in her mind.

Lauren, I wnt a divorce.

Ray

It was in the mid-1950s that things started to go downhill at the Flamingo Key Aquarium and Tackle. A new state-of-the-art marina was built at the eastern tip of the key, one that dwarfed the Flamingo Key Marina, which fell into disrepair and then eventually closed in 1960. People still came to the aquarium, but its status was relegated to roadside attraction, a sideshow, a relic of the past. The real aquariums, in Tampa and Miami and Orlando, had killer whales and penguins and sea lions. Flamingo Key Aquarium and Tackle only had some fish and invertebrates—the otters and gators all long sold to make much-needed yet still insufficient repairs to the infrastructure—and a manatee. A manatee who, after years of being adored by the people of Sunset, was now forgotten, hulking and silent at the bottom of the pool.

By the time I arrived on the scene in 1984, the aquarium was a shadow of its former glorious self. Still, I have spent most mornings on that ship for the past thirty-five years, arriving before dawn, hauling open the wooden service-entrance door and immersing myself in the darkness of its belly. Every time I do, it feels like I am cracking open something ancient and mysterious, with its own ecosystem, its own set of rules.

I was fresh out of trade school and eager to work. My life was new then: my job, my city, the little cottage at the tip of the key we called home. You and me. Raymond and Rayna. The priest could barely get through our wedding ceremony without laughing, do you remember? *Raymond and Rayna. If you have a son, you could call him Raylan.* But you preferred Joseph. That was your father's name. You wanted to pass it down, keep a part of your family alive.

I was twenty-four years old, and I thought I knew everything. But the minute I set foot on that ship, I realized I knew nothing. That first day, Mrs. Appleby, who had started with Sharples as his personal assistant and was now the guest services manager, showed me around, telling me stories about how they trapped this crab under a dock in Venice after he bit a local celebrity on his genitals, or how that grouper was donated by a local fisherman who caught it the day after his mother died and was convinced her soul lived inside the fish. But I barely heard any of her stories, mesmerized as I was by the strangeness of it all, by the realization that while I had spent my entire young life on the surface of the ocean, I had no idea what it held in its depths. At the end of the tour, she pushed open a door at the stern of the ship and we stepped into the shade of a green-striped canvas tent not unlike the one erected in 1932 by Sharples himself. I didn't know yet that this was the manatee enclosure, or that this would be where I would spend most of my life. All I remember is the unbroken surface of the water, scummy with vegetation, a shadow circling slowly around the bottom.

My job at the aquarium was to assist with morning maintenance, under the guidance of Jorge Pereira, who would become my mentor. Jorge taught me everything I know about aquarium maintenance, about fish and aquatic habitats and what they need to survive. And he truly loved all the fish, he did. But the manatee was nothing but a nuisance to Jorge. He preferred the intricate work, the beauty of the coral reefs, the silvery scales of an angel-fish or the spiny bloom of a sea urchin. To him, the manatee was just a mammal in a tub.

"Useless sea cow," he would call her. "Mowing through let-tuce like it's the end of the world. Just think, Ray, how many more tanks we could fit in this space if it weren't for this concrete pit."

Because I admired Jorge so deeply, for a time his beliefs were my beliefs. When Jorge railed against the manatee, I would nod my assent, and I grew to dread the moments of each day I had to spend in the enclosure, with its smell of rotting lettuce, the sickly green hue of the light coming through the tent, the grey blob of flesh that languished on the floor of the pool. All the manatee tasks, delegated solely to me by Jorge, were anathema to me, and I longed for the pristine beauty of the tropical aquariums, the magic of the jellyfish, the antics of the invertebrates. I would rush through my cleaning and water testing, dumping the crates of lettuce in almost as an afterthought. I stayed as far away as possible from the manatee—which wasn't hard, as she stayed as far away as possible from me. Most of the time, I couldn't even bring myself to look at her. It was all just too sad, too real, too much of a visceral reminder of our failed attempts to capture the sea, to possess something that was unpossessable. Too much of a reminder of how wrong we had gotten things.

But as the months wore on, it became apparent that Jorge lived in the past. He truly believed that one day the aquarium would be restored to its former glory. And with each passing year—with each fish that died and was never replaced, with each mechanism that broke and was scrapped, with each amenity that was liquidated once it was determined we could live without it—instead of facing reality, he gripped that belief tighter and tighter. Some days he would spend the entire morning polishing the pebbles in the crab habitat, or arranging the seagrass that was in with the pufferfish, or adjusting the lighting in the jelly-fish room. Eventually, as you no doubt remember, Rayna, I was doing most of the heavy work myself. I didn't mind. There was no acquisition involved, no designing exhibits, no public outreach or propagation—I was strictly maintaining the status quo. And it was comforting in a way, to know that I could keep this entire hulking beast of an aquarium running entirely on my own.

After I had been working at the aquarium for almost a year, Mrs. Appleby asked me if I wouldn't mind staying after my shift to redo all the educational signage for the displays. The ones they had at the time had been handwritten by Sharples himself, in elegant calligraphy, but had faded over the years. I painstakingly typed up all the facts and tidbits about each display, faithfully conserving the text that Sharples, now well into his nineties, had written so many years before. But there was nothing there for the manatee. When I approached Mrs. Appleby about it, she told me there had been a plaque, but it had been stolen years ago and never replaced. She couldn't even recall the manatee's name. We had to look it up, rummaging through the filing cabinet in the office for old promotional materials.

In the back of the bottom drawer, Mrs. Appleby came across an old brochure from the 1950s that Sharples had made to distribute to the local hotels. "*Behold the magnificent Sirenia, Pebble,*" she read aloud, frowning down at the page. "Oh, right, Pebble, I remember now. Such an absurd name for such an enormous creature, don't you think?"

On the front of the brochure was an illustration of the aquarium's exterior, and beneath that a smaller illustration of the manatee pavilion, with people standing around the manatee, who was hoisting herself out of the water by her flippers and balancing a ball on her snout. The back of the brochure told the story of how the manatee came to live at the aquarium, and described all the exciting tricks she could perform. "*Her name is Pebble because when she was first born, she was no bigger than a tiny grey pebble at the bottom of the pool.*" I had heard the story of Sharples and the harpoon by then, and I knew what had happened to the mother manatee. But I had never really understood what it must have meant—this small, helpless creature, alone in the world, with none of her own kind around her.

"What else is in the drawer?" I asked. Mrs. Appleby pulled out a long tube of thick, matte paper secured by an elastic, and we unrolled it together, spreading it out over the desk. It was a poster featuring a drawing of a larger-than-life manatee wearing a top hat and a bow tie, hovering in a galaxy of stars over a much smaller Flamingo Key Aquarium and Tackle. Crowds of tiny people on the decks, dressed in tuxedos and evening gowns, peered up at her in awe. On one side, the words *Pebble: Star of the Ocean* were written in large, looping cursive, and at the bottom was information on how to procure tickets to this magnificent event, at $20 each—a hefty sum back then.

"This can't be the same manatee that's in the tank," I said. It was hard to imagine that surly creature I reluctantly fed each day interacting with anyone, let alone performing for an adoring crowd.

"The very same," Mrs. Appleby replied. "She used to be quite the little starlet. Well," she chuckled, "not little, I suppose."

I ran my hand over the poster. "What happened to her?"

She shrugged. "We had to let her trainers go, and no one else really had the time to work with her. And anyway, no one was interested in those shows anymore. Too old-fashioned, I suppose." She rolled the poster back up and slipped the elastic over it. "After she stopped performing, people just forgot about her."

Later that afternoon, I went down to the manatee enclosure and stared down into the water, watching Pebble circling the base of the pool, the way she always did, day after day. I tried to imagine her performing for a crowd. It seemed impossible, seeing her now. But at the time, it had been all she'd ever known, and to have that suddenly taken away from her—I couldn't even imagine what a loss like that would have felt like.

I slipped off my shoes and socks and dipped a toe into the water. Pebble didn't react. I was alone in the enclosure—the aquarium was closed to the public on Mondays, and the only other person on site was Mrs. Appleby, locked up in her office doing paperwork. I flicked the water gently, but still Pebble didn't move. I plunged my foot into the pool up to my ankle, stirring it around and around. The water was warm and viscous, and stringy green algae clung to my skin. Pebble started drifting toward me. I kept stirring, and she came so close to the surface that I could see the cross-hatching of lines on her weathered skin. Then she dove and, with a heaving undulation, slapped her tail against my foot with such a *thwack* that it sent me flying backward, skidding across the platform on my rear.

I sat there, stunned. It clearly hadn't been an accident. Pebble was upset that I had invaded her space. And why wouldn't she be? She had been alone in that water for her entire life; of course she would want to protect it. But this also meant that she was aware of me, that she was reacting to me. That, more than anything, sparked something inside me.

You made me sanitize my foot with vinegar that day, do you remember, Rayna? I knew you were worried about keeping us both healthy, taking every possible precaution, so I compliantly dipped my foot in the bucket, the sharp tang bringing tears to my eyes. I worked with chemicals every day at the aquarium, but none made my stomach heave the way that did—that, and the lavender you began mixing with Epsom salts and baking soda for my clothes, which I would leave in a hamper by the back door after stripping down in the yard when I got home, allowed only the dignity of my underwear.

You blamed everything that happened afterward—or didn't for us—on those chemicals I worked with, and maybe you were right. I'll admit it's hard for me to think about that possibility, and the implications of it. But I also know it's easier to have something tangible to imbue with your pain, rather than face the fact that sometimes things just don't work out the way that we want them to, for no reason at all.

That's enough for today, Rayna. You need your rest. And there will always be tomorrow.

Dove

After she locks herself in the bathroom, Dove puts the toilet lid down and sits on it, leaning her head against the wall beside her with her eyes closed, wishing she could just fall back into that black abyss of dreamless sleep. She'd still be there if she hadn't been woken at basically dawn by her mother banging around in the bathroom, which is about half an inch from her head, on the other side of a wall that might as well be cardboard.

Now she is awake and wired, her mind racing. All she can think about is how much she wants to go back to Lennox Heights, to Worley Academy, to have everything be the way it was. She wants to sit in the library with Dex and Kait after school and find cool drawings to trace. She wants to come up with excuses to get out of class at 10:45, right when the cookies are coming out of the oven in the caf. She even wants to smell that weird air-freshener stuff they use in the bathroom on the second floor. Nothing else in the whole world smells like that air freshener, and now she's never going to smell it again. And the worst part is, the only thing people are going to remember her for is that stupid bee stunt. It's not like she made any amazing contributions to the school while she was there or anything. But she was *there*. She did more than just set loose a bunch of bees. At least, she hopes she did.

Dove knows she has to tell her mother what happened. But it's been so easy to not say anything, to just let time slip past in silence, every opportunity for her to come clean drifting along with it. And now it feels like it's too late, as though telling her would be an admission that she's been lying. Although she *hasn't* been lying. She just hasn't told the truth. She knows there is a difference, although deep down, it doesn't feel like there is. Plus, she doesn't have the slightest clue how her mother will react. Three months ago, Dove would have said she'd lose her shit, drag her back down to Worley and make her apologize to everyone, and then force her to throw a bake sale to raise money for the Beekeepers' Society of America. But lately it seems like her mother is just going through the motions. She never answers her phone when Dove calls for a ride home, and at least once a week she sends her to school with empty Tupperware containers in her lunch bag. Often, Dove will catch her at the kitchen table just sitting there staring into space, a blank expression on her face. Sometimes it's like she doesn't even remember she has a daughter at all.

If her father were around, she'd talk to him about it. But he hasn't been home in weeks, and when he *is* home, he's been acting weird too. For instance, before he left this last time, he took her out for a fancy dinner, just the two of them—something he's never done before. They went to a steakhouse, even though he knows she's a vegetarian, and when she ordered a baked potato and salad his face collapsed in disappointment. "I'm so sorry, I don't know what I was thinking," he said, and she felt so bad she told him it was okay, she still ate meat on special occasions. She ordered the smallest steak they had, and when it arrived she cut it into tiny pieces and slipped it into a napkin in her lap when he wasn't looking. He ate a T-bone and didn't touch his sides, and the whole time he kept talking about what a special young woman she was becoming and how proud he was of her, which was nice to hear but also made her feel sad for reasons she couldn't quite put into words. Afterward, they went to the mall and he said she could pick out a new toy, but while they were walking through the toy store he suddenly stopped in the stuffed animal aisle.

"I'm so stupid," he said, his head hanging low. "You're too old for toys. I should have offered to buy you an iPad or something."

"It's okay, Dad. I love stuffed animals," she replied, and picked up a little elephant. "I want this guy, okay?"

Her father was silent for a moment. "That's a good guy," he said finally, and she was mortified to see his eyes were full of tears. When she got home, she put the elephant on the shelf next to her bed so he'd be the first thing she saw when she woke up in the morning, but she found she couldn't look at him without thinking about her father crying in the middle of the toy store, so she hid him in the back of her closet instead.

The person she really wishes she could talk to is her grandmother. But she made things very clear. *I'm not going to be able to talk to you anymore*, she wrote, over three months ago now. *I know it's hard to say goodbye, but sometimes we come into each other's lives for a certain purpose, and then we move on. This is just me moving on, keeping you close in my heart and treasuring the gift of this correspondence with you as I go on to my next big adventure.*

At the time, Dove was so angry. What the hell was that supposed to mean? *Moving on? A certain purpose?* Why did she have to be so cryptic all the time? Dove had poured her soul out to her grandmother in those emails, and this is how it ended? It was so unfair. And yet, she can't stay angry at her grandmother. More than anything, she just misses her.

She picks up her phone. The first thing she sees is a block of notifications from Kazu—countless comments and reposts of the video, and hundreds of new followers to her account. A wave of anxiety washes over her. All last night she dreamed about bees— coating the bedspread, filling the pillowcase, spilling out from under the bed. Her subconscious clearly thinks she should take the video down, but she still can't bring herself to do it. Taking it down feels like defeat, somehow. *Sticking to your principles doesn't always feel comfortable*, Nana told her once. *But in the end you'll feel more uncomfortable with yourself if you don't.*

Ignoring the notifications, Dove refreshes her email, but there's nothing new. She hits the button again, refresh, refresh, refresh, as if she can conjure an email from her grandmother by sheer will. Last night before bed, she searched the bedroom, thinking maybe she could find a clue to where her grandmother has gone. But there was nothing in the closet except a couple of flowery dresses and a straw hat, and nothing in the bedside table except a dead gecko, brittle and dry, its tail coiled into a spiral, and a large, rusty key with no keychain or markings. That was it. No tourist brochure for some years-long silent retreat in Bali, no book on a super-charismatic cult leader with notes in the margins, no photo of her grandmother and a handsome billionaire, not even a business card with just an *X* on it.

But there *are* the photos tacked up on the bathroom wall in front of her. Maybe there's a clue in there. Scanning the articles, her eyes stop on one, which she carefully unpins. The clipping is from a profile of her grandmother in an art magazine from 2010. In the very bottom corner, there is a photo of her sitting on a stool in a pub, a pint of beer and her camera on the bar beside her. There have never been any photos of Imogen around their house, but when Dove first started writing to her grandmother, she spent hours googling photos of her. She's never seen this one, though. Imogen is wearing jeans and an oversized white button-down shirt, open to reveal her sharp collarbones, the faintest line of cleavage. Her hair is loose and long, her feet perched on the bottom rung of the stool, her knees open, her hands dangling between them. Sitting like a man.

Dove straightens up on the toilet and tries the same pose, spreading her legs, letting her body take up space. She tries to copy her grandmother's expression—somewhere on the knife's edge between annoyed and amused—but it feels awkward, wrong. She can sense how ridiculous she looks. How did she not inherit one ounce of her grandmother's coolness?

"Where are you, Nana?" she whispers to the photo.

Imogen Starr, on a break between shoots, reads the caption on the photo. Dove tries to imagine her grandmother in some distant country, her camera slung around her neck, on a continual search for beauty and meaning, showing people all the things they can't see. It makes her feel better, to think of her out there doing what she loves to do. It gives her hope that the reason her grandmother stopped talking to her wasn't because Dove somehow chased her away, the way her mother did.

It happened by chance; Auntie Joy had accidentally emailed everyone in her contacts when she signed up for a photo-sharing site. There was a long list of names attached to that email, but Dove saw only one. *Imogen Starr.* When she clicked on the name, a "compose" window opened up with her grandmother's email in the address field.

The only things Dove knew, concretely, about her grandmother were that she was a photographer and that she and Lauren didn't speak anymore. Early on, Dove had learned that mentioning her grandmother resulted in an icy silence from her mother; even her father and Auntie Joy acted strangely whenever her name came up. Every now and then, Dove would come across a reference to her grandmother in a magazine or on television, or she'd see a photo of hers on the wall of a dentist's office, as the background to someone's inspirational quote on Instagram, as a print for sale at the poster store in the mall. Dove hadn't been curious about her, though, not really. She'd been a question mark in her head, a shapeless idea of a woman floating just outside her periphery. But now here was her grandmother—just a keystroke away.

Dove typed the word *Dear* and then stopped. What was she supposed to call her? She had only met her once, when she was four. They'd been at some kind of coffee shop or restaurant—Dove remembered big bright windows, comfy mismatched chairs, and an area with colouring books and blocks and little animal figurines for children to play with while their parents did parent things. They'd sat at a table with a woman with long grey hair braided loosely and draped over one shoulder, who gazed over the rim of her coffee cup at Dove in a way that made her anxious. She'd crumbled her cookie all over the table and spilled her juice and pulled at her mother's sweater until Lauren had shooed her off to the play area. Dove became engrossed in a puzzle, and when she came back to the table, her mother was alone.

"Where did the lady go?" she asked.

"She had to leave," Lauren replied, staring down into her coffee.

"Will she come back?"

"No," Lauren said, and there was such a flatness and finality to it that Dove's bottom lip began to tremble. Lauren pulled her up onto her knee. "It's okay, babes," she said, mumbling into Dove's hair. "We don't need her. Lots of kids don't have a nana."

Dear Nana,

   Hello. I'm sorry if it's weird for me to be writing you

out of the blue like this. My name is Dove Sandoval and
I'm your granddaughter. I'm writing you because . . . well,
I don't really know why I'm writing you. You don't even
have to write back if you don't want to, but if you do, it
would be really nice to talk to you.
    Sincerely,
    Dove Sandoval

Less than twenty-four hours later, an email appeared in her inbox.

Dearest Dove,
    Dove. What a beautiful name, and such a satisfying
one to say, to read, to type. I don't think I have ever spoken
your name aloud, or even formed the letters onto a page or
a screen, although please know I have held it within my
heart since the day I first heard it. I remember your mother
telling me you had named yourself. What a gift that is, to
know yourself so well.
    And to see myself referred to as Nana. My dear, I'm
not sure I have words for that.
    I would like nothing more than to continue to cor-
respond with you, but first, I need to know if your mother
knows you have written to me. She made it very clear to
me years ago that she didn't want me in your life, and
I want to abide by her wishes.
    Much love,
    Your Nana

Dear Nana,
    No, Mom doesn't know I'm writing you, and I'm
not going to tell her. I'm 12 years old, I can make my own

decisions, just like she did. And if you don't like that then maybe I shouldn't have written to you in the first place.

Your granddaughter,

Dove

Dearest Dove,

You're right, and I'm sorry. I relish the opportunity to get to know the young woman you've become. Now tell me, have you ever heard of a young musician called Drake? His PR team has been emailing me asking if I would shoot him for his Instagram, even though I keep telling them I'm retired—and even if I wasn't, I wouldn't do social media. Does that seem old-fashioned to you?

Much love,

Your Nana

Dear Nana,

Maybe a little bit? But I think that's a good thing. Anyone in the world can put something on social media. Even me, like I have this dumb Kazu account where I post videos of me and my friends doing dumb stuff. But only you can do what you do!

xoxo

Dove

Dearest Dove,

You are very wise, my love. Now where can I find this Kazu account? I would very much like to see videos of you and your friends doing dumb stuff.

Much love,

Your Nana

Dove was true to her word—for the two years she and her grandmother wrote to each other, she never told her mother. Another lie that wasn't really a lie, because her mother never asked her, never even mentioned Imogen's name until yesterday, when they arrived at Swaying Palms. Now, she suddenly seems to want to talk about her, and it's making Dove uneasy. That makes two secrets that are lies-that-aren't-really-lies. And it's getting harder and harder to believe she is doing the right thing—or to even know what the right thing is.

It's as she's reaching up to pin the photo back on the wall that she glimpses another photo beneath where the clipping was. It takes a minute for Dove to understand what she is seeing: a man, dressed in a wetsuit, floating in a tank of greenish water. To his left, a large sea creature. She unpins another clipping, and then another. There are photos underneath all of them, all of the same man and the same creature. A whale?

No, she realizes, not a whale.

Hurriedly, she peels one of the photos off the wall, then replaces all the magazine clippings. She races back to the bedroom, opens her backpack, and pulls out her laptop. Just before she went on her big adventure, her grandmother sent her a link to a webcam at a place called Halfiron Springs, where Florida manatees go when the weather gets colder. Over the past three months, Dove has spent hours watching it—putting it on in the background while she does her homework, when she's listening to music, when she can't sleep. Now she opens her laptop and brings up the site again. On the homepage is a video shot on an underwater camera, a school of silvery fish swimming through the frame. Far in the distance, she can make out the shape of something larger. She holds the photo up next to the video. The same body shape, the same tail, the same snout. It is definitely a manatee.

She flips the photo over. The back is gummy from adhesive, and in the bottom right corner her grandmother has written *Ray and Pebble, 2018.* Her fingers shaking, Dove opens another tab on her browser and types in the names. All that comes up is a news story about someone called Ray Romano playing golf at Pebble Beach. She assumes that Ray must be the man, so instead she types in *pebble manatee.* Her screen floods with old news stories about a manatee named Pebble, and a link to something called Flamingo Key Aquarium and Tackle.

The site looks like it was made in the '90s—one endlessly long page with yellow writing on a purple background, pictures either way too small or way too large, and annoying banners on the top and bottom. She wonders if the actual aquarium exists anymore, but when she brings up the address, not only is it still open, it's only a few miles away from the trailer.

She gets out of bed and crosses over to the window. Through the blinds, she can see the back end of the neighbouring trailer, a trellis of bougainvillea trailing up the side and across the roof. Beyond, over the tops of the palm trees, she can just make out the commercial landscape along the Tamiami Trail: a 7-Eleven sign, a billboard for a personal injury lawyer, a huge American flag flying over a gun store, and a green highway sign that says FLAMINGO KEY, with an arrow pointing diagonally up and to the right.

"Is that where you are, Nana?" she murmurs, staring at the sign. "This whole time, have you been right here?"

Lauren

Lauren and Dove's first couple of days at Swaying Palms are a fever dream—a messy, humid blur of heat rashes and broken things, insects and lizards and strange birds all running scattershot from behind cupboard doors and under patio furniture, only to creep back in under the shadow of night to reclaim their space. Dove finds a bike in the shed and rides it around the trailer park for hours, while Lauren rifles half-heartedly through the cupboards and closets and giant Tupperware containers, occasionally escaping into the carport to breathe something other than the stuffy trailer air. At night, she jolts out of sweaty nightmares in tangled sheets, wondering where she is, why the sirens that wail through the night sound different, why the light crawls across the ceiling at an unfamiliar angle. Then she lies awake listening to the rain pummelling the roof, watching the streetlights winking through the palms waving in the wind.

On their third day, Lauren is on her way back from the 7-Eleven across the Tamiami with a case of beer when her phone rings. She holds her breath, stopping in the middle of the sidewalk to check the caller ID, but she exhales when she sees it's only Joy.

On the other end of the line, she can hear the unmistakable voice of George Gray exclaiming *come on down!* "Isn't it a little late in the day for *Price Is Right?*"

"Lill's laid up with a knee replacement. We PVR'd all the episodes she missed while she was in the hospital," Joy says. "Are you home now? Can you check to see if you have a package? I ordered you one of those Himalayan salt lamps. It says it's been delivered, but I don't trust those FedEx guys."

Lauren bites her lip. "Actually, Dove and I are in Florida. At Swaying Palms. After I talked to you, I figured I should come down here and check things out for myself."

"Oh! That's wonderful!"

"Yeah." She considers whether she should tell Joy about Jason. The thought of saying the words out loud is almost unbearable. "Things are . . . not that great at home," she says finally. "Jase and I are having some problems, but don't worry, it's nothing we can't figure out. I just needed some time away."

"Oh, Lauren." Joy's voice is heavy with concern, but she doesn't say anything else.

"Anyway," Lauren says, eager to change the subject. "Turns out the trailer is falling apart. And the neighbour is a real bitch. I don't understand how Mom lived here."

"Ah, you must be talking about Carol Harvey." Joy makes a tsking sound. "She and your mother were close friends up until a couple of years ago. Then, suddenly, they weren't."

Lauren jams her finger on the button for the traffic light a few times, balancing the case of beer on her hip "Seriously? Do you have any idea what happened?"

"No idea, sweetie. You know how guarded your mother was.

She didn't even tell me they had a falling-out. But you know me," she adds, her voice lilting in that singsong way it does when she's about to say something she thinks Lauren will find flaky. "I'm very intuitive about these kinds of things."

"That you are," Lauren says. Her phone buzzes a notification against her ear. She lowers it to check the screen and sees a text from Hayley.

girl, where are you? Ron is getting on my case about the money, please text me back!

"Fuck," she mutters, her stomach tightening. She raises the phone back to her ear. "Joy, you don't think there's a chance Mom hid all that money *here*, do you? Like, buried under a palm tree or something?"

"Anything's possible. But I wouldn't go digging up the lawn just yet."

"You're probably right." The light changes, and Lauren steps out onto the crosswalk. "I guess I was expecting to find a collection of Fabergé eggs or a solid gold statue of Elvis or something. Or at least appliances that weren't a hundred years old. But it doesn't look like she's done anything to the place since Gran died." At the gates of Swaying Palms, Lauren pauses. "Do you think . . . do you think Mom was happy here?"

"Sweetie, I don't think your mother was ever happy," Joy says without hesitation. "It wasn't even something she aspired to."

Lauren rolls her eyes. "What else is there in life *to* aspire to?"

"Enlightenment, I suppose. It's different from being happy, you know."

"Come on, Mom wasn't after enlightenment."

"Fine. A deeper meaning, whatever you want to call it. Communicating something that tapped into a collective consciousness. Laying bare the artifice of the human condition. That kind of thing."

"That still doesn't explain what she was doing *here*."

Joy sighs. Lauren hears the fridge door open, and she pictures Joy standing in the middle of her kitchen in her yoga pants and mala beads, drinking her homemade kombucha straight from the bottle. Sometimes Lauren regrets giving her that Thich Nhat Hanh book. "She was tired. I think she just liked being somewhere where she could be ordinary."

"Really? That's your theory?" Reaching the trailer, Lauren puts the beer down on the patio table and kicks off her sweaty sneakers. "She moved here because she was tired of being rich and famous and just wanted to shop at Walgreens and buy her clothes at Dressbarn, the same as everyone else?"

"Oh, Lauren, you don't shop at Dressbarn, do you? You really should be wearing ethically harvested natural fibres."

"Of course I should."

"Sweetie, I know you want me to have answers for you, but I don't. I loved Imogen, but I don't pretend to have ever understood her. There are a million different things she could have done with that money. For all I know, she could have given it all away to a stranger."

Lauren turns to Carol Harvey's trailer and notices the blind lift ever so slightly away from the window. "Or maybe a neighbour stole it," she says, loud enough for her to hear. The blind drops abruptly. Her phone buzzes again in her hand, but she doesn't look. She doesn't have to—she knows it's Hayley, who never texts just once. "Joy, I've gotta go. I'll talk to you later."

"All right. Just . . . don't overthink all this, okay? Enjoy yourself a little. You are in paradise, after all." Joy pauses. "And Lauren? Maybe you should think about telling Dove about your . . . problems at home, if you haven't already."

"I'll keep that in mind." Lauren hangs up the phone and steps off the driveway and onto her side of the lawn, wiggling her toes in the dry, prickly grass. As a high-heeled shoe, when you're facing something that causes you anxiety—what Dr. Lightfoot refers to in *Putting Your Best Foot Forward* as a "sewer grate scenario"—you should ground yourself by visualizing the type of surface you would prefer to be walking on. She suggests imagining those metaphorical sewer grates are a sandy beach, or a plush carpet, or a mossy forest floor. But for now, this scrubby patch of lawn will have to do.

Suddenly, Lauren hears shouting. When she raises her head toward the noise, she sees a man running at her with a garden hose in his hand. He's motioning to her legs, and she glances down to discover that her feet have turned a shade of rusty red that is proliferating rapidly over her ankles and onto her shins. The pain reaches her brain at the same time as the horrifying realization that the rusty red is not spreading up her skin, but crawling. The man turns the hose on, and as the cold water hits her she screams and runs for the driveway, water everywhere as she stumbles onto the asphalt.

"Turn it off!" she cries, shielding her face from the spray. The water stops. Her feet and shins are now covered with bright red dime-sized welts. Growing lightheaded, she leans against the car. "Oh god."

"You're fine," the man says, chuckling. He's wearing dirty cargo shorts and a SPMHA staff T-shirt, and the smell of sweat and chlorine radiates off him. "A few fire ant bites won't kill you."

"A few?"

"Fine, a few hundred." He flicks a rogue ant off her knee. "You're new here, aren't you?"

"Why, because I've never been swarmed by fire ants before? That's a common occurrence around here?" Lauren tries to keep her voice steady, but she knows the pitch is rising.

"No, because you were on the grass in bare feet. Do you know what could be lurking in there?"

"I do now!" Light sparks in front of her eyes, and she tilts her head back, focusing on the corrugated tin roof of the carport. "I think my heart is beating too fast. And my lips are tingling."

"You're fine. It's just the adrenaline." He picks up the end of the hose and loops it over his shoulder. "Put some ice on your legs for the swelling. The pain should subside in a couple of hours. Then you'll have a nice set of blisters that you'll have to fight the urge to pop."

"Lovely."

"Calvin?" a voice calls from the trailer next door. "What's going on?"

"Just a run-in with some fire ants, Dr. Harvey."

Dr. Harvey cackles with glee, and her little beady eyes peer out between the slats of her closed blinds. "Don't let her distract you from your work, Calvin. That thatch palm at the end of the driveway badly needs trimming."

Lauren shakes her head. "She and I are going to be best friends."

He raises his eyebrows. "Dr. Harvey? She's harmless."

"Two days ago she tried to murder me with a toy gun."

He laughs. "Well, she wasn't a huge fan of the woman who lived here before you."

"She's not the only one."

She can see him studying her, and so she pretends to inspect her legs, running her fingers over the angry red welts already forming there.

"You're Ms. Starr's daughter, aren't you?"

"Maybe."

"Maybe?"

"There's no evidence I wasn't actually left on her doorstep by aliens."

"Ah. So it's like that."

"Yeah." Lauren can't think of anything else to say, so they stand in awkward silence. After a moment, he reaches up to a bent piece of lattice that has come free from the frame and bends it back, tucking it in and flicking away a piece of gunk. A realization dawns on her. "You're the one who washed the windows and painted the steps," she says.

He shoves his hand into his pocket. "I'm the maintenance guy. It's my job."

She regards him, eyes narrowing. "That seems like it's a little beyond your duties."

"I liked your mom. She was a nice lady. She used to give me a bottle of scotch every Christmas. Expensive stuff." He squeezes the hose nozzle gently, and a thin stream of water trickles out, splashing onto the asphalt pad of the carport. "I guess I just thought it was something I could do."

"Well, thank you," she says, crossing her arms over her chest. "I'm sure she would have appreciated it."

He gives a short laugh. "She would have told me to fuck off and do something useful." He raises an eyebrow. "Sorry."

Lauren's face flushes. Of course this random stranger knows her mother better than she does. "Yeah, no, that sounds more like her."

"I'm, uh . . . I'm sorry for your loss."

"I feel like I'm the one who should be saying that to you." Lauren clears her throat. "You'd better go finish trimming that thatch palm, Calvin."

"You'd better go put some ice on those legs, uh . . ."

"Lauren."

"Lauren," he repeats. "Call me Cal."

"Okay, then. See you around, Cal." She turns, feeling his eyes on her as she wobbles down the driveway. She can still hear Dr. Harvey laughing from inside her trailer.

Sitting at the kitchen table with a beer in her hand, Lauren mulls over her conversation with Cal. Did he seem a bit cagey? Had Imogen given him more than just pricey booze? Had he scammed her somehow, promising to make upgrades to the trailer and never following through? Or, heaven forbid, could he have seduced her? Convinced her to write a secret second will leaving all her money to him?

Lauren takes a long sip of beer. She knows she is letting her imagination get away from her. She makes a mental note to keep an eye on Cal, and then pushes him out of her mind.

She finds Dove in the bedroom, sitting on the bed in her underwear, playing some video game on her laptop, a fan blasting in her face. Lauren thinks about what Joy said. While she's certainly not going to tell Dove about Jason's text, she does owe her more of an explanation for why they're here. She gives a little knock on the doorframe.

"Come on, we're going to Taco Bell."

Dove doesn't look up. "No, thanks."

"Are you kidding? You love Taco Bell." At home, Lauren doesn't let Dove eat fast food, but if they're going to have this conversation, she needs her in a good mood. "I am your mother, and I am ordering you to come with me to eat cheese and refried beans, okay?"

With a sigh, Dove climbs off the bed and slides her feet into her boots. In the doorway she stops. "Eww, what happened to your legs?"

"Florida," Lauren says, ushering her out the door. "Florida happened to my legs."

At the restaurant, Dove picks at a bean burrito while Lauren ploughs through four soft tacos and her half of their Nachos

Supreme. "When your dad and I were young, we used to put our nachos *inside* our tacos," she says between bites. "Sometimes, I would sneak hot sauce inside your dad's. You know how he can't handle spice. He'd pretend he was fine, but his face would turn so red." She pushes the container across the table. "Have some before I eat it all."

Dove listlessly pulls a soggy nacho out of the container and lets it hang from her fingers, dripping grease. "There's meat on this."

Lauren closes her eyes briefly, then opens them again. "I told them to leave it off. Do you want me to take it back?" Shaking her head, Dove drops the nacho. "I'm sorry, babes. They probably don't even know how to make nachos without meat in this stupid state."

Dove takes a sip of her drink, then begins pulling the straw up and down through the plastic lid with an ear-splitting squeal. "Why are we even here if you hate it so much?"

Lauren crumples up the wrapper of her last taco and drops it on her tray, resisting the urge to snatch the cup away from Dove. "Honestly? I just want to get the trailer fixed up, sell it, and never have to think about Florida again." Dove stops playing with her straw and stares at her. "Things have been . . . a bit rough for me for the past few months. I've been trying so hard with Gordon Lake, and your dad's been gone so much, and your grandmother—"

"You're going to sell the trailer?"

"Well, yeah. You thought we were going to live here?" Lauren laughs mirthlessly. "I know Florida might seem super fun, babes, but it's all old people and guns and Mickey Mouse. You hate all those things."

Dove blinks, her face flushing. "You're unbelievable."

"What?" Lauren says, surprised. "Are you actually mad?" Dove presses her lips together, silent. There is an expression on her face that reminds Lauren of Imogen, and she is struck, not for the first time, at how alike the two of them are. She supposes she could say the same for Jason, too—the three of them like distant little islands, serene and unyielding in the middle of a vast ocean while Lauren struggles against a current to try to reach them.

"Do you even know *how* to fix up a trailer? Do you have any clue what you're doing?"

"I'm sure I'll figure it out."

"No, you won't," Dove hisses. She leaps to her feet, flinging the tray toward Lauren, spattering her in meat and cheese and grease.

Lauren leans back in the booth, slouching down as the other diners turn to stare at her. She gazes at her feet in her sandals, red and welt-covered, and tries to imagine herself barefoot on an expanse of clean, cool marble tile. *Fear is what happens when the ground beneath our sole is uneven, as it does when the ground beneath our soul is uneven,* Dr. Lightfoot says. *If you level the ground, you can eradicate your fear and embrace the unknown.* But Lauren can't look down at her feet without seeing them swathed in a wriggling mass of tiny red bodies, without feeling their millions of little ant fangs sinking into her flesh. She wraps up the rest of Dove's burrito in a napkin and follows her out the door.

That evening, when everyone else is tucked up in their trailers watching the news, Lauren and Dove go down to the pool. Dove still isn't speaking to Lauren, but she isn't able to resist the call of the cool water in the heat. Lauren sits on the pool steps and sips beer from a red Solo cup, watching Dove floating on her back with her head resting on the flutterboard, wondering how her baby girl suddenly became this fourteen-year-old headstrong young woman.

When Lauren got pregnant, she told Jason at the top of a roller coaster. It was the August before their senior year of college, and they both had summer jobs at Thrillville, an amusement park just outside Lennox Heights, where Lauren sold ice cream and sno cones and Jason worked as an operator on the Expedition G-Force. Lauren had been feeling off for weeks, the world around her taking on a muted quality, as though everything was shrouded in cotton. She craved peanuts and couldn't stand the smell of the hard lemonade Jason bought from his boss, who sold it out of a cooler for $3 a bottle. One time, she threw up on the Expedition G-Force, after having ridden it at least twice a day for months without so much as a swoon, and Jason had to clean it up while Lauren sat with her head between her legs.

But from the moment she found out she was pregnant, contentment settled into her body. Here was the start of their family, growing inside her. Here was someone they had made, someone who was going to have all the best parts of the both of them. And in her dreamy, hormone-drunk state, there was no doubt in her mind that Jason was going to be as elated as she was. Otherwise, she wouldn't have told him at work. Otherwise, she wouldn't have met him just as his shift was ending and asked, "Can we ride?"

He eyed her, taking a drink from his plastic Thrillville water bottle. "You're not going to puke again, are you? Because you're going to clean it up this time."

"I'm not, I promise."

Jason took her hand and muttered "sorry, security testing" as they pushed past all the kids waiting for the front car, the line snaking back from the gates and curling around itself within the corral. As the train chugged to the top, Lauren turned to face Jason as best she could within the confines of the headrest. She pictured herself as one in a long line of women opening their mouths to say this very thing—nervous or sad or scared or joyous, or none of these, or all of them; some whispering the news in bed from pillow to pillow, others shouting to the clouds from mountaintops or the apex of a roller coaster.

"I'm pregnant," Lauren said, before the wind took the words away from her.

Jason whipped his head toward her, the heavy plastic from the headrest digging into his cheek. "You're what?"

"I'm pregnant," she said again, and then the car began to drop, just as she'd imagined it. What an amazing story to tell their child, she thought—that her existence was made known to her father as he went over a cliff, willingly succumbing to the pull of gravity.

When the ride was over, Lauren laughed and pushed her hair out of her face, relieved that she hadn't vomited. Then she turned to Jason and saw him sitting there in the car, his hands white-knuckled on the safety bar, tears streaming down his face. At first, she thought it must have been from the wind.

"You're not supposed to ride the coaster if you're pregnant," he said softly. "It's right there on the sign."

"Are you crying because you're happy?" she asked.

Jason didn't answer. He just stared straight ahead until the safety bar raised, then climbed out of the car, wiped at his eyes, and walked away, leaving Lauren standing on the platform, swallowing furiously to keep from throwing up.

Lauren often thinks about the moment they plunged over the edge together—the drop momentarily lifting them from their seats before the G-force pinned them back down, their future laid out before them as smooth and fixed as the coaster's track—as the last moment she felt truly happy, truly free. She had believed motherhood would calm the unease she had felt in her own skin her entire life, but it only amplified it. Now, she wonders if Imogen felt the same—if she had been expecting

motherhood to make her feel whole, only to discover it frag-
mented her in ways she never could have foreseen. Suddenly,
Lauren is overcome with grief at the thought that she will never
be able to ask her.

As Lauren climbs out of the pool in the waning twilight, she's
startled by a man peering at her over the low fence. He is slight
and stooped, his bald head covered in a splattering of liver spots.
"Now, Imogen," he says. "You know you're not supposed to be in
the pool after dark."

Lauren crosses over to the fence. "I'm not Imogen. And it's
not after dark."

The man wags a crooked finger. "Don't try to fool me, Imogen.
I know it's you. And your daughter Laura is right over there."

"Lauren," she says. "Wait, no, *I'm* Lauren."

A woman appears behind him, as slight and stooped as he
is, a cloud of snow-white hair resting on top of her head. "Percy,
stop bothering this woman," she says.

"Oh, Maude, it's just Imogen. Breaking the rules again, as
always." He winks at Lauren.

"I'm Lauren," she repeats, this time for Maude's benefit,
although maybe a little for her own, too. "Imogen's daughter."

Maude takes Percy's arm in hers. "I know, dear. I'm sorry.
After sunset he has no idea what's going on. Most of the time he
thinks it's 1952 and we're still at war with the Russians."

"It's okay. It's actually kind of nice that he thinks I look like
my mom." Lauren glances over at Dove, who is still floating on
the other side of the pool, oblivious to the conversation. "I don't
know if my daughter would be as happy to know he thinks she
looks like me."

Maude smiles. "I'm sure you felt that way at her age, too."
She begins to steer Percy away from the pool and back toward
the street. "That's it. This way. It's time for the *Wheel*."

Lauren crosses back over to the pool, wrapping herself in a towel.

"I don't look anything like you," Dove says as she approaches, her face still tilted up to the sky.

"You can tell yourself that as much as you want. But it doesn't make it less true."

Dove's head jerks toward her sharply. Then she rolls herself off the flutterboard and dives under the water, her body disappearing into the depths of the pool.

Imogen

1986

mogen hates Prague, but she loves its bridges. Specifically, she loves the Charles Bridge and the rows of baroque statues of saints perched along the sides of the balustrade. She loves the effect they have on people, the tension and drama they bring to the air. She knows there are older, more ornate bridges in Europe, ones that aren't behind the Iron Curtain. But there is something about that bridge—the texture of the Bohemian sandstone, the way the light hits it in the late afternoon, the movement of the Vltava river below it—that lights people up in a way Imogen can't replicate anywhere else. Standing on that bridge with her camera, Imogen feels as though she can see the true essence of a person.

Zed, however, hates Prague, full stop. He doesn't give two fucks about bridges, as he makes very clear to Imogen as he leans against the balustrade, lighting a cigarette with a silver Zippo. "The light, you say," he says wryly, pocketing the Zippo and gesturing with the lit end of his cigarette toward the sky. "It's been raining ever since we got here."

He's not wrong. They've been in the city for three days and have yet to see the sun. That's just one in a string of problems they've encountered—Lauren vomiting in the cab on the way to the hotel, Imogen breaking a glass and slicing open her hand at dinner the first night, Joy getting her wallet pickpocketed in Wenceslas Square. Now it's their last day, and Imogen can't force the clouds to part.

"Just a few more. Maybe on the other side."

"You promised me my soul lit up from the inside. But in this country there is no light. No light!" Zed yells over the balustrade, his voice carrying along the river. He begins to pace, and Imogen continues to shoot. "Everywhere I go, it's dark. The sky, darkened by rain. The shops, darkened by power outages. The people, darkened by their lives in this hellhole."

People assume that women are the biggest divas and therefore more difficult to photograph. But in Imogen's experience it's men who have no tolerance for change, have no flexibility. They're resistant to venturing into the unknown, and they can't handle Imogen's unflappability, her endless capacity for reinvention. They're just like children.

"Don't be so dramatic. Just get back up on the wall," Imogen says, adjusting the aperture ring.

She hadn't wanted to take the job when Zed offered it to her—photographing him for some profile in an Italian magazine she was only vaguely familiar with. They loved Zed in Italy for his deep, sonorous singing voice, the indecipherable poetry of his lyrics. The money wasn't great, and she'd been trying to scale back her freelancing so she could focus more on her own work. But then Zed told her they could go anywhere she wanted, and she realized she'd never photographed him in Prague. She needed to do it, had probably needed to the whole time she'd known him, their relationship transitioning over the decades from occasionally romantic to profound friendship, interrupted by months of silence when one of them grew tired of the other's bullshit.

But Prague is against her. She wants a certain light, and with the weather prohibiting it, she can't adjust for it the way she usually would. She's spinning out, her head in a fog, overcorrecting one minute and slipping into apathy the next. Everything irritates her, from Zed's laugh to Lauren's incessant questions to the feeling of her camera strap around her neck, something that usually brings her comfort. No matter how hard she tries to focus, she can't find that opening she's constantly searching for—that tiny crack that lets her capture the truth of a person before it vanishes, or is folded back into the layers they've built up around themselves.

She's losing Zed's attention. *Just like a child.* "Look at me," she says. She takes out a bottle of bubbles she'd tucked into the pocket of her trench coat to keep Lauren occupied, unscrews the top, and whisks the wand around inside. Zed regards her, his curiosity clearly piqued, if only slightly. She plucks the cigarette from between his lips, takes a long drag and, without breaking eye contact, brings the wand to her mouth and exhales. A bubble begins to form, encasing the smoke in a fragile, iridescent orb that wobbles at the end of the wand as it grows and grows, before it closes off and lets go, floating in the space between them.

Zed looks at the bubble, then raises his finger and pops it. She takes another drag and exhales again. He extends his hand, but the bubble catches an updraft that pushes it beyond his reach and across the Vltava. "No more of this whimsical bubble shit!" he says, waving dismissively. "I'm done."

"I'm not done!"

"Well, you'll be photographing her, then," he says, gesturing to the statue of St. Ludmila hovering above them, young King Wenceslas tucked into her skirts.

Imogen clenches her fist, feeling the spot on her hand where the glass had cut her. It was the strangest thing. She'd picked up her glass to refill her wine, and it had shattered as if it were a thin layer of ice on a river's edge. She should have had stitches, but she convinced Joy all she needed was some gauze and a good stiff drink, and for Lauren—who had burst into tears at the first sight of blood—to stop crying. She got two out of three, Lauren's tears escalating to screams as Joy carried her out of the restaurant and up to their room.

When Imogen found out she was pregnant, she was sure she would be having a son. She'd imagined a whole life for this male version of her, a boy who would fall asleep on piles of clothing or in guitar cases, who would charm the men around her by asking them the innocent, ingenuous questions that only a child can get away with. He would grow up independent, intelligent, curious. He would love books and music and art as much as she did, and when they were able to meet as adults—over a bottle of wine at a bistro in Paris, or a pint sitting at the bar in a Dublin pub, or a coffee at the diner around the corner from his apartment in New York or L.A.—he would challenge her views on everything, and they would part ways for weeks or months, thinking of one another fondly in the interim. A relationship with a son—a boy, a man—was a relationship she understood.

When Lauren was born, screeching and angry, after seventeen hours of labour and with one more X chromosome than anticipated, Imogen felt that life she had envisioned trickle away from her, like water down a bathtub drain. The nurse placed the baby in her arms and Imogen could barely hold them rigid enough to keep the child from tumbling to the floor. She had no idea what to do with a little girl.

Now, on the north side of the bridge, Lauren stands with Joy beneath the statue of St. John of Nepomuk clutching his crucifix to his chest, his head ringed by a halo of stars.

"You know what's really cool? They say if you touch the statue, it will bring you good luck," Joy says, placing her hand on the plaque, the bronze worn smooth and golden by thousands of other hands searching for answers, for something higher than themselves. Joy took a leave from teaching when Lauren was born, after Imogen begged her to. After all, who could be a better nanny for Lauren than her own aunt? But Imogen hadn't anticipated what it would be like spending so much time under Joy's judgmental gaze. It's hard enough feeling guilty about her daughter; she doesn't need to feel guilty about her sister, too.

"I don't want to," Lauren whines through her toy dog's ear in her mouth. "He scary."

"He's not scary," Joy says, hopping up onto the balustrade and letting her legs swing. "He was a priest. And he will grant all your wishes." She reaches out her arms for Lauren. "Come on, look! He even has a dog, like yours!"

Lauren stops sucking the dog's ear. "He magic?"

"He's not magic, he's a martyr," Zed growls, swooping in behind them. "He was tortured and then thrown off the bridge from this very spot. Just like this." He hoists Lauren up by her armpits, drawing her back through the air as if preparing to throw her. She lets out a piercing scream.

"Zed!" Imogen yells sharply.

Zed flies Lauren, still screaming, around in a circle, then across the bridge, making airplane noises as he lands her in front of Imogen. "I believe this is yours," he says.

As soon as Lauren's feet hit the ground, she runs to Imogen, burying her head in her thighs. "Jesus, you scared the shit out of her," Imogen says. She puts down the bubbles and wraps her arms around Lauren, stroking her hair. "You're okay. He's just playing a game. Go back to Joy."

"No." Lauren's eyes well up. "You."

"Babes, you need to be a big girl while I work." Imogen peels her daughter away from her legs and swings her around by her arm. She can't spend one more second contemplating that face, those watery brown eyes, the matted, wispy cloud of her hair, her pudgy, tear-streaked cheeks. The longer she looks, the harder it will be to let go. "Go to Joy."

"Come here, Laur," Joy says, jumping down from the balustrade. "Let's go look at the other statues."

Lauren waddles across the bridge, ramming the sodden ear back in her mouth. As Imogen stands up, she knocks over the bottle of bubbles, the blue fluid trickling between the cobblestones. Below them, the Vltava flows on, and on, and on.

The bar at the Hotel Alcron is lit up even though most of Prague is still dark and powerless after the nuclear accident at Chernobyl a few months earlier. Onstage, a jazz singer in a slinky red dress runs through the standards beneath an ornate chandelier, while black-tie waiters light up plates of Cherries Jubilee in the glow of the wrought-iron wall sconces. Still, Zed's right, even with all that light, everywhere Imogen looks seems to be in shadow—the couple further down the velvet banquette, the faces of the musicians accompanying the singer, the hands of the bartender who pours her whisky.

Imogen joins Zed at his table, where he is hunched over a crock of French onion soup. "This is the only edible thing on the menu," he says, cheese hanging from his lip. "These communist fuckers have no idea how to cook a steak."

Raising her glass, she gives him a wry smile. "I'll stick with this," she says, tipping it toward him.

"Jelena doesn't let me eat cheese," Zed says. He peels a piece away from the edge of the bowl with his fingers and suspends it in the air above his mouth before lowering it, his face dissolving into pleasure. "She has no idea how to live well."

"She must have some idea, or you wouldn't still be with her." Zed has been with Jelena, a photojournalist, for almost two years, the longest relationship he's had since Imogen has known him. She likes Jelena, although she finds her approach to photography too aggressive, too sensationalistic.

Zed wipes his mouth with his napkin. "I've been meaning to ask you," he says, gesturing to the ceiling. "That little one up there . . ."

"She's not yours."

"Ah." He picks up his spoon again and gives her a crooked grin. "Well, that's a relief."

Imogen rests her hands on the table. "And what would you have done if I said she was?" Every once in a while, she thinks about lying to Zed, telling him he is Lauren's father. The three other men who could possibly lay claim to Lauren's paternity would be about as interested in being a father as she is in seeing them again. That was fine, when she thought she was having a fatherless boy—he'd become a man a little too early, sure, but it would solidify his independence, free him from the burden that all boys carry of having to live up to their father's expectations. A fatherless girl, however, is an entirely different creature.

But Zed is not the fatherly type either, she knows. He shrugs, shovelling a mound of broth-soaked bread and glistening caramelized onions between his lips. "I just don't understand why you'd do it," he says between chews. He swallows. "A child, Imo? At the peak of your career?"

Onstage, the singer says something in Czech, and there's a ripple of laughter from the tables around them. Imogen leans back in her chair. "How is that any of your business?" She takes another drink, letting the whisky bite her tongue before sliding down her throat. "I suppose, for one thing, everyone kept telling me I couldn't: I couldn't raise a child alone and still have a career, couldn't have a child without destroying my ability to create."

"So, you had a child out of spite."

"No. Well, partially."

"Ah, I see." Zed folds his hands behind his head. Imogen hates it when he gets this way, acting as though he knows her better than she knows herself. "You just don't want to tell me the truth."

"Not true." The truth is, she has no idea why she decided to have Lauren. She has no idea what deep-seated biological imperative had released the signal to her hormone-addled brain telling her that a child would make her life complete, would finally bless her with the meaning she's been searching for.

Zed eyes her as the singer launches into "Stormy Weather." "It has though, hasn't it?" he asks. "Destroyed your ability to create."

"What do you mean?" she asks sharply.

Zed wipes his mouth with his napkin and leans forward, close enough that she can smell the mixture of onions and whisky on his breath. "You didn't get what you wanted here, did you?"

"What do you think it is I want, Zed?"

"The photo. The one perfect picture. That moment of a window of time or whatever the fuck it is you call it." He waves his hand through the air. "The thing you always want."

"Oh." Imogen is quiet. "It was the weather," she says finally.

"The weather would never have stopped you before."

He's right. There was something holding her back today, blocking her vision. She hadn't expected how much of her brain would be occupied by Lauren's needs when it should be occupied with work. Even the love she has for her is stealing a part of her focus.

She fiddles with a breadstick in a basket on the table, clamping it between her fingers like a cigar. "Do you ever think about why you only fuck photographers?" she asks.

"I don't," he protests. "I fuck lots of women."

"Oh yes, of course. The virile, prolific Zamir Khouri, man of insatiable appetites." She twirls the breadstick in her fingers. "None of the others really count, though, do they?" She puts the breadstick down and leans on her elbows, staring into his eyes. "You fuck photographers because you like how we look at you. We find the best version of you, that person you wish you could be all the time. We *see* you, in ways that others can't."

Zed is silent.

"Another whisky?" the waiter asks, coming up behind her.

"How much for the whole bottle?" Imogen asks. The waiter stares at her blankly. She takes out her wallet and begins laying American dollars on the table, one after another, until he finally snatches them up, returning moments later with a full, unopened bottle.

"Can I bring you fresh glasses?" he asks.

"No," Zed says, before Imogen can answer. "We'll be taking this to go."

It's after 5 a.m. by the time Imogen makes it back to her own room. Their suitcases sit packed and ready just inside the door, and Imogen tries to remember what time the car is coming to take them to the airport. She hoped to sneak into bed for at least a few hours' sleep before their flight, but when she turns on the light, she sees Joy is still up, sitting in the dark by the open window, smoking. Imogen can tell by the overflowing ashtray she's likely been there for hours.

"Where were you?" Joy demands, stubbing out her cigarette on the pile.

"Working," Imogen replies.

"You didn't even have your camera with you!"

"There are other parts of my job."

"I bet."

Joy stands up and attempts to close the window, but it is stuck. Imogen watches her struggle until finally it comes free and clatters down the sash. Both of them still, listening for any stirring in the bedroom, but Lauren remains asleep.

Joy moves to the couch, wrapping herself in a blanket. "When we get home I'm going back to teaching, Imo. I can't do this anymore."

"Do what?" Imogen asks. She crosses over to the kitchenette and pours herself a glass of water. Her head is pounding, the hangover beginning to edge out the high.

"This. Watch you gallivanting around with men until all hours of the night while your daughter cries for her mother."

"Oh, come *on*, Joy. You make it sound so sordid. This is my *job*."

"It's not a job, it's an *obsession*. And it's hurting your daughter."

"It's not hurting her. She's seeing the world, having experiences that very few people ever get to have. How many four-year-olds have ridden on a camel in Egypt? Or got to play hide-and-seek with Keith Richards?"

"She doesn't want those things!" Joy hisses. "She wants you! You're a mother now, and you're still acting like . . . yourself!"

"So what? I should just give up who I am?" Imogen slams the water glass down on the counter. Every time she has this conversation, she thinks about their own mother, who had been a singer before Imogen was born. She even performed at the Grand Ole Opry, singing backup for some of the biggest country and bluegrass stars of the time. All of that gone once the children came, reduced to nothing but faint memories that fuelled her bitterness, her resentment. Imogen felt it every moment of her life. "What kind of lesson is that teaching her?"

"I don't know." Joy pulls the blanket around her emphatically.

"All I know is, we can't go on like this, Imo."

Imogen rubs her temple. "I know," she whispers. "Don't you think I know that?"

Joy stands and squeezes Imogen's shoulder. "Get some sleep, okay? The car's coming at nine." She turns and disappears into the bedroom.

Imogen watches her go, the pounding in her head growing more intense. As she downs another glass of water, she finds herself thinking about that morning in the hospital when she first held her daughter. Lauren's eyes were open, and she was staring at her as if Imogen was there to save her. To her surprise, Imogen had felt a twinge of that frantic, all-consuming, irrational love she knew she was supposed to feel for her child. Maybe she wasn't a complete monster, after all. But as quickly as it came, it disappeared again, and Imogen closed her eyes, overcome once more with the desperate need to put some distance between herself and this baby in her arms. *Her* baby, now outside of her body but no less hers to carry.

With all the strength she had left in her body, Imogen lifted her arms a few inches toward Joy, who had been there for the whole seventeen hours of labour. "Will you hold her?" she asked. She couldn't stand Lauren's weight against her chest. She felt like she was suffocating.

"No," Joy said. "You keep her a little while longer. She needs to be with her mother." But there was a hesitation in her voice, Imogen was sure. Joy had known then, just as she knows now, that Imogen was no mother.

Imogen puts down the glass and crosses to the window, staring out at the Prague sky, which is just beginning to lighten with the blush of a sunrise. It is, of course, supposed to be a sunny day.

Dove

*D*ear *Nana,*

    I'm so sorry to be writing you after you asked me not to. I know I said I would honour that, and I really want to keep that promise to you, so just know I wouldn't be writing you now unless it was an emergency.

    We are in Florida. Mom and me. At your trailer. I don't really understand why we're here, especially because you're not. Mom basically whisked me away in the middle of the night, while Dad was in South America, and now we're here in your trailer and she's talking about selling it. And I just thought that was something you should know? That Mom is trying to sell your home? I guess I'm just worried about Mom, too, like it really feels like she's gone off the deep end a little. Over the past few months, she's been steadily getting weirder and weirder. Like she still does all the psycho Stepford Wife-y things she used to do, but there's something off about it. Her fake plastic smile seems a little more plastic. And sometimes she just,

84

like . . . stares? Which is something she used to get mad at
ME *for doing all the time. "Be present in your life!" she'd*
say, like she was quoting a fucking throw pillow. And
she thinks I don't notice, that I just think she's regular old
Mom doing regular old Mom things, when in reality she's
basically been body-snatched. How does she think I won't
notice that? I'm worried about her but I'm also mad at her
for making me worried about her.

    Anyway, I really hope you get this. I don't want you
to come back from wherever you are and realize you have
no home, and then be like, "Dove, why didn't you stop your
mother from selling my house?" How am I supposed to
figure all this out on my own?

    xoxo Dove

It takes Dove three days after finding the photo to build up the
courage to bike to Flamingo Key, mostly because she is scared
to ride over the drawbridge. Each day, Dove pedals on wobbling
legs down the sidewalk beside the Tamiami—basically a highway
through the middle of the city lined with shopping plazas—to
the beach road. Then she stops at the foot of the bridge, her pulse
racing, hands clamped around the handlebars, until finally she
gives up and turns back, her face burning with humiliation, telling herself *tomorrow, tomorrow.*

But after her mother tells her she's selling the trailer, Dove
knows there are no more tomorrows. She needs to talk to her
grandmother now. After they get back from the pool, she sends
Nana an email and locks herself in the bathroom, where she
carefully removes every one of the articles tacked up on the wall,
then every one of the photos underneath, looking for any notes
Nana might have written on them. But there is nothing, so she

puts everything back up again. She spends the rest of the evening searching for more information about Pebble on the internet. She doesn't find much, and she finds nothing at all about Ray, the man in the wetsuit, or about Nana's connection to either of them. The most recent article she can find is a newspaper ad from the late '90s for an event where twenty strong men from a local gym were going to try to carry the manatee out of the aquarium and set her free.

Maybe she's not there anymore? she texts Dex later that night. *Maybe this whole thing's just a wild goose chase.*

I feel like if they'd actually set her free, there'd be an article about it or something, he replies. *Besides, didn't you say the date on the photo was from last year?*

Yeah.

You have to go. Post a Kazu!

I will. You up for Everrain again tomorrow afternoon? I really want to run that weird K'Ilith dungeon again.

I'm going to the mall, but I'll be around later.

K, tell Kait I miss them!!

I'm not going with Kait. But I'll tell them when I see them.

Who are you going with? Dove types, then deletes. This is *Dex*. He's probably just going with his moms, or his Uncle Greg, who isn't really his uncle but actually his biological father. It's not like Dex has made an entirely new posse of friends in the four days she's been gone. *Unless it's not someone new*, a tiny voice in her head says. But she pushes it away, texts back a black heart instead, their usual sign-off.

The next day, she checks her email as soon as she wakes up, but there's nothing. If the aquarium is her only clue to where Nana is, then Dove has to be brave. She slips out while her mother is still asleep and bikes furiously through the park, bearing down with enough force, she hopes, to expel any fear and doubt from her mind. When she gets to the bridge, she stops, takes a deep breath, and begins pedalling slowly up the incline, cars flying by her, boats whizzing beneath her, the clanging metal and rushing wind making her insides twist up into a ball. She crests the summit and begins gliding down the other side, and the ball begins to disintegrate. Once she's on the key, the road is flat and wide, with broad bike lanes peppered with tourists cruising leisurely along, and she starts to breathe again.

As she comes up on the address she googled, she has to check her phone again to make sure she's in the right place. There's nothing that looks like an aquarium—just an empty parking lot surrounded by a rusting chain-link fence. She bikes through the open gate, and as she gets closer to the water, she realizes it's some kind of marina. At one end is a grungy tiki bar, and attached to the pier on the other end is a hulking wooden ship, surrounded on the other three sides by a concrete barrier peeking just above the water's surface. One mast has cracked in half and there are three stumps where the other masts should be, and off the back of the boat's cabin is an octagonal green-and-white-striped tent that reminds Dove of a circus big top. A set of rickety metal stairs nearly a storey high leads down from a door on the deck to the pier, and at the bottom is a faded sign that says FLAMINGO KEY AQUARIUM AND TACKLE.

Even though she knows that must be where the manatee is, she can't imagine anything living in there. In her mind, she had pictured one of those fancy aquariums like the New England Aquarium in Boston, where she went on a school field trip—all architecture-y and pretty, with crowds of tourists flowing in and out, maybe a waterfall or koi pond or parking attendants outside. This aquarium looks more like an abandoned pirate ship, and the only other person in the entire area is a man working at the tiki bar, a cockatiel perched on his shoulder spewing a string of profanities at the football game on the television. Dove ducks her head and pedals past them, the cockatiel's *fuck you, fuck you* following her across the parking lot.

She hops off the bike and stares up at the door. It's heavy and wooden, with no hint of what's behind it, but she can see a faint light glowing through one of the portholes. She puts her hand on the railing, then tests the bottom step with her foot. It feels solid, so she continues climbing to the top. She tries the door, but it's locked. From her bag, she removes the key she found, which she grabbed from the bedside table at the last minute on a hunch. She slips it in and turns it. The lock clicks.

She pushes the door open and steps inside the cabin. Directly across from her, illuminated by the light through the door, is a giant crab staring out through the glass of its tank. He's at least two feet wide, and all by himself in a massive tank decorated with rocks and seagrass and a fake dock piling covered in barnacles and clusters of mussels. She walks over to the tank and presses her finger against the glass, and it leaves a foggy print that fades away after a couple of seconds. Ignoring her, the crab shuffles around, picking things out of the gravel that she can't see.

She steps back, and the floorboards creak under her feet. As her eyes begin to adjust to the dark, she sees the entire cabin is lined with tanks full of different kinds of aquatic life, sectioned off by a massive glass archway full of coral and tropical fish. There's no light other than the sun streaming through the portholes and the coloured lighting illuminating the tanks, which gives the room an eerie feel, like walking through your own dream.

"Nana?" she whispers.

There is, of course, no answer. Her voice echoes down the hallway, and she can sense things moving in the tanks around her, startled by the new presence in the gaping quiet of the ship. But other than the sea creatures, she is alone.

That's when she realizes that, yes, she really did think her grandmother was going to be here, waiting for her on the other side of the door. She wraps her arms around herself in the dank chill of the cabin, feeling foolish. This isn't some quest in *Everrain*, where you follow the clues and overcome obstacles and get the reward. She should know better than to believe that's how life works.

On the other side of the archway is a reception desk and, behind it, a closed door. She walks over and picks up a brochure from the counter, faded but clearly once glossy, with a man on the front dressed as a ringmaster pointing a cane at a marquee containing the words *Flamingo Key Aquarium and Tackle: Your Destination for Family Fun on Flamingo Key!*

When she opens the brochure, the first thing that catches her eye is a photo of a manatee, its pudgy little nose sticking out of the water. *Pebble, the oldest manatee in captivity*, the caption reads. Is this really the same manatee as in Nana's photos? How long do manatees live? Could she actually still be here?

At the other end of the cabin is a door, and when she goes through it, she's enveloped in a greenish glow from the striped canvas tent above. In front of her is a cement tub built into the floor, with a raised platform on one end. She climbs up onto it and peers into the water, which is full of floating lettuce pieces and has a greenish tinge to it, though she can't tell whether it's from algae or from the reflection of the tent. Beneath all the gunk, a dark blob moves slowly around in circles.

Dove holds up the brochure, then peers back down into the water. Brochure. Water.

"Are you Pebble?" she asks. Her voice sounds quiet, muted, absorbed into the heavy canvas of the tent. The blob doesn't move. "Pebble!" she says again, calling her as if she were a puppy, slapping her hands against her knees. Still nothing.

This is wrong, she thinks. Of course, nothing about this place feels *right*, but here under the tent it's worse, and her stomach flip-flops like when she's watching *Crime Files* and there's a victim who looks a little too much like her. She read online about Pebble's mother dying while giving birth to her, about her never being able to return to the wild. She knew she was going to find Pebble alone here. But she didn't know just *how* alone it would feel.

Dove sits down on the platform, pulls out her phone, and starts filming a video for Dex and Kait. "Hi friends," she whispers. "I didn't want to put this on Kazu because I'm probably trespassing. I mean, I *know* I'm trespassing. But I have to show someone what I found." She flips the camera around and points it at the water, where Pebble's shadowy outline is still lurking. "I'm pretty sure it's the same manatee as the picture, but I'm going to sit here and wait for her to come to the surface so I can know for sure."

She hits send, then stares at her phone. But no response comes, which is strange for a weekend, when she knows they both have their phones glued to their hands. Maybe it didn't go through. *Did you get the video?* she types. Still no response. She rests her head on the railing and watches the water, loneliness overcoming her. The mass continues to slowly circle the pool, skimming along the bottom, never rising any higher. "Come on," Dove whispers. "Come say hi. Please." It hits her then, how badly she wants to see the manatee up close, to see what her grandmother saw.

But it's more than that, she realizes, staring at the picture on the brochure. She wants to see Pebble's little snout poke up out of the water like that. She wants to look into her eyes and see that she is the same manatee who was here all those years ago. She wants the manatee to know she is here. She doesn't know why it matters so much to her, it just does.

But the manatee just keeps slowly circling, circling, circling.

Lauren

arb is a widow, she tells Lauren as they stand together in the shade of the carport. So many women in the trailer park are. Everyone keeps asking her when she is going to start dating again, but you know what? Barb is perfectly happy being by herself. Does Lauren mind if she just sits down for a second? Her sciatica has been acting up today and she's on her way to the pool to do some aqua therapy. Barb's seen Lauren at the pool with a young girl, is that her daughter? Barb has three daughters and five grandchildren, and she would have more if her youngest daughter would just settle down and get married like the other two. Is Lauren's daughter's father still in the picture? Men these days work so hard, barely any time to spend with their families. Gene was a car salesman, and he worked hard to provide for his family, but he was always home at 6 p.m. without fail, so they could sit down to a home-cooked family dinner together. Nobody has home-cooked family dinners anymore. Nowadays, it's fast food in the car on the way to soccer practice, or microwaved meals in front of the TV. Not that Barb minds a microwaved meal now and then, especially since she is alone. But she always makes sure she sits at the table, like a civilized human being. It's when the little things go that we start to completely degrade as a society, you know? And how hard is it to put a napkin in your lap before a meal?

"Truly," Lauren says, the first word Barb allows her to get in. It's late in the morning, but Lauren is still in her pyjamas, having only just roused herself from bed. She'd stepped out into the carport with her coffee to check if Dove had taken the bike when she was accosted by a woman in her mid to late seventies wearing a bright, flowered bikini top and white canvas shorts, a plastic visor with a Speedo logo nestled in her coiffed grey hair, skin tanned and leathery, lips, fingernails, and toenails all painted the same electric pink. "Can I get you something to drink? An iced tea, maybe?" she adds reluctantly.

"Oh, no thank you, hon, I can't stay. I'm already running late."

Lauren nods, relieved, and starts moving toward the trailer door.

Barb doesn't budge. "So, how long are you planning on staying?" She leans forward and clasps her hands together in a way that reminds Lauren of a daytime talk show therapist, and she wonders if Barb has cultivated this pose for gossip purposes.

"I'm not sure yet. I'm just assessing things, seeing what Mom left here."

Barb arranges her face into an expression of concern. "Of course, dear. It's all so tragic. You poor thing, you must be completely overwhelmed."

"Thanks. I . . ." Lauren means to say *I'm fine*, but the words get stuck in her throat. "Thanks," she repeats, sitting down.

"You'll find we have a very supportive community here in Swaying Palms," Barb says, patting her hand. "Have you met any of your neighbours?"

"Just Dr. Harvey," Lauren says, gesturing to the trailer next door.

"Oh, she doesn't count." Barb gives a dismissive wave. "I'll introduce you to my shuffleboard girls: Rosa and Mariam across the street from you, and Helen, who's just behind you and over a few doors. And her brother Frank, who really is the sweetest man. He's one of the few widowers in the park, and he's been so good to me since Gene passed." She glances around to make sure no one is listening. "I think a few of the other ladies might be a little jealous."

"Well, I hope I get to meet him," Lauren says.

"Oh, you will. Do you play shuffleboard? You must come out and play with us. You could take over your mother's spot. She was a wonderful shuffleboard player."

A snicker comes from behind the blinds of Dr. Harvey's trailer.

"Oh god, I'm sorry," Lauren says. "I think she's listening to us."

"Of course she is. She's got nothing better to do than sit at that window judging everyone." Barb pushes back in her chair, angling herself around the trellis. "You have something to add, Carol?"

The blinds move slightly, and Dr. Harvey's beady eyes appear in the crack. "Just laughing at your characterization of Imogen as a 'wonderful shuffleboard player.' I don't even think she had the mental capacity to understand the rules of the game."

"She's just mad because your mother once went after her with her shuffleboard stick. Remember that, Carol?" Barb calls. "You jumped over the fence to get away and ran right into the pool." She turns back to Lauren and leans in conspiratorially. "I hate to be one to gossip, but I heard they were fighting over a man," she whispers.

Lauren laughs. "My mother? Got into a fight over a man? No chance."

"Well, that was just one of the rumours. I also heard it was a money thing."

93

I knew it, Lauren thinks. "What kind of money thing?"

"Oh, I don't know," Barb says, waving her hand through the air dismissively. "I don't like to get too involved."

Yeah, right. Barb's clearly what Dr. Lightfoot would call a "classic flip-flop"—looks comfortable but is really right up in your business. "Come on, you must have some idea."

"All I know is, it was a big deal. Those two were at each other's throats for years." She drops her voice to a stage whisper. "A reliable source told me your mother paid a float plane pilot to fly over the beach at sunset with a banner that said *Carol Harvey Is a Traitor*."

"No wonder she hates me," Lauren says. "You know, when we first got here, she shot me with a toy dart gun for accidentally stepping on her lawn. And I'm pretty sure she sent a bunch of fire ants to attack me." She reaches down and absently scratches her shin, where the bites have begun to dry into itchy scabs.

"Now *that* I believe," Barb says. "She was a bug scientist . . . what do you call it? An entomologist. She's retired now, but I imagine she could summon a bunch of awful creepy-crawlies if she wanted to."

"I don't need to," Dr. Harvey says. "That trailer is already infested."

Lauren inhales sharply.

Barb takes her hand again. "Don't worry, dear. She's just trying to get under your skin."

Behind the blind, Dr. Harvey chuckles but doesn't say anything else.

Long after Barb finally leaves, Dr. Harvey's comment keeps echoing in Lauren's head. If the trailer really is infested, she can't let Dove know, or she'll end up sleeping in the car or running away to the Motel 6 on the Tamiami. Dove shares her father's fear of bugs—in their household, Lauren is the fly killer, the bee trapper, the one who puts down ant poison and sweeps away cobwebs, the one who Dove screams for at night when a moth flutters around her light fixture or in the morning when a house centipede slinks across the bathroom sink.

She presses her ear to the wall of the living room, and sure enough, she can hear something scuttling. Above the television, she spots a hole, and as she is staring at it, a pair of antennae emerges, followed by the long black body of a beetle.

"What the fuck are you?" she says in a low voice, even though she knows Dove is off on the bike somewhere, completely out of earshot. The beetle crawls out of the hole, and Lauren kicks off a sandal and crushes it against the wall. She knows it's futile, that there are likely hundreds more burrowing through the walls, but it's worth it for that one moment of satisfaction, feeling its hard shell yield under the force of her shoe.

Further inspection reveals several other holes, contained to the inner walls of the trailer. She remembers seeing a can of Raid under the sink and hopes the fact that it expired in 2016 doesn't have any bearing on its effectiveness.

She's just about to check the bedroom for more holes when there's a knock at the door. Through the window, she sees it's Cal, the maintenance guy.

"Hi," he says as she opens the door, then scrunches up his face. "Are you okay in there? It smells like chemical warfare."

He's wearing the same staff T-shirt she sees him wear every day, but instead of his usual cargo shorts, today he's wearing a pair of board shorts, teal blue with bright pink flamingos. Lauren imagines him riding around the park in his little golf cart, fixing things and chatting with the residents, then clocking out at 3 p.m. and heading down to Flamingo Key for a quick surf before his early evening set playing acoustic covers at the oyster bar. Of course, she doesn't know for sure that he surfs and plays guitar, except somehow she does. She knows how easy his life is, free from responsibility, doing whatever he wants whenever he wants to.

"It is." She shakes the can of Raid.

"The only thing you'll kill with that garbage is several of your own brain cells." His eyes travel down to her legs. "How are those ant bites treating you, anyway?"

Involuntarily, she reaches down and scratches her knee. "Can I help you with something?"

"Oh, yeah." He glances around the carport. "It's just . . . well, I saw someone on Ms. Starr's old bike. I thought maybe it had been stolen."

She sighs. "A girl, about yay high, with dark hair and a bloody cross on her backpack?" Cal nods. "That's Dove, my daughter. I told her she could ride it around the trailer park."

His mouth drops open in mock indignation. "Trailer park! Oh *no*, Lauren. It's a *mobile home community*."

She peers out the door at the trailer and its foundation of cement bricks. "These homes don't seem very mobile to me."

"Don't tell the residents' association that," Cal says. "They'll run you out of town."

"They might do that regardless."

"Anyway," Cal continues, "if this was your daughter, you might want to double-check where she went, because she was out on the beach road and definitely not in Swaying Palms."

"Son of a bitch." Lauren retreats into the trailer and puts down the can. "Where the hell is she going?"

Cal shrugs. "The beach?" When Lauren scoffs, he throws up his hands and says, "Okay, maybe you should ask *her*."

"Ha ha, very funny." Turning on the faucet, she begins soaping up her hands, trying to scrub out the smell of the insect poison.

Cal leans against the doorway. "Ah, well, she is a teenager." He runs his hand through his hair and it stays raised, buoyed by either hair product or sweat, or both. "When my kid was that age she didn't talk to me for weeks at a time, other than a few grunts."

"You have a kid?" She's unable to hide her surprise, and in her head she rewinds the tape of Cal the Maintenance Guy/Surfer/ Acoustic Guitarist to try to figure out where to fit in a kid.

"Brody. She's seventeen now. Lives with her mom in Fort Lauderdale, but she's thinking of coming to Sunset for college."

The fridge kicks on and begins to rattle, almost imperceptibly, with all the beer bottles shoved too close together inside. "Well, Dove has never talked to me. That's just how she is."

"Everyone has to talk to *someone*." His eyes land on the hole above the television. "Termites?"

"Some kind of beetle, I think."

"Powderpost, probably. May I?"

"Be my guest."

He crosses the room and peeks into the hole. "Doesn't look too bad, but you might want to think about hiring an exterminator."

"I'll get right on that."

"Your mother told me the same thing. That was almost a year ago."

She joins him at the hole, drying her hands on a damp dish-towel. "It seems like you knew my mother pretty well."

"I'd help her with stuff around the house sometimes. Once in a while we'd have a beer together. She was a nice lady, like I said." He touches the edge of the hole with the tip of his finger, pushing against the ragged drywall. "Not all the residents here treat the staff like human beings."

Lauren nods. If there's one thing she does know about her mother, it's that the ruder the others were to Cal, the nicer she'd have been to him. "Earlier, you said something about how

Dr. Harvey wasn't a fan of hers. Do you have any idea what happened? My aunt told me they'd been good friends."

"There were rumours. But neither of them ever talked about it. It must have been something dramatic, though, 'cause they did all kinds of crazy things to each other. One time Dr. Harvey called me over because she thought she was getting some weird interference on her radio. Turns out your mother had hidden a tape recorder in her ceiling that played a recording of an old-timey radio play, to try to convince Dr. Harvey her trailer was haunted." He chuckles.

"It's been suggested that Dr. Harvey retaliated by infesting this trailer with bugs," Lauren says.

"Now that would be a pretty sweet trick." As he pulls his finger back, another beetle emerges from the hole. Lauren grabs the can of poison and sprays the beetle, which drops to the floor, writhing on top of a pile of drywall powder.

Cal covers his mouth and moves toward the door. "That's one way to handle it," he says from behind his fingers.

"No mercy," Lauren says solemnly.

"Well, if that doesn't work, let me know. I can recommend a good pest control company."

"Thanks, I'm good!" she calls to his retreating back just as it starts to pour—big, heavy droplets that slam off the carport's metal roof. She opens all the windows, hoping the fresh, clean scent of warm rain will replace the pesticide fumes, but the air outside just smells of exhaust from the Tamiami.

Her phone buzzes in her pocket, and she takes it out, expecting it to be Dove texting for a ride home in the rain. But instead, it's a notification that Jason has posted a new photo on Instagram. She clicks on the notification and lets out a sharp exhale. The image that pops up is one she recognizes—Jason, standing on a beach in Mexico against a backdrop of startlingly blue water, wearing a wet white tank top, board shorts, and mirrored sunglasses, his arms tanned and muscular, his skin glistening with water. He's holding a bottle of Corona in one hand, and the other is clenched into a fist with his thumb and pinky extended.

Fun in the sun, the caption reads, followed by *#tbt*.

She knows this photo. *Dove* took this photo. They were on a family trip to an all-inclusive resort in the Mayan Riviera. It was much nicer than they could ever have afforded, but Jason got a discount through the airline. They had a view overlooking the ocean, big fluffy robes, and a marble bathtub. Every day when they got back from the beach, their fridge was restocked with beer, the bed was made with clean sheets, and there were fresh towels folded into the shapes of animals on the bathroom counter. Dove made a friend who she swam in the pool with while Lauren and Jason lay on the beach under resort umbrellas, drinking endless piña coladas that seemed to just appear in their hands.

Sometime on that trip, Dove took this picture. Which Jason has now posted again, for reasons Lauren can't fathom. Is he using a picture *his daughter* took as a thirst trap? Is there someone he's trying to impress? *Oh god, what if there's someone else?* This is something she hadn't even considered until now.

"Mom?" She raises her head to see Dove standing in the doorway, soaked from head to toe, little half-moons of mascara streaked under her eyes. "Are you okay?"

"Yes, babes. I'm fine," she says, tucking her phone away. As she stands up, the blood rushes back into her legs, and her skin fizzles with an almost unbearable itchiness. "Where did you go today, anyway?"

Dove shrugs. "Just did some loops of the trailer park."

"Must have been fun in the rain," Lauren says. She opens the linen closet and pulls out a towel that must have been her grandmother's, thin and frayed and smelling faintly of tobacco, a giant Walt Disney World logo on the front.

"I went to the rec hall," Dove says, reaching for it.

"Oh yeah?" Lauren holds it back. "Play a little bingo, did you? Or maybe check out a couple of Tom Clancy novels from the library?"

Dove snatches the towel from Lauren and rubs it over her face, smearing her mascara into little Rorschach tests on her cheeks. Then she bends over and drapes it over her head, scooping up her hair and winding it into a knot in such a grown-up way Lauren can hardly bear to watch.

"What's for dinner?"

"You didn't answer my question," Lauren says, but Dove just turns and goes into the bedroom.

Later, Lauren heats up a frozen pizza and they sit in front of the television watching some reality show about librarians while they eat, although Lauren makes Dove put a napkin on her lap in deference to Barb.

"She's captain of the shuffleboard league or something like that," Lauren says. "She just lives a few doors down."

"Is she the one with the Republican bumper sticker on her car? Or the one with the lawn sign that says DON'T NEW YORK MY FLORIDA?"

"Why are you so grumpy?" Lauren asks, trying to keep her tone light, even though inside she is quietly freaking out, going through a rolodex of every woman Jason knows and imagining them having an affair. *Plush carpet, plush carpet.*

"Because we're surrounded by a bunch of Trump supporters?" Dove frowns. "I think you're sitting on the remote. The channel just changed."

"It's right here," Lauren says, grabbing it off the coffee table and chucking it onto the couch. Taking a bite of pizza, she opens the Instagram app on her phone and starts scrolling through Jason's millions of photos of plane wings and airport coffees, all the selfies with the flight attendants at the hotel bar. If Jason is cheating, there must be some evidence somewhere—a like or a comment by a stranger, someone sitting a little too close, a reflection in his mirrored sunglasses.

"Mom? I think the TV is broken."

Lauren glances up from her phone. "It seems fine to me. See, there's good old Guy Fieri, about to take us to Flavourtown."

"Yeah, except I was watching *Librarians of Florida*, not the Food Network." Dove picks up the remote again, flicking through the channels. Suddenly, she shrieks and pulls her legs up on the couch. "There was a rat!" she says. "It's behind the television."

Lauren puts down her phone, sighing. "It's probably just a mouse, babes."

"I know the difference between a mouse and a rat!" Dove squeezes herself up even tighter. "I heard one the other night, too. We're going to get, like, the plague or something."

"It's not a rat," Lauren says. "There's no way it's a rat." She gets up and pulls the stand away from the wall. As she does, a large, furry rodent scurries across her feet and shimmies under the door to the sunroom before she even has a chance to scream.

"I told you!" Dove grabs a throw pillow and buries her face in it before flinging it across the room, shrieking even louder. When Lauren picks it up, she sees it's covered in beetles. She runs for the door and opens it, throwing the pillow out into the carport, then turns back around just in time to see Dove lean over the arm of the couch and throw up.

"See?" Lauren says, resting her head against the wall as Dove straightens up, wiping her mouth. "We're basically in paradise."

Ray

forgot to tell you, Rayna, what it was I wrote for Pebble's plaque.

> Born in 1933, Pebble was one of the first manatees born in
> captivity, and she is currently in the *Guinness Book of Records*
> as the oldest captive manatee in the world. Her name is
> Pebble because when she was born, she was no bigger than
> a tiny pebble at the bottom of the pool. But now she has
> grown to almost 1100 pounds! Manatees are herbivores, and
> their diet consists of seagrass, mangrove leaves, and algae.
> Here at Flamingo Key Aquarium and Tackle, Pebble eats
> lettuce, carrots, and sweet potatoes. She will eat 10 per cent
> of her body weight a day.

After staring at it day after day for almost thirty-five years, I can recite it by memory, though I have grown to loathe it. It doesn't even begin to capture Pebble's magic. But maybe that's the way it should be. Even a manatee needs to keep her secrets.

After that first encounter, I found myself returning to the manatee enclosure at the end of my shift, routinely staying an extra hour or two. I didn't put my foot in the water again; I would just sit on the viewing platform and watch her. My instinct was to get her used to my presence, to see what would happen. I had no idea what Pebble did when she was alone. Did she stay at the bottom of the pool? Did she surface, performing all her old tricks to the empty enclosure? I thought perhaps if I waited long enough, was patient enough, I would find out the answer. I don't know why it was easier for me to be patient with her than with you, Rayna, but in retrospect I am ashamed I never extended you the same generosity. You are my wife, and you deserved so much more.

For over six months, Pebble ignored me. It was clear she'd been neglected for so long that she had forgotten how to interact with people. She would only surface when she had to breathe. Occasionally, she would meet my eyes, and I would think that we were making a connection, only for her to turn away and slowly sink down further into the depths of the pool. But I didn't give up. I started moving closer, day by day, dipping my toes tentatively back into the water. Eventually, I moved to sit on the edge of the tank, my work pants rolled up to my thighs, my feet dangling. She never tried to push me out again, as she had that first time. But the closer I moved into her space, the further away she seemed.

I knew nothing about animal behaviour or training or biology then. I still know very little, even after all this time. I was just a plumber, a squeegee holder, a chemical mixer, dumping heads of lettuce into the pool and hoping for the best. I've always believed that all of God's creatures are searching for the same thing: someone to be kind to them, to treat them with tenderness, to come to them at their level. So, eventually, that's what

I decided to do. I came to Pebble at her own level. One day, I clutched the lettuce to my chest like a talisman and slid off the side and into the pool.

I was terrified, Rayna, make no mistake about that. Manatees are gentle giants, but they are still giants. If she wanted to hurt me, she could have hurt me. But she stayed as far away from me as possible. I held on to the edge and kicked my feet gently, waiting. She didn't move. I took the head of lettuce and tossed it toward her.

Minutes passed. I was about to give up and get out when I suddenly saw her begin to rise through the water. Her snout broke the surface, and from that eye-level vantage point I could see the gaping abyss of her maw, the massive blocks of her teeth beneath her whiskered snout as she took in a breath. Then she grabbed the lettuce in her front flippers and disappeared back into the pool.

It was a small thing, but it felt like a victory, and enough to make me want to keep going. I did the same thing every day, for months, before she began to trust me. No one knew what I was doing except Jorge, who told me I was crazy, that even Sharples hadn't been able to get the baby manatee to engage in recent years.

"Well, of course," I said. "Sharples killed her mother."

"Her mother would have died anyway," Jorge said, shrugging. "And she would have died along with her."

Jorge wasn't wrong. Even though Florida had begun legally protecting manatees in 1907, threats from fishing lines, boat strikes, red tide, and declining habitat made their odds of survival in the wild slim. At the time, I didn't think about whether it was better to die free or live in a prison—and to be honest, I still don't think I know the answer. But nothing Jorge could say would have deterred me from trying to make her life in the tank at least a tiny bit better.

After a year of my getting in the pool with her, she no longer hesitated before moving toward the lettuce. Some days she would eat it, other days she would slap at it with her front flippers, sending it swirling back across the pool toward me in a gesture I could only assume was annoyance or frustration. She was growing to tolerate me, but really, she still wanted me gone. Sometimes I would let myself sink beneath the water and listen to her vocalizations, trying to figure out her moods, but all her grunts and squeaks sounded the same to me—sad, hollow, lonely.

I don't think it's a coincidence that this all began after we lost the first baby, Rayna. It felt more possible to bring Pebble back to the surface than it did you. I remember the days I would come home to find you in the bathtub, the water cold to my touch, sitting there, staring at the wall in front of you. It was as though you were lost in a vast ocean within yourself, and I could not reach you. Much to my shame now, I didn't try. Even months later, when you were mostly back to your old self—baking in the kitchen, sweeping the palm berries from the steps, reading in your favourite chair on the porch in the evening—I would catch you staring off again, and I knew you were adrift on that same ocean. When I called your name, you would turn and look straight through me.

If only I had immersed myself in that ocean with you—had waited, as I did with Pebble, for you to come to me on your own terms. But instead, I would turn my back to you, and leave you to descend again to the depths, alone.

Aside from my own cowardice in facing you, there was another reason I was spending so much time with Pebble. I was worried that her reclusiveness was going to become a liability. I had seen the aquarium visitors excitedly enter the manatee enclosure, only to turn around and leave moments later, disappointed. Florida is a place where your worth is judged by your entertainment value. The orcas at SeaWorld jumped in the air, the penguins dove and somersaulted, the sea lions honked on command, balanced balls on their noses, imitated human gestures. No one was interested in staring down through cloudy water thick with decomposing lettuce at an unmoving shadow lurking at the bottom.

And as it turned out, my worry was not unfounded. One afternoon, after I had been in the water with Pebble and was getting ready to go home, Sharples's grandson, Tom, came into the manatee enclosure. As his grandfather had gotten older, Tom had taken over most of the day-to-day operations of the aquarium. Usually, I tried to stay out of his way. Tom wasn't a bad man, but he had a poorly hidden drug habit that drove most of his decision-making. The less I was around him, the fewer bad decisions he would try to involve me in.

Tom walked around the perimeter of the pool, staring thoughtfully into the murk. "Ray," he said, "does she ever come to the surface?"

"Yes," I replied. It wasn't a lie—she had to come to the surface to breathe. But I knew that wasn't what Tom meant.

"Hmm," was all he said, and then he walked the rest of the way around the pool and back out the door. After that brief interaction, I had a feeling that Pebble was in danger, though I wasn't sure from what, quite yet. Sold off, if anyone would have her, or possibly even euthanized. I told myself at least Tom wasn't considering setting her free.

"We'll set her free," he said to me and Mrs. Appleby the next day, as we were going over some invoices in the office. His eyes were red-rimmed as he paced in front of the desk where the two of us sat, stunned.

"What?" I finally asked, dumbfounded.

"You can't be serious," Mrs. Appleby said.

"We'll make an event of it!" Tom continued, his pacing growing more frantic. "We'll call the papers and advertise it on the radio, so people can come out and see us, the progressive Flamingo Key Aquarium and Tackle, world leaders in animal welfare, releasing one of its captive mammals back into the wild. We'll be heroes. Plus, we'll sell tickets. We'll make a boatload of money at the same time as we're saving ourselves a boatload of money."

"We can't," I said faintly. "She'll never survive."

"Of course, she will," Tom said, clapping me on the back. "She's an animal, she'll adapt."

There was a part of me that wanted to believe him. I had so often watched her skimming along the walls of the tank, imagining her instead skimming alongside the mangroves in the Intracoastal Waterway. But I knew, *I knew*, that it was a bad idea. It was more than a gut feeling. It was an understanding of how being in that tank had shaped her. What it had given her, and what it had withheld. There was no way she would make it out there on her own.

"It will kill her," I said, more assertively. "She has no idea how to fend for herself."

But it was as if Tom didn't even hear me. "We'll schedule it for next month," he said. "I'll have to find the right equipment, bring in some people to help lift her. I know!" He snapped his fingers. "Maybe we could do a cross-promotional event with the weightlifting gym that just opened up in the village." He rummaged through Mrs. Appleby's desk for a pen and a pad of paper, and as I watched him scribble down his ideas, I realized: he didn't care. He wasn't doing this out of the goodness of his heart. It wasn't altruism driving him—it was greed.

For the next few days, I spent as much time as I could with Pebble. I didn't get into the water with her again; instead, I sat by the pool and read to her from books about manatees that I'd taken out of the library. After working with Pebble for so many years, I was embarrassed to discover how little I knew about how manatees lived in the wild. The extent of my knowledge was what I had written on that sign. I knew she couldn't understand what I was saying, but I had to do something. No one had taught her how to be a manatee, and this was my deluded attempt to rectify that. I could only hope that, somehow, something would sink in.

I learned through Mrs. Appleby that Tom had arranged the cross-promotion with the gym and was in the process of figuring out the logistics. The plan was to lift Pebble out of the enclosure and lower her over the side of the ship into the water, with the aid of the weightlifters and some sort of pulley system that would need to be designed from scratch. I began hearing ads for the event on the radio on the way to work, Tom's voice echoing through my truck, sombre and unusually low-pitched. *Pebble the manatee has given us so much. Now it's time for us to give her something: her freedom*, followed by swelling orchestral music. I never knew what came next, because I always turned it off.

"In the wild, you'll have to use your flippers to scoop vegetation from the substrate to your mouth," I whispered into the water. "None of this floating lettuce stuff. Make sure you find warmer water once the season turns. There's a refuge at Halfiron Springs where you can stay safe and warm all winter, but you'll have to figure out how to get there on your own. And for god's sake, avoid boats. Avoid anything driven by a human, actually. We are the enemy."

"That part is true," I heard a shaky voice say, and lifting my eyes from the book I saw a man standing just inside the entrance to the enclosure. Harry Sharples.

I had only met Sharples twice before, and each time had been an event. He rarely came to the aquarium, and when he did, Mrs. Appleby would run around for days making sure that everything was in perfect order—the reception area organized, the displays clean and polished, every burnt-out light bulb replaced, every garbage can emptied. It was like a celebrity was coming to visit, and I had been appropriately intimidated, preferring to stay as far away from him as possible lest his famous temper pick me out of the crowd.

But this time, I hadn't been aware he was coming, otherwise I would have left the second my shift was over. I certainly wouldn't have sat with Pebble, reading books to her like a fool. And yet there he was, watching me with his small, rheumy eyes, the tremor in his hands visible from across the enclosure. Far from the formidable man I had made him into in my mind.

As he crossed the enclosure, I rose to my feet. When he reached me, he took the book I was reading from my hands and regarded the cover. "*The Magnificent Florida Manatee.* I haven't read this one."

"I think it's a children's book," I said quietly. "But this was all I could find."

Sharples opened the book. "*The manatee calf will stay with its mother for one to two years, long enough to gain information about travel routes, feeding areas, and warm water refuges.*" He glanced up at me. "Did you read her this part yet?"

"No." I shifted uncomfortably. "I left that part out."

He handed the book back to me and stepped to the edge of the pool, gazing down into the water. Pebble continued to circle slowly, her shadowy outline coming in and out of view beneath the rafts of floating debris. Every time she reached our side, I could feel my pulse begin to race, but she never stopped, never broke her pace. The moment felt so oddly intimate I wondered if I should leave, but the second I took a step away Sharples turned to me, and I was surprised to see his eyes were wet with tears.

"The manatee stays where she is," he said.

I paused before I spoke. "Your grandson has other plans."

"I'll speak to Tom. But promise me, no matter what happens in the future, you will make sure the manatee stays where she is."

Who did he think I was, Rayna, that I could make such a promise? Still, I knew that I would always do everything in my power to make sure that she did. "Yes, sir," I said.

Sharples crouched down and dipped his hand into the water, swirling it around. For a second, I thought he was going to jump in, but he just kept pushing his hand back and forth, as though he were stirring a bath, making sure it wasn't too hot. His lips moved, and though I couldn't hear the words he spoke, I'm fairly sure he was saying *I'm sorry*.

Pebble continued circling, slowly, slowly, slowly, until finally he straightened back up and, without another word, walked out of the enclosure.

After he left, I immediately changed into my wetsuit and got into the pool. As I lowered myself into the water, I could hear Pebble chirping below the surface, a longer, less sharp noise than the frustrated grunts I was used to hearing from her. I stayed under as long as I could before rising for air. Suddenly, I realized she too was rising through the depths, and she was getting closer. I stayed by the side of the pool, treading water as gently as possible, not even daring to breathe. Then there she was, her snout huffing above the waterline a foot in front of my face. Still holding my breath, I held out the lettuce head. She regarded it, and me, for what felt like an eternity. I thought she would swim away, as she had done so many times before when I was getting too close. But on this day I swear I saw something flicker in her eyes, a flash of recognition, or of resignation, as she carefully and gently opened her mouth and took the head of lettuce from my trembling hands. Then she reached up with her front flippers and held the lettuce to her chest as she descended through the water column.

Until then, Rayna, I hadn't known what it meant to really accomplish something—to put work and effort into something I dearly wanted, and see that rewarded. But I guess I don't have to tell you that. You know that better than anyone. Every day for more than a year, I had gotten into that pool with Pebble, and every day I got an inch closer to her trusting me. I believed, then, that I could cover miles that way. Maybe part of me still does. Maybe part of me believes that, by telling you this story, I can cover some of the millions of miles that I let stretch out between us. But to travel that slowly takes time. When I was twenty-four, I believed I had all the time in the world. Now I know that while I have been inching toward my goals, time has been speeding away from me at a mile a minute.

It wasn't until I left the pool and was on my way home that I realized what Pebble had been doing, what her chirps meant. She had been calling out to another manatee. She had been trying to find more of her own kind.

Lauren

After she cleans up Dove's vomit, Lauren offers to go ask Cal for help. "He'll know what to do about the rat," she says to Dove, who eyes her skeptically. "He said he'd helped Mom with stuff like this before." Secretly, she's glad to have an excuse to see how he lives. If he's shacked up in some Spanish revival mansion down by the Intracoastal, she'll have a pretty good idea of where he got the money for it.

At the maintenance shed, an older man washing a golf cart directs her and Dove—who refused to be left alone in the trailer—to Cal's apartment. To Lauren's disappointment, his place is above the main office near the entrance to the park, in a rundown pale yellow stucco building facing the Tamiami. An ambulance screams by as they climb the stairs and knock tentatively on the door.

"Hi," Lauren says when he answers, shirtless and still in his flamingo board shorts, holding a half-eaten bowl of cereal. "Remember when you said you knew a good pest control guy?"

"Sure." He leans against the doorframe and shovels a spoonful of cereal into his mouth. As he drops his arm, Lauren notices his biceps have dramatic tan lines bisecting them. Maybe not a surfer, then. "What do you want to kill first?"

"Nothing!" Dove blurts out. "You can't kill it!"

Lauren puts her hand on Dove's shoulder. "We have a rat. And my daughter would like it to live, just not in our trailer."

Cal turns his attention to Dove. "Ah, a humanitarian," he says through a mouthful of Cheerios.

"An *animalitarian*," she says hotly, shrugging off Lauren's hand. "Humans are terrible."

"Ain't that the truth," Cal says, grinning. He tips the bowl against his lips and slurps down the last of the milk. "Let me see what I can do."

They follow him back to the maintenance shed and wait outside while he rummages around. "Babes, you don't have to stick around here. I can meet you back at the trailer," Lauren says, while Cal has his head in a cabinet full of tools.

"What, and hang out alone with the rat? No, thank you."

"Oh come on," Lauren says, exasperated. "Don't be such a wimp."

Dove doesn't respond, but red splotches appear beneath her temples as she stands there glowering, a clear sign that Lauren has embarrassed her. But she makes no move to return to the trailer.

"Here we go," Cal says, finally emerging from the cabinet. "A humane trap." He holds up a long wire cage with an elaborate door, which he pulls back. "Rat buffet goes in here, then rat comes in the door, and boom, the door closes behind her." The door snaps shut with a loud clank. "Then you can do whatever you want with her. Take her to the next county and set her free. Whatever."

Dove snatches the trap from Cal's hand and starts walking back toward the trailer.

"Sorry," Lauren says. "She's a little on edge. Hey, I was wondering . . ."

She wants to ask him about her mother. If he cleaned her gutters for her in the spring, repaired the broken latticework, gave her advice about her garden. If, when he stopped by for a beer, they would sit in the carport together and she would tell him about her life, the places she'd been, the people she met. If she told him about Lauren. If she was happy.

"Mom!" Dove stops in the road and turns around, glaring at Lauren impatiently.

Lauren sighs. "Thanks for your help," she says. Her questions will have to wait for another day.

The next day, Lauren wakes Dove at 8 a.m., before she can take off on the bike again. "Get up," she says, throwing a tote bag onto the bed. "We're going to spend some quality mother-daughter time at the beach."

"Ugh, *why*?" Dove asks, rolling over.

"Because we're in Florida, and that's what you do." Lauren barely slept last night, and when she did, she had strange, tangled dreams about Jason having an affair with a rat. She's been too closed in, here at the trailer, staring at her mother's face on the wall every time she sits down to pee. Plus, she feels badly for how she handled things with Dove last night. "It'll be good for us to get away from this place for a bit," she adds.

"That's what you said when we left Lennox Heights," Dove mutters.

While Dove gets ready, Lauren packs the car with all the beach necessities she can find: a couple of folding chairs and pool noodles dug out of the sunroom, bags loaded up with sunscreen and Doritos and bottles of water. When Dove finally comes out of her room, she's wearing a long black sleeveless dress and her black boots, but Lauren resists the urge to comment. By this point she knows better than to say anything about Dove's outfits.

Lauren drives out of the park, onto the Tamiami, and then turns onto what must be the beach road Cal was referring to, given the giant sign that says BEACH. She tries not to think about Dove riding her bike along the narrow shoulder, past the shirtless men fishing on the shore of the Intracoastal, fighting her way through traffic. Why hasn't she asked Dove where she goes? She has no idea. It's as if the line between giving her daughter too much and not enough independence keeps shifting, and she's always on the wrong side of it.

On the key side, the bridge is flanked by towers of speedboats stacked in dry dock. There were fewer condo towers the last time Lauren was here, but the hotel with the pink-and-green archway, the giant shark sculpture advertising deep-sea fishing expeditions, and the swath of tennis courts baking in the sun are all familiar. They pass the wrought iron gates and stucco walls of the gated beach clubs, candy-coloured villas with names like Crystal Cove and Casa del Mar, and sky-high condo towers overlooking the Gulf, until they reach the long stretch of parking lots adjacent to the public beach. As the ocean winks in and out of view, it all comes back to Lauren in a rush: the sensation of salt drying on her skin after a swim, the tangy smell of the seaweed washed up on shore mixed with the French fries and hot dogs from the concession stand, the surprisingly cold water against her legs as she waded through it, searching for sand dollars as the tide went out. The storm clouds that blew in one afternoon and drenched her and Imogen as they ran up to the pavilion with towels over their heads, and then stood under the eaves and watched the lightning crack open the bruised sky. The beautiful, gauzy beach cover-up Imogen was wearing. Her coral-painted toes. How much they laughed as they ran.

She's so caught up in her thoughts she almost misses the parking lot. She turns into the last driveway and circles four times before she realizes they're not going to find a spot. She drops Dove off with the chairs and the beach bags. "Set up near that lifeguard station," she says, pointing over the wall to a blue building with a green flag flying from the top. "I'm going to park in the village."

"I can't carry all this stuff," Dove whines.

"Yes, you can. I believe in you," Lauren calls out the window.

She drives into the village, with its T-shirt stores and oyster bars and ice cream shops, and parks illegally behind a yoga studio, doing her best to appear like she's on her way to class as she crosses the parking lot. When she finally makes it back to the beach, she scans the sea of umbrellas and is annoyed but not surprised to see that Dove is not where she told her to be. She kicks off her shoes and makes her way through the tents and coolers and beach chairs, the kids playing frisbee and building giant sandcastles, teenage girls lying on their stomachs on towels. Eventually she finds her, standing at the shoreline, talking to a man with his back to Lauren.

"They nest at the top of the beach, and when the babies are ready, they run from the nest into the water," Dove is saying to the man as Lauren approaches. "But then if there is a light some-where? Like from one of these houses along here, or someone with a flashlight? It makes them all confused and they can't find the water and then they *die*."

"I did not know that was the reason for the no-lights rule," the man says. "That makes a lot of sense, though."

"Yeah! And sometimes people do it on purpose? Like these kids were taking selfies with a turtle that had come up to make a nest, and the turtle got so scared it went back in the water and just, like, dropped its eggs and they died. But those kids got fined a bunch of money, like five thousand dollars or something. Here." She holds up her phone. "Let me find the article."

"There you are," Lauren says. The two of them turn toward her. The man is about eighty years old, shirtless, and wearing a pair of stained cargo shorts that are damp around the hem. Around his neck hangs a pair of headphones, and he's holding a long metal pole of some sort.

"Hi Mom," Dove mumbles.

"Hello, you must be Lauren," the man says, offering his hand. "I'm Frank. I live a few houses down from you in Swaying Palms. I saw your daughter and recognized her from the pool. I thought I would come over and introduce myself."

Lauren smiles, taking his hand. "I couldn't find parking. It's nuts down here."

"It'll be like this until after Easter." Frank waves in the direction of the parking lot. "There's a back alley behind the grocery store just over the bridge that has a few free spots that no one really knows about, if you're stuck again."

"Thanks," Lauren says. Water swirls around her ankles. What she really wants is to sit down in a beach chair, open a beer, maybe read that book Joy sent her, a new self-help paperback with *fuck* in the title. But instead, she's stuck here talking to Frank the widower lady-killer, who has somehow found them at the beach in the middle of a crowd of thousands. Well, fine. She points to the contraption in his hand. "What's that?"

"This"—he hoists it into the air—"is a metal detector. I was just showing Dove how it works. And she was asking me if I had ever found any sea turtle nests on Flamingo Key." He smiles at her. "Your daughter knows a lot about marine ecology."

She does? "She does. She's very bright," Lauren says. "She's on full scholarship to Worley Academy, one of the most prestigious private schools in the Northeast." She reaches out to touch Dove's arm, but Dove shrinks away. "Do you find a lot of stuff out here with your metal detector?"

"I do. You'd be surprised at the things that tourists leave behind." He digs around inside the pocket of his cargo shorts, then opens his palm to reveal a cheap-looking watch, a silver hair clip with a butterfly on it, a cross hanging from a gold chain, and several rings and coins. "I take all the things I find and weld them into sculptures. Just a little hobby of mine. Maybe you've seen some of them around Swaying Palms? I've given them to several residents."

"We haven't really spent much time exploring."

"I think this is real sterling silver." He hands the hair clip to Dove.

"Cool," Lauren says.

Dove holds the hair clip back out to Frank, but he waves her off.

"Keep it," he says, winking at her. He turns to Lauren. "Say, maybe you'd like to stop by sometime for a drink? I have something I'd like to show you."

Is he hitting on me? Lauren tries to smile, but it comes out as more of a grimace. "Uh, I'm pretty busy with the trailer. We've got a lot of work to do."

"Nonsense. I won't take no for an answer. Stop by any time—I'm always home, unless I'm here." He gives them a salute. "I'm off to find more buried treasure. Enjoy your beach day, ladies." He slides the headphones over his ears and heads off toward the lifeguard station.

Lauren motions to the hairpin. "That's pretty. Remember to thank him next time you see him." She glances around. "Where's our stuff?"

Dove points back toward the parking lot. Lauren sees all their things leaning against the boardwalk fence. "Seriously?"

"It was too heavy," Dove says, shrugging.

"Come on," Lauren says, sighing. "There's a good spot right over there."

Although it's early, once they've set up, Lauren sits down in one of the chairs and pours a beer into a red Solo cup. After she downs half of it, she picks up her phone and, ignoring the flurry of text and call notifications on her home screen, opens Instagram and navigates to Jason's profile. There is nothing new, so she clicks on her own profile and scrolls through her grid. The most recent picture is from the day before she got Jason's text—a promotional post for Gordon Lake, with a link to some stupid two-for-one diffuser sale. The rest is mostly pictures of coffee cups and Christmas lights, her toes at the yoga studio, and cute neighbourhood cats, interspersed with a few selfies with her girlfriends.

She glances over at Dove, who has her head bent over a comic book, cream soda in the sand next to her, the bag of Doritos wedged between her knees. A little self-consciously, Lauren snaps a few selfies, but she doesn't like any of them, so she deletes them and starts again, trying to get the white sand behind her, catch her hair while it's blowing in the breeze. After a moment, she feels Dove's eyes on her.

"How many selfies are you taking?" she asks.

"Just one," Lauren says defensively. Then she adds, "The first ones didn't work for some reason."

"Uh-huh."

"What?"

"Nothing."

"No, what's *uh-huh*?"

"It's just—how come you always have to try to make everything seem so perfect?" Dove reaches into the bag and pulls out a chip. "Why can't you just be, you know, *authentic*?"

"Jesus. I just wanted a nice picture of me on the beach." Lauren brushes some sand off her legs. It feels good on her ant bites, so she grabs another handful and begins rubbing it against her shins, like she's seasoning a piece of meat. "It's not like anyone else is going to take one."

"But, like, why do you have to make it *perfect*? Life isn't perfect."

Lauren raises an eyebrow. "Oh? Tell me more."

"You're just like all the annoying rich girls at my school, posting all their fake shit to try to appease the almighty algorithm." Dove waves her chip in the air. "When in reality they're the pawns of, like, capitalism and the patriarchy, getting suckered into a version of a perfect life that's being *sold* to them . . ."

Suddenly, a seagull swoops down and snatches the Dorito out of Dove's hand. She shrieks and drops the bag, spilling chips onto the sand, as three more seagulls come flying in from behind her.

"Watch out!" Lauren yells.

Dove covers her head but not in time, and one of the seagulls lands on her, squawking as his foot gets tangled in her hair. "Mom!" Dove screams.

Lauren grabs a towel and starts whacking at the bird. Everyone around them watches, benignly curious, but no one moves to help. Finally, the bird dislodges itself and flies away, but more are coming in its place, so Lauren takes Dove's hand and they run, weaving in and out of people until they are out of bird-collision distance.

"Jesus," Lauren says, collapsing on the sand. "What kind of seagulls are those?"

"Seagulls from hell," Dove says. She brings her hand up to her head. "I think they ripped out a patch of hair." Lauren snickers. "What? You think this is funny?"

"A little." Lauren holds up her phone. "Do you want me to take your picture? You look pretty authentic right now."

"Rude." Dove picks up a handful of sand and lets it flow through her fingers. "I hope they all get heartburn from those Doritos."

"Me too, babes." Lauren pushes her feet through the sand, making little trenches with her heels. She thinks about Frank with his metal detector, unearthing all the things that people leave behind. "How do you know so much about sea turtles?"

Dove shrugs. "I've been watching videos. Did you know that sea turtles don't pull their heads into their shells like other turtles?"

"I didn't know that." Any minute now, Lauren realizes, Dove will be a grown woman, out on her own. And Lauren will have even less to do with her life than she does now. "You know if there's anything you ever want to talk to me about, you can, right?"

"I know," Dove says, avoiding her eyes.

"It's just . . ." Lauren thinks about the past few days, together but apart in the trailer. "We never hang out anymore. You're always going off on your own."

Dove is quiet. "Did we ever really hang out before, though?" she asks eventually.

"Of course we did!" Lauren lightly kicks some sand at her. "We used to go to the mall together all the time, and those yoga classes. And I chaperoned all those dances at Worley, remember?"

Dove brushes the sand from her leg. "I hate the mall. And yoga. And I didn't even go to those dances. I'd drive over there with you and then I'd just go to the park next door."

"No, you were there. I remember seeing you! Dancing with your friends! Dex and Kait?"

"Dex and Kait wouldn't be caught dead at a school dance."

"Right." *What was I doing, then?* Lauren thinks. *Talking to the other moms. Sneaking vodka into our punch. Posting fake perfect pictures to Instagram.* She clears her throat. "Okay. What about this. You were about eight, right about the time when Daddy started doing long-haul flights, and he wasn't around as much. You had a really bad nightmare, so instead of taking you to school in the morning, we went to the Oxford Theatre and watched movies and ate Dairy Queen Blizzards that we snuck past the usher." Lauren stops abruptly. Can this really be her last good memory of being with her daughter? When she was *eight*? "You were probably too young to remember, I guess."

"It was *The Princess Bride*, followed by *Willow*. Some kind of Gen X nostalgia film fest. That was fun, I guess."

"Maybe we can do that again sometime when we get back," Lauren says. "Worley won't miss you for the afternoon."

"Yeah." A cloud passes over Dove's face, but it's gone as quickly as it arrived. "Hey, did we catch the rat?" she asks.

"Nope. Turns out he's a bit of a food snob. Cal said we might need to try a few different types of bait before he takes anything."

"That Cal guy is weird."

"Are you sure you think he's weird?" Lauren nudges her. "You don't think he's cute?"

"Gross, Mom," she says, trying to suppress a smile. "He's, like, almost as old as Dad." She squints at Lauren, her dark eyes crinkling in the corners. "I wish he was here."

"Cal?"

"Dad."

"Oh." Lauren stares out at the ocean, past the crowds at the shore and the boats out beyond the buoys, to the horizon. "Me too." She puts her hand on Dove's leg, expecting her to shrug it off like she always does. But she doesn't move. They stay like that while the gulls devour the rest of the Doritos, screaming and squawking at one another until they finally fly away, their feathers stained neon orange.

Lauren is just about to make up the couch and go to bed when her phone starts buzzing. She glances down at the caller ID.

Jason.

It takes her by surprise, even though she's been keeping track of his movements in her head, like she always does. *Connecting to*

Houston, deadheading to Philly, in the Uber by 9:30, home in Lennox Heights by 10:15. Then, one minute to realize Lauren and Dove aren't home, and five more to figure out that they haven't been home for days.

You'd think by now Lauren would have figured out what she's going to do. Whether she's going to answer the call, what she's going to say. You'd think she'd be better prepared for things. But under-preparation is common in high-heeled shoe types. What would Dr. Lightfoot think of her now, sitting here without any kind of strategy like the wedge heel she is, instead of meticulously planning things out like the low-heeled pump she is trying to be?

The phone stops ringing, making Lauren's decision for her. Then it buzzes again with a notification. One voicemail.

She changes out of her clothes and into her bathing suit. She knows it's past sunset, but she just wants to be submerged in water, with nothing to think about other than swimming. The streets of Swaying Palms are eerily quiet—the air is still and the palms barely rustle, the streetlights are glowing, and there is a faint reggaeton beat coming from somewhere outside of the park. Lauren gets to the pool and slips into the chlorine blue. It's cold but it feels like a balm. She dives beneath the water, and it fills her ears, her nose, her eyes.

As she swims for the surface, she can make out a watery figure standing by the pool. Dove. Holding out her own phone.

"Dad wants to talk to you," she says as Lauren comes up into the night air.

Slowly, Lauren makes her way across the pool to the steps, letting the heaviness sink into her body as it emerges back into gravity. She takes Dove's phone and stares at it, Jason's face gazing up at her from his contact photo, eyes squinting, cheeks puffed up like a chipmunk, the face he makes in all his selfies. She can hear him breathing on the other end, and she tightens her grip, squeezing the phone in her hand so she can feel the almost imperceptible vibration of his breath in her palm.

Then she hangs up.

Dove

Dear Nana,

   It's the middle of the night and I'm at the Flamingo Key Aquarium.

   I know you're probably wondering why I'm here at all. The short version is I found your photo of Ray and Pebble. I still don't know who Ray is or what your connection is to this place, but something happened and before I knew it, I was on a bus at 11 o'clock at night, empty except for some guy dressed up as Abraham Lincoln, or maybe it actually WAS Abraham Lincoln. I mean, at this point anything is possible. I just needed to get away from Mom, and I was on this bus and then I saw the sign for the marina and I suddenly knew that was where I had meant to go all along.

   The thing that happened is Dad called. I guess deep down I knew there was something going on the whole time, you know? I'd look at Mom and she just didn't seem . . . right. She always wanted to be there when Dad

*got home before, all dressed up and ready to take off his coat
and bring him his slippers and a martini, like some kind
of '50s housewife bullshit. She never would have taken off,
knowing he would come home to an empty house, if she
wasn't running away from something. If she wasn't running away from him.*

*Anyway, I guess Dad has been trying to call Mom and
she's been avoiding him, so he called me. He was crying,
and I think he might have been drunk, and every single
cell in my body wanted to hang up that phone. But I didn't,
because what kind of person hangs up on someone who is
drunk and crying? Especially if that person is your father?
"Dove," he said. "Where are you?" And when I told him
Florida, he laughed and then said a bunch of things about
Mom that only half made sense, about how he couldn't
make her feel loved enough, I mean, I don't even know.
Then he said, "I hope you know that none of this has anything to do with you, we both still love you so much, lots of
parents get divorced and everything turns out okay."*

*And that's when I said, "Okay, I'll go get Mom," because
suddenly my parents were getting divorced, and apparently that was not something I needed to be told. I mean,
WHAT THE FUCK. Am I not even a part of this family? Do
I not deserve to know these things? Anyway, I brought the
phone to Mom, and what does she do? She hangs up on him.
She hangs up on poor drunk, sad Dad, sitting at home in
Lennox Heights all by himself. It was too much for me to
take, and so I ran. I ran and I got on a bus with Abraham
Lincoln and then ran some more, across the marina parking
lot, into the aquarium, and straight to Pebble.*

*When I came into the manatee enclosure, the moon-
light was coming in at a slant through the tent covering*

and it made everything feel like a black-and-white movie.
I sat down and dipped my feet in the water, and when
I did, Pebble immediately began floating up. I couldn't
believe it, Nana. The first time I came here, I sat watch-
ing her for hours, and she barely came to the surface at all,
except to take a breath and then go right back down again.

But this time, she poked her head out of the water and
looked right at me. I could see, in perfect detail, the twitch-
ing of her little whiskers, the creases on her face, the rolls
around her neck, the tiny pocket of her eye puckered into
her leathery skin like a button on a couch. And for the first
time she was a real living, breathing creature, and not just
this manatee-shaped blob at the bottom of the pool. And
it was as if, in that moment, we were in a tiny, separate
world from the real world we live in, a place where the air
was like air but not quite the same as air, and I wondered
if this was like the place that you had gone to, or if this WAS
the place you had gone to, that maybe this ship is a portal to
another realm and all I have to do is immerse myself in it
long enough and it will take me, too.

I know you said you were going somewhere you
couldn't check your email, but Nana, please, write me back.
I'm so lost right now. I sometimes feel like Idira in the
Hollowgirl series, after she discovers that she is just a cre-
ation of the Juniper League's imagination, brought to life
so they can have a little plaything to make dance for them
and put on a shelf when they're done with her. Except Idira
gets to escape and just become pure consciousness, leav-
ing behind her hideously perfect human body for them to
manipulate while she goes off and lives in the ocean and
the moon and the glass of windows and the pages of books.
Me, I'm stuck in this body, pretending to be a human being

*while I am actually a howling spiral of matter hurtling
through the universe.*
   xoxo Dove

Dove wakes up on the viewing platform at the aquarium with
someone else in the room with her.

She didn't mean to fall asleep here. Her mother kept calling
and calling, but Dove didn't answer, and she knew if she didn't
go back to the trailer soon, eventually her mother would come
looking for her, or call the cops, or something even worse, if
there is such a thing. But she just needed a little more time, just
one more minute in the cocoon of the manatee enclosure, away
from her mom and the trailer and everything out there beyond
the tent. Then she lay back on the platform and closed her eyes.

It is still dark outside, and her feet have shrivelled to the
consistency of soft prunes from being submerged all night. She
pulls them out of the water, heavy and waterlogged, and wiggles
her toes. The man watches her from a distance. He is wearing a
baseball jersey and cargo shorts that look like they're thirty years
old. In one hand he has some kind of long vacuum, and perched
on his shoulder is a lizard, its eyes wary.

She knows she should be scared, but she isn't. "You're Ray,
aren't you?" she asks.

"Yes," he replies. His face is kind, inquisitive. "Who are you?
What are you doing here?"

She says the first thing that comes into her head. "I'm trying
to find my grandmother."

Ray doesn't say anything for a long time. Dove wants to take
out her phone to see what time it is, but she also doesn't want
to be rude.

"You're Imogen's granddaughter," he says, finally.

"Yes!" She sits up straighter. "Do you know where she is?"

"No. I'm sorry, I don't."

Dove slumps back down. In the glow of the ship's light, she watches the lizard on the man's shoulder flick his tongue in and out. "What's his name?"

"Toby. He's an iguana."

Dove pokes at the bottom of her foot, which is bloated like a dead fish, and peels away a piece of decaying lettuce. "I'm Dove."

"Dove," Ray repeats, sitting down next to her. "Do you want to hold him?"

Dove holds out her arm and Toby crawls onto it, his little talon feet digging into her skin as he climbs over her and tucks himself into her lap. She touches his head and then runs her finger down Toby's back. It feels like stroking a dinosaur. She thought it would feel hard, like plastic, but it is almost spongy, a slight give under the pressure.

Ray smiles. "He misses my wife."

"Where is your wife?"

"She's in the hospital. She probably won't come out."

The way he says it makes her so sad, like it is just a matter-of-fact thing that he has to live with every day, but really it's like boiling water being poured on his skin. "So why are you here, then?"

"I work here."

"In the middle of the night?"

"It's four a.m.," he says, checking his watch. "Well, it's four-thirty. I'm a little behind. You're welcome to stay. It's nice to have the company."

She imagines her mom frantically pacing the trailer, calling her over and over. Then she remembers her father's voice on the phone, how small it sounded, how far away. "Okay."

As Ray vacuums the pool, she sits with Toby, listening to the hum of the motor and the gurgling of the water through the hose. She takes a picture of Toby in her lap and texts it to Dex and Kait with the caption *New BFF!* but she doesn't get a response. She hasn't even heard back from them about the video she sent on Saturday. *They're probably both still sleeping*, she thinks. Soon they will get up and shower, eat breakfast, run to catch the bus. She wonders if they're planning to go to the sandwich place on 23rd for lunch or if they're just going to split fries in the caf; whether Kait will go to Dex's after school or if they have their karate class. If anyone will follow the two of them in the halls, jeering at them about their clothes, or their hair, or the way they walk, talk, breathe. If they'll finish that last dungeon level in *Everrain* without her, and which one of them will get to loot the Sword of Calandrinia off Morwraek.

When Ray is done clearing the pool of lettuce, he sits down beside her again. Toby wakes up and flicks his tongue at him, then closes his eyes. "You know, your grandmother used to sit right here and watch me, just like you are now. You look so much like her."

She blushes, even though she knows it isn't true. Nana was beautiful—*is* beautiful—and Dove is just this too-tall, stringy-haired, acne-covered freak. She wonders how her grandmother knows Ray. Are they friends? Do they work here together? There are so many questions she wants to ask him, but when she opens her mouth, nothing comes out. "I only met her once, when I was little," she says eventually. She shifts her weight, and Toby's claws dig into her leg, holding him in place. "Do you really not know where she is?"

"I'm sorry, Dove. I haven't seen her in months. But that's not unusual. She'll be gone for a while and then just show up out of the blue." He pauses. "Usually around this time I get in the water with Pebble, before I do the rest of my work. Just for some social interaction." He holds out his finger, and Toby loops his tail around it. "Would you like to join me?"

Dove bites her lip. Ray is asking if she wants to swim with Pebble. If she wants to get into that pool, share the same water with her, swim inside those same concrete walls. She stares down into the murky water. She wants to say yes, but a small hard ball of fear ricochets through her veins. What if she can't get out? What if she gets stuck in there too, swimming around and around in circles forever and ever?

"Thanks," she says. "But maybe I'll just watch from up here."

Ray nods. "I'll be right back," he says, and disappears into what appears to be a storage room. When he returns, he's decked out in a full wetsuit with a little hood, goggles protecting his eyes. As soon as he walks over to the pool, Pebble swims up to the surface and flaps her flippers, then rolls onto her back. Ray leans over and rubs her belly with a gloved hand before lowering himself into the water. Once he's submerged, he dives down, and Pebble chases him, barrel-rolling around him as they make their way across the tank. Dove feels a twinge of jealousy—not of Ray, but of Pebble, for having Ray. What would it be like to have someone care about you that much?

When Ray gets out of the water, Toby scuttles over to him, and Ray holds his arm out for him to climb. In the pool, Pebble sinks to the bottom, as though she knows that the fun is over for another day. Dove wonders if she anticipates Ray's arrival. Do manatees look forward to things the way humans do? Do they get disappointed when something gets in the way of that, when the routine doesn't play out the way it's supposed to?

Ray offers to drive her home. When they get to Swaying Palms, he pulls over by the entrance and lets her out there. "Come back whenever you want," he says. As she walks back toward the trailer, she turns and sees him staring past the sign, through the rows and rows of trailers, as if he were trying to see right into Nana's.

Just before she reaches the trailer, she stops. She knows she should go inside and deal with her mother, but she walks straight past it toward the pool. It's still early, and the pool is empty, the water barely moving, and there is a yellowy-orange reflection on the surface from the sun through the trees that makes it look like honey. She jumps in, fully clothed. She doesn't know why she does it. It just feels right. But as the water closes over her head, the anxiety comes rushing back, sinking her deeper into the pool. Her parents are getting a divorce. Her grandmother is missing. She's been kicked out of school. All around her are secrets—it's like she's drowning in them.

Then her face breaks through the surface just like Pebble's. And suddenly it all seems a little easier, just knowing she has a good secret, alongside all those other secrets that are so heavy to carry.

Pebble.

Lauren

Lauren sits on the pullout, another of her calls going straight to Dove's voicemail. Every time she closes her eyes, all she can see is the look of betrayal on Dove's face as she calmly hung up on Jason. All she needed to know about their conversation was right there—Dove knew, possibly even more than Lauren did, about what Jason wanted to do. But the hurt she saw in Dove's eyes wasn't because her father wanted a divorce. It wasn't even because Lauren had hung up on him. It was because Lauren hadn't told Dove the truth. And if she hadn't told the truth about that, what other secrets could she be keeping?

As the hours tick by, Lauren grows more frantic. She wonders how much longer she should wait before calling the police, every possible scenario playing out in her head: Dove dead in a ditch, Dove headed north on a Greyhound, Dove kidnapped by human traffickers. *Just one more hour*, she thinks, staring at the door. She doesn't need a self-help book to tell her that sitting there panicking won't do her any good, but she has no idea what else to do.

It's in moments like this, when she's feeling helpless and out of control, that she wonders if this is what Imogen was trying to avoid. "Having a child means you'll never stop worrying again, for the rest of your life," her mother said when she found out Lauren was pregnant. But Lauren didn't believe that for a second. Whatever concerns about Lauren her mother might have had disappeared the second she left her with Joy. She imagines her mother driving to the airport on her first child-free trip, windows open, breeze in her hair, some classic rock song on the radio, freer from worry than she had ever been.

When Lauren was younger, it was easy for her to come up with excuses for Imogen—she had to make sacrifices for her art, she'd done what was best for Lauren, she still gave as much of herself as she could. But after Dove was born, all of those excuses grew hollow. As she held her daughter in her arms, she knew she could never leave her, even if it did mean worrying about her every day for the rest of her life.

Just after sunrise, the door opens and Dove slinks in. Her hair is wet and slicked back from her face, and her dress drips water across the floor as she slips into the bedroom. Lauren is bleary-eyed and wired, her nerves as shot as they've ever been, and her relief dissolves into rage as she chases after Dove into the bedroom, almost knocking the door off its hinges.

"Where were you?" she shouts. "Why didn't you answer my calls? I was worried sick about you!"

Dove doesn't answer; she just climbs onto the bed and puts her earbuds in her ears, a tinny bass beat pounding through them. Lauren snatches the cord and rips them out of her ears.

"Those are mine!" Dove says, reaching for them. "Give them back!"

Lauren holds them over her head. "Not if you're going to use them to ignore me! You're grounded. You are to stay in the trailer unless I tell you otherwise."

"You can't do that!"

Lauren laughs. "Oh yes, I can. I'm taking your bike, too. I know you've been leaving the trailer park, after I explicitly told you not to. I know you think you're all grown-up now and can do whatever you want, but you're still my daughter, and you still have to do what I say." She tucks the cord of the earbuds into her fist and holds it up. "I'm keeping these, too."

Dove's face turns bright red. She screams and lunges at her, and they both tumble onto the bed in a tangle of flailing arms and kicking feet. The earbuds snap, flying across the room and landing on the dresser, the frayed cord dangling over the side.

"You bitch!" Dove screams, pushing Lauren backward against the pillows. "You lied! You told me you missed Dad. You told me you wished he was here, when really you ran away from him!" She chokes back a sob. "You tell me to stop running away but you're the one running away!"

"I am not running away!" Lauren yells back. "Your father is . . ."

"Is what?"

"It's complicated!"

Dove slumps down onto the bed, and for a moment Lauren thinks maybe this is over, maybe she has given up. But Dove jumps to her feet. "Get out of my room."

"This isn't *your* room."

"You're right, it's Nana's room! This whole trailer is Nana's trailer, and you think you can do whatever you want with it!"

Dove runs out of the room and slams the door, then the bathroom door slams as well. A second later, the shower starts running. Lauren sits on the bed, the broken earbuds in her hand. She pinches the cord together where it's been torn out, desperately trying to push it back in, but the damage is too great. There's no coming back from it.

By the afternoon, Jason has left Lauren thirteen voicemails and eleven texts. She sees the notifications when she wakes up on Dove's bed, which is how she thinks of it now, despite what she said earlier. She doesn't read or listen to any of the messages; she just deletes them. She knows what they must say. *Come back, come back. Come back so we can talk about ending our marriage. Come back so I can leave you.*

Still, she knows she has to talk to him before things go any further. While Dove is still asleep, flung out across the pullout like a starfish, Lauren takes her phone down to the rec centre so she can speak to Jason without Dove overhearing. On the way, she passes Frank, who is out in his carport with a welding torch, a mask pulled over his face.

"Hey, Lauren!" he calls. He lifts the mask and waves the welding torch in salutation. She waves back but doesn't stop. "Lauren!" he calls again, lightly jogging to the end of the driveway. "How about that drink now?"

She holds up her phone, waving it gently in the air. "I'm sorry, Frank, I was just on my way to make a call."

"Of course, of course." He peels the mask away from his head, then smooths his hair back. Drops of perspiration line his forehead. "Maybe later this evening?"

"I'll try, Frank," she says. As she backs away down the road, she glances around to see if anyone might have overheard their interaction. The last thing she needs is the single ladies of Swaying Palms coming for her.

When she gets to the rec hall, she sits on a bench in the community garden. As she is trying to psych herself up to call Jason, her phone vibrates in her hand.

Hey girl! I've been trying to reach you by phone but I can't

seem to get through to you. I hope you're not ignoring me,
haha! We need to make arrangements for you to get that
money to me by the end of the month, okay? I don't want
to have to bring Ron in on this but you know we've all got
bills to pay, right? Love you, xo

Lauren bites her lip. She's never met Ron, but she pictures a big, bald white guy with a moustache, a Harley-Davidson tank top, and a matching set of knuckle tattoos, who will track her down to the ends of the earth to get Hayley her money. She has a feeling Ron would love to take a business trip to Florida, catch up with some old cronies, wrestle a few alligators, and break Lauren's kneecaps. But she'll have to deal with that later.

She takes a deep breath and brings up Jason's number.

He answers on the second ring. "Where the fuck are you?" he asks, without so much as a *hello.*

"Florida. Didn't Dove tell you?"

"I mean where the fuck are you in your head that you just went to Florida without telling me?"

A loud screech comes from the pool area, and when she glances over the fence she sees a child in a swim diaper running on the deck, precariously close to the water. Likely someone's grandkid come to visit for the weekend, who's now about to fall into the pool and drown if whoever is supposed to be watching him isn't more careful.

"I tried to call you," she lies. "Imogen left me a trailer in Florida in her will. It was the only thing she had left, and now it's mine."

"That's not something you could have handled from here?"

"Didn't you hear me? There was no money left. She spent her last days living in this crappy trailer park in Florida and I have no idea what happened to her."

The build of Jason's anger is palpable even through the phone. "Who gives a shit? That's more than she deserved."

Lauren's shoulders tense. She hates when he does this. "Don't put me in a position where I have to defend her!"

"She was terrible to you!"

"She was my *mother*!" From the pool, there is a splash, followed by crying. Lauren is struck with the urge to run out of the rec hall and scoop the little boy up herself. Maybe she could start over with this one. Maybe she could take that boy and run.

"A text, Jase, really?" she asks quietly. "What is wrong with you?"

An adult voice joins in the chorus in the pool area, and then another, and soon the crying has stopped. Lauren pictures the three of them, a little happy family wrapped up in towels in the Florida sun, planning their trip to the fish shack for dinner, coming home and dreaming of sandcastles and water wings, the sun on their face, sand in their shoes. She was once part of a family like that. Or maybe she never was, and she just didn't realize it.

"Just come home, Lauren," Jason says. "We need to talk."

"I can't do this right now," Lauren says, and hangs up.

She stays sitting on the bench, unsure what to do next. She briefly fantasizes about a future in which she keeps hiding from him, so he can never actually confront her, and they just carry on like that forever. It's not an ideal marriage, but at least it's not divorce, which she imagines will always hang over her head like a giant neon sign advertising the fact that she failed. She doesn't want people to know about the train of mistakes that billow out behind her like the bridal veil she dreamed of but never had. They got married in Joy's backyard, which at the time seemed so sweet and quaint. How had they thought that was a proper start to their life together? Lauren nine months pregnant, in rain boots and a parka because it was a cold spring, the cuffs of Jason's pants getting covered with mud. The guests were mostly Jason's family, and a few friends from school, anyone they could get to come at short notice—Lauren had purposefully planned it to be last-minute, at a time when she knew Imogen wouldn't be able to come. It was just easier that way. Still, she tried to make it nice. She ordered a beautiful cake and put vases of flowers all around the yard and gave all the guests butterflies that had been frozen in little boxes and thawed out before the ceremony, so that when they were pronounced husband and wife everyone could open the boxes and set them free. But the butterflies were confused, probably stunned from the months spent unconscious, and they went crazy, flying into the ground, into the backs of chairs, into people's hair. One flew straight into the candle that Jason and Lauren had lit together, and went up in a flash of blue flame.

"Is that a bad sign?" Jason asked. But he was laughing. They all were.

Now she thinks they should have known better: how ridiculous to think something could be frozen like that and then brought back to life.

Lauren makes it about half a block back toward the trailer before she hears someone calling her name.

When she looks up, a small round woman with a buzz cut and wearing purple bike shorts and a neon green FLAMINGO KEY FISHING TOURS T-shirt is power-walking toward her. "You're headed in the wrong direction!" the woman says, linking her arm with Lauren's and pivoting her around. "We've got a shuffleboard game in an hour."

"Uh, who are you?"

"I'm Rosa. Barb wanted me to invite you to play shuffleboard with us today, but I completely forgot." She makes a circular motion with her head, like she's shaking something loose. "My brain is a sieve these days, I swear."

"Oh, no, I can't," Lauren says. "I've got to get back."

"Of course you can," Rosa says with a laugh. "You're on vacation! You can do anything you want!"

"I don't actually know how to play."

"It's easy," Rosa says as she steers Lauren through a gate into the shuffleboard area. "You'll catch on in no time." She picks up a tall plastic glass with flamingos on it from a tray on the bleachers and hands it to Lauren. "Drink," she commands.

Lauren takes a sip, lacking the energy to fight back, and her throat immediately starts burning. "What is this?"

"Just a little tipple," Rosa says, nudging her with her elbow.

"More than a little," Lauren says. She takes another sip, fighting the urge to down the whole thing at once.

The rest of the team—including Barb, who waves enthusiastically when she sees Lauren—are lounging on the rec centre patio furniture, holding the same plastic glasses, their shuffleboard sticks propped up against the fence.

"Ladies, this is Lauren. She's going to be our alternate today," Rosa says. "You already know Barb. And this is Helen and Mariam."

Barb hands Lauren a stick with a double-pronged fork end. Lauren holds up her hand. Part of her would love to stay, get drunk, and play a low-stakes game with strangers and not think about anything. But Dove is back at the trailer, grounded and probably bored out of her mind, and even though Lauren is still upset with her, she has softened a little. Maybe they could watch a movie together or play cards. Maybe she'll even take her down to the pool, if she seems remorseful enough.

"Thanks, but I can't stay. I'll have a quick drink with you, but after that I have to get back to my daughter."

"You mean *that* daughter?" Barb asks, pointing out to the road.

Lauren follows her finger and sees Dove cruising along on her bike, heading toward the park exit. Something breaks inside her, a glass shattering. She knows she should chase Dove down and bring her back, but she just doesn't have the energy anymore. She snatches the stick from Barb with a force that surprises both of them.

"I guess my afternoon just freed up."

It turns out that Lauren is good at shuffleboard. She is good at this silly game with its little pronged sticks played only by people twice her age, that she doesn't understand how to score and likely the other women don't either. But they are drinking and they are outside and the sun is shining and Lauren is wearing a T-shirt that says KEEP CALM AND SHUFFLE ON, and that's all that matters to anyone. Who cares what the score is? They've already won.

At some point, they make their way to the rec hall, where dinner is meatloaf and mashed potatoes, served promptly at 5 p.m. They eat together on uncomfortable metal chairs and tell stories about their husbands, all of whom are dead except hers. "Except sometimes I wish he was!" she says at one point, to a supportive response of giggles. Then they move into the lounge for bingo night, and Lauren somehow wins a macramé wall hanging without even really paying attention, but who cares? Take the wall hanging, take the rum and Cokes, make up your own rules to the game; they are all retired, their husbands are dead, and they have no responsibilities other than Aquacize in the morning, if they feel like it, or maybe a trip to the hairdresser.

Afterward, they bring their rum and cokes out to the pool deck and pull the lounge chairs into a circle. It's after dark, so there is no one in the water, but the radio still plays softly, an

Elton John song that Lauren somehow knows all the words to. She sings along, *I can see the red taillights heading for Spain*, leaning back in her lounge chair and staring at the moonless sky.

"Do you guys do this every night?" she asks carefully, trying not to slur her words.

"Only on days ending in Y," Rosa says, cackling at her own joke.

Barb grins over the rim of her glass. "We've only got so many nights left, you know."

Next to Lauren, Helen pulls an ornate silver cigarette case out of her purse and pops the lid open, revealing a row of slender, perfectly rolled joints. When she sees Lauren watching her, she says, "Oh, they're medicinal. For my glaucoma." She slips one out of the case and lights the tip with a mother-of-pearl Zippo. "Well, my *potential* glaucoma. Because you never really know, do you?" She takes a delicate toke and then holds it out to Mariam. "And for everyone else's potential glaucoma, of course."

"Thank you, darling," says Mariam, taking it between trembling fingers. Mariam is tiny as a bird and dripping in turquoise jewellery. "You are nothing if not charitable."

"Hey," Lauren asks. "Did, uh, my mother have potential glaucoma?"

The women exchange glances. "Occasionally," Helen says. "At least with us."

"Did you all . . . hang out? Like were you friends with her?"

"She was very hot and cold," Helen replies. "But yes, I would say we were friends."

Rosa nods. "Sometimes she was the life of the party, and sometimes she wouldn't even acknowledge you if you saw her on the street."

"She was an introverted extrovert," says Barb. "Depending on her whims."

"What else would you expect from a Gemini?" Mariam

asks, passing the joint to Rosa. "Especially with an Aries rising."

Helen waves her hand dismissively. "Would you cut it out with that astrology stuff, Mare? No one wants to hear it."

"You know it's true. What other astrological combination would only be interested in you as long as you had something to offer?"

"A sociopath with narcissism rising," Helen says dryly.

"Helen, this is Imogen's *daughter*," Rosa says, waving the joint in Lauren's direction. "Could you please show a little more compassion?"

Helen glares at Rosa. "She was the one who asked," she says. "I assume she wants to know the truth."

"The truth is subjective," Mariam says.

"It's okay, it's okay," Lauren says, struggling to sit upright, her limbs heavy with rum. "I mean, I probably would have said 'psychopath,' but yours could be right, too."

Barb smiles gently at her. "You would not, dear."

The women's eyes are all on her as she slumps back down. "Maybe not."

"If you really thought that, you wouldn't be here, would you?" Barb takes the joint from Rosa and pinches it daintily between her thumb and forefinger. "You wouldn't be on this journey that you're on, to discover who your mother was."

"I'm not here for that . . ." Lauren trails off, meaning to leave it at that, but the alcohol has smoothed out her edges too much. "I guess I *am* here for that. Partially. I thought I didn't understand my mother when she was off travelling around the world making art. But I feel like I understand this retired-in-Florida version of her even less."

"Hon, your mother might have been living in Florida, but she certainly wasn't retired," Rosa says. "She'd go off with her camera at least a couple of times a week."

"What? Where did she go?"

Rosa shrugs, and glances at the other women, who all shake their heads. "She never talked about her work with us at all."

"I didn't even know how famous she was until Frank told me," Helen adds.

"*I* knew," Barb says. "But only because I was such a big fan of Zamir Khouri when I was younger. I had a photo Imogen took of him framed in my guest bathroom back in Milwaukee." She giggles. "Gene bought me a few more Imogen Starr prints over the years. He thought I was really into art, but actually I was really into men with sexy singing voices and eyes that looked right into your soul." Sighing, she takes another puff of the joint, then holds it up to Lauren. "Do you have glaucoma, dear?"

Lauren heaves herself upright. She hasn't smoked weed since high school, and even then she only tried it a couple of times. But when in Rome, she supposes. "Only on days ending in *Y*," she says weakly. The women erupt with laughter, and she smiles, although it feels half-hearted. She can't stop thinking about what Rosa said, about her mother not actually being retired. *What were you up to, Mom?* she wonders. Then she takes a puff of the joint and the marijuana closes down her vision, like a curtain being drawn.

Lauren wakes up with a hangover and the strange sensation that she's not where she should be. She rolls over and buries her head in the pillow, which has an unpleasant smell—something like motor oil mixed with grilled meat. She opens one eye and, seeing an unfamiliar room, shuts it again quickly. As long as her eyes are closed, she doesn't have to face what's on the other side.

As if on cue, she hears footsteps. "Good morning."

She knows that voice. She shuts her eyes tighter. "Don't talk to me. I'm not here. I was never here. I'm at my mother's trailer, asleep on the couch. Dr. Harvey is outside banging around with her garbage cans, and Dove is banging around in the kitchen." Her eyes fly open. "Shit, Dove!"

"Relax," says Cal, from the doorway. "I saw her this morning. She asked if I had seen you and I told her that you got up early to go for a swim."

"And she believed you?"

"Think so."

Breathing a small sigh of relief, Lauren flops backward onto the bed and begins sifting through the remnants of her shattered brain. Everything is moving too slow. "How did this happen?"

Cal looks amused. "You don't remember?"

She does, but only in flashes: shutting down the rec hall with the shuffleboard ladies, walking home through the dark streets of the trailer park, which somehow had gotten all turned around on her, a maze whose walls kept shifting. "You brought me here?"

He chuckles. "You banged on my door at two in the morning. You said you didn't want to go home. Something about someone named Jason coming to find you?"

Her conversation with Jason comes back to her in pieces she needs to tape back together, but she can't remember him saying anything about coming to Florida. She wonders what other conversations she is forgetting. Did she say anything stupid to the shuffleboard team? Send any embarrassing texts? She grabs her phone from the bedside table, bracing herself, but there's nothing from last night.

"Wait," she says, squinting at the screen. "It's two p.m.?"

"Yep. I've worked my whole shift already."

She shuts her eyes again. "I'm not here. I'm at home, on my couch, and it's eight a.m."

"If you're going to make stuff up, you might as well be somewhere better than Swaying Palms."

"Fine. I'm in Paris, in a huge four-poster bed, somewhere on some arrondissement. Any minute now, a handsome Frenchman will deliver me some warm croissants and an espresso."

"Well, I can't do espresso, but I do have a coffee maker."

"I guess it will have to do." She sits up again, and the effort makes her head throb even harder. "Actually, some Advil too, if you've got it."

While Cal makes coffee, Lauren goes into the bathroom to splash water on her face. As she dries it off in the mirror, she cringes to see Imogen's features emerge from beneath the towel. She told Maude she didn't mind people thinking she looked like her mother, but now she puts a hand on either side of her jaw and pulls the skin back, wondering if she should consider a face-lift. Or maybe she should just get complete facial reconstruction surgery. They do that for people in witness protection, don't they? Why couldn't they do it for people who didn't want to turn out like their mother?

The smell of coffee lures her into the kitchen. Cal hands her a mug, and she takes a sip. It's strong, and so much better than the instant stuff she's been drinking at the trailer. She knows she should leave, but being at Cal's apartment makes all her problems feel so far away. "We're never going to talk about this again, right?"

"If that's what you want."

"It is." She takes another sip. "From now on it'll all just be lawn care and pest removal, I promise."

"Speaking of which, you catch that rat yet?"

Lauren grimaces. "Oh, trust me, you'll know if I have. I will be hiding out here until you get rid of it." The coffee has begun to work its way into her bloodstream, and she can feel the fog lifting from her brain. "I just don't know how my mother lived in that place."

"It wasn't always like that. It was just in the past few years that she started to let it go."

"Really?"

"Yeah." He pauses, as though considering whether he should say more. "It was still filled with junk from your grandmother, but she did a lot of gardening and kept up the maintenance. She even had the bedroom redone. And she'd hang out with the other ladies, play shuffleboard, that kind of thing. But then she seemed to lose interest in it all. I got the feeling that something else was pulling her focus."

It's coming back to her, some of the things she heard last night. "The shuffleboard ladies said they thought she was still working."

"She was."

"What? How do you know?"

"I'm the all-seeing eye around here." He grins, sitting down at the kitchen table. Lauren sits down across from him, wrapping her hands around the mug. "She was renting a darkroom in a plaza somewhere. I saw her there once when I was picking up cleaning supplies, and she asked me not to tell anyone. Don't ask me why."

"But why would she keep it such a secret? And if she was still taking photos, where are they?" A thought occurs to her. "Maybe there's still stuff in that darkroom she was renting?"

Cal shakes his head. "The whole plaza was torn down four or five months ago. But I think Imogen cleared out of there long before that."

Missing money, and now missing photos. Lauren spins her mug on the table, and a drop of coffee splashes out. "You ever feel like the more you get to know someone, the further away they actually feel?"

"I guess, yeah." They're both silent for a moment. Then Cal reaches across the table and takes her hand. At first, she thinks he's going to lace her fingers with his, but instead he opens them and places two Advil in her palm. "They're regular-strength. It's all I've got," he says.

As he is closing her fingers back around the capsules, a young blonde woman appears in the doorway. "Hey Dad, I'm going to the gym."

"Okay, honey," Cal says, withdrawing his hand. "Hey, this is my friend Lauren Sandoval. Lauren, this is my daughter, Brody."

"Hi," Brody says. She seems unfazed that Lauren is there. She grabs an apple from a bowl on the counter. "Dad says you have a daughter around my age? You should bring her over; it's nothing but old ladies around here."

"Maybe," Lauren says. Watching Brody—happy, relaxed, all-American in her bike shorts and T-shirt, with her blonde hair and healthy tan, her tiny gold locket around her neck, biting into her apple without a care in the world—she feels a terrible stab of jealousy. *How easy it must be to have a daughter like that.* She takes another sip of her coffee, trying to wash the thought away. "Dove's not exactly the social type."

Brody stops, mid-chew. "Your daughter is Dove Sandoval?"

Lauren freezes, her coffee cup hovering in front of her lips. "How do you know Dove?"

"Dove. The Kazu star."

"What's Kazu?"

Brody laughs. "A video sharing app. Here." She pulls out her phone, and after a few seconds, brings up a video. It's Dove, sitting on a platform next to a pool that appears to house some kind of sea creature. She's talking earnestly into the camera, but the sound is off, so Lauren can't hear what she's saying.

"Can I see that?" Lauren asks. Brody hands her the phone, and Lauren turns up the volume. " . . . like the pacifists of the ocean, neither predator nor prey, just vibes," Dove is saying, smiling so widely Lauren almost doesn't recognize her. Not a trace of Imogen there, or Lauren, even. Right now, she is all Jason, his huge dark eyes, his cupid's bow mouth. "She uploads videos of herself?"

"You seriously didn't know?" Brody chucks her apple core into the compost bin. "She has like 800,000 followers."

Lauren starts scrolling backward through the feed. Video after video, post after post. Nausea washes over her, and she has to put the phone down. Dove has been sharing all her most intimate thoughts online for months. Years, maybe. *How did I not know? How did I miss this?* Then an even more distressing thought enters her mind. *How could she share so much of herself with strangers, and keep so much from me?*

Picking up the phone again, she navigates back to the most recent video. Dove is sitting next to what looks like a grimy indoor pool. Cal leans over her shoulder and squints down at the screen.

"Hey, I know that place," he says. "Isn't that the old Flamingo Key Aquarium? I thought it closed down in the nineties."

Brody shrugs. "Guess not, 'cause this was posted like two minutes ago."

"I have to go," Lauren says, jumping to her feet and running for the door.

Imogen

1995

In Joy's backyard, Imogen sits in a lounge chair drinking pink lemonade and thinking about her first boyfriend, David.

It's early summer, which means it's time for Joy's honeysuckles to bloom, time for her birdfeeders to be overrun with finches, and time for her to lay her annual guilt trip on Imogen. This passive-aggressive siege always coincides with the advent of summer vacation—Imogen can only assume that once Joy has been released from the daily business of interfering in her students' lives, she needs some place to put all that officious energy. Of course, Joy would never come right out and tell Imogen of all the ways she disapproves of her life choices. That wouldn't be in keeping with the kind, nurturing, selfless person she wants the world to think she is.

"I just can't imagine living the way you live," Joy is saying now. "It's like you're a hummingbird flitting around from flower to flower. It's exhausting."

Imogen doesn't know what it is about this time of year that

makes her think of David. She supposes it's how everything is sweet and new, the burgeoning summer still swollen with possibility. She remembers David with a bright vividness that eclipses her memories of even her most recent lovers. The soft down on his jawline, the freckles on his back, the curve of his clavicle. His playful smile turned up at one corner as if it were being tugged by a string. The flutter of his eyelids when he kissed her, thin purple veins threaded through pale skin. He gave her a watch inscribed with the words *a kind of blind love*—lyrics to a song they considered to be their song, though now, looking back, she knows it was everyone's song.

Joy pops a browning marigold head off its stem and tosses it across the garden. "But of course you can't keep going like that forever. Sooner or later, even hummingbirds touch down."

It's the same thing every time: Joy just doesn't *understand* Imogen. If it were her, and she was the big, famous artist, she'd make people come to *her*. After all, what is the point of all that money if it doesn't make your life any easier? She certainly wouldn't be able to handle all that travelling the way Imogen does, jet-setting off to foreign countries all willy-nilly. She just isn't that sophisticated. All *she* wants is a simple life: a place to call home, and her family around her. That's all *she* needs.

"You know I have a condo and a house, right?" Imogen says, unruffled as she stirs her straw in her lemonade, little flecks of pink pulp swirling around the surface. Long ago, Imogen learned the best way to handle Joy is to remain unfazed in the face of her judgment. If Imogen doesn't let her sister get to her, Joy loses interest in her provocation soon enough.

"Those are places to live, not a *home*."

Imogen raises her glass and taps it against Joy's shoulder. "Well, that's what I have you for." She wishes there was tequila in the lemonade, but Joy hasn't kept liquor in the house for years, since Manny was killed by that drunk driver. Imogen does feel bad for Joy about that, losing her husband so young. But it's been almost twenty years. Now it just feels like an excuse.

"Well, aren't I lucky," Joy says dryly. A trickle of condensation from Imogen's glass runs down Joy's arm and lands in her lap, a darkened splotch on her light yellow sundress. "Lauren's really looking forward to going to Florida with you, by the way. It's going to be so good for her to get out of here for a while."

"Oh, shit," Imogen says. She completely forgot about that—or maybe she just chose not to think about it, pushed it out of her mind on purpose in the hope that everyone else would forget too. She leans forward in her lounge chair and drops her head against the cushion. "Joy, oh Joy. No. I can't."

"What do you mean, you can't?"

Rolling her head sideways, she knits her eyebrows together and pouts up at Joy. "I'm shooting in London . . ."

"No."

"I already agreed to it. I'm sorry, I just can't—"

"No!" With more strength than Imogen would have thought her sister capable of, Joy pushes against Imogen's shoulder, forcing her upright. "I don't care if you're photographing the Queen of England."

Imogen bites her lip. "Well, Elton John, so kind of."

"Imogen! This is non-negotiable. Lauren has been looking forward to this all year. I'm sure Mr. John will understand."

Sighing, Imogen takes a sip of lemonade, trying to think of another excuse. It's not that she doesn't love her daughter; it's just so hard to be around her—she can't handle Lauren's infatuation with her, or her fanatical enthusiasm for everything about Imogen's life. If Imogen is being honest, the depth of Lauren's love scares the shit out of her, the weight of it driving her deeper into the earth every second they spend together. "She won't like it," she says. "It's going to be really hot. And Mom's started hoarding again. There's barely even room for her in the trailer, let alone us."

"Make room, then." Joy's voice is steely, resolved. "You're not backing out of this. Lauren's been spending way too much time with Jason. It's not healthy, at their age. They need some time apart."

"Jason? The neighbour?" Since she's been here, Imogen has seen them together, playing Nintendo in the basement, eating ice cream sandwiches, lazing around on the porch. They are at a movie together now, trying to escape the heat in the air conditioning of the theatre. There is nothing unhealthy about that. If anything, it eases some of the pressure Imogen feels, having Lauren's wide, adoring eyes focused elsewhere. "They've been close for years. They're just kids, doing kid things."

Joy stares at her. It's the same stare she gave Imogen the year she came home from art school for Christmas break and tried to convince Joy that their mother's sudden obsession with keeping empty tin cans and burnt-out light bulbs was just her leftover Depression-era frugality kicking back in. "You don't know. You haven't been here. They're together all the time. And they're not kids anymore, in case you haven't noticed," she says. Then she whispers, "I think they're having sex."

"Well . . . so what?" Imogen pulls her knees up to her chest, trying to disguise her shock. "They should be able to take charge of their own sexuality."

"For god's sake, Imo, they're fourteen! They're not even in tenth grade yet."

Imogen tries to find meaning in Lauren being fourteen, but she can't wrap her head around it. Where was she at fourteen? With David, she realizes. His hand up her skirt in the back of his older brother's Thunderbird, Connie Francis on the radio. Skinny-dipping at Rose Bay, moon high over the ocean.

"Even if they're not having sex yet, they will be soon enough," Joy says, settling back into her chair. "They're two little writhing balls of hormones. They can't help themselves. They need to be physically separated."

"And you think Lauren going to Florida for two weeks will somehow break them up?"

"You don't know teenagers. Their infatuation burns hot and fleeting. Two weeks apart and that bond will snap like a twig."

David moved away with his family at the end of that summer. They promised to write to each other, but she can't recall sending him even one letter. It's so strange how clearly she can bring to mind the shape of his fingernails, the softness behind his knees, the exact shade of gold his hair shone in the sun. Why has she carried all this with her for so long? Why did it mean so much to her? Was it just the sheen of first love? Will Lauren remember Jason this way as an adult, an apparition who appears to her on a sunny afternoon in June as she is sitting in her backyard, as real as if he were standing in front of her?

No, she realizes with a start. She won't. Because it isn't David she's remembering—or, at least, he's not the catalyst for her memories. Fourteen is the age she was when she got her first camera, the age she was when she first learned how to see people through the viewfinder. Of course she saw him more clearly, because it was the first time she was really *seeing* anyone.

"She just needs to find something she loves more than being loved," Imogen says.

"Well, maybe she'll find that in Florida." Joy adjusts the wide brim of her sunhat over her eyes. This conversation is over, Imogen knows. Joy has already mapped out all the moves in her head, and there's no way for Imogen to win. Joy is always going to have the upper hand because of the sacrifice she made for Imogen: raising her daughter while Imogen runs off chasing a stupid dream, a kind of blind love.

In Florida, things go just about as well as Imogen expected they would. Lauren mopes around the trailer, writing postcards to Jason, listening to the mix CD he made her, calling him from the pay phone at the rec centre when she thinks Imogen isn't paying attention. Every second word out of her mouth is his name: Jason would love these cinnamon buns. Jason is so good at *Mario Kart*. Jason made the funniest joke the other day. Jason's father is a direct descendant of Francisco Goya, the artist, have they heard of him? She's even driving her grandmother mad with it. By the third day, Jeannette claims to "know more about that boy than even his own momma."

This doesn't mean that Lauren is paying any less attention to Imogen. She can sense Lauren's eyes on her—in the carport while she's drinking coffee, by the pool as she's trying to read a novel, at the Ponderosa on the Tamiami where Jeannette takes them for dinner. Imogen knows she is searching for approval, for some indication that things are going well, that Imogen loves her. Imogen wants to give it to her, she does. But she can't help it—it drives her crazy.

One day while they're at the beach, she catches Lauren smiling at her as she puts on sunscreen and she finally snaps, leaning toward Lauren, smiling widely, mockingly. Lauren shrinks away, busying herself by rummaging through her bag, and it's not until she's disappeared into her headphones that Imogen realizes she's been crying.

Fuck, she thinks.

She taps Lauren's shoulder. Startled, Lauren jumps, spilling her Coke over onto her towel. "Sorry," she mumbles. She picks up the can and slurps from the top where the liquid has bubbled over.

"I was thinking maybe tomorrow we could take Mom's canoe out in the Intracoastal? Carol next door was telling me there's this place where the mangroves are all twined up into tunnels that you can paddle through."

"Okay." Lauren brushes some droplets of Coke off the towel and onto the sand. Her eyes are still red, but the tears have receded. "I don't really know how to canoe, though."

"I can teach you." It's been years since Imogen was last in a canoe, but she's pretty sure she can safely manoeuvre one through the relatively calm and shallow waters of the canals around Sunset. "It'll be fun." She forces herself to smile, genuinely this time, trying to convey warmth through her eyes. When Lauren smiles back, it's with her whole mouth, revealing a row of straight tiny teeth fresh from their orthodonture, the soft pink of her gums.

The next day they head out, the canoe bouncing around in the bed of Jeannette's truck as they cross the drawbridge onto the key. They launch across from a bird sanctuary, in a lagoon flanked by two mangrove islands crowded with pelicans roosting on the twisted branches. Imogen situates Lauren in the bow of the canoe and shows her a quick J-stroke and then they push off, the hull raking against the crushed shells at the shoreline before they swing free into the canal. The key was busy with beachgoers fighting for parking spots and streaming across the road, arms laden with coolers and umbrellas, but once they are on the water it is quiet; nothing but the smell of Imogen's coffee and the soft rhythm of their paddles, the heat of the afternoon sun on their backs.

They don't speak as they glide across the lagoon and past the islands, toward the spot Carol marked for them on a map of the waterways. Imogen watches Lauren's shoulders working beneath the thin cotton of her T-shirt, her dark hair salt-tangled and snagged in the tie of the bathing suit she has worn underneath, her thin, tanned arms moving up and down with each stroke. Maybe she has just made things too complicated. Maybe she could love Lauren in the way that she needs her to, if they could just stay like this.

After about fifteen minutes, they reach the entrance to the tunnels, where gnarled branches have formed a warren of latticed canopies in the middle of the shallow waterway. As they enter, the air becomes still, the soft splash of their paddles echoing through the silence, the dappled sun through the leaves projecting patterns on the water's surface, bright sparks of light winking like stars about to go supernova. Anoles skitter among the branches, and Imogen thinks she spies a raccoon rummaging among the vegetation. Ahead of them, a fish heaves itself into the air and flops lazily back into the water, sending ripples across the surface that gently break against the hull of the canoe.

Using her paddle to push off from the roots, Imogen leads them along a narrow section of the tunnel toward the exit. When they finally spit out into an expanse of sky, painfully blue after the darkness of the tunnels, Imogen spots a flash of grey beneath the water.

"Laur." Imogen taps her shoulder with the paddle and gestures several feet ahead of them, where the whiskered hillock of a manatee's snout is now protruding from the water, huffing bubbles against the surface. Slowly they guide the canoe toward her, their paddles barely touching the water. When they get closer, Imogen can see the manatee is just a baby, not even four feet long, curiously peering up through the brack like a puppy.

"What is it?" Lauren whispers.

"A manatee," Imogen whispers back. "A really young one, it looks like."

Imogen skims the tips of her fingers across the water's surface, and the manatee noses against them, at once soft and sharp, the sponge of her snout and prickle of whiskers. Their eyes meet, the manatee's a tiny round black bead sunk into leathery folds of skin, an orb that flickers with light that could be the whorl of a galaxy, an entire expanse of a universe caught in the watery curve of her cornea. Resting her paddle gently over the gunwales, Imogen lifts her camera from her lap and holds it to her eye, but with the glare on the water, she knows she will never be able to capture what she's seeing. She bends toward the water, but there is no angle that will give her what's she's looking for.

The manatee ducks back beneath the surface and does a long, leisurely barrel roll under the canoe before gliding away toward the canal. From the bow of the canoe, Lauren watches her go, her eyes bright as they follow the shadow in the water. That's when Imogen shifts the camera to focus on Lauren. It's the first time she has seen her daughter through a viewfinder. She's not proud of this, but she supposes she has always been afraid of what she would find there—the darkness behind the devotion, the fear behind that bright smile. Evidence of just how deeply Imogen has fucked her up. But here, from behind, with her face in profile, Lauren glows from within, full of youth and promise. Imogen's finger finds the shutter release, clicking furiously until the manatee has disappeared from sight.

On the way home, they stop at the Flamingo Key Fish House and sit out on the rickety patio under a Corona umbrella, eating conch fritters and onion rings off a plastic red-checkered tablecloth. Lauren drinks a chocolate milkshake and Imogen a PBR in a frosty draft glass, the beer so cold it's almost slush. Lauren is buzzing from the manatee encounter, and there's an easiness between them that can only be born of a significant shared experience—one of those moments that you know is going to become a cherished memory while it's still happening.

"I almost wanted to jump in there and follow her," Lauren says, jabbing her straw into her milkshake to break up a clump of ice cream. "Like I was just about to . . ." She presses her palms together and points them away from her chest, making a diving motion.

Imogen squirts a small puddle of ketchup onto her plate and drags an onion ring through it. "It does seem like quite a peaceful life. Just floating through the canals all day, snacking on seagrass and surprising tourists." She pops the onion ring into her mouth.

"And then every now and then just being like, hello paparazzi."

"I wish I could have gotten a photo," Imogen says. She's trying not to let it bother her, but she can feel it there, worming its way under her skin. *Let it go*, she tells herself. *You don't need it. Life will go on.* "Maybe we can go out another day, when its more overcast."

"Sure," Lauren says.

"Just try once more. See if we see her. You never know." Despite her frustration at not getting the photo, she's surprised to discover she's actually happy to be here, with Lauren. It's nice to have someone to share things with. Maybe, now that Lauren's older, she could be good company. She could come along on some of Imogen's trips, maybe even stay with her in Chicago for a bit. That wouldn't be so bad.

"I wish Jason could have seen the manatee," Lauren says. A white ibis stalks along the rocky shore below the patio, waiting for handouts, and she tosses him a piece of conch. "He'd be so into it."

"Do you have any idea how much you talk about Jason?" Imogen means it jokingly, but Lauren's face darkens. "I just mean, you seem to like him a lot."

"I *love* him," Lauren says hotly. The change in her demeanour is so abrupt that Imogen is briefly taken aback. "We're soulmates."

She rips off another chunk of conch and whips it over the side. The ibis hops across a spit of rocks and snatches it in his long curved beak, tipping it back into his gullet. "You're not going to give me a stupid speech like Joy did, are you? About how I'm too young to know what I want and I should just be having fun and blah blah blah?"

"I don't know. Maybe."

"Oh my god. Why does everyone always treat me like a child?"

"Because you *are* a child." It's true, she realizes. Minutes earlier, she was thinking about Lauren as an adult, but she is still so young—too young to understand the consequences of her choices. Imogen was foolish to think that the time they had together on the water changed things.

"You're just jealous because you're old and alone. You and Auntie Joy both. You want what Jason and I have."

Imogen has to keep herself from laughing out loud. "Oh, no. I certainly do not."

"Is this why I'm really here? Is this some plan you and Auntie Joy had to get me away from him? Because it's not going to work. We can withstand *anything*."

Wiping a drop of ketchup off the back of her hand with a napkin, Imogen thinks back to those bright, vivid moments with David. Had she felt like this? As though the two of them were soulmates, and no one else in the world understood their love? It's possible. But that part of the image has faded. "I just don't want you to limit yourself," she says, softening.

"You don't know anything!" Lauren shouts, picking up her plate and flinging the rest of her food over the railing of the patio.

"Hey!" their waitress yells. "No feeding the birds! Don't you see the sign?"

Lauren sets her plate back down on the table. A red flush creeps up her neck, her eyes wobbling with tears. Imogen knows she should say something. Tell Lauren she's right, that she and Jason have an unbreakable bond that no one else can ever truly understand; that she's never seen two people more in love. And then let their teenage infatuation peter out, as all teenage infatuation is wont to do. Let Lauren cry on her shoulder, tell her sincerely that she's sorry, never say *I told you so*. Invite her on a trip, introduce her to some interesting people, let her get a taste of what's out there for her in the world. There is so much more out there for her in the world other than what she sees in that boy's eyes.

But she can't find the words, and the silence between them stretches on, Imogen drawing patterns in the ketchup with her last onion ring, Lauren sitting with her arms crossed over her chest, watching the ibis wolf down the last of her lunch. When the waitress brings them the bill, Imogen leaves her a massive tip, hoping it will make up for the fact that she's going to spend every shift for the next week chasing that ibis away from unwitting patrons.

Out there on the water, Imogen thought Lauren had found something she loved more than being loved. But now she realizes the only thing Lauren would ever trade Jason's love for is Imogen's. And no matter how much she wants to, that isn't something Imogen will ever be capable of giving her.

Dove

Dear Nana,

Do you think Mom ever had any dreams?
I know we've had this conversation before and you said her
dream was to have a family, and even though you encour-
aged her to dream beyond that, it was the only thing she
ever cared about. But I can't accept that, mostly because she
doesn't really seem to like having a family very much. And
I'm not saying this because I'm her daughter and I'm mad
at her, but as a totally objective outsider seeing three people
who live COMPLETELY SEPARATE LIVES. She never asks me
what my favourite true crime series is, or my favourite
comic book, or what I want to be when I grow up. It's hard
to believe someone really cares about you when they don't
ever seem interested in what you have to say.

For example, a few months ago, just before Christmas,
I was supposed to go to Dex's rock camp concert, but at the
last minute, Mom said I couldn't because she wanted us all
to go to this stupid Christmas carnival, and when I told

her that I had something else to do she just went on about how we needed to have a nice family outing while Dad was home. And then Dad said, "It's not going to be a nice family outing if two out of three of us don't actually want to go." Then they closed the door to the kitchen so I couldn't hear the rest of the conversation, and when Dad came out he said, "Dove, maybe we'll just go for a little bit, to make your mom happy?" I got so frustrated that I grabbed a book off the shelf next to me and threw it, and it hit Mom as she was coming out of the kitchen.

Nana, I swear to you, it was just this small floppy thing, but when it hit her she screamed like I had shot her, and she started to cry and was blubbering on about how she "tried so hard to make things nice for us" and "everything was ruined now" and she didn't even want to go anymore. So I was like, cool, and tried to leave to go to Dex's concert. But then Dad was like, "We are going to that carnival and then after that you're not going anywhere," and basically grounded me for the rest of the weekend, so that not only would I not be able to go to Dex's concert, but I also couldn't go to the winter solstice party his moms were throwing or see Kait before they went to their grandmother's in Maine.

And I know Dad was the one who grounded me, but he did it because of Mom and this stupid picture in her head of the perfect family she wants us to be. I mean, she spends so much time on the Instagram accounts of those dumb fake moms with their picture-perfect pretty lives, but does she ever even look at my Kazu? No, of course not, why would she? It's messy and crazy and she would probably be embarrassed if she saw it, me talking about serial killers and aliens and video games instead of fucking candles and makeup.

There's this other thing I can't stop thinking about. You know how Mom always tells that stupid story about how, when she found out she was pregnant with me, she told Dad on a roller coaster and it was "the beginning of our beautiful lives together"? And yet somehow it always seems like that was the moment when everything got screwed up, like Mom and Dad were happy and in love and then I came along and suddenly it was all ruined. And I know parents always say "it's not your fault" in like every after-school special about divorce ever made. It's not your fault. It's not your fault.

But what if . . . it is?

xoxo Dove

After her fight with her mother, Dove falls into a deep sleep on the pullout couch, waking up in the afternoon when the garbage truck comes by. Her mother is nowhere to be found, but when she peeks out into the carport, the bike is still there. *She can't take it away if she doesn't know where it is,* Dove thinks.

She rides the bike around until she finds a secluded spot to lock it up, at the back of the cemetery next to the trailer park. When she returns to the trailer, her mother still isn't there, so she microwaves a burrito and eats it while watching a documentary about Vikings. By 9 p.m., when her mother still isn't back, Dove slips into the bedroom, amazed and relieved that she has somehow been able to evade her for a whole day. She falls asleep watching Kazu videos, letting them load one after another—a mix of song covers, dance routines, and people explaining how every character in *Star Wars* is actually gay, all of which contributes to the chaos of her dreams, a montage of peculiarities that quick-cut from one slightly disturbing scene to the next.

Early the next morning, the scrabbling on the roof is back, and this time it sounds like the creature is right above her head. The sound is so quiet she might have missed it, but now that she's conscious of it, it's the only thing she can hear. She knows it must be the rat—or, at least, she hopes it is. Even though she helped set up the trap, there's a part of her that is rooting for the little guy. After all, he was here first. If anything, he should be trying to get rid of *them*.

But the more it scratches, the more she starts to worry it's going to break through and land on her face. She goes into the living room, thinking that maybe she can sneak onto the pullout next to her mother without waking her up. She doesn't want her to think she's come running to her for protection—she just wants to go back to sleep. But Dove feels it before she sees it: the air in the room undisturbed by another presence, that hollow feeling of being alone.

Her mother isn't there. The trailer is empty, the couch still neatly tucked into couch form, the sheets and pillows untouched on the rattan loveseat.

Dove sits down on the couch. She has no new messages on her phone, no missed calls, nothing. It occurs to her that maybe this is just her mother trying to get back at her—maybe she's left Dove alone to teach her a lesson for not coming home herself the night before, so she can understand how worried she was. This thought is quickly usurped by another: her mother has found out she's been kicked out of school and has abandoned her here.

Instead of texting her mother, she texts Dex. *Are you up?* Minutes pass, and she doesn't get a response. She's beginning to panic a little, imagining what will happen if her mother is really gone for good: she'll have to become self-sufficient, living off food from the 7-Eleven and spending her days on the beach selling the fruit from the trees in the backyard to tourists.

She starts scrolling through Instagram, trying to stop her mind from spiralling, and she sees Kait just posted a photo five minutes ago: their cat, Pineapples, curled up by their feet on the end of the bed. *Jealous of his sleeping talents*, the caption reads.

Dove switches back to text and types: *I am also jealous of Pineapples's sleeping talents.*

Hey! Kait replies almost instantly. *Nice to have some company in Insomniaville. How's Florida?*

Not good. I just woke up and my mom's not here.

What do you mean not there?

Like gone. Not here. I think she found out I got kicked out of school and just left me here to die.

OMG you're so dramatic. She's probably just out for a walk. Or maybe she made some friends there!

We're in an old persons' trailer park.

Well, old people need friends, too. Don't panic, okay? It's going to be fine. Is the car still there?

The car. Of course. Dove jumps to her feet and runs to the window. *Yeah*, she texts back. *I don't know if that's good or bad.*

Well, the good news is, she didn't abandon you. The bad news is, she might have been abducted by aliens. I hear that happens a lot in Florida.

Fuck you!! But Dove is grinning in spite of herself. The thing she loves about Kait is they are always able to stay light when things get heavy, in contrast to Dove and Dex, who tend to get lost in their own misery. *I'm glad you're awake. I miss you guys. I keep imagining you're having all these cool adventures without me. Like, Dex told me he was going to the mall with his dumb uncle, and I was jealous?? And you know how much I hate the mall.*

Three dots appear on the screen, then disappear for a long time. Finally, they reappear, followed by a new text: *He didn't go to the mall with Uncle Greg, he went with Emily C.*

Haha, Dove texts back. *I've gotta go*, she adds before Kait can text back and tell her it's not a joke, that Dex really is hanging out with Emily C. Emily C, who is friends with Chelsea and Madison. Emily C, whose father is Wendell Carter of Carter Homes, the company responsible for the swaths of identical ugly houses multiplying on the other side of the highway from Worley. Who is on student council and the yearbook committee. Who wears sneakers that cost more money than Dove has ever seen. Who cares about no one but herself. Who is the epitome of everything they hate—or so she thought.

But then she thinks back to the rock camp concert she wasn't allowed to go to. When she saw pictures afterward, whose glossy blonde head did she see in the audience? Emily C's. And who did Dex say he sat with at lunch once and *she isn't as shallow and air-headed as people think she is*, and he *feels kind of bad for her because she has to put on this persona at school because people expect her to be a certain way*? Emily C. And who is still a student at Worley while Dove is a student nowhere, stuck here in Florida a million miles away from her life? Emily C. Emily C.

After everything Dove has done for him, Emily C.

In the silence of the empty trailer, Dove begins to hear more sounds outside, sounds she doesn't recognize, that are so different from the sounds at home—wild sounds, animal sounds, *Florida* sounds. Her eyes begin to fill with tears. She is so alone. How did she end up so alone?

Dove is out in the carport putting on her bike helmet when that Cal guy appears at the end of the driveway. It's still early, and she hasn't slept, but she's decided she has to at least make an effort to look for her mother, who so far hasn't answered any of her texts.

"Oh, hey Dove," Cal says, rubbing the back of his neck. "Your mom wanted me to tell you she just got up early for a swim."

Relief washes over Dove, followed by a record-scratch of wariness. "No, she didn't. She wasn't even here last night."

Cal's face reddens. "Okay, fine, she got really drunk and crashed at Helen's. She didn't want you to know, so don't tell her I told you."

Who the fuck is Helen? she wants to ask, but instead she just shrugs. "Whatever," she says. She doesn't want to give him the satisfaction of knowing what he's said has affected her. But her mind is churning. *Is this a person he invented? Did he kill Mom and, like, chop her up into little pieces with all his weird tree-cutting equipment and then sink her in a swamp or something?*

"Well, your mom should be home soon, okay?"

"Sure." Dove watches Cal push a wheelbarrow full of palm fronds along the road, whistling a tune that she doesn't recognize. She thinks about the night they went to his place to get the rat trap, the way he looked at her mom. *You watch too many true crime documentaries,* she tells herself. *The simplest explanation is usually the most likely, right? So why would he lie about someone named Helen? Why would he make up a place where Mom stayed last night?*

The answer sucker-punches her, knocking her so off balance she has to grip the car for support. Helen is Cal. Her mother slept at Cal's.

Her mother slept *with* Cal.

Of course she did. Everything makes sense now—her mother's secrecy around coming here, her sudden obsession with home maintenance, her disappearance. Her abandonment of Dad. She must have known Cal from before, maybe when she came to Florida with Nana when she was a kid. They probably reconnected over Facebook, like sad old adults do when they're bored with their lives, stirring up all those feelings from their past. She wonders how long her mother has been planning this. She wonders how long she has just been a pawn in her mother's twisted game.

Dove makes her way back to her bike and rides straight to the aquarium. When she gets there, she searches until she finds Ray in the staff room, drinking a coffee.

"Dove, hey," he says. "I didn't think I was going to see you today."

"I want to swim with Pebble," she says abruptly.

He studies her for a few seconds, and it's as though he's right inside her brain, trying to figure out what it was that made her change her mind. *Because my mom is having an affair and I've been kicked out of school and my best friend abandoned me for my worst enemy and the world sucks and I have nothing left to lose*, she thinks. *Because I need a friend.* She meets his gaze, daring him to say no. But he doesn't.

"Come on, then," he says.

She follows him to the manatee enclosure, where he gives her a wetsuit. She changes in the supply room, surrounded by crates of romaine lettuce and carrots, dizzy with anxiety. The wetsuit is too big and bags around the crotch, but it's better than swimming in her dress.

Ray is already in the pool when she gets back. He motions for her to come in, and she sits on the edge. There is scum on the surface that she didn't notice before, and pieces of lettuce floating around. The water looks murky and dark. She starts to panic, but before she psychs herself out again, she squeezes her eyes shut and launches herself into the pool.

The water closes over her head; it's bathwater-warm and smells much different from the pool at Swaying Palms. She kicks her legs and for a moment she's not sure which way is up. Her throat constricts, and she starts thrashing, trying to find something to grab on to. But all around her is water, and she is sinking, the surface getting further and further away, just like in her dream.

Suddenly, it's as though she is caught in an upward current, and a second later she bursts out of the water, gasping for air, grappling for the wall. When she turns around, there is Pebble with her snout less than two feet away from Dove's face. She knows she should be scared, being this close to an unfamiliar animal. Dove is just a little speck of dirt Pebble could flick away with her tail. But she is completely calm. They stare at each other for a long time, and everything feels so still around them it's as though Dove could melt into the water and not even make a ripple.

Ray swims over and hands her a red ball. "Here. Sometimes she likes to play with this."

With one hand still on the wall, Dove takes the ball and throws it across the pool. Pebble zips past her in the opposite direction and then dives beneath her, coming up underneath the ball and batting it with her snout back across to Dove. It lands with a splash in front of her, and Pebble reappears at the surface, whiskers twitching.

"She's showing off for you," Ray says, grinning like a proud father. "I rarely get that one out of her anymore." Dove reaches for the ball and throws it again. This time, Pebble barrel-rolls across the bottom, and when she reaches the ball, she holds it in her front flippers and turns over onto her back.

"This one I know," Ray says. He swims over to Pebble and rubs her belly with a gloved hand. He motions to Dove, who reaches out and tentatively runs her hand along Pebble's side. Her skin feels leathery and rubbery at the same time, and dense, like she is pure muscle.

"Do you think she likes it in here?" Dove asks.

"Would you?"

"No." Dove lets her fingers trail over the manatee's side. "Could she ever be set free?"

"You sound like your grandmother." Ray skims his hand across the surface of the pool. "She wouldn't survive in the wild. She's too habituated to human contact."

A drop of water trickles over Dove's nose, and she wipes it away. Her eyes are beginning to burn, either from the chemicals or the algae, and she resists the urge to rub them. "Did my grandmother come here a lot?"

"Quite a bit—in the last few years, anyway."

"Did she ever get in the water like this?"

He shakes his head. "She always said she was happy to just sit up there with Toby and watch. She took a lot of pictures of Pebble, though, with this huge underwater lens."

Pebble lets go of the ball, and it rolls down the taut curve of her belly.

"I found some of them," Dove says. "The photos. That's how I knew who you were."

Ray's face lights up. "You have them?"

"Yeah. I can give them to you, if you want."

"I'd like that. I didn't even know if she'd kept any of them."

Dove chews on her lip. It tastes sharp, metallic. "Do you really not know where she is?"

"No," Ray says quietly. "I have no idea."

With a heave of her tail, Pebble flips back over and dives to the bottom, the momentum enough to send waves rippling across the pool. Dove momentarily ducks under the surface as well, slicking the hair back from her face. She thinks about something Nana said to her once, about how she sometimes felt as though life were just a series of rooms she kept trying to get out of, and that each new room felt like freedom until that room became a prison, too. Watching Pebble, Dove thinks maybe Nana knew how she felt. Maybe Dove does, too.

After Ray leaves, Dove sits on the bleachers, her head in her hands. Her stomach feels tight and swirly, the way it does when she gets carsick. If even Ray, someone whose entire life has been spent working in an aquarium, thinks it is wrong to keep creatures in a tank, then what is it even all for? Why do people scoop up fish and crabs and manatees and make little worlds for them behind glass? *Do we need to see them that badly?* she thinks. *Do we really have to know everything about everything? Can't there just be some mysteries left out there?*

She takes her phone out of her bag and opens Kazu. Then she presses record.

When she's finished, she closes the app, then lies down next to the pool, letting her hand fall into the water. Moments later, Pebble rises up and nudges her fingers. "I know," she whispers. She holds her phone in the air and presses the record button on her camera. This one will be just for her.

She doesn't know how much time has passed when she hears the door to the manatee enclosure creak open. She raises her head. A figure is standing in the doorway, her face tinged green from the sunlight coming through the tent.

"Dove?"

"Hi Mom."

"What are you looking at? What's in there?"

Dove sits up. "Come meet Pebble," she says.

Ray

You might remember, Rayna, that Harry Sharples died in 1996, at the age of 104, passing sole control of the aquarium over to Tom, who began cutting the aquarium's hours and downsizing the displays and the staff. I knew my job was safe, as Jorge had retired two years earlier, leaving me as the sole maintenance person. Nothing had ever been modernized, and much of the aquarium operations were so archaic that information could only have been passed from one person to another. After Jorge left, I became the only soul in the world who knew how everything worked. I was the Rosetta Stone of the Flamingo Key Aquarium and Tackle.

I know this period isn't one you like to think about. You were so far along before that third miscarriage that we had already prepared the back room as a nursery, a wallpaper border of cartoon zoo animals parading across the tops of the walls. When you came back from the hospital, you sat in that room for hours, painstakingly unravelling all the sweaters and hats you had knitted for the baby. "I can reuse the yarn," you said when I asked what you were doing.

A few weeks later, I came home to find you sitting in the middle of the nursery surrounded by remnants of the wallpaper border, which you'd managed to tear off two walls, strip by strip, before you gave up. You were tearing the scraps into smaller and smaller pieces, letting them settle in your lap.

"I'm busy," you said as I entered the room, your head still bent over your work. "Please leave me alone."

I watched you for a moment, unsure of what to do. "I want to show you something," I said finally, and you raised your head. "Come with me."

I don't know why I thought that this was the right time to bring you to the aquarium. In retrospect, bringing you to a place where life persisted against the odds was not exactly the kindest decision. I could be so selfish sometimes, Rayna. I couldn't conceive of a perspective outside of my own. But when I was grieving, Pebble helped heal me. I suppose I hoped she could heal you, too.

You'd asked to visit me at the aquarium a few times, especially in the early days, but I had discouraged it. At work, I was a different person than I was at home. Maybe I was worried that if you saw me there, you would realize this was where I put most of my energy and mental resources. Maybe I was worried you would see how compassionate and patient I could be with Pebble, and wonder why I wasn't that way with you. "What is it about Pebble that makes you love her so much?" you used to ask, the tone of the question evolving over the years from genuinely interested to passive-aggressive to openly hostile. *Why Pebble? Why not me?* I would always deflect, but the truth is, I never had an answer for you. And I'm not sure I have one, even now.

The aquarium was closed, but I led us in through the service entrance and up the dark, dank stairs through the belly of the ship to the storage room. You warily eyed the crates of half-rotten lettuce and shrivelled carrots, the scummy buckets and the leaking bottles of chemicals, but I could tell you were also curious as you ran your rubber-gloved hand over the wooden hull of the ship. I opened the door and we stepped into the manatee enclosure. Pebble must have heard us coming—she was used to me emerging from the storage room, and so she had risen to the surface, her spongy snout snuffling in the air. You weren't expecting to come upon her so immediately, and you took a step back, almost falling back into the storage room. I grabbed your elbow to steady you, but you shrugged me off.

"I'm fine," you protested.

I backed away, and you strode confidently toward the tank, the heels of your shoes clacking against the boards. Pebble's snout disappeared below the water.

"She'll be back," I said. "She does this. It's really cute. It's like she's playing hide-and-seek with you." I knew I was babbling, but I wanted so much for you to like her. "I've taught her a few games, actually. She can chase a ball and play tug-of-war, and she'll even come out of the water to get her lettuce. And before this she never even moved from the bottom of the tank."

"That must have taken a lot of work," you said.

Had I been paying more attention, I would have seen your fingers twitching in your gloves, itching to rub against one another, and your mouth moving as you chewed on the inside of your cheek, your tongue probing for edges to grasp. But I was too caught up in my own self-congratulatory bubble to see any of it. "Wait here, I'll go get some toys, and we can play with her," I said, retreating into the storage room once more.

I returned moments later with an armful of balls and ropes, expecting to see Pebble at the surface again, lolling on her back, waiting for belly rubs. But she was nowhere to be found. I peered into the pool and saw her lurking at the bottom on the opposite end.

That's it; she's gone, I thought, deflating. I had seen a bit of improvement over the years in the way she interacted with people, but there were so few visitors to the aquarium that it was impossible to measure the change. But for some reason I thought that with you, Rayna, she would relax. I thought she would realize you were a person she could trust, as she trusted me. Instead, she was back to stalking the bottom again, as recalcitrant as she'd been when I met her.

I kicked off my shoe and dipped my toe in the water, splashing it around a bit, trying to entice her to the surface. "What are you doing?" you asked, alarmed.

"This? This is nothing," I said sharply. I was annoyed with Pebble, yes, but also with you—unfairly, to be sure. I had such high expectations for the day, and it wasn't going the way I had hoped. Pebble had failed to acknowledge you, but you had also failed to adequately marvel at Pebble, even in her petulant state. I was so foolish, so full of pride. "Sometimes I spend hours swimming with her. Hours, Rayna. Swimming in this soup of lettuce and algae and excrement."

"Please stop," you said softly.

"Stop what?" I dipped my leg further into the water. "Stop doing my job? Stop caring about something other than you?" Even at the time, I knew my words were harsh; now, in retrospect, they seem catastrophically cruel. "I've accommodated you and your wild demands for years. I wash every speck of this place off my body in the yard. I keep my clothes in a plastic bag and cover the car seats with plastic wrap. I leave everything work-related at work. I've taken a million steps toward you, and you can't even take this one step toward me?"

"I'm here, aren't I?" you shot back. "For the first time in years, you asked me to come somewhere with you. And I did. I came with you. I'm here in this falling-down ship standing next to this disgusting pool, to see this stupid sea creature you love so much who won't even come to the surface." Your eyes bore right through me. "I think I've taken a few steps too, Ray."

You were right, of course. But I couldn't see it. In that moment, all I saw was someone scared of the world and projecting those fears onto me. And now, with you here in my domain, that expression of disgust mixed with defiance on your face, it took all my willpower not to shake you, to try to rattle some sense into you. "Those aren't steps," I replied. "That's like saying you woke up, or you took a breath. Just basic, human things."

You opened your mouth to speak and then shut it again. Your eyes still on me, you leaned over and began pulling off your shoes.

"What are you doing?"

"Just basic, human things," you said. Standing there in your now-bare feet, you reached behind your neck and pulled at the zipper of your dress, letting it fall to the floor, then stepped out of it in just your underwear, your thin arms crossed over your chest.

"Rayna . . ."

You hovered your foot over the water. "Is this what you want, Ray?" you asked. "You want me to take another step? Is that what I have to do to get you to hear me?"

I hesitated. Part of me wanted to call your bluff; I knew you wouldn't step off the edge into that water. You expected me to stop you, and I wasn't sure I wanted to. We stared at each other in a stalemate, my arms still full of Pebble's toys, your foot dangling over the pool, a steely glint in your eyes that I hadn't seen in months, maybe years. Suddenly, I realized I was wrong. Underneath it all, you were the same smart, fiery woman I'd married, who would go to any lengths to challenge me, to put me in my place. Even ones that terrified you. You would have stepped off that ledge in a heartbeat if I'd let you.

I dropped the toys on the viewing platform and reached out my hand. "You will go a long way to make a point," I said.

You smiled. "That's because you are a stubborn man."

I kissed you then, your shivering body small and vulnerable in my arms. When we finally moved away from each other, there was a light in your eyes that I only realize now was masking a deeper sadness.

Afterward, I left you to wander the halls of the ship while I cleaned up the enclosure and put everything away. When I found you, you were sitting on the floor of the jellyfish room, staring at the largest tank, which reached almost all the way to the ceiling.

"How do you clean it?" you asked. "Without getting stung, I mean."

"I have a divider I can move around, to keep the jellys away from wherever I'm working," I said, sitting down next to you. "It doesn't always work that well, though."

Keeping your eyes trained on the tank, you pulled your hands further into your sleeves. "It's funny," you said. "Every month, I start out with such hope. Even after everything that's happened, even after all these years, after all the tests, after everything the doctors have said. After all that lived experience, month after month, year after year, I can't stop myself from hoping. Miracles happen, right? You hear about them all the time. Why not to me? Why not to us?" You took a breath. "Every day as the month progresses, I hold my breath when I go to the bathroom, when I wake up in the morning, when I feel an ache or a cramp or a twinge. I hold my breath and check for blood. And every time there's none, the hope grows. Until the one time there is. There's no being *almost pregnant*. You either are or you aren't. There is hope, and then there's none." You turned your head toward me slowly, and I could see the fear behind your eyes, as if you were being pulled out to sea in a riptide. "But how do you go on without it? Knowing you will never have the only thing you've ever wanted?"

"I don't know," I said, even though I knew that wasn't enough. You had never said anything like this to me before, Rayna. Had never let me into the extent of your pain. Perhaps you were protecting me, but more likely I had just never asked, never given you the space to express it. Just one more thing I regret, now.

"You know, I think so much about being pregnant. But I've never been able to think past that, and I can't help but wonder why. Why can't I picture it? Us being parents?" You turned to me. "Maybe, deep down, it's because I know it wasn't meant for us."

"Don't say that," I said, taking your hand. "I don't know much, but I know that's not true."

You were quiet for a long time. Finally, you gestured to the tank. "What do you do if one gets through?" you whispered. "When you're cleaning it?"

"I let myself get stung," I whispered back.

Tell me a story, you said, before the light kicked out in your eyes. *Don't just sit there, watching me die.* I don't know if this is the story you were expecting. But I do know that I should have told it sooner, that so much could have been different between us if I had.

Lauren

Once Lauren reaches the aquarium, there is a moment when everything she's been feeling is erased and replaced by a pure sense of confusion, as though she has inadvertently walked through a portal into another reality. She wonders briefly if she is still stoned from the night before, or whether perhaps her brain has completely broken and she is still back in Cal's apartment, having a very elaborate hallucination. This is a *ship*, with *fish* living in it. And somewhere inside is her daughter. Her daughter the *internet celebrity*. It's like the entire world has turned upside down.

When she finally finds Dove next to the same grimy pool from the video, relief floods her. In her state of bewilderment, she had imagined Dove transformed into something else, some mysterious creature like the ones she saw as she raced through the halls of the ship, slimy and gilled and tentacled and trapped behind a wall of glass. But here is her daughter, in her natural state with her phone in her hand, tossing heads of lettuce into a pool from a crate on the floor next to her.

"Come meet Pebble," Dove says, as Lauren gets closer, as though it were just another day and she was introducing her mother to a friend from school.

As quickly as Lauren's confusion shifted to relief, her relief shifts to anger. How can Dove just sit there, contentedly playing with vegetables, while Lauren is clearly losing her mind? She can't even remember what she was angry about originally, what primal rage propelled her from Cal's apartment and across the key, careening through red lights, breaking all the speed limits. All she knows is that she has to get out of this horrifying fever dream. She flies across the room and grabs Dove's arm. "Get up."

"Let go!"

"You do not get to tell me what to do, Maya Rose."

"Don't call me that!" Dove wrenches her arm away. She still hasn't lifted her eyes from her phone, scrolling through page after page of thumbnail videos—videos that likely everyone in the whole world has seen, except Lauren.

"Give that to me!" she says, trying to snatch the phone out of Dove's hands.

Dove holds it back, surprised. She clutches it to her chest. "No!"

"Fine, at least turn it off and look at me!"

Glowering, Dove shuts off her screen and puts her phone in her pocket. "Are you happy now?"

"*Happy*?" Lauren laughs out loud, aware that she sounds slightly unhinged. "No, I'm not happy. I just found out my daughter is a secret internet star who is breaking into abandoned aquariums. Would you be happy?"

"Yes. That person sounds awesome."

"Well, I am *not* happy. You're in a lot of trouble." A chill rips through her. "What the hell are you doing in this place, anyway?"

"I'm feeding Pebble!"

"Who or what is Pebble?"

Dove points. Lauren shifts her gaze to the pool. Breaking through the surface of the water is a set of whiskers snuffling at the air. As Lauren looks closer, the outline of a creature begins to appear beneath them. The creature somersaults slowly and languidly, then disappears under the lip of the pool, reappearing several moments later, lazily paddling her tail up and down. A half-formed memory floats into Lauren's mind of being in a canoe with Imogen, a flash of grey skimming past them in the shallow water.

"A manatee?" Lauren asks.

Dove nods. "A famous manatee."

"What is she doing here?"

"She lives here. She used to perform for people, but then the people stopped coming. So now she just swims around in this pool."

In the murky water, Pebble does a slow barrel roll, her flippers pinned to her sides. Lauren watches Dove watching Pebble: this greenish-glowing Dove, soft Dove, manatee-whisperer Dove. She is struck by this girl, this beautiful, smart, compassionate girl who has suddenly appeared in front of her—this aquarium Dove, this watery shadow of Dove. It's clear that Dove is smitten, in her element. But there are still so many pieces that Lauren can't make come together.

"How did *you* find her?"

"There were pictures," Dove says, giving her mother a sideways glance. "At Nana's trailer."

A strange wave of dread comes over Lauren, and she reaches for Dove's arm again, tries to pull her to her feet. She doesn't know why, but she needs to get out of there. "Okay, I've had about enough. This is trespassing."

Dove shrugs Lauren's hand away. "I'm not trespassing! I'm allowed to be here. Ray said."

"Who's Ray? Does he work here?" Dove doesn't respond. "Who the fuck is Ray, Dove?"

Dove turns to her sharply, her eyes flashing with anger. "Who the fuck is *Helen*?"

"Helen?" Lauren says, surprised. "Who's Helen?"

"Just like I thought. She's no one, right? She's just someone you made up to cover up your gross affair!"

"Dove, what are you talking about? Why on earth would you think I was having an affair?"

"Where were you last night?" Dove's hands clench into fists, and Lauren can tell she is fighting back tears. "You didn't even call me!"

"Babes, I'm sorry, I—"

"You *left* me. I was alone in the trailer with the rat and god knows what else." The tears spill over. "I thought you *abandoned* me. Just like you abandoned Dad."

"I didn't abandon him."

"I heard him, on the phone. He said you were getting divorced. He was so sad, and you just left him at home and hung up on him when he called!"

"Dove—"

"You always say this family is the most important thing to you, but you don't really care about *either* of us." She leaps to her feet. "Well, we don't care about you either!" Before Lauren can stop her, she disappears through the door.

Lauren takes a few steps to follow her, then stops abruptly. She tells herself that Dove needs to cool off before they can talk about this, but the truth is Lauren just doesn't have the energy to chase her. All her anger has left her, and her body already feels wrung out like a dishrag, her nervous system in overdrive. The thought of having a conversation with Dove about divorce sends fresh waves of anxiety through her veins. She needs a minute. Or maybe several hundred.

She sits down on the platform. The hard wood causes her already tense muscles to cramp, but she can't keep herself upright anymore. *Breathe*, she tells herself, and closes her eyes. The tent is filled with gentle sounds: the buzz of the lone light bulb, the shy splash of the ocean as it laps against the bulkhead, the low rumble of the tank's machinery belching up from the belly of the ship. She peers down into the pool, where the manatee is circling the bottom, and has a sudden urge to slide in there with her, let the water close over her head, blocking out everything else.

After a few minutes, Lauren gets up and backtracks through the ship, searching for Dove. Everywhere she goes, she feels watched, fishy eyes following her from behind the glass. In the reception area, she pushes open a door to reveal a small, dusty office that appears as though it has been untouched for decades. "Are you in here, babes?" she calls. She circles behind the desk and peeks beneath it, as though she and Dove were playing hide-and-seek. But she finds nothing but a massive cockroach, who stares her down for a few seconds before scuttling away beneath the filing cabinet.

Further down the hallway, she finds what appears to be a staff room, with a sink, a fridge, and an ancient vending machine, but Dove isn't in there, either. When Lauren drops some coins into the vending machine, surprisingly the coils whirr to life, dropping a bag of Cheetos and a Kit Kat bar.

She wanders back out into the hallway and sits down on a bench, popping open the Cheetos, trying to regroup. There must be a million nooks and crannies on this ship for Dove to hide in. All around Lauren, things hum and bubble and gurgle and spit. In one tank, a porcupine fish chases a yellow butterflyfish, an angelfish plays in an anemone, and schools of bright blue tang swim back and forth. Another is filled with dozens of clownfish, their bodies striped orange and white like Creamsicles. A single lionfish, its lacy fins rippling lasciviously, props up the invasive species display, a scapegoat for his entire kind. Between the displays, the walls are covered in old framed newspaper clippings, and waterlogged fact sheets printed on plain computer paper and pinned to the wood with thumbtacks, ink bleeding from cartoonish depictions of different marine life. She can't stop thinking about what Dove said, about how she found photographs at the trailer. Could her mother somehow be connected to this place?

She pulls out her phone and calls Joy. "I have a question," Lauren says when she answers. "Do you know anything about an aquarium in Florida?"

"Your mother did take me to an aquarium when I visited a few years ago. In Tampa, I think. It had a huge shark tank with a moving sidewalk through it."

"No, that's not it. The one I'm talking about is on the key. A really creepy place in a ship. No sharks." Lauren crosses to a tank occupied by a giant grouper whose sign says her name is Paloma and she's over fifty years old. When she touches the glass, Paloma swims over. "What about someone named Ray?"

"That doesn't sound familiar either, sweetie. What's this about?"

"I'm not sure yet. I'm following a hunch about Mom's missing money." She moves her finger back and forth across the glass, and Paloma follows it, transfixed by the movement. Bringing her face close to the tank, Lauren stares into Paloma's eye as she swims past. How did she get here? Was she just swimming along one day in the bay, minding her own business, only to be scooped up by a net, transported here, and dumped in this strange new universe, miles away from her home and her family? Or was she born here, shut up behind the glass of a tank, not knowing that there is a place where the water is endless, where she could swim forever?

"Lauren?" Joy's voice sounds loud, too close. "Are you all right?"

"Yes, fine," Lauren says. "I'll call you later."

After she hangs up, she watches Paloma's mouth open and close behind the glass. "I know how you feel, Paloma," Lauren whispers, dropping her hand. Her source of interest gone, Paloma swims away.

A loud knock on the main door startles her. Dove must have left and locked herself out. Lauren makes her way across the reception area, stuffing another handful of Cheetos in her mouth. When she hauls the door open, she comes face to face with two men wearing Florida Fish and Wildlife uniforms.

"Ma'am," one of them says, tipping his hat.

Fuck.

Dove

*D*ear Nana,
   It's been more than three months since I've heard from you. It feels weird, like there is this giant steel orb that follows me around everywhere I go, and it's as big as the room but I'm the only one who can see it, and every now and then I say something about the giant orb but everyone just keeps on talking as if I haven't said anything at all. There are just so many secrets. Emailing with you was a secret. Getting kicked out of school is a secret. Mom and Dad getting divorced is a secret. Pebble is a secret—or at least, she was a secret until now. And it's all just too much to carry. Maybe that's where the steel orb comes from. Maybe it's the weight of all the things I can't talk about—the, like, every-day heaviness of it. And maybe that weight is why I posted the video of Pebble, why I had to put her out there for people to see. I couldn't carry one more secret on my own.
   A lot of the time I feel really invisible, which is why I post the videos, and I guess also why I can't stop writing

to you, even though you don't want to talk to me anymore. At least on Kazu, people see me the way I want them to see me, the way I really am. It might sound stupid, but in my videos I am the hero, not just the sidekick or a background person. IRL *most of the time I feel like I'm just a prop for Mom and Dad to use in their fights, or just a nerd hiding behind her hair in the hallways at school, a cardboard cut-out of a person. Even to Dex and Kait, I'm just going to become someone they used to know, who used to go to their school, who they chat with online sometimes. They were the only people who made me feel like a real person, but I guess that's over. Or maybe it was all a lie. Maybe we were never really friends to begin with.*

You made me feel like a real person too, but the whole time you were writing me I couldn't help but wonder if there was some kind of catch. And now that you're gone, I keep thinking maybe you didn't even exist in the first place. Maybe I was just being trolled, Nana-catfished by Chelsea or Madison or some jealous bitch on Kazu. Or maybe YOU *were trolling me, pretending to give a shit and then using all the things I told you for, like, research into the disturbed teenaged mind or something.*

I don't know why you stopped talking to me, but I hope it's not the same reason you stopped talking to Mom. Because that would mean that it was forever, and I don't know how to think about forever right now.

xoxo Dove

In the video Dove posted on Kazu, she is sitting at the edge of the pool in the manatee enclosure, her legs in the water, her camera reversed to film her face. "Manatees don't think about who they are," she says into the camera. "They don't think about their fathers or their mothers, they don't think about what happens when they die, they don't think about whether they gained two pounds last month or whether someone posted a video of them online or even whether other manatees like them or not. They just follow their natural instincts and some deeply ingrained manatee collective consciousness that tells them to travel to this particular spot at this particular time, or that the best thing for them to eat is leafy greens, or that they should stay away from humans because we are the fucking enemy to everything. They just swim around and eat and sleep and chill. They're like the pacifists of the ocean, neither predator nor prey, just vibes."

She holds out the ball and Pebble appears at the surface. "This is Pebble. All her natural instincts have been taken away, by us. No one taught her to be scared of us, because we've kept her from her own kind. And because of that, she carries this ache around in her body, knowing that she is missing something, but not knowing what it is." Dove lobs the ball into the water, panning the camera down to show Pebble chasing it across the pool, then gripping it in her front flippers and depositing it at Dove's feet.

Later that day, as Dove sits on the beach outside the marina, replaying the video, she thinks about what else she could have said. She doesn't really know what she hoped to accomplish with her post, other than to let people know about Pebble, the simple fact of her existence. Everyone seems to think there's nothing they can do to change her situation. But Dove doesn't believe that. There has to be *something*.

She's rewatching the video to avoid thinking about her fight with her mother at the aquarium, but the anger keeps sneaking back in. How dare her mother be mad at *her* after everything *she's* done? She is such a hypocrite, going around pretending she's all

perfect and happy, when in reality everything is messy and horrible. Maybe that's the reason her mother sent her to Worley in
the first place—so Dove could learn how to be all fake and plastic
like she is. No wonder Dove can't bring herself to tell her about
getting kicked out, or about what happened with Chelsea and
Madison. She probably wishes *they* were her daughters instead.

Dove shoves her feet into the sand and starts scrolling
through the comments people have left on the Pebble video. It
hasn't been doing the same numbers as the bee post—which still
hovers on her grid next to it, making her stomach turn every
time her eyes skim over it—but she's hoping that some bigger
accounts will pick it up. Maybe even her grandmother will see it.
The possibility is slim, but it doesn't stop her from imagining it:
her grandmother sitting in some tiny restaurant on a beach in
Fiji, the news playing on a black-and-white TV behind the bar,
background noise in a foreign language until a voice comes on
that she recognizes, catching her attention. She looks up and sees
Dove and Pebble on TV, and then immediately throws down a
few Fijian dollars on the bar and says, "Can someone call me a
cab to the airport?"

As Dove is scrolling, she gets a text from Dex. She stares at
the notification, wiggling her toes free of the sand. He texted her
a few times earlier in the day, but she didn't even look at them—
she was still too mad. Now, though, she uses the knuckle of her
pinky finger to open it.

I just saw your video. So you're a marine biologist or something now?
She considers how to respond. Finally, she types a simple *Yup.*
Three dots appear, then disappear. Then nothing happens for
a few minutes. A new text eventually pops up. *Are you mad at me?*
I don't know. How's Emily C?
Kait told you?
Because you didn't!!

Fuck, Dove, because I knew you'd be like this!

I'm not being like anything. I just asked how she was, that's all.

Emily's cool. She's not like you think. You should check out the dope Kazu she has with Logan, where they rate movies based on flavours of Jolly Ranchers, it's really funny.

At the mention of Logan, Dove's fists clench. Does Dex really think she doesn't already know about that stupid Kazu account and have it blocked? Emily C is one thing, but Logan. Fucking *Logan*.

Hey, she types, *remember that time Logan posted a pic of a period stain on my shorts with the caption "What do Dove Sandoval and a hockey goalie have in common? They both change their pads every two periods"?*

Come on. That was like a year ago.

Next thing, you're going to tell me you're hanging out with Chelsea and Madison.

Another long pause, dots flashing. Then the text comes: *They're really not that bad, once you get to know them.*

Blood rushes to her head, filling her ears, flushing her cheeks. Not that bad? After everything they've been through together, after everything she's done for him, he is telling her they're *not that bad*? And all for what? The attention of a vapid blonde with a rich daddy and a perfect life? A girl who was, if not the instigator of all the hateful things that were done to them, still standing by and cheering them on. How long has this been going on? Has he been secretly hanging out with them all this whole time? Has he been going to parties at Logan's house when he's said he's studying or visiting his uncle, sitting around with their mortal fucking enemies, laughing at her behind her back?

Fuck you, Dex, you fucking traitor.

As soon as she hits send, she jumps to her feet, overcome with the urge to throw her phone into the sea. She squeezes it, knuckles turning white, until her arm starts to cramp, then pockets it with a shaking hand, not even bothering to check if Dex has texted her back. She knows he won't. Why would he? He has someone else to protect him now. Not only someone who still actually goes to his school, but someone who can do a better job of it. Someone who can turn him into a person who doesn't need protecting at all.

Standing at the shoreline, she looks out over the horizon. It's so disconcerting, after spending so much time staring at that concrete pool, to find herself next to the ocean. *How many manatees are there out there?* she wonders. Hundreds? Thousands? She wades in a little further, then a little further. *Manatees don't care how cool you are, or who you hang out with. They don't care if their best friend betrays them. In fact, there's probably no such thing as betrayal in the manatee world.*

She stretches her arms out, raises her face up to the sun, and lets out a howl that comes from a place inside her she didn't even know existed. Maybe it's Pebble, speaking through her, calling out to her family.

If Dove were given the choice to be either a manatee or a girl, she wonders if she would make the right decision. Would she give up all the good things about life, like fresh raspberries and hanging out in Dex's treehouse and dogs that look like they're smiling, just so she could be a manatee and not know about any of the bad things, like the climate crisis or assault rifles or internet trolls or that feeling you get when you know that something's over and you can't get it back? Could she be happy just living her life following her natural manatee instincts?

The thing is, if you chose to be a manatee, you would never know if you'd made the wrong choice because you would be a manatee, and you wouldn't have the ability to think about yourself the way a human does. But if you chose to be a human, and you made the wrong decision, you would always know. You could have been a manatee, but instead you are just you, and you have to live with that for the rest of your life.

Lauren

The two Florida Fish and Wildlife officers are in beige uniforms, badges gleaming on their chests. One is carrying a reinforced clipboard, which he unfolds with an air of ceremony.

"Ma'am, we have some reports of an unlicensed protected species being housed on this ship," Clipboard says.

"Oh." Lauren takes a step back, wiping her Cheetos-dust-covered hands on her shorts. "Well, as you can see, there's nothing here. Unless you mean that big guy over there." She gestures to the crab in the tank behind her, who is busily digging through the sand.

The second officer, her eyes hidden behind mirrored sunglasses, holds out a phone, and Lauren recognizes the video of Pebble from Dove's Kazu account. "Care to explain this, then?" she asks.

"Oh, that's just my daughter. She likes to post things on social media."

Sunglasses puts her phone away. "So you work here?"

Dove appears on the stairs behind the officers. "What's going on?"

"Here's the thing," Lauren says, reaching for Dove's hand and pulling her inside. "We were just out exploring the key and we found this ship, and when we came inside, we discovered that manatee here. We're just visiting. We don't know anything about this place."

"Mom!" Dove yanks her hand away and glares at her.

Clipboard closes his clipboard. "Ma'am, we're going to have to ask you to leave while we investigate this further."

Lauren stares into the nearest tank, where a pufferfish is skimming along the bottom, picking up tiny rocks in his mouth and then spitting them out. Trying to build something, but really only futilely moving pieces of his tiny world from one place to another. She turns to Dove. "Come on, babes, let's go."

"No," her daughter says, with tears in her eyes. "I'm not leaving."

Sunglasses takes a step toward them. "Unless you want us to arrest you for trespassing, you'd better do what he says."

Dove starts to shake, and Lauren puts her arm around her. "We have to go," she whispers.

This time Dove doesn't argue, although the look in her eyes is one of pure wrath. As they wordlessly descend the stairs, Lauren can feel Sunglasses and Clipboard watching them from the doorway.

Dove unlocks her bike from the fence and they load it into the trunk without speaking. As soon as they're seated in the car, she whips around to face Lauren. "Why did you let them in?"

Lauren puts her key in the ignition, and the engine shudders to life. "We're lucky we're not in jail. I can't believe I let you pull me into this."

"*Pull you into this?* I didn't ask you to come here!"

"Dove, you do not want to do this with me now." Lauren manoeuvres out of the parking lot and onto the road. "Put on your seat belt."

Dove angrily pulls the seat belt across her chest. "This is such bullshit! I finally find something I love, and then you come and fuck it all up!"

"This isn't my fault."

"You let them in! You opened the door to those monsters, those fucking *sea cops*!"

"I'm pretty sure you were the one who led them there in the first place, with your videos!" As soon as Lauren says it, she regrets it. "Those wildlife officers were just doing their job, babes," she adds, softening her voice. "They were right to tell us to leave. We shouldn't have been there."

"Since when are you on the side of *cops*?" Dove smashes her fist against the door with a crack that makes Lauren jump. "At least I care about something. You don't care about anything."

"I care about you."

"You say you do, but you don't."

"Dove!"

"It's true! This is just like the winter carnival. You didn't care if any of us wanted to go, you just had this picture in your head of what we were supposed to want and you didn't care if it was true or not!"

"The winter carnival? Dove, what are you talking about?"

"You know exactly what I'm talking about! You only pretend to care about other people because you don't want anyone to know what a horrible person you are. You drove Dad away. You probably drove Nana away. I can't wait until I'm old enough to get away from you, too." Her words slice Lauren open, an exquisite pain that momentarily takes her breath away. "Why won't you say anything? You never tell me anything!"

"Fine!" Lauren jerks the wheel, pulling the car over. "What do you want to know?"

"Nothing. Just forget it."

"No, what do you want to know?" Her daughter doesn't respond, but her hand snakes toward the door handle. "Don't even think about jumping out, or I swear to god I will run you over."

Dove's hand moves back to her lap. "Why did we come here?"

"You know why we came here. You talked to your father."

"You're still not answering me! You never answer me!"

"You're asking me about things you already know! Come on, Dove, you say I never answer you. Tell me what you want to know about me so badly!"

"Why did you even have me?" she yells.

"I don't know!" Lauren yells back.

Dove recoils in her seat as though she's been slapped. "You don't know?"

Outside, a family on bikes whizzes by, father, mother, and daughter all in matching teal bike helmets. The daughter rings her bell as she passes, each chime ricocheting around Lauren's head like a pinball. She slips the car back into drive, her limbs still sticky with adrenaline.

"We're both tired," she says feebly. "Let's just go home." But her words are drops of water on a vast, burning landscape. They evaporate long before they even reach their destination.

They drive back to Swaying Palms in silence. As they reach their street, Lauren sees a rental car in the driveway and someone sitting in her lawn chair, over on Dr. Harvey's side of the lawn.

It's Jason.

Lauren stops the car in front of the trailer. Every cell in her body is telling her to reverse out of there and run. But then Dove is out of the car and dashing through the carport, yelling "Dad!" Lauren puts the car in park gently, mechanically, and gets out, her ears ringing so loudly she barely hears the door when she closes it.

"Hi, kiddo," Jason says as Dove flings herself into his arms. He is wearing a plain white T-shirt and the board shorts he bought when they were in Mexico, and Lauren feels a brief surge of desire that immediately repulses her. He has one of her beers in his hand, and she imagines herself snatching it away from him and smashing it on the driveway. It would be nice if Dr. Harvey were preparing to shoot him with the Nerf gun, but Lauren assumes that horrible woman's wrath is reserved just for her.

"Hey, Laur."

"Hi."

"I hope you don't mind," he says, indicating the bottle. "The door was open, by the way."

"When did you get here?" Dove asks.

"About an hour ago."

He presses his face into Dove's hair. She leans against his shoulder, and that's when Lauren realizes that Dove is taller than her father, which means Dove is also taller than her. Lauren can't understand how this happened, how two short people made such a tall girl, and then it occurs to her that there will be a myriad of other ways Dove is going to surpass them, become a better version of them—or something new, something just for her that has nothing to do with them at all.

"I missed you, Dad," says this extraordinary person they somehow made together.

He kisses the top of her head and sets his beer down on the table, then sweeps a few palm berries onto the ground with his hand, as though this has been his trailer all along and Lauren is just a guest. "I bought some veggie dogs at the 7-Eleven. Want me to cook some up for you?"

"The barbecue doesn't work," Lauren says flatly.

"I got it going earlier."

"Well, I guess you've really made yourself at home."

He touches Dove's shoulder. "Hey, kiddo, I have a present for you inside. It's in my bag in the bedroom if you want to go open it."

Dove glances back at Lauren and then disappears into the trailer.

Jason and Lauren stare at each other. She doesn't know what to do or say, but here they are. Just like they have been a million times before.

"Lauren . . ." Jason begins.

She snatches her bathing suit and towel from the drying rack in the carport, and before he can say anything else, she's gone.

At the pool, Lauren hops over the fence in the twilight and changes into her bathing suit behind a huge potted hibiscus. Then she jumps into the water and floats on a noodle that someone left on the deck and stares up at the sky. Something has snapped inside her brain, crushed under the weight of everything she's been carrying. It's too much, and now she can't feel anything, she can only stare, and float, and wait for someone to come and kick her out.

For some reason, she finds herself thinking back to what Dove said in the car about the winter carnival. She doesn't know why Dove brought it up, but she was right: she *had* made a big deal about the entire family going, even though she knew neither Jason nor Dove wanted to. Maybe Dove was too old for it, but Lauren had been sure that once she got there, she'd remember how much she'd loved it as a kid—how her eyes would light up when the Christmas train came by and the conductor honked the little horn at her. How she used to make them stop and listen to the carollers in their Victorian garb singing "O Come All Ye Faithful." How afterward they would go to the Lakeside for perogies and plan their Christmas-morning breakfast. Jason had been away for so long, and it was ages since they had done anything together as a family, and her mother had died only two weeks earlier—was it asking too much for her family to put aside their own feelings for one lousy minute and think about *her*?

But they had fought in the car about what route to take, and they had fought in the parking lot about whether that spot was *really* a spot. The wind was cold and none of them had remembered their mittens. Dove thought the train was stupid and didn't want to ride it, and Jason spilled hot chocolate all over his coat. By the time they left the carnival they weren't hungry—or speaking to each other—and so they just went home. Dove disappeared into her room and Jason into his laptop, and Lauren was left in the kitchen, eating leftover pad thai from the takeout box and wishing she had just gone to the Lakeside by herself, eaten her own weight in perogies, and washed it down with a shot of vodka or seven. At least there, she could be alone with the gnawing hollow feeling that had been growing inside her ever since she got the call about Imogen. There, she wouldn't have to pretend that everything was okay, that she didn't care, that life continued as normal. There, she could just be a daughter, grieving her mother.

She hears someone clearing their throat. She spins herself around on the noodle to find Dr. Harvey watching her over the fence. Of course.

"Fine," Lauren says, propelling herself toward the stairs. "I'm getting out."

"Don't mind me," Dr. Harvey says. She rests a notebook on the fence and scribbles something inside it.

"What are you writing?" Lauren climbs up the ladder and crosses the pool deck. "Are you writing something about me?"

Dr. Harvey hides the page with her arm. "Resident . . . in pool . . . after hours," she says as she writes.

"Okay. I'm out. God." Lauren picks up her clothes and hops back over the gate, still in her bathing suit, dripping pool water on the asphalt. "Are you happy now?"

A smile plays on Dr. Harvey's lips. "Resident . . . in public area . . . without . . . proper attire."

"Are you fucking serious?"

"Resident . . . using profanity."

Her face growing hot, Lauren moves toward Dr. Harvey. "I'm going to shove that notebook up your ass."

"Resident . . . threatening . . . innocent . . . bystander."

"Oh my god, stop!" She lunges for the notebook, but Dr. Harvey is too quick, tucking it under her armpit. Then Lauren grabs hold of a corner of the notebook just as Dr. Harvey doubles over, shielding it with her body, and they commence a ludicrous tug-of-war.

"Give it to me," Lauren says.

"Never," Dr. Harvey growls, strengthening her grip.

Lauren feels a hand touch her back. "Oh, hello Lauren. What are you doing out here?" Helen's face appears next to hers. "The book club meeting is this way."

Lauren lets go of the notebook and straightens up. "The book club?"

"Oh, dear." Mariam appears on the other side of her. "Did we not tell you that the pool party portion of book club was cancelled?" She removes a long flowery shawl from her own shoulders and drapes it over Lauren's. "We're just meeting in the rec room. Come on."

"Residents . . . running unsanctioned organized clubs . . . at park facilities . . ."

"Oh, go suck a dick, Carol," Helen says. Mariam and Lauren both stare at her. She shrugs. "Hey, it might loosen her up."

Inside the rec room, Barb and Rosa are sitting on a well-worn loveseat covered in floral-patterned upholstery, deep in conversation. Helen and Mariam steer Lauren over to them.

"We picked up a stray," Mariam says, clapping her hands lightly before sitting down next to her.

Helen pulls a chair over from one of the card tables. "She was about to go a few rounds with Carol Harvey."

"Ah, out for a little late-night dip, were you, darlin'?" Rosa asks.

Shivering in the arctic blast of the air conditioner, Lauren adjusts the shawl over her arms. "I just needed to get away from the trailer. I didn't think anyone would mind. But then that bitch out there had to ruin it." The volume of her voice is rising, and she takes a breath, steadying it. "My husband's here. He wants a divorce." The words tumble out before she can stop herself, and she's surprised at the sudden rush of relief that comes with them.

"Oh, hon, I'm so sorry," Barb says. "He must be a complete fool."

"A first-rate toolbox," Mariam says.

"What's he even doing here, then?" Rosa asks. "Let's run him out of Dodge."

"Right?" Lauren knows she sounds unhinged. She's not even a high-heeled shoe anymore; she's something more ridiculous, like a pair of stilts or those platform boots with the goldfish in the heel—something that would topple over at the slightest breeze. But she doesn't care. These women are the first people who have asked her anything about herself, the first people who have cared even a little about what *she* is going through. "Like, don't freak me out with a stupid text about *oh, I want a divorce* and then just show up at my doorstep like nothing happened!"

The women exchange glances. "He asked for a divorce by text?" Helen asks.

"Yup. And there was even a *typo* in it!"

"Well, that is just next-level rude," Rosa says.

"Absolutely disrespectful." Barb pulls a flask out of a giant beach bag at her feet and hands it to Lauren. "Here, have some of this."

"Thanks." Lauren takes a swig, glancing around. "Hey, am I interrupting something? Helen, didn't you say something about a book club?"

"Oh, don't worry about that," Barb says. "This is much more important."

Mariam reaches for the flask. "You should stride back in there in that sexy bathing suit and show him what he's missing," she says.

"He doesn't even merit that," says Helen. "Ungrateful pig."

"He's not!" Lauren wraps the shawl more tightly around herself. "I mean, Jason hasn't always been the best husband. But maybe I haven't been the best wife, either."

"Now, Lauren," Barb says sternly. "You gain nothing from playing the martyr here. You've given him a home, a child, and what does he do? He turns around and abandons you. With a *text*."

"A *text*, Lauren," Helen echoes. "Don't you think after all these years, you deserve better?"

"Yes. I do. I just . . ." She picks at a loose thread on the couch cushion. "I've known Jase almost my whole life. No one knows me like he does."

"The people who have known us the longest aren't always the ones who know us best," says Rosa. "Sometimes they never see past the person we were when we first met them."

"And even if they do, it doesn't mean they're the only ones who ever will." Helen takes Lauren's hand. "Your mother once told me you were the most loyal person she knew. And she worried that loyalty would be what broke your heart."

Lauren pulls her hand away. "That can't be true. She never talked about me."

"Not a lot," Helen admits. "But when she did, you could see why. If even you, the most loyal person in the world, had pushed her away, then what must that say about her?"

Helen's words, on top of everything else, are almost too much to bear, and Lauren buries her face in her hands. "She was wrong, though. I'm not loyal at all. I'm just . . . I'm just scared."

Rosa waves her hand through the air dismissively. "Everyone always says that. But look at you! You just stood up to Carol Harvey!"

The flask makes its way back to Lauren, and she regards the women as she drinks, each of them smiling at her, waiting with all the patience in the world to see what will happen next. These are women who are finally at ease with themselves after years of putting it on for everyone around them, being who everyone else needed them to be. After years of soothing their husbands' neuroses and nurturing their children's dreams and mollifying their condescending bosses who probably believed that a man really would be better for the job, these women no longer give a fuck what people think of them. And part of Lauren wishes she could fast-track to this point, skip all the middle stuff and retire to Swaying Palms.

But she knows she can't. She takes the shawl off her shoulders and hands it back to Mariam. "Thanks. Really, I mean it. I'd probably have murdered Dr. Harvey if not for you all."

"If that does happen, we can help with that, too," Rosa says, winking.

Dove

Dear Nana,

    Do you believe in parallel lives? Like, when you make a decision between two things, your life goes off in the direction you've chosen but a shadow you goes off in the other? And maybe in that shadow world, the same splitting-off happens when your shadow self has to make a decision, until there are infinite versions of your life happening all at once? I guess maybe the problem with that is, would it happen with only the big decisions, or every decision? Would there be a parallel life for the Dove who chose to put cinnamon sugar on her toast instead of peanut butter? I mean, how different would that life really be? Or if it was only for the big decisions, where would the line be drawn? What if the small decisions turned out to be the big decisions? What if the Dove who chose to put peanut butter on her toast ended up falling off the stool trying to reach for it on the top shelf?

    And what about the decisions that other people make

for you, the ones that you have no control over? Like, what would have happened if Mom had never had me? What would happen to me in that scenario? Like the me in my brain, the voice that lives in there now? Where would I go? Where would all these thoughts go? Do you ever think about this too?

Sometimes I feel them out there, those parallel lives, all overlapping this one. Sometimes, with complete clarity, I can see another Dove living a completely different life, going to school and having friends and a family that understands her. And I wonder, where was the juncture? What was the decision that led that Dove to that life, instead of the miserable one I'm in now?

Did I fuck it up, or did someone else?

I tried to do something good today, and it ended up being a huge mistake. Stuff happened and words were said and blah blah blah, none of it matters. Tomorrow, I'll just go make another decision that will send my life hurtling down another path, and then another, then another, until those parallel lives overlap so thickly I can't see them anymore. And then I will just succumb to the mediocrity of life. I will be just like Mom.

xoxo Dove

When Dove goes inside to find her father's gift, she expects it to be some trinket, a souvenir like the little woven change purse he brought back from Peru or the shell necklace from Costa Rica. But when she sees the iPad on the bed, it's as though an anvil has fallen from the sky the way it does in those old cartoons, and she is on the floor with birds circling her head. Forget about all those other parallel lives. This is it. This is where her life splits in two: the before and the after; stuffed elephant on one side, iPad on the other.

When Dove goes back outside, her mother is gone, and her father is sitting at the table drinking a beer. He's smaller than she remembered, and all she can think about is him sitting at home alone, crying on the phone because Mom is leaving him for some guy called Cal.

"Are you hungry, babes?" Dad asks.

"Don't call me that," she says. "Mom calls me that."

"Okay, sorry."

He really looks it, too, and she is overcome with guilt. Just another thing to pile on top of all the secrets and lies, she supposes. Maybe that's part of growing up, too—feeling bad about your parents all the time.

He rubs the back of his neck. "Are you having fun here?"

Dove shrugs. She thinks about telling him about Pebble, and the aquarium, and those stupid sea cops, but just thinking about it makes her eyes start to water. "We went to the beach," she says instead. "That was pretty cool."

Her father smiles. "The beach, eh? I would never have taken you for a beach person."

"Yeah, me neither. But I liked it."

"Well, we should go to the beach at Marty's Cove when we're home."

When we're home. She bursts into tears, right there in the carport. Her father jumps up and puts his arm around her, sitting her down at the table.

"I'm sorry," she says, ugly-crying, snot dripping everywhere, a disgusting blob of emotion. "I'm sorry, I'm sorry."

"Babes . . . Dove. Honey. You don't have to be sorry. What are you sorry about?"

It all comes rushing out—Dex and Emily C, Chelsea and Madison, the bees, Principal Matharu. Getting kicked out of school. Her father crouches in front of her, holding her hands in his as she talks, his eyes never leaving her face.

When she's done, he rubs his hands over his face, as though he is wiping away the residue of her confession. "That's why I had all those calls from your school. I just assumed it was a fundraising thing." He drops his hands, and his expression is grim. "What did your mother say?"

Dove takes in a juddering breath. "I don't think she knows."

His eyes widen. "What do you mean she doesn't know?" he asks, straightening up. "Didn't the school call her, too?"

"At first, I assumed they did, but now I'm not sure. Or she didn't bother answering either."

"And you didn't tell her?"

"I was going to, I swear. She was out at some candle party and I was going to tell her when she got home, but before I had a chance to she was like 'we're going to Florida' and then we were here and she was acting so weird and I didn't know how to tell her." Tears spill from her eyes once again. She'd thought telling her father everything would make her feel better, but instead she feels worse. *The right thing isn't always the easy thing*, she hears her grandmother say. "I've wrecked everything."

"No, no, of course you haven't." He hugs her tight, then pushes her hair out of her face and tilts her chin so he can meet her eyes. "We'll figure it out, okay? I promise."

"I just want everything to go back like it was. I don't want to be kicked out of school and I want us to be a family again." She hesitates, wondering if she should say what she wants to say next. "I don't want Mom to divorce you."

"Oh, honey. Your mother . . ." He purses his lips. "It's me. I'm the one who wants the divorce. Not your mother."

A strange tingle creeps up her spine. "But on the phone, you . . . you were so upset."

"Of course I was upset, honey. I had no idea where you were. I was scared."

"Oh," she says, her mind spinning. "Well, I just wish things were different, I guess."

"Come on," her father says, rubbing her shoulder. "We don't have to solve this now. Let's get you some food."

"Okay." Dove does her best to smile at him, and he goes over to the barbecue and puts on some veggie dogs.

As they finish eating, her mother reappears in the carport, her hair all wet like she's been in the pool, even though it's after dark. Dove holds her breath, waiting for her father to tell her mom what happened. But instead, he just smiles at her and asks, "Do you want one?"

"Do I want one?" she replies. "Do I *want* one?" Then she just goes inside, and Dove hears the bedroom door close.

The veggie dog flips around in Dove's stomach, and she worries she might throw up. When they were leaving the aquarium, and she realized she would probably never see Pebble again, all she wanted to do was dive back into the water with her and never get out. She wanted to live in that tank with her forever, though she knew it was a bad place for them to be.

Her mother, though, had run away from the thing she was losing. At first, Dove thought that meant she didn't care, but after seeing the expression on her mother's face just now, she wonders if maybe the opposite is true, too. Maybe sometimes it feels like the only way to keep something you love is to run as far away from it as you can.

Lauren

The Florida Fish and Wildlife offices are in a nondescript white stucco building sandwiched in between an urgent care centre and a store that sells honey-baked hams. When Lauren arrives, a receptionist leads her to an empty meeting room, where she sits at the furthest end of the mahogany conference table, the surface oily and smelling of furniture polish. On the wall is a poster admonishing her not to feed wildlife in national parks, featuring a photo of a large alligator with its jaws wide open to reveal the massive scoop of its palate leading into the darkened abyss of its gullet.

It's not how Lauren had imagined spending her day when she got up at dawn, unable to sleep. Dove's body was a lump beneath the comforter as Lauren shifted gently out of the bed. She slunk through the kitchen making coffee, trying to avoid waking Jason on the other side of the trailer, sprawled out under a thin sheet on the pullout. As soon as she poured the coffee into her mug, there was a knock at the door. She checked herself briefly in the mirror: hair an unwashed, chlorine-fried tangle, eyes swollen from crying, yesterday's clothes wrinkled and sweaty. *Beyond fixing*, she thought. *I guess I've found the title of my own self-help book.* She was still chuckling mirthlessly to herself as she opened the door to Clipboard.

"Oh, it's you," he said when he saw her, as surprised as she was. "You're Imogen Starr?"

"Uh, no." Lauren stepped outside and closed the door behind her. The sky was grey, and a hot, dank wind swirled through the carport, rattling the loose grill on the barbecue, left open since last night. "I'm her daughter. Lauren Sandoval."

"Oh." Clipboard peered down at his namesake. "Is Imogen Starr here?"

"No," Lauren said, crossing her arms. "She's dead."

"Oh," the officer said again. He bit his lip, and Lauren realized how young he really was—likely only in his early twenties, a fresh and shiny life ahead of him, so many mistakes yet to make. "I think you're going to have to come to the office with me."

"Why?"

"We have some stuff to sort out here, about the aquarium."

"The aquarium? What?" But Clipboard just blinked at her. She peeked through the window but didn't detect any movement inside. Whatever was going on, it was probably best that Dove and Jason didn't hear it.

Now, at the office, Lauren waits for Clipboard to arrive and fill her in. But when the door opens, another man enters the room—older, with a grey moustache, dressed in khakis and a polo shirt. He is followed by Clipboard, as well as Sunglasses.

"Ms. Sandoval? So, just to be clear, are you the owner of the mobile home at 145 Swaying Palms Boulevard?"

"Yes. I mean, it was my mother's, like I said. But she left it to me."

"And this was the only property left to you by your late mother?"

"It was. She didn't own anything else. Can you tell me what's happening?"

Moustache sits down and pushes a piece of paper across the table to her. "Your mother is named as the owner of the property located at the civic address 4527 Rising Sun Court." Lauren stares at him, uncomprehendingly. "Otherwise known as Flamingo Key Aquarium and Tackle."

"You think my mom owned that aquarium?" Lauren laughs. "Of course she didn't. She just . . ." *What? Visited a lot? Volunteered there?* "Wait, she *owned the aquarium*?"

"That's what this says."

"I think you must have made a mistake."

Moustache points to the paper. "As you can see here, she obtained it in 2009. This is a title transfer from a Thomas Sharples. We also have records of her operating the aquarium as a tourist attraction up until the end of 2018, although she never filed any paperwork with the department or submitted to any inspections." Moustache pulls the paper back and puts it into a binder. "Something must have slipped through the cracks. Our investigation has shown that her staff were all let go in November."

"But that was months ago. Who has been caring for the fish all this time? There must have been someone."

Moustache studies the papers in front of him. "There are four employees listed on the payroll account: Patricia Ling, Rashida Simpson, Eliza Hart. There's also a Ray Malik, but I don't see any reference to him in the termination documents."

"Oh. I think there is a Ray there, still," Lauren says. "Maybe?"

Moustache hands her another piece of paper. "We have an order here stating that the ship is a hazard and will be torn down. I guess this can go to you."

"What will happen to the fish?"

"Some of them can be released. The rest will be transferred to other aquariums."

"What about Pebble?" Moustache just stares at her. "The manatee."

"Oh. Well." Moustache touches his moustache. "There's not a lot we can do. She's too old to be moved, and even if she wasn't, I don't know if there's anywhere that could take her. There's not a lot of facilities that can handle a thousand-pound marine mammal on short notice."

An uneasy feeling slowly spreads through her body. "So . . . ?"

"So. She'll likely be euthanized."

"Excuse me?"

"I know it sounds harsh, but it's for the best." Moustache folds his hands in his lap.

The paper grows damp in her clammy grip. "And there's nothing I can do about it?" she asks, swallowing back the bile rising in her throat. "I mean, technically, the aquarium is mine now, right?"

"Is there something you would *want* to do about it?"

In a brief flash of optimism, she imagines herself scrubbing the aquarium clean, building a shiny new gift shop with manatee keychains and mugs and snowglobes, hiring students from the university to do research. But when she looks into Moustache's eyes, all she sees is the piles of paperwork beyond them—the estate lawyers and the licensing board and the government mandates and the bureaucratic red tape. She slumps back into her chair. "I guess not."

"We also had to close the associated bank account," Clipboard says. He slides another piece of paper across the table. "This is yours."

It's a cashier's cheque for $25,000. "This is what was left?"

"It was opened with over fifteen million dollars," Clipboard replies. "It costs a lot to run an aquarium."

Lauren stares at the cheque in shock, Imogen's signature staring back at her, the unmistakable capital letter *I* followed by a line and a quick five-pointed star. $15 million. *$15 million.* She unfocuses her eyes until the ink begins to dance on the page, the letters forming and unforming until the words make as little sense as their meaning. She doesn't hear anything else the wildlife officers say, their voices tinny, far away. She nods, staring into space until they're done, then she walks back to her car in a trance, the image of the cheque and of Imogen's signature burned into her retinas. On automatic pilot, she pulls out of the parking lot and chugs back down the Tamiami, past chain restaurants and gun shops and laser hair-removal clinics, past condo towers rising up between scrubs of palmettos, huge pines dripping with Spanish moss, vultures perched in their upper branches. None of this feels real—it's like a movie set, a fake version of Florida, and she has been living a fake version of her life inside it, oblivious. She could knock those sets over with one quick breath. But what would she find behind them? What is waiting for her, in the desolate wasteland of her mother's bizarre legacy?

What the hell were you doing, Mom?

She steps on the gas, pulls a U-turn, and heads back toward the key.

When she reaches the aquarium, she rips down the caution tape across the entrance to the ship. Then she smashes the shiny new padlock on the door with a brick she scavenged from the detritus in the parking lot, the soft wood of the door yielding easily beneath her blows. From across the parking lot, the bartender at the tiki bar gives her an enthusiastic thumbs-up as the bracket pops off and the padlock clangs down the metal stairs.

Once inside, she goes straight to the office and begins searching through the desk. She doesn't know what she's looking for—something with Imogen's name on it, a bank statement or a newspaper clipping, concrete evidence that what the Fish and Wildlife people told her is true. When she finds nothing, she moves on to the filing cabinet. Finally, after sorting through purchase order after purchase order signed by someone named Patricia Ling, she finds one with a different signature on it, for a new vending machine. That capital letter *I* again, seared into her brain forever.

She flops back into the desk chair. None of this makes any sense to her. What drove Imogen to spend her life savings pumping ocean water into tanks for fish to live in, mere steps away from an actual ocean? Did she think she could make money off tourists? Or was it just for her? Did she want to keep those fish for herself, capture them like a subject in one of her photographs? Why doesn't anyone have any answers for her? "Why, Mom?" she murmurs. But in that moment, she understands that she will never know what her mother was doing with this aquarium; the same way she will never know how her mother felt about her; the same way she will never get an apology, not even so much as an acknowledgement, of the mistakes Imogen made. Her mother has died and left behind all these things that Lauren doesn't want—the trailer, the aquarium, the questions, the regret—without giving her any of the things she wants most. She runs her finger over the signature, a low moan escaping through her lips.

Then, from behind her, she hears a sneeze. She is surprised to see a man in his late fifties or early sixties standing in the office door. On his shoulder, there is a large lizard, scaly and prehistoric, its long spiny tail dangling around his neck.

"Sorry," the man says. "Toby isn't feeling well."

"Toby?"

The man gestures to the lizard. "I think he has a cold."

Lauren narrows her eyes at him. "Are you Ray?"

He nods. "You must be Lauren. I've heard all about you." He takes in the open filing cabinet, the desk strewn with paper.

"Right. I guess you've met my daughter." She wonders what Dove has told him about her—her horrible, mean mother, who keeps secrets from her, abandons her, pushes her away so she's forced to confide in strangers in weird aquariums. With shaking hands, Lauren starts arranging the papers, stacking them on the desk. "I just came from the Fish and Wildlife office. They're shutting this place down for good."

A brief flash of pain crosses Ray's face. "I figured as much, given the lock on the door," he says. "Can I ask what is going to happen to Pebble?"

His face is expectant, worry and hope mingling behind a tentative smile. Lauren knows she should tell him the truth, but she's not sure she can get the words out without crying.

"Another aquarium, somewhere up the coast or something."

"Oh, well. That's good." Ray slides his hand along Toby's tail over and over, until the lizard gets annoyed and flicks it away. "I'm sure that's good."

"Yeah." She considers what to say next. There are so many questions swirling around in her head. How well did he know her mother? Does he know how she came to own this place? More importantly, does he know *why*? She closes her eyes. How ridiculous, that she has to pin her hopes of understanding her mother on this stranger, this man with an iguana who she didn't even know existed until yesterday. Instead, she says, "Well, thanks for keeping this place going after my mother died."

"Your mother is dead?" Ray's expression doesn't change, but his voice pitches down half a tone and his hand starts to tremble almost imperceptibly. "I suppose I assumed she was. She told me . . . well, I just didn't know for sure."

She told you what? But she's not sure she wants to know. "Three months now."

Ray is silent, and Lauren has to look away, blinking back the tears that have sprung to her eyes. She knows she should feel sorry for him, but all she feels is angry. How many more people will she discover her mother has hurt?

"Do you need help with any of this stuff?" Ray asks, taking a step forward.

Lauren stands. "Nope. I was just leaving." She surreptitiously wipes a tear from the corner of her eye. "The Fish and Wildlife guys will probably get in touch with you about the logistics. I'm sure they'll need your help."

"I'll give them a call now," Ray says. He turns to leave, then stops. "Lauren, I don't think Dove knows."

"About what?"

"Your mother dying."

Lauren sighs. "Of course she does. She's just a weird goth kid. She probably thinks her spirit is still here at the aquarium or something." Lauren runs her finger over Imogen's signature. "Anyway, it doesn't matter. She didn't know my mother."

"I see." He pauses. "I'll go make that call now. It was nice to meet you, Lauren."

"You too." She picks up the vending machine purchase order, pretending to study it, until she hears his footsteps disappear down the hall. Then she folds the paper in half and slips it in her purse, before walking as quickly as she can through the lobby and out the door, down the steps, and into her car. She turns up the stereo and opens the windows, trying to shake off the fog of Ray's sadness, but it clings to her as she drives away.

Ray

One day, sometime in the late 2000s, Tom Sharples came to the aquarium and told us we would be pivoting to a conservation model. He was applying for a grant, he said, that would let him bring in grad students from the University of Sunset to study the aquarium's marine life and their longevity within captivity. I was thrilled. I had never been to college, only trade school, and I was excited to participate in such a project. I think a part of me believed that the more I learned about conservation, the better I would feel about what I did for a living. Science would prove the fish were better off here. Science would assuage the guilt that pressed up against me every time I opened the door to the ship and stepped inside.

But, as it turned out, Tom had no intention of using the money for research. Once the grant paperwork went through, he cashed the cheque and took off. I heard that he had gotten involved with some kind of yoga-healer type who convinced him to flow all those misappropriated government funds into his ashram in India. Another rumour was that he had gambled it all away in Vegas, but I preferred the former. I liked to imagine that Tom thought he was doing some good in the world.

The remaining staff went through the motions of trying to keep the place afloat. We had few exhibits, and even fewer employees—me, the two part-time girls who worked as guides and helped in the office, and Patricia the administrator, who had taken over from Mrs. Appleby. The aquarium's hours were reduced, and often I would find myself completely alone for weeks on end. Occasionally, I would run into one of the girls as I was leaving and she was arriving, and I would see Patricia maybe once every two months; if she needed anything from me, she would leave me a sticky note on my locker in the supply room. It was an odd way to work, but I preferred it. Alone, the work was meditative. I didn't give much thought to who owned the aquarium at this point. I kept getting paid, so I kept coming in. I had grown to think of the aquarium as my own private sanctuary—one that I increasingly turned to as life at home grew more difficult.

There had been years of doctors by this point, all of them saying the same thing, but we couldn't afford any of the procedures they suggested. "Keep trying," they told us. "You never know." But as our thirties passed into our forties, our chance at having a family receded into the distance until it was barely visible, a speck on the horizon that seemed impossible to reach.

I remember the day they finally stopped saying "you never know." A virtually zero per cent chance of a viable pregnancy. *Virtually*. How I wished they had never used that word.

"Virtually," you whispered to yourself on the car ride home. "Virtually. Vir-tual-ly."

"Rayna, stop."

"It doesn't mean it's over," you replied. "Remember when the last doctor said that yoga could help? I'll sign up for a class, and start with the folic acid again . . ."

I pulled over to the side of the road and cut the engine. When I took your hands in mine, they trembled so violently it reverberated through my body. "No," I said. Month after month, year after year, I had watched your hope peak, then crash. I couldn't do it anymore, Rayna. I couldn't participate in that kind of slow, horrific dismantling of your heart. It was over. It had to be over. "Enough. This is enough. We have to move on."

Our eyes met, and in yours I saw a fear so deep that I couldn't even name it, like a dying star at the edge of a far-off galaxy. *To what?* they asked. *What are we supposed to move on to?*

I don't know what you saw in my eyes. I don't even want to think about it.

You began to cry. I tried to hold you, but you pushed me away, curling into the car door. I placed my hand on your back, feeling your lungs expanding and contracting, your breath laborious, your body choking on your sobs. Once your breathing began to return to normal, I pulled back onto the road and drove us home without saying another word. You kept your head against the window, facing away from me. It was days before you were able to look me in the eye again.

After that day, I started staying out a few nights a week at the marina tiki bar, drinking Coronas and watching baseball, crashing in the staff room at the aquarium. I'd listen to the constant rhythm of the waves breaking on the beach outside and try not to think about you in our house on the other side of the key, lying in our bed alone.

Some nights, when I couldn't sleep, I would creep into the manatee enclosure. My shift started at 4 a.m., so I was used to being there in the dark when there was no one else around; but there was something different about being there at midnight, with the moon high in the sky and glowing through the canvas tent. Most nights, I would just sit on the side of the pool, watching Pebble swim. She was much more active at night, skimming so close to the walls of the tank I worried she might crash into them. But she never did. That tank was an extension of her body, and she could navigate it without sight, without sound, without touch.

On those nights, I would occasionally get into the pool with her, submerging myself in the water and listening to her squeaks and chirps, feeling the darkness become even darker as it enveloped me. I wish I could explain that feeling to you. How the water can be whatever you need it to be: a heavy blanket, a suit of armour. An embrace. But there are so many things I wish I had told you. Instead, I hid inside that ship, my own concrete tub. Safe, but captive, just like Pebble.

One morning, when I roused myself from the staff room couch and opened my locker, I found a note from Patricia. *Imogen will be here at 7 a.m. Please show her around.* I had no idea who Imogen was, but I assumed she must be someone important to warrant a private tour. I tried not to think of it as an intrusion, although it was impossible to quell my irritation at having my sanctuary disrupted. I only hoped I would have enough time to complete my morning routine.

I heard the delivery bell ring promptly at 7 a.m., and opened the door to a woman perhaps a decade older than me, dressed in a simple cotton dress and sandals and carrying a large satchel. She didn't look like a student, or a rich investor—up until then, I had thought she would have been one of the two. After we introduced ourselves, I asked her where she would like to start the tour.

"I don't need a tour, Ray," she said, pulling out a camera. "Just do what it is you do, and I'll follow along."

Of course, a journalist, I thought. "It's not very exciting," I said, apologetically.

"I'll be the judge of that," she replied with a smile.

I was just about to do my collection for water testing, so I gathered my equipment and climbed up out of the belly of the ship into the main aquarium. Imogen followed behind as I collected my samples, taking pictures of everything—the rotting wainscoting, the weathered wooden railings, the cracked concrete. I thought she was documenting the damage, perhaps for insurance purposes, but she told me later she thought broken things were beautiful.

Finally, it was time for me to collect from the manatee tank. I felt a tiny rumble of dread as I led her down the hall to the enclosure. I'm not sure if it was because I wanted her to be impressed with Pebble, or if I wanted to keep Pebble all to myself. Perhaps a bit of both. Perhaps pride and possessiveness go hand in hand. And I still held the memory of your visit to the aquarium in the back of my mind—my high hopes, your lukewarm reaction, Pebble's refusal to come to the surface.

We entered the enclosure and Imogen walked directly toward the viewing platform, then kneeled by the edge and gazed into the water. But the only thing that gazed back up at her was her own reflection—her face, with mine peering over her shoulder.

"She comes up to breathe every five minutes or so," I said, gauging my words carefully. "But she'll go longer when other people are around. Unless she's with someone she trusts."

Imogen met my eyes in our reflection, then dipped her fingers into the water, our faces dimpling with tiny ripples. "She trusts you."

"Yes," I admitted. "But it wasn't easy." I waited for her to ask me what I had done to gain Pebble's trust, but she said nothing, just dragged her fingers back and forth across the surface of the pool. "I can show you how I did it, if you'd like," I said.

I didn't know how Pebble would react to me getting into the water with someone else in the room again. I pictured her sulking at the bottom the way she had with you, upset that I had brought someone else into our time together. But I got into the water anyway. To my surprise, she swam over to me immediately, waiting for me to throw the ball. I tossed it over her head and she swam across the pool in pursuit. By this time, Pebble had learned to grab the ball in her front flippers and carry it back to me. When she deposited it in front of me, I took it and threw it again. I admit, I was showing off. I couldn't help it. I was imagining a future where people would come from far and wide to see the miraculous manatee from the photographs. Maybe there would be repercussions—I still didn't know whether I was allowed to be in the pool with her—but it would be worth it, to live in a world where Pebble was loved.

Eventually, as she always did, Pebble tired of the game and began swimming in circles beneath me. I was flushed with adrenaline; I could have pulled the *Prins Viggo* out of the bulkhead with my bare hands. I climbed out of the water and dried off, excited to see what Imogen's reaction would be. But she stayed crouched on the platform, her body still. When her eyes met mine, I knew that she had seen the entire universe in that pool, the way I had, and that she felt the weight of what I had been carrying alone all these years.

It's hard for me to say this, Rayna, but even in that brief moment, being able to share all this with someone else—it was the first time I felt as though a little bit of that weight had been lifted. It makes me sad, to think of all the things I wasn't able to share with you. I know it was my fault we didn't communicate better. I tell myself that I didn't want to add to your burdens by sharing my own with you, but that feels like an excuse. Maybe, had I been less closed off to the world—to you—I would have seen that there are so many different ways of doing things. Maybe, in the end, this is why we ended up where we were, with silence growing between us instead of the life that should have been.

The nurse is here now. I can see her outside the door. It's strange, after all these years, to have someone else controlling when I can and cannot see you. For so long, I made the choice on my own. Perhaps I often chose poorly, but it's too late to change that now.

Imogen

2009

Whenever Imogen is in Las Vegas, there are two things she must do: play poker at Andriy's, and see Lulu LaFontaine. This time she's only in town for twenty-four hours, so she arranged to meet Lu here at the club before her set, intending to have a quick drink and catch up before moving on to the poker. But there's always something with Lu—costume problems, this time—and so four hours later Imogen finds herself in the second-floor VIP area of a club somewhere on the Strip, drinking very expensive vodka straight from the bottle and waiting for her friend to finish performing.

Below her, on the dance floor, young bodies churn together to a primal EDM beat. The sight reminds Imogen of when she was a child, and her father would come home from smelt-dipping in the spring with a bucket full of the long, silvery fish writhing together in a rippling mass of scales and flesh. It's both mesmerizing and ridiculous, and she perches on the edge of the plush velvet couch, allowing herself to zone out as the vodka freezes then warms her throat.

"Imo!" Lu appears at the top of the stairs. She's still in full drag, although she's traded her massive Marie Antoinette updo for a sleek teal bob. Imogen met Lulu in 1979 at Studio 54, where they spent the evening locked together in a back room watching Frank Capra movies with a bottle of tequila and a mound of cocaine. They've been friends ever since. Imogen has probably shot more photos of Lulu than anyone else. There is an unknowability to Lulu that captivates Imogen—the layers of identity she builds around herself a nearly impenetrable fortress. The rare occasions that Imogen can break through, even for a split second, have been her best work. "I'm glad you waited, chère." She studies Imogen's face. "You look like shit. How was Lennoxville?"

"Lennox Heights," Imogen corrects her. "And I'd rather not talk about it, if it's okay with you."

"No, it not okay with me. But never mind, I'll get you talking." Lu takes her hand. "Let's go find Sandro. He's got a bottle of Veuve Clicquot that was salvaged from a shipwreck from the 1800s."

Imogen pulls back. "I was due at Andriy's half an hour ago."

Frowning, Lu puts her hand on her hip. "Don't you want to taste champagne that's been underwater for two hundred years?" Imogen widens her eyes. Lu sighs. "Okay, fine, chère. But that fucking meathead had better not try to grab my tits again." She reaches into her dress and grabs her silicone breastplate with both hands. "If he's going to feel me up, he should at least be grabbing a part of me that's real."

"Is *any* part of you real?" Imogen asks.

Lulu winks. "I'll never tell."

Andriy's poker game is played in the basement of a Ukrainian legion in an industrial park, in a room adjacent to the kitchen where the babas cook the holubtsi and varenyky they sell on Fridays, the walls thick with the smell of cabbage and potato. Physically and spiritually, it's as far from the Strip as you can possibly get. It's also the most prestigious and highest-stakes game in the city, and nearly impossible to get into. Imogen has had a standing invitation since the '80s, after she took some nude photos of Andriy's second wife for him for his birthday—photos that still adorn his office walls even though he is now onto wife number four. Tonight, he puts Imogen and Lu at a table with three middle-aged men she doesn't recognize, all of whom appear slightly aggrieved to be joined by an aging hippie artist and a six-foot-four drag queen, although two of them nod in their direction as they sit down. The third man—in a golf shirt and khakis, his hair gelled into spikes that could puncture skin—is clearly hammered and in the middle of telling a story, acknowledging them with only a glance and not so much as a pause in his oration. "Come on, honey, let's get this party started," the man says to the dealer, who doesn't respond. He finally turns his attention to Imogen and Lulu. "How wonderful to have a couple of lovely ladies joining us." He squints. "Or, er, is that what I'm supposed to call you?"

Lulu lifts her hand, fingers outstretched. "You can call me Lulu LaFontaine."

"Miss LaFontaine," he says, lips brushing her knuckles. "I'm Thomas Sharples, but *you* can call *me* Tom." He looks at Imogen. "And you are?"

"Surprised at how Andriy's standards have gone downhill," she says, not looking at him.

"Ah, a purist. I see. Well, let me tell you the story of how I came to be here."

"His sister is Andriy's third wife. They were separated at birth and he tracked her down just to get in on this game," one of the other men says flatly in a deep, Southern drawl. He's wearing a cowboy hat and appears to be just about ready to punch Tom out. "There, I just saved you three hours of your life."

"Separated at birth! You card." Tom elbows the other man jovially. "She just didn't want to have anything to do with me. But you know what, that's all right, because I didn't want to have anything to do with her either, the stuck-up little bitch. But then our mother died, and she came back for the funeral with this big burly Greek god for a husband." He taps his finger to his temple. "Lemme tell you, I've been around a bit, and I knew *exactly* who he was."

"You like to gamble, Mr. Sharples?" Lulu asks. Imogen nudges her, but she pretends not to notice. Poker bores Lu. Stirring up shit does not.

"I am a *businessman*," he says, as if that answers Lu's question. "I own an aquarium in Sunset, Florida, among many, many other things."

"He owns all the creatures in the sea," says the man with the cowboy hat as he lifts the edges of his cards. "All of them. So don't even ask."

"Why would you make that up?" says the third man, small and wiry, with round glasses and close-cropped silver hair. "Of all the things you could have told us you owned."

"The Flamingo Key Aquarium and Tackle," Imogen says, her eyes on her cards. She knew she recognized him from somewhere. Those billboards over the Tamiami in the late '90s, with him dressed as a ringmaster, his thin, reedy face and gummy smile looming over you as you turned onto the beach road, and the radio ads where he sang a nonsensical, off-key version of "Under the Sea," the lyrics and music altered just enough to avoid copyright infringement. Imogen hasn't spent that much time in Sunset with her mother, but she can still recite those radio jingles by heart. *Come drop your anchor, down where it's damper, beneath the waves.*

"You've been!" Tom claps his hands together, delighted. "What was your favourite exhibit? The jellyfish? Everyone loves the jellyfish." He waves his arms through the air, in an apparent attempt to imitate them.

Imogen studies him. She can't imagine this fool running a hot dog stand, let alone an aquarium. "The manatee," she says.

Tom's face darkens. "Oh, that," he says. He lowers his eyes to his cards, finally silent. The others all exchange glances, a silent pact not to break the spell. Lulu opens her mouth, but the man with the cowboy hat raises his finger to his lips, and so she closes it again.

The previous day, Imogen had spent twenty-four hours in Lennox Heights, too. She went at Joy's request, ostensibly to talk about how to get their mother into a nursing home, but it was nothing they couldn't have discussed over the phone. When Imogen arrived, she realized Joy's real intention was to reconnect her with Lauren, who she hadn't seen in almost three years.

"She wants to see you," Joy said when she picked Imogen up at the airport. "But she doesn't want you to come to the house. She wants neutral territory."

If she was being honest, Imogen had no idea why Lauren was mad at her—other than her usual level of resentment that simmered under her skin, always on the edge of boiling over. How was Imogen supposed to know the difference? The last time she saw Lauren, the baby, Maya, wasn't even talking yet, although she sang to herself almost constantly, in a made-up language only she could understand. Imogen had brought her a kaleidoscope decorated with drawings of birds that, one by one, she named for Maya—nightingale, cardinal, goldfinch, so many others. Then she held the kaleidoscope up to her granddaughter's eye, spinning it slowly while the child mumbled her tuneless nonsense under her breath, pausing every few moments to giggle. They'd ordered pizza and watched a movie, and the next morning Lauren drove Imogen back to the airport, told her she'd think about spending Christmas in Chicago. Imogen couldn't think of a single thing she'd said or done to deserve the silence since. But, of course, she hadn't asked either.

Neutral territory, it turned out, meant Local Joe's, a coffee shop in a building that used to be a drugstore, one of the last in the city with a soda fountain. The fountain was still there, behind the counter, although now it was just for show, and instead of root beer and cherry Coke, they served lattes and organic teas. When Imogen arrived, Lauren was already there, sitting at a table by the window, her back to the corner. Maya was with her, her soft brown hair pulled back in elaborate French braids. Imogen wondered if that was for her, or whether Lauren did that every morning, Maya sitting patiently at the kitchen table, letting her mother yank her hair into place.

Imogen set her mug of Earl Grey on the table and patted Maya's head. "Hi, babes," she said, then glanced at Lauren. "Hi, other babes."

"Mom," Lauren said. "How was your flight?"

"Peachy. At least, until I got to the shithole you folks call an airport. It's like travelling back in time to the 1970s, but without all the fun party drugs." She directed the last sentence to Maya, putting on a babyish voice. The child stared at her, a chocolate chip cookie melting in her hand.

Hoisting Maya onto her lap, Lauren pursed her lips. "Do you have to do that?"

"Do what?"

"Say stuff like that in front of her."

"She doesn't understand what any of that means."

"According to all the books I've read, children start retaining memories around this age. Do you really want her first memory of her grandmother to be you talking about your drug use?"

Imogen burst out laughing. "My drug use? Laur, I was making a joke." Lauren's mouth set in a hard line. "Besides, you can't keep her sheltered forever."

"*Forever?*" Lauren yelled, ignoring the heads turned toward her. "She's four years old, for god's sake."

"You could already mix a drink at four years old."

Lauren slid Maya off her lap. "Why don't you go over and play with those toys in the corner? I'm just going to talk to the nice lady here for a minute."

As they watched Maya waddle off in the direction of the kids' area, Imogen was transported back in time to when Lauren was that age, toddling around with her stuffed dog's ear in her mouth. She turned back to Lauren. "Nice lady? Do you not want her to know who I am?"

Wrapping her hands around her mug, Lauren gazed at Imogen over the table in a way that was so theatrical Imogen wondered if she'd practised it in front of the mirror. "Mom, I just... I think she's better growing up without you, that's all."

Imogen gave a short laugh. "Well, I can't argue with that."

"You always do that. You always just shut down when I try to talk to you."

"That's because you're always criticizing me. You're a better parent than I was, I get it."

Disappointment creased Lauren's eyes. "You don't get it," she said, fiddling with the tag from her teabag.

Over the speakers in the coffee shop, Imogen could hear the sound of Debbie Harry singing "The Tide Is High." She remembered how much Lauren had loved that song when she was a kid, how the two of them had made up a dance for it, acting out all the words in the song.

"What happened, Laur?" she asked. "We used to have fun."

"When? When did we have fun?"

Imogen held her arms out in front of her like a tide rising, then wrapped them around herself, singing, "The tide is high, but I'm holding on."

"Mom . . ."

She raised her index finger and waved it back and forth in Lauren's face. "I wanna be your number one."

"Mom."

"Nuuuuuumber one . . ."

"Mom!" Lauren slapped her hands on the table, making their mugs tremble. Across the room, Maya looked up, her face crinkling with concern. "You're not listening to me."

"Of course I'm not listening to you. You're saying something crazy. You don't want me to see Maya? At all? Ever?"

"Her name's not Maya anymore," Lauren said quietly. "It's Dove." When Imogen raised her eyebrows, Lauren gave her a wry smile. "It's the only thing she answers to, so we just went with it."

"That's surprisingly . . . flexible of you." Imogen regarded Maya—Dove—from across the coffee shop, her mind fumbling with this new information. She had never thought the girl was a Maya, and her new name draped over her like a blanket, bringing the outline of her into sharp relief. "It suits her," Imogen said. As she turned back to Lauren, she was overcome with a surge of grief for what she was losing.

"Look, Mom, I'm sorry. I just want to eliminate as many negative influences as I can."

Lauren turned away, out the window, and in her profile Imogen saw every person her daughter had been since she was that tiny baby placed in her arms. If, in that moment, Imogen could have foretold this one, would she have done anything differently? She honestly doesn't know. "Negative influences. I see. Well, I suppose that's that, then."

Without meeting Imogen's eyes, Lauren stood and beckoned to Dove, who dashed across the coffee shop and slipped her hand into her mother's. Watching them as they walk out, Imogen remembered how she used to think that men were the ones who guarded their vulnerability, and that women gave themselves away too quickly. How wrong she had been. There was no end to the depth of a woman's mystery, a vast expanse that you could get lost in forever.

By 5 a.m., the basement of the legion is nearly empty. Everyone else has tapped out of their game, and Lulu is at the bar, flirting with the bartender. It's just Imogen and the man in the cowboy hat and Tom, who has been growing increasingly panicked. Imogen can tell by the way Andriy is watching them that he's into him for a lot of cash already. Her greatest gift as a photographer is being able to suss out people's vulnerability; this is also her greatest gift as a poker player.

"I'll raise," she says, throwing ten $50,000 chips into the pot.

At the sound of the chips dropping, Lulu's attention whips back toward Imogen. In two strides, she is across the room, her hand gripping Imogen's elbow. "Chère, can I talk to you?"

"I'm in the middle of something," Imogen says, not looking at her. Yes, it's much more than she would bet on a normal night. But this is not a normal night. And she really doesn't have anything to lose. Not anymore.

"I can fucking see that." Lulu leans in closer, and Imogen can smell the whisky on her breath. "Are you sure you want to do this?" she whispers. "That's half a million dollars."

"It's already done," Imogen says, motioning to the centre of the table. Turning to Lu, she mouths, *Trust me.*

The man with the cowboy hat places his cards on the table. "I'm out."

Tom wipes the perspiration from his brow. Imogen can tell he has a good hand by the way his leg bounces under the table. "I don't have enough," he says, fiddling with his last $500 chip.

Imogen folds her hands in front of her, waiting. She can't rush this. She knows he only has one thing left, but she's not sure if *he* knows it. He sits there, sweating under her gaze, until finally she says, "What about the aquarium?"

Tom laughs. "You can't have the aquarium. My grandfather *started* that aquarium."

"Throw in the aquarium and we'll call."

A bead of sweat rolls over Tom's temple and splashes onto his shirt collar as he regards Imogen, who remains impassive— her second greatest gift as a poker player. Next to her, Lulu twirls a chunk of her wig between her fingers, and Imogen knows she is jonesing for a cigarette, even though she quit almost a decade ago. The room is silent as Tom reaches into his pocket and pulls a large square key off his keychain. He tosses it into the centre of the table. "Happy?"

Imogen purses her lips. "Let's see what you've got."

The room collectively holds its breath as Tom fans his cards out in front of him triumphantly. "Full house, queens over fives." He leans back in his chair so far that Imogen expects him to topple over. "Sorry, sweetie."

Imogen shrugs. "You win some, you lose some." She drops her cards on the table. "Kings over sevens. So I guess this time, you lose some." She finally exhales, her body awash in dopamine. This is what she comes here for—the release, the feeling that she can't get from anything else anymore. And even still, it fades as quickly as it comes, and as she glances down at her cards, she realizes she is already back to feeling numb.

Tom, however, is anything but. His face flushes a deep crimson and with a roar he jumps to his feet, slapping his hands against the underside of the table and pulling upward in an attempt to flip it over. But Andriy is no fool—the table is bolted to the floor, and after a moment of struggling against it, Tom finally gives up. He falls back against his chair, just in time for Andriy and his man to flank him. Andriy puts a hand on his shoulder.

"Tell them I'm sorry about the money," Tom says as they drag him toward the door.

"My lawyers will be in touch with your lawyers," Imogen calls after him.

Ten minutes later, Imogen and Lulu are outside, waiting for Andriy's driver to pull around. The sun is just beginning to come up, and the industrial park is coming to life, trucks and occasional commuters passing by on the road in front of them. From somewhere in the distance comes the smell of commercially baked bread, making Imogen's stomach growl.

"Want to hit the breakfast buffet at my hotel?" she asks.

Lulu only stares at her. "What happened to you in Lennoxville?" she asks.

"Nothing," Imogen says. "I visited my sister. That's all."

"Uh-huh." She keeps staring at her, then shakes her head. "Only you would come to Vegas and walk away with an aquarium."

Imogen fingers the key in her pocket. When she closes her eyes, she can see her: the manatee, hovering around the bottom of the pool, a relic hidden away in that aquarium so that no one can know her owner's shame. "That man did not deserve to have an aquarium."

Lulu cocks an eyebrow. "And you do?"

Andriy's car pulls in front of them, and Imogen opens the door. "I guess we'll see," she says.

Lauren

When Lauren gets back to the trailer, Jason and Dove are gone. There is a note on the kitchen table, in Jason's handwriting. *At the pool. Come join us!*

"Not on your life," she says to herself, crumpling up the note and throwing it in the garbage. Instead, she grabs a bottle of water out of the fridge, holding the door open for a moment too long, just to feel the stale air cooling her skin. Her brain feels like an overloaded computer, a continually spinning wheel on the screen as the processor grinds away in the background. Imogen owned that aquarium and used her entire life savings to keep it running. And for what? What did she think she was accomplishing?

As Lauren closes the fridge door, she hears a noise behind her. Turning, she sees the rat sitting on the kitchen table, a piece of hotdog bun in its mouth, and she jumps back, startled. "Oh, it's you," she says. "Hey, I put out some cheese for you in the sunroom. Wanna go get it?" She crosses the trailer and opens the door to the sunroom, gesturing inside. The rat doesn't move.

"Whatever. You know, you're actually the least of my worries right now. I've got to lie to my daughter about her favourite manatee being euthanized."

She takes a sip of water. The rat keeps watching her, its whiskers twitching. "Don't judge me. It's better this way. I'll just tell her Pebble's gone to another aquarium. Like telling her the dog has gone to a farm upstate." She tips the bottle toward him. "Or that a rat's been set free from a humane trap."

It could all be so easy. The ship will come down and the fish will return to the sea. She'll sell the trailer, go back to Lennox Heights, and use the proceeds and the $25,000 from Imogen's account to pay Hayley. Everything will go back to normal.

Except Jason will still want to leave me. And Pebble will be dead.

She lets out a scream, deep and guttural, that bubbles up from somewhere deep inside her lungs. The rat scurries off the table and wriggles through a hole in the baseboard.

"Resident . . . violated section 3, article 2, of the park charter, regarding acceptable noise levels," she hears a voice say from across the carport.

Lauren clenches her fists and throws her head back. "Are you kidding me? You have the actual charter now?" she yells at the ceiling. "Can you please just give me a fucking break, Dr. Harvey?"

"Resident . . . used profanity. A second time. That's a violation of section 3, article . . ." She pauses, and Lauren can hear pages flipping. "Article 6," she says triumphantly.

"Will you stop? I know you're not going to actually do anything. You're spineless."

"Defamation," Dr. Harvey says. "That must be in here somewhere."

"Jesus Christ!" Lauren jumps to her feet and whips the door open. On the other side of it, Jason and Dove are standing in the carport, wrapped in towels, their eyes wide with surprise. Lauren freezes, then turns around and goes back inside the trailer. "You might have just prevented a murder."

"Of you or by you?" Jason asks. Lauren glares at him over her shoulder.

"Were those the Fish and Wildlife guys here this morning?" Dove asks, pulling her towel closer around her body. "Did you find out anything?"

With her back still turned to them, Lauren begins to put away the dishes that have been drying in the rack for three days. "No, babes, sorry," she says, stacking the plates noisily on the counter. "That was about something else completely."

"Lauren, can I talk to you outside for a second?" Jason asks. Lauren shoves the stack of plates into the cupboard, trying to think of an excuse not to. But there's nowhere left to hide. She closes the cupboard door, then follows Jason outside, avoiding looking at Dove's face. He shuts the door behind her and turns to her angrily. "What's going on?"

"You wouldn't believe me if I told you."

"Where have you been all morning? What the hell is wrong with you?"

"Wait, are you really mad?"

"Yes, I'm mad! You can't just keep running away from me."

"I wasn't running away! I had to go take care of something." How does she explain the past week and a half? She wants to tell him that she can't remember why she came here in the first place—except she can, his words continually surfacing from the storage locker of her brain, no matter how hard she tries to forget them. *Lauren, I wnt a divorce.*

"You don't return my text. You take off to Florida without telling me. Then, when I get here, you won't even talk to me."

"You wanted me to *return your text*?"

"I was hoping we could be adults about this."

Lauren's so stunned she can only repeat his words back to him. How dare he, after everything she's been through, be angry at *her* for leaving? Isn't he the one who wants to leave? Isn't he the one who is running away from *them*?

"We should get Dove out here," she says. "If we're going to be doing this now."

"She doesn't need to hear this."

"Doesn't she? I mean, you want to talk about the dissolution of our family, don't you? I think that concerns her as much as anyone."

"Don't do that, Lauren. This is about you and me."

"This is about our *family*. You want to rip apart our family!"

"Oh, *now* you're worried about our family?"

"What the hell is that supposed to mean? I do everything for this family! Everything!" Her vision has narrowed to a pinpoint, sweat is dripping down her back, and there's a tinny hum ringing in her ears. Maybe she's having a heart attack. She *hopes* she's having a heart attack. If she died right now, here in this carport, Jason would spend the rest of his life wracked with immeasurable guilt, which is the only thing he deserves. "I'm here, trying to hold a million things together while you're out frolicking on a beach somewhere—"

"I was *working*. At my *job*." Jason steps forward and puts his hands on her shoulders. "Listen to me very carefully. You have got to get it together." He pauses. "Did you even know our daughter has been expelled from Worley?"

Lauren laughs. "What are you talking about?"

"There were some girls at school who were bullying her and her friends, so she sicced some apiary club bees on them and posted it on some video app. Then when the principal tried to get her to apologize, she dumped coffee on his lap."

Lauren sits down on the step, all the fight drained out of her. "She told *you*? I've been here with her all week. Why wouldn't she tell me?"

Jason sits down next to her. "She was scared. She didn't know what to do."

"I just assumed all those emails and calls from her school were because I didn't tell them I was taking her out for a while."

"I got them, too. I guess we've both just been wrapped up with our own stuff."

"You have absolutely no right to say anything to me about being *wrapped up*. If I have been *wrapped up* in anything, it's because of you. I've been making myself crazy all this time because you decided it would just be cool to end fourteen years of marriage with a fucking text." She's worried she might start screaming; more than that, she's worried that if she starts, she will never stop. "I can't do this," she says, standing up.

"Lauren, where are you going now?"

She holds her hand up and starts backing away.

As soon as she is out of view of the trailer, she sits down against the base of a palm tree in someone's front yard and types *Dove Sandoval Kazu* into the search engine on her phone. The video that comes up is the one that Dove posted right before the Fish and Wildlife officers showed up at the aquarium. Lauren scrolls back until she finds what she's looking for: a video captioned *Mean Girls Get What They Deserve*. The video opens with Dove entering a school washroom, where four girls are standing around talking. They say something to her, and even though Lauren has the sound turned off, the contempt on their faces tells her everything she needs to know. Then the camera jostles, and a swarm of bees appears from somewhere below, flying straight for one of the girls and congregating on her head. Her mouth opens, and Lauren can sense her scream pulsing through the shot. Two of the girls run away, but the screaming girl grabs the arm of the one who's left, holding her there. A bee flies up and lands on the camera, crawling over the lens, and then the screen goes blank.

I've seen this before, Lauren thinks. She opens her book club group chat and scrolls backward until she finds it: a screenshot of the video, the girl screaming, her head covered in bees. Across the top of the image it says *When the book club suggests a short story collection.*

Jesus. That was from Dove's video?

"Hello! Lauren! Are you here for that drink?"

Lauren glances up and realizes the lawn she's sitting on is Frank's. He's in the shed at the back of his carport, wearing welding gloves and a face shield, which he pushes up as he beckons her over. She blinks slowly, his face disappearing and then reappearing in her vision. She pockets her phone and walks slowly toward him. Even though the carport is crammed full of junk, it's all fastidiously organized. Crates full of kitchen utensils separated by type—forks, knives, spoons, corkscrews, can openers, spatulas—are lined up along the edge of the driveway. A shelf has boxes of pull tabs, rings, coins, keychains, zippers, lipstick tubes, and more bottle caps than she has ever seen. It's oddly soothing, being around all these reclaimed objects.

"My sculptures, like I was telling you. It's such a silly hobby," Frank says. He turns the gas off and tosses the mask onto a small table. "But after I retired I got bored. I tried so many things to keep myself occupied. I built trellises, I birdwatched, I even busked for a while at the farmers' market down on the key." He gestures to a patio chair. Lauren sits down, and he sits opposite her. "I played mostly Jimmy Buffett songs, some Beach Boys, that kind of thing. 'Summery nostalgia,' I like to call the genre. I went by the name Flamingo Frank, just in case people didn't completely get it from the music."

"Jimmy Buffett has more songs than that 'If you like piña coladas' one?"

"My dear, that song is Rupert Holmes, not Jimmy Buffett. The good ladies of Swaying Palms will have your head." He takes off his gloves. "At least with the sculptures I feel like I'm doing something. Making something out of the things people leave behind."

Lauren touches a sculpture made of several spoons welded to a Bud Light can and arranged like a bouquet. "I can't believe this many people bring spoons to the beach."

"I once saw a family bring their entire Christmas tree and presents to the beach on Christmas morning. For a lot of people around here, the beach is kind of like a second home." He claps his hands together. "What can I get you? Lemonade?"

"Oh, no, I'm sorry. I can't stay."

"Come on! How about a beer?" He glances at his watch. "I know it's early."

She sighs. "Actually, a beer sounds good."

He gives her a quick salute and retreats into the trailer. Through the open door, Lauren can hear him rummaging around in the fridge.

"Listen, Frank, I'm really flattered, but I'm a married woman," she calls, then winces, realizing she won't be able to use that excuse much longer. "Also, judging by what I've heard from the ladies around here, you're way out of my league."

Frank reappears with two Coronas and an envelope tucked under his arm. "I wanted you to come by because I have something for you." He puts the bottles on the table, then holds out the envelope. "I'm sorry, were you saying something? I don't have my hearing aids in."

"It was nothing," Lauren says, feeling foolish. She eyes the envelope. "What is it?"

Frank smiles. "Open it."

Lauren takes the envelope and pulls out a photograph of two women sitting next to each other. "Is that my mother?"

"You probably don't have a lot of photographs of her. I know she hated to have her picture taken, ironically. I thought you might like to have this one."

She studies the photo. It appears to have been taken at one of those chain Tex-Mex restaurants—there are chili pepper lights hanging behind them, above a shelf lined with bottles of hot sauce. Both women have massive margaritas in front of them and beer-branded straw cowboy hats on their heads. Imogen's mouth is open wide in a laugh, and she's looser and more relaxed than Lauren has ever seen her.

The other woman has her eyes crossed and her tongue out. Lauren points to her. "Who's that?"

"Carol Harvey."

"Seriously?" Lauren examines the photo more closely. So it was true. They *had* been friends. "Do you know what happened between them?"

Frank shakes his head. "It was only about two years ago, but I swear it felt like they'd been enemies for an eternity. I don't even know if *they* remembered how it started. But before then, they were nearly inseparable. They'd be out in the carport together constantly, playing cards and drinking and giving everyone shit. Pardon my language."

Lauren runs her fingers over the photo. Who is this woman, who sat around having *fun*? With another *woman*? Lauren doesn't know her at all. It's not that her mother was always a serious person, but she always kept a part of herself away from everyone else. But this woman in the photo is so open, so unreserved. Realizing her mother had that in her all along and Lauren never saw it—it's almost too much to bear. "I wish I'd known her. This Imogen, I mean. She feels like a stranger."

"She wished that too," Frank says.

Lauren snickers. "I'm sorry, Frank, but I find that hard to believe."

"Oh, Lauren, she *did*. She agonized over getting in touch with you. In the end, she decided it was better for you if she didn't. There was too much baggage there. But she really wanted that connection back. That's why she was so happy when your daughter reached out to her."

Frank seems to interpret the noise that comes out of Lauren in that moment as a sigh, instead of what it really is, which is the sound of her deflating, like a pool toy that's gotten caught on a nail. He keeps talking but she can't hear him over the noise in her head.

"Frank," she says, interrupting him. "Thank you so much for this photo. I will cherish it forever. You are a good person and I hope that you are happy making your sculptures. But I have to go now."

As she pushes her chair back, she stumbles, and it falls against the asphalt driveway with a clang. "Are you okay, my dear?" Frank asks, but Lauren just picks up the chair and waves him off, shuffling her feet, now strangely heavy, toward her mother's trailer.

Dove. Imogen. Dove and Imogen. Dove reached out to Imogen.

From down the street, she can see Jason still sitting on the stairs in the carport. "You came back," he says as she approaches. "Well, that's a surprise."

She doesn't even acknowledge him; she just pushes past him and into the trailer. "Dove, I'm coming in." She opens the closed bedroom door without waiting for a response, but there's no one inside.

She stares into the empty room. Her whole world feels tilted somehow, like a ship taking on water, listing to its side. From this angle, nothing makes any sense at all. *Dove and Imogen.* How did this happen? And where has her daughter gone?

"What's going on?" Jason asks, appearing behind her.

"Where's Dove?"

"She's not in there?" Lauren pushes the door open wider so Jason can peer past her. "Is she in the bathroom?"

Gesturing to the door behind him, Lauren says, "*You're* basically in the bathroom."

"The pool?"

"I doubt it. *Fuck*." She glances out the door. "The bike's gone." She turns back to Jason. "You didn't see her leave? How could you have missed that?"

"I don't know, I was here the whole time." He puts his hand on her arm. "She's probably just biking around the trailer park."

Lauren lets out a short, loud laugh. "Well, that's just *priceless*," she says. "Amazing suggestion, Jase. Have you ever even *met* our daughter?"

"Laur, I think you're freaking out about nothing."

But Lauren already has her phone out, trying to work her way back to Dove's Kazu. *The aquarium. Dove. Imogen. What does Dove know about Imogen and the aquarium?* "She knows it's closed up. She wouldn't go back there, would she?"

"You know that's exactly where she's gone." The voice comes from across the carport. The hairs on the back of Lauren's neck stand up. "You didn't give her any other choice."

"What are you talking about?" Lauren yells, running back outside. "Tell me what you know!"

"Who is that?" Jason asks, following her. "Go back *where*?"

"The aquarium," Dr. Harvey says, appearing at the end of the driveway.

Carol

GRIEVANCES — SPMHA

FILE #201908

FEBRUARY 28, 2019

Ladies and Gentlemen of the Board,

To begin, a brief follow-up on my letter from earlier this year, File #201903. As you may recall, with regards to the incident on 01-15-19 involving Mr. and Mrs. Sharma and guests at the Swaying Palms Pool and their disregard for the "no beverages within 6 feet of pool edge" rule clearly posted both inside and outside the facility, it was determined at this week's board meeting that water does not fall within the definition of "beverage," and is therefore to be allowed, in closed containers, at the pool's edge, for the hydration of swimmers. I am hereby giving notice that I will be filing an appeal of this decision, in which I will be reiterating that, according to Merriam-Webster (which, unlike the random unverified internet sources referenced by Mr. Sharma, is a trusted source on the meaning of words, better known as a *diction-ary*, and as such is something you should make yourself familiar with if you are at all interested in the residents of this community taking you seriously as a governing body), the word *beverage* is defined as "a drinkable liquid," and, seeing as Mrs. Sharma herself has categorized the water as something she brought with her for the sole purpose of consumption, it would therefore be included within that definition. As you may recall, Mrs. Sharma also indicated that she had a "condition" that required her to drink water at regular intervals. If this is a factual claim and she does, indeed, suffer from polydipsia, then I must insist she be immediately examined by a medical professional as she is most likely exhibiting early signs of diabetes, and should be undergoing treatment rather than cavorting around in a swimming pool.

Secondly, while I understand that under the agreement we made in 2017, I am only allowed to submit one complaint per letter, per week, I hope that you will understand why I am asking you to make an exception this week, as the complaint stated previously in this letter was not resolved to my satisfaction and required an immediate follow-up to avoid further undermining of the Association's rules, as well as any potential damage to the pool property, which we all pay to maintain. And the new complaint I am bringing to you is time-sensitive—dare I say urgent—and therefore cannot wait until next week.

As you know, the property formerly owned by Ms. Imogen Starr has, after several months of abandonment, recently become occupied by Ms. Starr's daughter and granddaughter, who have subsequently been flouting several of the SPMHA bylaws. Over the course of the past week, I have recorded violations of rules related to trespassing (Files #201905, #201906), excessive noise (File #201907), fraternizing with SPMHA staff (Files #201905, #201907), unlawful use of park facilities (Files #201905, #201907),

PEBBLE & DOVE

and failing to adhere to park dress code (Files #201905, #201906, #201907). I have, however, tried to extend my compassion to them and not demanded immediate action from the board due to the sensitive circumstances surrounding their visit, by which, of course, I mean the death of Ms. Starr. I had hoped their presence—while technically a violation of article 4 subsection 1 of the SPMHA tenancy agreement (File #201905)—would lead to the repair of the property at 148 Swaying Palms Boulevard, which I have been fighting to have deemed an unsightly premises for quite some time now (Files #201832–#201847).

I might remind you that this is a persistent problem with this family, and that I lodged similar complaints against Ms. Starr herself, dating back to 2017. But it is my wild (and likely, at this point, deluded) hope that, this time, my complaint will not go unheeded, and something will be done to permanently address the menace currently living next door to me, which has detrimentally affected my ability to live my life in the way that I was promised in the SPMHA tenancy contract, and forced me to, time and time again, take matters into my own hands.

Today, while attempting to prepare a meal in my kitchen (which, unfortunately, faces the carport of 148 Swaying Palms Boulevard), I heard a terrible commotion. Upon further investigation, I discovered an argument ensuing between Ms. Sandoval and a male individual who I ascertained to be her husband, Mr. Sandoval (who, as far as I am aware, was not officially registered as a guest with the SPMHA administration). The volume and proximity of the argument was such that I felt forced to leave my home, under the threat of being exposed to graphic details of their relationship that I had no interest in knowing, and indeed should not have ever had to hear about, even though I prefer to remain inside after 9 a.m. As my car is currently being serviced, I set off on foot, and was soon overcome by the heat and the humidity and had to stop at the recreation hall to take a drink from the water fountain.

While inside, I discovered the younger Ms. Sandoval sitting in the library, alone. Because the SPMHA bylaws state that minors under the age of 16 must be accompanied by a parent or guardian at all the recreational facilities, I approached Ms. Sandoval and told her she needed to vacate the premises immediately and return with a responsible adult. But as I was speaking to her, she began to cry, and I remembered what the "responsible adults" who called themselves her parents were doing.

I know that most people in this park consider me to be heartless, but I will assure you that beneath this wrinkly old bosom there is, in fact, a left and right atrium, a left and right ventricle, and all four of the requisite valves. And so, I made it clear to the young woman that, while technically she was not allowed to be unaccompanied in the recreation facility, perhaps if I were to sit with her I could stand in as a guardian for the purposes of following the spirit of the bylaw.

The young woman did not immediately respond, likely due to the velocity of her tears, and so I sat down anyway, assuming her choice to not immediately remove herself from the premises could be construed as consenting to my plan. But after a moment, she stopped crying and stared right at me and said, "You're a bitch."

It wasn't what I had been expecting her to say—I had imagined her snivelling to me about her problems, and me immediately regretting my choice to sit with her. I must say that part of me was impressed by her directness. "Yes, I am," I said, because I am tired of people thinking this is an insult—my professors, my so-called colleagues at the lab, even you, esteemed ladies and gentlemen of the Board. Being a bitch got me where I am in life, and I wear it proudly. "I assume you heard that from your mother."

"And Nana. She told me all about you."

I could only assume that "Nana" referred to Imogen Starr, although thinking of her in any kind of motherly or grandmotherly role is laughable. "She was a bitch, too," I said. "But you would do well to take anything she told you about me with about a thousand grains of salt."

The girl's eyes were dry by this point. "Why did you stop being friends?"

I will admit that the question caught me off guard. After all, the feud between myself and Ms. Starr was well known and well documented around Swaying Palms, but no one ever had the guts to look me directly in the eyes, the way this young woman did, and ask me to explain its genesis.

And what *had* the genesis been? It was so long ago, I had convinced myself it didn't matter anymore.

"I told her something she didn't want to hear," I said, the words surprising me.

"What?" Dove asked.

What, indeed. I can recall every detail about that night. It was cold for Sunset, and we drank tequila to keep ourselves warm in the carport. Imogen had her hair arranged in one long, ropey braid, draped like a heavy strap over her collarbone. I still had my sunglasses pushed back on the top of my head, even though it was dark out. We could hear the hockey game blaring out of the television at Percy and Maude's three doors down, Columbus at Tampa Bay, the announcer yelling as though the world were ending. I joked about sneaking into their trailer and stealing their remote while their hearing aids were out for the night. Her laugh, like a braying donkey—the absolute worst sound in the world, and the only thing I ever wanted to hear.

How did we end up where we did? Where did the conversation turn? From stealing remote controls, to work, to friends, to family. Family, that was it, that was always it. But when I try to pin down the exact words, my memory always fails me. Did I say *you should have been a better mother?* Did I say *you wasted what you were given?* Did I say *you don't deserve the life you have?*

No. As I looked into this young woman's eyes, the words came back to me at last, as raw and loud in my head as when I first uttered them.

She's better off without you.

I have always known myself to be unlovable. Perhaps with those words, I proved it. Imogen had tried to love me, in her way, and I lashed out at her. But isn't love supposed to be honest? Isn't love supposed to reflect the truth we're too afraid to face?

"I told her the truth," I said to Dove. "I told her she had the whole world in her hands, and she let it slip through."

Dove blinked at me. "She already knew that," she said.

"Of course she did," I replied, but the thought grew hard and heavy in my gut.

We sat in silence for a few minutes. Dove picked at her cuticles, and I resisted the urge to clap my hands over hers. "Have you ever heard of the assassin bug?" I asked, finally. She shook her head. "It kills ants, sucks out their insides, then glues all their exoskeletons together and carries them on its back to use as armour."

"Gross," Dove said. "Did you know that manatees replace their teeth throughout their lives, and the new teeth just grow in behind their old teeth at the back of their mouth and push them forward until they fall out?"

"That's pretty gross, too," I said. "How do you know so much about manatees?"

"I guess I'm kind of friends with one."

Just then, the door opened, and Barb and her gaggle of geese waddled in, squawking their heads off. "Oh, hello," Barb said when she saw us. She glanced at me and then at Dove. "Are you okay?" Barb asked her. "Is the mean lady bothering you?"

This isn't the first time she has said such things to me—as you may recall, I have complaints lodged in Files #201824 through #201850—and they no longer elicit a response from me, other than to mentally make a note for further administrative action. However, I am not going to lie and say that it didn't give me a sweet thrill when Dove stared right at her and said, "Not unless you're talking about yourself, in which case, the answer is yes."

"Young lady," Barb said, tilting her chin to the sky. "My goodness, you are rude. Your grandmother must be turning in her grave."

Dove's face froze in shock. Barb and her harpies walked on and left her there, motionless and expressionless. But as I watched her, the realization began to dawn on me that somehow this young woman had not been aware that her grandmother had passed.

I thought then about family, and love, and the lies we tell to protect them. I thought about all the secrets trapped in the carport between my trailer and Imogen's, and how out of all of them, this would be the one that I failed to understand. Would I have told her, had I known? Probably, if only to save her from having to sit there devastated in the rec room while the Swaying Palms gossips sat in the corner, whispering to one another behind their wrinkled hands.

Then it occurred to me that, although it was too late for me to save the girl from this moment, there was another, potentially more devastating one I *could* save her from. "This manatee you're friends with, did your mother tell you about what is going to happen to her? Something about going to a farm upstate, maybe?"

"No," she whispered.

But I couldn't bring myself to repeat what I had overheard her mother say. Instead, I said, "She needs your help. Now."

"Can you drive me?" Dove asked, and her voice sounded

a million miles away, as though it were echoing across a vast expanse before reaching my ears.

"I can't. I lost my licence." You may as well know the truth, although I can imagine this will lead to much ridicule against me within the ranks of the Board. I was deemed unfit to drive four months ago, and surprisingly, it has affected my life very little. Until now.

"Never mind." She started to walk away, then turned around and studied me. "Nana told me she hated you," she said, "but you were all she ever talked about in her emails. I think you were the only person who ever understood her. You were her family, and she loved you." Then she pushed open the door and walked through it, and I was alone.

So what, then, is my complaint, you ask? How about the cruelty of existence? Its evanescence, its sorrow, its ultimate meaninglessness? How about how time is marching on and will soon leave us all behind? How about the fragile, transient beauty and innocence of youth, and how it will inevitably be corrupted, and no matter what we do, we can't stop it from happening? How about the fact that three words, uttered by a child, can completely strip you to your core? How about the fact that, most times, we will never know the impact of the acts we commit in the world before we decompose into the earth? Or the fact that, most times, the acts we commit in the world have no impact at all?

How about the fact that life is just piling the corpses of our enemies on our backs, higher and higher, until we can no longer bear the weight of them? Or that we spend our lives buckled under an armour made of the things we fear the most?

I don't know what you'll file that one under, but you're all semi-intelligent individuals, you'll figure it out.

Sincerely,

Dr. Carol Harvey

Lauren

The day she found out her mother had died, Lauren was woken by her phone ringing at 6 a.m. As soon as she saw it was Joy calling, she knew it couldn't be good news.

"It's your mother," Joy said. "She passed away." Joy's voice broke as she said it, a crack that Lauren could hear echoing through her mind for weeks afterward.

"What happened?" Lauren asked, her voice garbled and slow, as though she were underwater. She was sure Dove was still asleep, but there was always a chance she had heard the phone and thought it was her father calling on his layover. Lauren didn't want her to hear this conversation. "Was there an accident?"

"No, sweetie. She just died in her sleep. I don't think she'd been to a doctor in about twenty years, so it could have been anything." Joy stifled a sob, and the phone went momentarily silent. When she spoke again, her voice was hoarse. "I'm sorry. I just can't believe she's gone."

Lauren tried to let her body absorb the words, but all she could think about was how mundane they were, the phrases people used to describe something so intimate and personal. *She's gone, she's dead, she's passed away*—they all carried an entire universe of meaning. There were thousands of ways to grieve, Lauren thought, but so few words to talk about it. "Do you need me to do anything?" she asked, while thinking *please say no, please say no.*

The reluctance must have come through in her voice, because Joy hesitated and then said, "No, no. Imogen specifically said she didn't want a funeral. I can deal with everything else."

When the phone call was over, Lauren stared at the wall in front of her, unable to move. She wasn't crying, but her body was shaking as if she were. Nothing felt real—not the bed she was sitting on, the phone in her hand, the air she was struggling to breathe. It was as though everything around her had been replaced with a slightly different version of itself. She was still the same, but a slightly different version of herself. A motherless version of herself.

She stayed that way until she heard Dove come out of her room, walk down the hall to the kitchen, and the fridge door open and close. Then she heard the zipper to her wallet, from which she assumed Dove was taking money for lunch, since Lauren hadn't made her anything, and eventually the front door shut as she left for school.

Lauren went through the motions of her day. Laundry. Christmas shopping. Mindful Barrelates, and coffee afterward with Hayley, who was super excited about her new business venture selling Gordon Lake candles. Every now and then, Lauren would find herself staring at something ordinary—an inflatable Santa Claus swaying back and forth on a lawn, or two birds fighting over a piece of bread—and suddenly have no idea how long she'd been watching it. *My mother is dead*, she thought over and over. *My mother is dead, and nothing has changed in my life, except that my mother is dead. My mother is dead.* But no matter how much she tried to understand those words, she couldn't make sense of them.

"Don't you want something that's just for *you*?" Hayley asked, like a finger prodding the tenderest part of her heart. The candy-cane scent of her coffee made Lauren dizzy, casting her back to Christmases at Joy's, Imogen appearing on the doorstep on Christmas Eve with a beautiful gift from somewhere far away—a set of Russian nesting dolls, a box of delicate pastel macarons from Paris. *Yes, yes*, she thought. *Something just for me, that no one can ever take away.* It was only once she got back into her car that she realized she'd bought fifteen boxes of product from Hayley, with fifteen more boxes to come every month, the order sheet wrinkled and damp in her hand.

At home that evening, she found Dove lying in her bed, reading a comic book. "Babes, can I talk to you for a second?" Dove slid her feet over so Lauren could sit down. She hesitated. She hadn't said the words out loud yet, and she had no idea what was going to happen when she did. But when Dove turned to face her, Lauren saw a scratch down her right cheek, which her daughter tried, too late, to cover with her hand.

"Wait, what happened to you?"

Dove lowered her eyes. "I got in a fight."

"A fight? With who?"

"Some girls at school."

"Why on earth would you do that?"

"It doesn't matter." She picked at a thread on her bedspread. Lauren waited. She knew better than to push with Dove. "They just . . . they've been picking on us all year. Me and Dex and Kait. We don't, like, worship the ground they walk on like everyone else, so they hate us, and they want to make everyone else hate us."

"Oh, babes," Lauren said. She moved closer to Dove, holding out her arms. But Dove didn't move.

"It was okay when it was just name-calling and stuff, you know? Or putting stuff online or whatever. Like, who cares about that. But then today . . ." She began picking the thread more frantically, ripping it apart in her fingers, her voice growing more and more high-pitched. "Today we had the fun run, and Dex has asthma, right? So he can't run for very long. So everyone was lapping him, and these two girls, they started chasing him, running behind him and yelling at him and telling him if he stopped they were going to make him lick all the bird shit off the fence. And he tried to keep going, but he couldn't, and so they made him do it. Lick the bird shit, I mean."

"Dove, that's horrible! Where were all the teachers?"

"They wouldn't do anything even if they saw it. They don't care what those girls do." She looked up at Lauren, and her eyes were filled with tears. "I tried to stop them, Mom."

Lauren took out her phone, seething with anger. *What kind of school is this, anyway?* "I'm going to call Worley."

"No!" Dove reached out and grabbed her arm. "That'll just make it worse." She wiped at her eyes. "I don't care what they do to me. But Dex is just so . . . helpless, Mom. I don't know. I just hate it. I hate that they did that to him. Every time I think about it, it makes me so mad."

Lauren put down her phone. She wished she could think of something to say, but there was nothing, just a big, empty hole where her maternal instinct should have been. She knew she couldn't condone the fighting, but she couldn't help but feel proud. Somehow, despite Lauren and Jason's inability to set any kind of good example, Dove had become a deeply principled and compassionate young woman. And with this realization came a fierce need to protect that part of her, to keep the world from squashing it down.

"Dove, those girls are all assholes. I hope they all get ravaged by angry bees." She put her arm around her daughter, expecting her to pull away; instead, she laid against Lauren's shoulder and closed her eyes. They stayed that way until they both fell asleep. When Lauren woke up at 3 a.m., her arm was numb from where Dove had rested her head, pins and needles prickling under her skin.

On her way back to her own room, she tried to think back to their conversation, to remember how Dove had reacted to the news about Imogen. She couldn't remember talking about it, but she knew they must have. They must have.

Lauren bursts into the manatee enclosure, but Dove isn't there.

It hadn't occurred to Lauren that Dove would be anywhere but here. She glances down into the water but can only see Pebble's hulking shadow against the concrete floor. She runs to the storage room and yanks open the door, but there is nothing but crates and crates of vegetables stacked up against the back wall. She makes her way behind the bleachers on the viewing platform, her eyes scanning the ground beneath them, but there is no sign of Dove at all. Finally, she returns to the edge of the pool.

"Where is she?" she shouts at Pebble. "What did you do to her?"

As Pebble swims away into the darkest corner of the pool, something catches Lauren's eye: another shadow, on the opposite side of the tank. It's probably just her eyes playing tricks on her, because Dove wouldn't have gone in there, would she? She stares hard at the shadow, focusing so intensely that everything around it begins to blur, and slowly it morphs into the outline of a human body, legs and arms floating.

It's Dove. It is unmistakably Dove.

Lauren throws off her hoodie and hurls herself into the pool. The world mutes as the water closes over her head, lukewarm and almost gelatinous. Her mouth and nose fill with it, a sensation of something bright and alive infiltrating her body. She forces her eyes open and, in the light flickering through the ripples, the mammoth bulk of Pebble glides across her field of vision. A cold, primal fear licks at her extremities. She kicks awkwardly, flailing her way down through the depths, arms stretched out. Her only focus is Dove, her body suspended, lifeless, inches above the bottom of the pool.

But when at last Lauren's fingers meet the shadow, she's surprised to feel not her daughter's body, but something hard, unyielding. It's not Dove, but some kind of duct, part of the filtration system fixed to concrete. It takes a moment for the situation to register, her head fuzzy as her oxygen levels drop, but when it does, relief washes over her. She laughs involuntarily, expelling her air in robust bubbles that gurgle out through the murk. Lungs burning, she makes to swim toward the surface, but she is all turned around, and in every direction is concrete, concrete, concrete. Her brain begs for air and she begins to panic, her T-shirt ballooning out around her body, her feet slipping and arms scrabbling against the slimy edges of the tank. As her vision goes dark, the water begins to move around her, and she has a sensation of being lifted, her last thought is that she must be ascending to heaven.

When she regains consciousness, she is lying on her back on the viewing platform, staring at the striped underside of the tent, pool water stinging her eyes. As the world comes into focus, three concerned faces appear above her own, and she realizes she can't be in heaven because, alongside Jason and Dove, she is staring at the face of Dr. Harvey.

"Mom, can you hear me?" Dove asks.

"Lauren, say something," Jason says.

Lauren gives a sputtering cough, and a warm gush of water drools over her chin. "What's going on?"

"Oh, thank god," Dove says, sitting back on her heels. "I thought I was too late."

"Too late?" Lauren struggles up onto her forearms, then collapses back down, lightheaded. "Too late for what? What happened?"

"You almost drowned," Jason says. "What were you even doing in there?"

More gently this time, Lauren pushes herself up. Her lungs and throat are burning, and water sloshes against her eardrums, making everything around her sound like a staticky radio. "I thought . . . I thought I saw Dove in there. I thought she was drowning."

"Me?" Dove asks.

"I didn't know where you were, and I guess I was imagining things. But then I got turned around, and I couldn't find my way to the surface." She glances at the three of them, hair and clothing still dry. "Who rescued me?"

"Pebble," Dove says. "When I got here, she was down there with you. She pushed you to the surface. She even helped me drag you out." She wipes at the tears streaming down her cheeks with the palms of her hands. "I tried to give you CPR, but I don't really know how, so I was just kind of pressing on your chest. Then Dad and Dr. Harvey showed up." Dove glances sideways at the woman. "She gave you mouth-to-mouth."

"It's not something I'm keen to repeat," Dr. Harvey says.

Lauren wipes her mouth with the back of her hand, trying not to think about Dr. Harvey's lips on hers, her breath in her lungs. "What are you even doing here?"

"You drove off so fast," Jason says, "and I had no idea where you went. She wouldn't tell me unless I brought her with me." He rubs his arms with his hands, shivering even in the humid air of the enclosure. "I still don't really understand where we are."

Lauren gestures weakly with one hand, a game show hostess presenting a brand-new car. "Welcome to my mother's aquarium."

His face scrunches up into an expression of pure confusion. It would be funny if she wasn't still coughing up aquarium water. "What are you talking about?"

Dove's eyes widen. "This is Nana's aquarium?"

"Oh my god, so it was true," Dr. Harvey murmurs, straightening the buttons on her blouse. "Imogen told me one night that she had an aquarium. She even offered to bring me here. I thought she was just drunk." She shrugs. "She was often drunk."

"Well, the state has declared it a hazard," Lauren says. "And they're going to tear it down."

"What's going to happen to Pebble?" Dove asks.

"Babes," Lauren says, gently. "I'm sorry. They have to put her down."

"They're going to *kill* her?"

"She's too old to adapt to another environment. There's nothing they can do."

"No." Dove rises to her feet. "That's not true." She turns to Dr. Harvey. "Tell them it's not true. You told me to help her. It can't be true if you wanted me to help her."

"I'm not a marine biologist." Dr. Harvey pauses. "Actually, you're right. There's a lot they *could* do. They probably just don't want to put in the effort or money to move her."

Dove turns back to Lauren, panic on her face. "We have to do something. We have to free her."

Lauren rubs her hands over her face, thinking about Pebble's massive body propelling her through the water. For the first time, she wonders if Pebble has more awareness than they give her credit for. Maybe she understands more of the world beyond her tank than they could ever imagine. "We can't free her. You know that."

"Then what do we do?"

Then what do *we do?* What would her mother have done? It occurs to her that, out of all of them, it's Dove who might know the answer, who knew Imogen best—at least *this* Imogen, this Florida-loving, aquarium-owning Imogen. She reaches for Dove's arm, as though she might somehow make a connection, bridge the gap between them. *What do we do, Mom?* In the hazy green glow of the tent, it almost feels as though she might answer her.

But no epiphanies come, no magical ideas. What did she expect? That Imogen would somehow transmit her thoughts from beyond the grave? Ridiculous. There is no magic here. It's just an old ship. *Her* old ship, apparently. At least for now.

She scrambles across the viewing platform to her hoodie and retrieves her phone. She tucked Moustache's business card into the back of her phone case when he gave it to her, and now she pulls it out, dialling the number. He answers on the second ring.

"Hi, this is Lauren Sandoval. I was in your office earlier today. I just wanted to let you know that I've decided I want Pebble the manatee moved to another aquarium. Somewhere where she will be able to live out the rest of her years in comfort and safety." She pauses. Three faces look at her expectantly. "And we're not leaving here until you agree."

"You're trespassing, Ms. Sandoval. I hope you know that."

"Am I?" she asks. The phone shakes in her hand, and she hopes her voice doesn't betray her fear. "I mean, this place was my mother's, so technically it's been passed on to me, right?"

"Technically," Moustache admits. "But we're putting through the paperwork to have it seized."

"Putting through? What does that mean?"

"It's processing. We should have it in order by the morning."

"So I guess this place is still mine until morning," she says. "Which means if you come here before then, you'll be the ones trespassing." She hangs up.

"Laur—" Jason says.

"We're staying," she says, interrupting him. "I think there are blankets in the staff room. We should also try to push some stuff in front of the door, in case they try to come in."

"Thanks, Mom," Dove whispers. Then, quickly and without warning, she throws her arms around Lauren, gripping her tightly.

Lauren momentarily tenses in surprise. It's been so long since Dove spontaneously hugged her that it's almost like her body has forgotten how to react. But then she softens, and puts her hand on Dove's head, pulling her closer. She knows their fight hasn't been forgotten, but, at least for now, they are on the same side.

Dr. Harvey sighs. "Good thing I brought my heart medication."

Ray

For the next few years, Imogen would show up at the aquarium once a month, although in the last year she came more frequently. She would wander throughout the ship, her camera in one hand, poised and ready. I would go about my morning routine and she would follow me, or sit in the manatee enclosure taking photos of Pebble. I assumed she was working on an article, or perhaps a book, but I didn't think it was my place to ask. After years of these visits, I lost all hope of there being any miracles that might save the aquarium, but I knew I would continue to do my job until there was no longer a job for me to do.

Sometimes she would bring the photos back with her to show me, to get my help in correctly identifying what was in them. They were printed on thick, glossy paper and smelled faintly of developer, and the subject was always some aspect of the aquarium I had passed by a thousand times but had never noticed—a rusty hinge on a porthole, the curve of a PVC pipe, the bent tentacle of a crayfish, the slight droop of Paloma's dorsal fin. I wished I could have seen what she did, that I could see the world through eyes that found such beauty in ruin.

Occasionally, I would even catch her pointing her camera at me. I didn't mind. When she looked at you through that camera lens, it was as though no one else had ever looked at you before. As though she were staring directly into your soul. I hoped that what she saw there was good—or, at least not completely bad. I hoped that there was still some remnant of the good intentions I had started out with. But beneath all the dust and film that had built up over the years, I had no idea who I had become.

She would tell me stories about her life every now and then—places she'd travelled, people she'd worked with. It all seemed so glamorous, and so far removed from my small life here in Sunset. But it also made me feel as though we had a connection. Here was another person who understood what it meant to devote yourself to your work. Here was another person who knew what it meant to search for meaning in service to something greater than yourself.

She asked questions about the fish and where they came from, but mostly she wanted to know how they made me feel. I'd put my hand in the seahorse tank to adjust the output nozzle on the filter pump, and she'd ask, "What does it feel like?"

"Cold?" I'd say, confused.

"The water feels cold. Your hand feels cold when it touches the water." Click, click, click. "What about the action? What does it feel like when you do the thing you've reached in there to do?"

"It feels . . . easy?" Adjusting the nozzle wasn't a complicated job, just something that I did, without thinking about it, every time I noticed it had been knocked askew.

"Easy." Imogen would watch me, not saying anything else. She'd never tell me the answer I'd given was wrong; she would just wait to see if there was more. And there almost always was.

"It feels like I've accomplished something," I'd continue, pulling my hand out of the water and drying it on my towel. "It feels like I am doing my job, taking care of the things I need to take care of. It makes me feel good about myself to do those things, those small tasks I have to do every day to keep this place running. That my job is a series of many, many small tasks that add up to one big undertaking." Click, click, click. "It's silly," I added.

"You feel silly?" She lowered her camera and looked at me quizzically.

"Not about doing it . . . about saying it."

Imogen smiled. "It only feels that way because you're not used to it," she said. "Everything feels a little silly when it's new and you're not good at it yet."

The only time it didn't feel silly, though, was when I was talking about Pebble. I had spent so many years quietly thinking about how I felt—although I never would have put it that way—that it was a relief to speak the words aloud.

"What does it feel like when you're in the water with her?" she'd ask.

"It feels big," I'd say. "Important. It feels meaningful."

"Why?" Imogen asked me once. "Why is it meaningful?"

We were in the manatee enclosure, and I had just finished feeding Pebble. Leaves of lettuce bobbed on the surface of the water like little toy boats. I stared through them to the bottom, where Pebble hovered above the tank's drab grey floor. "Because . . . because she's special."

"Why?" Imogen asked again. "Why is she more special than the seahorses? Or the jellyfish? Or Paloma? What is it about Pebble that makes you love her so much?"

I heard your voice echoing in her words, Rayna. She was asking the same question that you had asked me a million times, a question that I had tried but failed to answer to your satisfaction. But when

Imogen asked me, it felt different somehow. There was no accusation in her tone, no years of baggage weighing down her words. She gazed at me impassively, only a benign interest behind her eyes.

"Because she has no one else. She needs me the most. She needs my love the most."

Imogen raised her camera to her eye, her face obscured by the lens. "She loves you, too."

"No," I said. "She trusts me. But only because I worked to prove it to her. Year after year, I showed her I wasn't going to hurt her. I was going to feed her and clean her environment and entertain her. So she stopped being afraid of me, and started expecting me to do the things that I do for her. I do them out of love, yes. But she responds out of instinct."

Imogen lowered her camera. "At some point, though, doesn't that become love?"

Pebble drifted across the bottom of the pool, and even though she was no more than an outline, I knew her so well that my mind reflexively filled in all the details—every hair, every crevice, every fold of skin. I knew how she was going to move before it even happened: when she would turn, when she would duck, when she would paddle her tail or extend a flipper to guide herself away from the wall.

"There are so many things that will kill a manatee in the wild," I said, finally. "Boat strikes. Red tide. Disappearing habitat." I kicked a rogue piece of lettuce back into the water. "Pebble is over eighty years old and is as healthy as the day I met her. Part of me thinks that, without all the dangers of the outside world, she might never die. Manatees are neither predators nor prey, so maybe, if it weren't for humans, no manatees would ever die."

"I like that thought. That manatees were meant to live forever."

Pebble began moving, rising through the water column like a submarine. "If that's true though, what does that mean for her?"

I asked. "Living in this concrete tub, after I'm gone, after you're gone, after the aquarium is gone? Does she just stay trapped here, for the rest of eternity?"

"What's the alternative?" Imogen asked softly.

"There isn't one. Everything I've read about freeing mammals born and raised in captivity says the same thing. *Too habituated to human contact. Lacking crucial survival skills. Unable to adapt.*" I paused. "She'd never survive out there," I added. "She's not equipped for it."

"Everyone always says that," Imogen said. "But how do we actually know?"

I also had that doubt, still a beating heart inside me after all these years. I knew that it would always be there, but I also knew that it was a delusion. Maybe other manatees born in captivity could be released into the wild, but not Pebble. "She won't survive because there has never been another manatee here to teach her how," I said, quietly. "Because as far as she knows, she is alone."

Imogen's eyes went momentarily dark. She kept her hand on my arm but looked away, down into the depths of the pool. Then she abruptly stood and walked out of the enclosure, her camera dangling from her hand, the strap dragging through the shallow puddles on the ground.

I have devoted my life to keeping living creatures behind glass for humans to marvel at—not necessarily by choice, but it's still something I have grown to feel pride in. But I still don't know how to resolve this. How can I love something so much, knowing it creates such harm? There have been times, Rayna, when I've been so angry at it all—the aquarium, Harry Sharples, myself—that I thought of destroying the ship: smashing it open with a wrecking ball, shattering the glass, allowing the fish to be free. Other times, I want to protect it so fiercely that my bones almost ache with the desire. I can't reconcile the two urges, which live inside me at all times, and every time I look at Pebble, I'm reminded of that.

Watching Imogen walk away that day, I wondered if she, too, had felt opposing forces pulling her apart inside, and what it had cost her. If when she looked at Pebble, she too saw everything she had lost.

Lauren

n the silence of the manatee enclosure, they wait. They've barricaded the door with a filing cabinet dragged from the office and a couple of benches piled with crates of sweet potatoes from Pebble's food stash. Still, they are all on edge. Every new noise—the clang of the mast on a passing boat, a shout from the tiki bar—jolts them to their feet. Lauren has no doubt that if Moustache and his cronies want to break through the door, they will, but at least the barricade makes them feel as though they are doing something.

She watches Pebble floating in her pool. Did she really save Lauren's life, or was she just trying to get her out of her tank? For over eighty years, it has been her whole world. Lauren thinks about all the things that have happened during that time. The world outside changing, season after season, yet everything in the tank remaining the same, a still point around which the rest of life revolves. Different faces peering into the water, holding out the food, cleaning out the algae. Maybe crowds of visitors in the aquarium's heyday, the happy chatter of tourists, the laughter of children. Does she miss all that? Or maybe she doesn't even experience time linearly. Maybe everything in her life is happening all at once, days overlapping with other days, faces overlapping onto other faces, while the water around her transforms, molecule by molecule, the way that a human sheds the entirety of their skin every seven years. Things changing but not changing, moving forward yet staying exactly the same. What would that be like? Lauren wonders. Not to be constantly thinking back over your life, obsessing over the choices you made, analyzing all those building blocks that made you who you are?

"She's not a very attractive animal, is she?" Dr. Harvey appears beside Lauren. She bends over and, with considerable effort, manoeuvres herself down to sit. "Not like, a horse, say, or a tiger. She's not even that cute. Or smart. She's just a big floating flesh sausage."

"Yeah. But somehow it works for her," says Lauren.

Dr. Harvey rolls up the bottoms of her pants and takes off her sandals, then slides her feet into the water. "I bet in some countries this would be considered a luxury spa treatment." She adjusts her sitting position, leaning back on her arms. "I guess your mother saw something in her, anyway. All those photos."

"What photos?"

"Of all this." Dr. Harvey sweeps her hand in front of her. "Boxes of them."

Lauren turns to her in surprise. So *that's* what her mother had been working on. All this time, Lauren has been plagued with questions about why her mother would spend all her time and money on this aquarium. Of course it was because of her work. Of course it was. What else was there, for her? "Did you see them?" she asks.

A half of a carrot bobs along in the water, and Dr. Harvey kicks at it gently. "A couple of years ago, I bought a remote and programmed it to her television. She just kept the volume so loud, I thought I could turn it down on her. But sometimes I would get carried away. Change the channel on her while she was watching the news, or turn the TV on while she was cooking dinner. It drove her crazy."

"You did that to us," Lauren says. "We thought it was the rat."

Dr. Harvey chuckles. "I couldn't resist." She shifts forward, clearly uncomfortable on the hard platform, but she doesn't get up. "One night, she was really annoying me. I could hear her shuffling around, talking to herself, playing this one old song over and over, 'I Only Have Eyes for You,' which has to be the most irritating song in the world, all those *sha bop sha bops*." She shudders. "The next morning, to get back at her, I turned her TV on. I was ready to keep turning it on all day, but for some reason she didn't turn it off. For an entire day, the television stayed on. At first, I thought maybe *she* was trying to mess with *me*, but then it just went on far too long. Finally, I went over. And sure enough, she was dead." She is quiet for a moment, her eyes far away. "Anyway, there were all these boxes of photos around, so I took them. I knew she wouldn't want strangers pawing through them, especially if they weren't ready. I figured I'd hold on to them until Joy came down to sell the trailer. But then you came instead."

There are so many things Lauren wants to ask Dr. Harvey, none of them about Imogen's photographs. *Where was my mother when you found her? Did she look peaceful? Did it seem like it had caught her by surprise, or was she prepared?* But she decides maybe there are some things she doesn't need to know. So instead, she says, "Did she ever tell you why we stopped talking?"

"She might have hinted at it a few times. But I don't know the whole story."

"She tried to convince me not to have Dove." A hot flush creeps up Lauren's neck. She's never told this to anyone, not even

Jason. It's as though the words are bubbling up from some fetid place inside her, where they have been locked away, unspoken, for years. "She told me I was making a huge mistake, that I was ruining my life." She stiffens at the memory: Imogen in the passenger seat of Lauren's car on the way to the airport, the reflection of her face in the windshield, her expression unchanged as Lauren told her she was going to be a grandmother. *You're making a mistake*, Imogen said. *You have so much more to offer the world. Motherhood will take everything from you.* Even now, remembering the words makes her stomach twist into knots. "We saw each other a couple more times after Dove was born, but then I just couldn't bear for her to be around her, knowing how she felt. I didn't want Dove to ever feel like she wasn't wanted." She hesitates, considering her next words. "I always assumed she said it because she felt she'd made a mistake having me. But now I think it was because she thought I would be a terrible mother."

"I don't think Imogen was in any position to judge anyone else's parenting abilities." Dr. Harvey pulls her legs out of the water and struggles back up to her feet. "There's a third option, you know," she adds. "She told me once she was terrified of how deeply you loved, how much you gave of yourself, how hard you tried to make things work. Maybe she was trying to protect your heart."

"From *what*?"

"From this." She gestures to the space between Lauren and Jason, who is sitting with Dove on the bleachers, looking at the iPad. Lauren stares at him, trying to imagine Imogen as the protector of her heart. Jason glances up and their eyes meet across the manatee enclosure. In a flash of sheer clarity, Lauren sees her relationship with Jason through her mother's eyes: irrational, starry-eyed young love that should have ended when her teenagehood did, but instead evolved into year after year of them falling complacently toward each other, never really questioning why they were together, just staying where it was comfortable, each of them filling a void in the other. But wasn't that how all relationships worked? Wasn't that the very definition of a marriage? Maybe her mother *had* been trying to protect her heart, but that was only because she knew she'd broken it first.

"My mother didn't understand anything about relationships," Lauren says.

"I loved your mother," Dr. Harvey says. "And I don't love many people, as you might have guessed. But she was different. She knew what it was like, to be a woman who didn't fit into a particular mould. She didn't give a shit what anyone thought about her. I always thought that was a blessing, but sometimes it also turns out to be a curse." She leans over to unroll her pant legs, then straightens back up. "Besides, the love of her life was a *manatee*."

As Dr. Harvey shuffles away, Lauren folds her torso over her thighs, bringing her face as close to the water as she can. A shiver runs through her body as she thinks about that water in her lungs, the weight of it pushing down on her. "How did you do it?" she whispers. "How did you make her love you?"

Pebble floats languidly up through the water column until her snout protrudes into the air. For a moment, Lauren thinks she is going to answer her, but Pebble just takes several huffing breaths before descending once more.

Imogen

2016

November 2016 hadn't been a good month for anyone in America, except maybe spray-tan manufacturers. But on the last day of the month, Imogen receives an email that gives her hope.

Sitting on the couch in her trailer, she stares at her phone, her mind flooding with the memory of a little girl in French braids watching her from across the table as a chocolate chip cookie melted in her hand. A little girl who, because time is the greatest thief, is now a young woman, with a mind and email address of her own.

Dear Nana, the email starts. *Hello.*

"What are you doing?" Carol calls, through the open window. "It's torment time." After the election, they renamed happy hour, although the purpose remains the same. "I've got the tequila all ready."

"Be out in a second," Imogen says. She reads the email one more time, a small smile tugging at the corners of her mouth, before putting her phone away and heading outside.

In the carport, Carol has set out shot glasses, salt, and limes on the table. They used to buy expensive tequila and sip it, but then they agreed that torment time should be tormenting, so they switched to the cheap stuff. But it is getting to be too much for Imogen, who misses her Rey Sol Añejo.

"Are we really going to keep shooting this crap until that sentient potato is out of office?" she asks, as she takes a sniff of the bottle, then holds it away from her face, wrinkling her nose.

"Good tequila is for joy, Imo. Cheap tequila is for pain. And this presidency is going to be nothing but pain."

As they down their shots, the carport fills with the sounds of a hockey announcer calling a play-by-play. "It's going to be extra painful if we don't figure out what to do about *that* racket," Carol says. "Didn't Percy get a new hearing aid last week?"

Imogen spits the lime out onto the table and tucks her hand in her pocket, caressing the edge of her phone. She wants so badly to read Dove's email again, to let every word sink into her body. *Dear Nana. Dear Nana.* How could those two words have such an effect on her? In the years since Lauren cut her out of her family's life, Imogen hasn't let herself think much about being a grandmother. It's less painful not to. But those words have opened up a whole world of possibility.

"What if we somehow got our hands on their remote control?" Carol says, pouring two more shots. "I bet if we turned down the volume, they wouldn't even notice."

"Probably not." Imogen takes her phone out of her pocket and starts spinning it absently on the table. *Dear Nana. Dear Nana.*

"Or we could just get our own remote and program it to their television. Then we could do whatever we wanted."

"Mmm."

Carol studies her. "What's going on? You seem distracted."

Imogen stops spinning her phone. She debates making something up, but Carol always knows when she's lying. "I got an email from my granddaughter."

"Oh." Carol passes the shot glass over to Imogen. "What did it say?"

"It was nice. She wants to get to know me."

"So, what are you going to do?"

"I'm going to write her back, of course." Imogen knocks back the shot without even bothering with the salt. She wedges a lime under her lips, smiling a green-peel smile, her hands out in front of her, palms up and fingers splayed, like Vito Corleone.

But Carol doesn't laugh. Imogen spits out the peel.

"Don't do it," Carol says finally. Imogen looks at her sharply. "I mean it. Don't."

"Why the hell not?"

Carol takes her own shot before answering. "I just think it's a mistake. Lauren doesn't want you in her daughter's life."

"*Lauren* doesn't get to make that decision. *Lauren* is not the one who reached out to me."

"What's her name?" Carol asks.

"Dove," Imogen says. She flings her lime peel into the garden instead of at Carol's face, which is what she'd prefer to do.

"Dove is still a child. She's not old enough to understand what she's doing."

"She's twelve. I think she understands quite a bit."

"Maybe just wait a few years? Until she's an adult? There's lots of time."

"There's never *lots of time*, Carol, you know that! Anything could happen. Hell, Trump could blow this whole place up before then." Imogen is dumbfounded. How could Carol, who has lived just as much of a life as Imogen, think that time comes in an unlimited supply? How could she suggest Imogen *wait*, after she has already waited so long? She grabs the tequila and takes a slug right from the bottle, the liquid burning the back of her throat.

"Imo." Carol takes the bottle from her and sets it gently on the table. Then she covers Imogen's hand with hers. "I say this as someone who cares about you deeply: you are not an easy person to love."

Imogen snatches her hand away. "I fucking know that," she says, wiping her mouth with the heel of her palm.

"So maybe starting up a relationship with a twelve-year-old whose mother you abandoned is not necessarily the best thing for either of you."

Did Carol just say *abandoned*? After all the conversations they've had about Imogen's decision—how hard it was, how it was ultimately the right one—she has the gall to say the word *abandoned*?

"You're one to talk," she says, leaning back in her chair and crossing her arms.

Carol gives her a warning look. "Don't."

"Don't what? Remind you that you're the one who *really* abandoned your daughter? That she's out there somewhere with her adoptive parents, knowing that her real mother didn't want her?" There's a twinge in her gut that feels something like guilt, but she pushes it aside. She knows she's being cruel, but Carol should have known better than to tell Imogen her secrets. After all, Imogen is not an easy person to love. "Maybe you're just jealous because you'll never even know if you *have* a granddaughter." As soon as the words come out, she knows she's gone too far. They land like a rock, reverberating in the silence between them.

"At least I gave her a chance at a good life," Carol says quietly. "You've been ruining Lauren's life since the day she was born. And now you want to ruin Dove's, too. She's better off without you." Carol stands up and pushes her chair back, staring at Imogen. "You're selfish, and you're heartless. And yet people keep giving you chances that you don't deserve. But rest assured, Imogen, I will not." Then she turns and retreats into her trailer.

Imogen takes another swig from the tequila bottle. "You say that now!" she yells after her. But her voice echoes through the empty carport, the only response coming from the hockey announcer, despondently calling a win for the other team.

That night, Imogen can't sleep. After hours of tossing and turning, she gets up and goes out to her car. She doesn't set out with any plan, but as soon as she turns onto the Tamiami, she knows where she is going.

She's never been to the aquarium at night, and she's surprised by how alive it is. Fish that appear sluggish and bored during the day are now alert, swimming frantically around their tanks, their eyes watchful as she makes her way down the hall to the manatee enclosure, where she takes off her shoes and sits down on the edge of the pool. She's brought her camera with her—whenever anything goes wrong in her life, she needs to work. Maybe in the dark, with just the glow of the moonlight filtering through the tent, she'll be able to capture that glimpse into Pebble's soul.

"If you even have one," she says, kicking her feet lazily through the water as she adjusts her lens. She bought an expensive underwater DSLR camera a couple of years ago and has spent a lot of time with her hands submerged in the water, waiting for the right moment. But she still hasn't gotten the photo she wants. It's like Prague all over again, except this time it's not the weather standing in her way.

Pebble comes to the surface, eyeing her warily. Even after all these years, Imogen hasn't spent much time alone with her, and it's clear the manatee is looking for Ray, the warm, caring centre of her universe. There have been times when Imogen has felt jealous of their bond, although deep down she knows it's because she wants something uncomplicated to put her feelings into, something to focus on besides herself. The closest thing she has is her camera, and as much as she loves it, she also understands it's not the same. Her camera is an extension of her, and everything she sees through the lens is clouded by her own perspective. It took her a long time to understand that her photography doesn't take her outside of herself—it brings her more deeply inside, to the very places she is trying to escape. This realization was, partially, why she decided to retire. She just couldn't bear to look inward anymore.

She lies down on her stomach and submerges the camera in the water, squinting at the display. It's challenging enough in the daytime to see through the murky water, let alone by moonlight. Whenever she thinks she might have Pebble in her focus, the manatee moves out of frame to a part of the pool Imogen can't angle her lens to see. Frustrated, she sits up. "Why are you so difficult?" she asks Pebble, who bumps her snout playfully against the side of the pool. Imogen sighs. "You're really going to make me do this, aren't you?"

She strips down to her underwear and gazes into the water. She's never swam with Pebble before—not because she's afraid, but because it's Ray's thing, and she doesn't want to get in the way of that. She likes Ray, so quiet, so competent, so principled, and so different from the men she's used to being around. No bravado—just honesty, and a devotion to his work. Their conversations have always stayed on the side of the philosophical, so she doesn't know much about his life. He's never talked about having a family, or any outside interests, but she gets the feeling he doesn't have much else to bring him the kind of happiness the aquarium does.

Looking down into the water, her head begins to spin, and she realizes she might still be a little drunk. "This is probably not a good idea," she says to Pebble. "But I'm going to do it anyway."

Imogen takes in a deep breath and steps off the edge. When she opens her eyes, all she sees are shadows. Suspended, she brings the camera up to her face and moves in a slow circle until she locates Pebble. As the manatee swims, Imogen trails after her, photographing hundreds of micro-movements. She may not get what she wants tonight, but she'll be able to study the photos and figure out what it is she should be looking for the next time.

Beneath the water, with the camera in her hand, a sense of peace washes over her. She's going to write to Dove. It's not just curiosity, although there is plenty of that. It's this melancholy she's had lately, a restless feeling that nothing she does these days has any real significance. She wants to write to Dove for the same reason she's been thinking so much about her childhood, about her early career, about Lauren. She tells herself it's nostalgia, but really she knows it's regret. For the first time in a long time, reading those words from her granddaughter, she felt the regret fade away, replaced by something else: hope.

Carol will probably never forgive her. But that's a sacrifice she's willing to make.

Lauren

The aquarium at night feels like another planet—humming, creaking, shimmering, all shadowy corners and strange nocturnal noises. Lauren and Dove spread their blankets out on the viewing platform, while Jason claims one of the remaining benches in the reception area that hasn't been pushed against the main door. They leave the couch in the staff room for Dr. Harvey, even though she protests that she won't sleep.

"I don't imagine any of us will," Lauren says, although once they are back in the manatee enclosure, Dove is out within minutes, her phone still lit up in her hand.

Lauren spends a couple of hours tossing and turning on the viewing platform, having lucid dreams about manatees that can walk, fish that can speak, and every lobster she ever ate coming back to haunt her. Eventually, she gives up and creeps out of the enclosure. Once more, she feels eyes on her from all sides as she makes her way down the hallway, watchful and wary, unsure whether this new nighttime presence is a threat or not. A few tanks are illuminated with a bluish light, but most of them are dark, except for the flashes Lauren catches out of the corner of her eye, silvery scales lit up by the moonlight through the portholes. She emerges into the glow emanating from the jellyfish room, where the three large, floor-to-ceiling cylindrical tanks are bathed in purple light. She watches, mesmerized, as the translucent moon jellies gently pulse together, as though moving as a single organism.

"Laur?"

She turns to find Jason sitting on the floor, his back against the wall, arms wrapped around his knees. His face looks almost ghostly, eyes sunken into caverns.

"Sorry," Lauren whispers. "I thought you were out in the lobby."

"I was, but that bird at the bar never shuts up. Besides, how many people can say they've spent the night in a jellyfish room?"

Lauren touches her hand to the glass, feeling the subtle vibration of the water filters from the belly of the ship. "They look like little wisps of smoke, don't they? Like after you blow out a candle." She drops her hand. "I'm sorry. I'll leave you alone."

"No. Stay. We should talk."

"I can't, Jase. Not right now. It's too much."

He stares up at her, exasperated. "All I want is to have an honest conversation about our relationship. But suddenly I'm trapped here at an aquarium in Florida with a crazy lady and our obviously traumatized daughter, trying to . . . what, save a giant fish?"

"She's not a fish, she's a mammal. And Dove is not *traumatized*. She's fighting for something she believes in."

"Come on, please just sit. We're stuck here together. You can't run away from me anymore." He pats the ground beside him, and reluctantly she lowers herself to the floor.

She can't remember the last time she was this close to him. He's wearing the same clothes he had on when he arrived at Swaying Palms, and it occurs to her that he probably didn't think he would be here longer than a day. She can smell a faint trace of the cigar he smoked in Lima, the laundry detergent they use at the hotel, the hand soap from the airport bathroom—the smell of him newly home.

"Lauren, we're not happy. You know we're not."

Lauren laughs in spite of herself. "Happy? No one is *happy*. Why do you think that we get to be *happy*?" She turns to him, and she can see the scar on his chin from when he fell off the merry-go-round at recess in fourth grade, the three freckles on his cheek that his freshman dormmates connected into a smiley face with permanent marker when he was passed out drunk in the lounge. How strange it is, to know someone else's body so intimately. "You know, for the longest time I thought it was me? That I must be a bad person, and that's why no one loves me."

"Jesus Christ." He runs his hand through his hair in frustration. "You don't even understand how loved you are. You never have."

"So I *am* a bad person, then."

"The world is not full of good people and bad people. That's not how life works."

"I'm sorry, now you know how life works?" Her eyes start to sting with tears, but she rubs them away. "In case you don't remember, when I got pregnant, we decided together to get married and start a family. That's not a temporary arrangement. It's not contingent on happiness."

"Did we decide *together*, Lauren? Really think about it."

"I do think about it. All the time." The sound of the coaster clanging over the tracks, the screams of the riders. The smell of the caramel corn at the food stand, cloyingly sweet, making her stomach roil with nausea. Jason's water bottle, which he kept squeezing and then letting go of, the plastic cracking as it contracted and expanded. The two of them sitting next to each other on the Expedition G-Force at the end of the ride, waiting for the safety bar to rise, their bodies still caught up in the momentum of it all. The idea of the future as this vague outline, something they could mould into whatever they wanted. But what if they had made a different decision?

"I don't regret any of it," Jason says. "I just . . ." He trails off, and Lauren knows he doesn't know how to finish the sentence. "I don't know how to fix anything, but I know we have to try. Because this . . ." He makes a circle with his index finger. "This is not working."

"Why?" she whispers. "Why isn't it?"

He shakes his head. "I don't know. But it's not. And I think you know it's not."

Neither of them says anything else. She wishes she could rewind their lives back to that first night they kissed, and kiss Tim McConnell or Dylan Fraser instead, and let her and Jason just walk home as friends, laughing at how sloppy Tim's or Dylan's tongue had been, how he hadn't been able to find the clasp of her bra. What might their lives have been like, travelling through it together as friends instead of lovers?

"I was stung by a jellyfish once," she says, staring down at her hands. "At Marty's Cove, when I was twelve or thirteen. I was just walking on the beach searching for sand dollars, and I saw this jellyfish wash up on a wave. It wasn't one of these cool-looking ones, just a plain old gelatinous disc of purplish goo. But I don't know, I guess I felt bad for it. It just had no capacity to save itself. I knew if I touched it, it was going to sting me, but I couldn't just leave it there. So I slid my hands underneath it and picked it up." She stretches her hands out in front of her, palms up, then curls her fingers inward. "I can still remember that split second between picking it up and the pain hitting. It seemed like an eternity, and I kept thinking there was something wrong with me that I couldn't feel the pain." Balling her hands into fists, she shoves them back into the pockets of her hoodie. "Then, when it finally did hit, it was like it was doubly painful because of that delay, that split second where I thought the impossible had happened and I was going to be okay."

Jason smiles. "But you saved the jellyfish, though. We watched it float back out to sea."

"Right, you were there. Of course." She remembers now, how they didn't know what to do, so Jason dug a hole at the shoreline and buried Lauren's hands in it, the cool sand rough against the burn, her jaw clenched and eyes watering as she rode out the worst of the pain. Jason has been there for all her mistakes, all her bad decisions, all her flailing attempts at life. How is she supposed to fumble through it all without him?

Slowly, Lauren is overtaken by a roiling sorrow for their past selves. What became of them—that boy and that girl who protected each other, who stumbled together toward adulthood? Was it the mundanity of marriage that destroyed them? The challenges of parenthood? Or were they doomed from the very beginning, two people who just needed someone to love them, trying to force the other into a shape that neither fit into? She gazes at him, and it suddenly feels as though she is looking at a stranger. When was the last time she was able to read the thoughts behind his eyes? Was she ever able to, or was she just projecting her own thoughts and desires onto him?

They sit in silence. The jellies continue to float, their luminescent bodies rippling, tentacles trailing after them like spectral trains. It's hard to believe they are alive, and not just vapour, formless and ethereal, slinking through the inky water.

"How can something so beautiful cause so much pain?" she asks softly.

"Maybe just don't overthink it." He rests his head against hers, and in that instant she knows.

It's time to let him go.

The pounding on the door wakes Lauren up. She stretches, her body cramped and stiff from sleeping on the floor, the jellyfish still undulating on their never-ending journey through the cylindrical tank, top to bottom, bottom to top. She gets up and rouses Jason from the bench across the room. A sliver of light is making its way down the hall, but it can't be much after sunrise.

"I didn't expect them so early," Lauren says softly.

Neither of them speaks as they make their way to the reception area. The air feels heavy and still, and Lauren is surprisingly calm as she opens the porthole next to the door. Clipboard and Sunglasses are standing at the top of the stairs, silhouetted by the rising sun behind them.

"Let us in please, ma'am," Clipboard says. "We have the paperwork."

Lauren presses her hand against the ship's wall, its solidity pressing back. Decades of carrying people, cargo, weapons; now carrying this tiny, delicate shard of hope. "No," she says.

"You guys can't be in there," Sunglasses says, leaning forward on the railing, and Lauren wonders if she is trying to gauge whether she could fit through the porthole.

"I don't care." Jason gives Lauren an almost imperceptible nod. "You're not coming in."

Clipboard rattles the door, which is still locked. "Ma'am, this is not going to end well for you."

"We're not leaving," Jason says. He's still rubbing sleep from his eyes, but his jaw is set and his shoulders are squared. He's as ready for this fight as she is, and with a pang of sadness she realizes she has never loved him more.

"Do whatever you want," Lauren adds, "but we're staying here until you agree to find another place for Pebble to live."

———

Clipboard and Sunglasses glance at each other. Clipboard sighs. "I'm calling the sheriff."

"Oh, you mean the real police?" Lauren says. Jason elbows her. "It's true."

Sunglasses leans even further over the railing, getting her face as close to the porthole as she can. "You'll be arrested for trespassing."

"Good." Lauren closes the porthole, watching through the glass as they trot down the stairs and back to their car.

Jason starts pacing behind her. "This isn't going to work. They're just going to break in here and arrest us."

"Well, do you have a better plan?"

Dr. Harvey appears, followed closely by Dove. They both look far too well-rested—Dove because she's young, all perpetually smooth, elastic skin and bright eyes, and Dr. Harvey because she is clearly a witch, her clothes unwrinkled, her hair as coiffed as if she had slept in rollers.

Jason puts his arm around Dove. "Are you sure you want to do this?" He is asking the question for all of them. And of course, there is only one possible answer.

"What's going on?" a deep voice asks.

Lauren jumps, thinking Clipboard has found another way in, but when she turns, she sees Ray in the hallway. He's holding a bucket and Toby is perched on his shoulder, his long tail winding around his arm. "Jesus, I thought you were the cops," she says, her hand on her jackhammering heart. "How did you get in?"

"The service entrance. No one told me not to come to work, so I came to work." He gestures to Dove. "I saw this one sleeping in the manatee enclosure, but I didn't know anyone else was here. Is that Fish and Wildlife outside?"

"We're trying to save her," Dove blurts out.

"Save who?" Ray asks. Then Lauren sees everything click

—

into place, suddenly and completely, behind his eyes. "Oh," he says. He eyes the furniture piled up in front of the door. "That's what this is for?"

"They've called the real cops on us," Lauren says. "But we're not going to let them in. You should go. You don't want to be involved with this."

"Hey!" Dr. Harvey says. "Why wasn't I given that choice?"

"You can leave too, no one's stopping you."

Ray is quiet, studying the door.

"If you're worried about them seeing you, I think they're too preoccupied with the front door," Lauren says. "You can sneak back out the service entrance."

"Oh, I'm not thinking about how to get out. I'm thinking about what else we can put in front of it."

"It's too late," Jason says from over by the porthole. "They're here."

They all crowd around and watch as several cops get out of cars and walk up the steps, led by Clipboard and Sunglasses. Clipboard is carrying a bullhorn, and he raises it to his mouth. "Ma'am, this is your last chance to open the door," he says, his voice echoing out across the parking lot.

"Not going to happen," Lauren says.

"What's that in that one guy's hand?" Dove asks.

Ray squints. "It's some kind of battering ram."

"Quick, come sit on the benches," Lauren says. Dr. Harvey and Jason sit on one, Ray and Dove on the other, pushing aside the crates of sweet potatoes and bracing their feet against the floor. Just as Lauren is about to sit down, the ram hits. The force reverberates through the ship, but the door remains intact, and Lauren presses her hand to the cabin wall once more, a gesture of gratitude. With the second hit, the benches inch forward, and a crate falls over, sweet potatoes tumbling to the ground.

Everyone on the benches digs their feet further into the floor as the third hit comes, making the filing cabinet wobble. Lauren leans her back up against it, her legs wide, the handles pressing into her skin. With every blow, the cabinet wobbles a little more, and Lauren knows it's only a matter of time before it tips over and crushes her.

Suddenly, her phone rings.

"Answer it! Maybe it's them," Dove says.

Lauren fumbles in her pocket for her phone and pulls it out, then hits accept and puts it on speaker.

"Hey girl! Wow, can't believe I caught you!"

Hayley. Jesus Christ. "Uh, I'm kind of busy right now," Lauren says.

"You are a hard one to get a hold of!"

"Really, Hayley, this is a super-bad time." Another hit knocks Lauren forward and sends the phone flying out of her hand.

"Who is that, Mom?" Dove calls.

"Just a wrong number, sweetie."

"Lauren? Lauren?" Hayley's singsong voice rises up from the phone on the floor. "You still there, girl? I really need that money . . ."

"How does a wrong number know your name?" Dr. Harvey asks.

Lauren manages to reach the phone with her foot and drag it back toward her. As she reaches down to pick it up, the ram hits the door again, and the filing cabinet tips over, falling against her back. She screams, and Jason and Ray both leap from their seats to lift it off her. She scrambles out from underneath just as the battering ram jolts the filing cabinet out of their grasp and spills Dove and Dr. Harvey off the benches and onto the floor.

That's it, she thinks. *We're done.*

They all stand, motionless, waiting for the final blow. Lauren prays for a miracle, although she knows that tiny sliver of hope will only make it worse when the blow does come. She breathes in and readies herself, and she can sense the others doing the same.

But nothing happens. From the other side of reception comes the sound of rocks clicking together as the crab scuttles in front of the glass. Outside, though, there is nothing but silence.

"What's going on?" Dove asks. "Why did they stop?"

Jason crosses over to the porthole and peers out. "Uh, I think it might have something to do with this."

They all crowd around the porthole once again. At the base of the stairs is a group of people who have engaged the cops in a shouting match. The crowd consists of mostly young women and a few young men, Dove's age or older, and a few parents. Maybe forty people in total, with more cars coming in behind them, parking wherever they can around all the junk.

"I can't believe it," Dove whispers, backing away from the porthole.

"Who are those people?" Lauren asks.

"They're here," Dove says, a hint of a smile on her lips. "They saw my videos."

"Your videos?"

Dove's cheeks begin to redden, but her eyes are bright and wide with disbelief. "Last night, I posted on Kazu about what was going to happen to Pebble, and I asked for help."

"Wait, what is going on? What's Kazu?" Jason asks.

"You don't know what Kazu is?" Dr. Harvey says, shaking her head. "Luddite." She takes a surprisingly new phone out of her pocket and begins tapping the screen, then hands it to Jason. "Your daughter has quite the following."

Jason stares at the phone. "How did I not know about this?" he asks Lauren.

"I didn't know either, until a couple of days ago."

Ray motions to them. "It seems like the police are standing down."

Through the porthole, Lauren sees that the cops have retreated down the stairs. Clipboard is on his phone, speaking animatedly with someone on the other end. The crowd has continued to grow. Some of the people have signs that say FREE PEBBLE or SAVE THE MANATEES; one person even has a SAVE DOVE sign, which Lauren finds a bit disconcerting. As she's watching, a news van makes its way into the parking lot, followed by another, and then another.

In a daze, Lauren and the others begin to push the furniture away from the door. Before she reaches for the lock, she turns to Dove, who nods, the expression on her face a mix of wonder and fear. Lauren reaches out and squeezes her arm, then takes a deep breath, lifts the latch, and opens the door. After the dark of the aquarium, the sunlight hits her like a flash of lightning. She shields her eyes and steps out onto the landing. Dove follows her, peering around her shoulder.

"It's Dove!" a voice calls out from the crowd.

"Dove! We're here for Pebble!" someone else shouts.

"We want to help Pebble!"

Dove ducks behind Lauren and presses her head into Lauren's back, her breathing ragged and shallow. "What do I do, Mom?" she asks.

"I think they want you to say something," Lauren says, squinting as another Fish and Wildlife truck pulls up, and Moustache gets out. "You don't have to, babes. We can just go back inside."

Then Dr. Harvey steps out onto the platform beside them, and Lauren can hear her whisper something in Dove's ear. Dove inhales deeply, gives Lauren's back a gentle tap with her forehead, and manoeuvres herself out in front. She pulls out her phone and opens her Kazu account, then holds it out to Lauren. "Can you film me?" she asks.

Lauren nods, taking the phone and holding it up. Dove opens her mouth to speak.

Dove

Dear Nana,

Remember when I was saying all that stuff before about parallel lives? I keep seeing this one parallel life where you and Mom didn't stop talking to each other. It's not like you're best friends or anything, but you come up to Lennox Heights at Christmas and we go to the craft fair at the Lennoplex and eat all the food samples, and we have some kind of crazy sandwich we make when Mom inevitably screws up the turkey she insists on cooking even though we're both vegetarians. Then in April we come visit you in Florida and spend all day in the pool and then eat tacos in the village like tourists. You teach me to play Gin Rummy, and I teach you to play Speed. Mom drinks a little too much every night and gets bitten by a different weird bug every time. You occasionally tell me stories about people you've met or places you've been, but only unprompted, never if I ask. I've learned never to ask.

I used to dip into this parallel world a lot, whenever

I was feeling like I didn't want to be in this one. But now, I just keep thinking about how that parallel-world Dove is going through exactly the same thing I am. Or at least, she will eventually. There is no parallel world where people live forever.

I know you weren't lying to me when you said you were going off on a "grand adventure." I'm sure you were trying to think of it that way. And I guess there must have been a part of me that knew the truth, ever since you stopped emailing me. But somehow it was just a lot easier to keep believing you were like on a spaceship or under the sea or something. And even though I now know what happened, it kind of feels the same. You're just . . . gone. And I miss you.

Anyway, I'm 95% sure I haven't processed it yet, since I'm still writing to you. But also it would just bug me too much to leave everything unfinished. And who knows, you could still be reading this, wherever you are. I mean, I obviously don't believe in heaven or an afterlife or what-ever, but I'm just a human being, I don't know anything.

That seems like a good place to leave it, don't you think?

xoxo Dove

By the time Dove stepped out in front of the crowd to speak, there must have been a hundred people there, all waving signs, holding up their phones, chanting Pebble's name, and gazing up at Dove expectantly. And while she was glad so many people came, there was also something sad about it. Like some kind of boundary had been destroyed.

"I'm grateful you're all here," she said, standing on the steps of the aquarium. "Pebble is special. And we're going to save her." But her words felt crooked somehow, weighted wrongly, as though they were about to tip over. Dr. Harvey had told her to speak to the crowd as though she were speaking to her grandmother, but she had never spoken to her grandmother. At least, not out loud. "When I first came here, to this aquarium, I was trying to find answers. I was lost and confused about a lot of things." She glanced at her mother, who gave her an encouraging half-smile, manoeuvring the phone so she could better film Dove's face. "Anyway, I met Pebble, and when I found out what was going to happen to her, all of a sudden all those things didn't seem to matter anymore." She turned to face the sea cops at the bottom of the stairs. "How about you tell my 800,000 followers about how you were going to euthanize a protected species for no reason at all?"

The sea cop with the moustache stepped forward, to a chorus of boos. "We were never going to euthanize her," he said. "You must have been mistaken."

"So what's going to happen to her?"

"My colleague is on the phone with another aquarium right now." He gestured to the other sea cop, who raised two fingers in a peace sign. Dove turned to the camera in her mother's hand and stuck her finger in her mouth, miming vomiting. "They're working out the details now."

"And the other fish? You're not going to kill any of them?" Dove asks.

"Well . . ."

"Fish killers! Fish killers!" the crowd began to chant.

"We'll find homes for all of them. Okay?"

The other sea cop stepped forward, holding his phone up. "I'm happy to say we've come to a deal with the Cincinnati Aquarium in Ohio, where the manatee will be moved immediately. She'll even be introduced to another manatee born in captivity!" He raised his arms triumphantly, waiting for cheers. The crowd remained silent.

"She'd better be. Because I'm streaming this live, right now, and if you're lying—"

"I'm not lying!" He glanced at his own phone, then climbed the stairs and handed it to Dove. "Here, they just sent the formal offer."

She took the phone tentatively and read the email. Then she passed it back to the sea cop. "She's going to Ohio!" The crowd erupted in cheers.

Dove took her own phone back from her mother, kissed the camera, and closed the app. Then she stared at the blank screen for a moment. Ohio. So far from Pebble's home. Dove wondered what the move would be like for her, whether there would be an opportunity to see the sky or whether she'd be shrouded the entire time, transferred from tank to tank to tank until she was in her new home under a new tent, wondering why the sky was now blue or red or yellow instead of green-and-white striped. Then Dove looked back at the crowd, jumping up and down, hugging each other, snapping selfies with the ship in the background.

Did they do the right thing? How could she ever know?

Now, she waits inside the aquarium, watching Paloma in her tank, while her mother and father talk to the sea cops outside. Dove crouches down and brings her nose up to the glass, so that she is eye-level with Paloma. Where will she go? Back to the ocean? To another aquarium? Paloma doesn't move, her body swaying in the current of the filter, her huge fish lips turned down in a perpetual frown. Under different circumstances, this could have been Paloma's story. But no one falls in love with a giant grouper.

Dove's phone buzzes in her pocket. A text from Dex.

I just saw your livestream!!! Holy shit, Dove, that was epic. Thanks.

She's being abrupt, but as much as she wants to forgive him, she's not sure she can. She did it all for him—the bees, the video. She got *expelled* for him. And it feels like he just threw that all out the fucking window at the first smile from a pretty girl, at his first opportunity to fit in.

He doesn't reply to her for a long time, though she sees the three dots reappear, and eventually, a message pops up. *I'm sorry. I miss you.*

Part of her wants to yell at him, tell him how much he's hurt her. But she misses him, too. And she knows that, no matter what's happened in the past ten days, he hasn't forgotten how she sat with him while he puked in the boys' bathroom after the fun run, or how they locked themselves in a stall afterward and she held him while he cried. He's just trying to figure all this out, too. And it's not like she had explicitly told him the revenge was on his behalf—she just assumed he would know, intuitively. But that's not how life works.

Finally, she types, *My parents are getting a divorce.*

After what seems like forever, Dex texts back. *Mine too.*

Dove stares at her phone, not comprehending. His moms? Divorced? *But they seemed so happy*, she types and then deletes. Of course they seemed happy. Everyone seems happy to the outside world. That's how people survive.

That really blows.

I know.

When I get home can we go to Junkies and shoot things with laser guns? We can pretend we're shooting our parents.

I'd be pissed if we didn't.

Dex and Nana are two of the only people who have ever really understood her. And now her grandmother is gone, and Dex is all she has left. She thinks again about what Nana said, about how the right thing isn't always the easy thing. But maybe, sometimes, the easy thing is to keep fighting, and the harder thing is to make the decision to let it go. And maybe that was what Dex had wanted all along. To let it go.

She hesitates a moment, then types a black heart emoji. Almost immediately, he sends one back.

She opens her Kazu. She hadn't expected anything to happen when she made those posts about Pebble. Even though she knew she had a lot of followers, she didn't really understand that of course people in Sunset would see it and share it with their friends, and their friends' friends, and their friends' friends' friends. Of her 800,000 followers, that crowd out front was only a tiny fraction. She scrolls back to the bee video. As she watches the bees fly toward Chelsea and Madison, Dove cringes at the memory of how angry she was when she posted it—so intent on evening the score, on getting revenge. With a soft tap of her finger, she hits delete. She knows that it's still out there, that the shares and the memes will keep going until the next thing comes along. But if the past few days have taught her anything, it's that she'd rather be remembered for putting good things out into the world.

As she tucks her phone back in her pocket, the door to the manatee enclosure creaks open, and Ray comes into the hall with Toby. He's got his windbreaker on and a duffle bag over his shoulder.

"Well, I'm off," he says.

"Are you going to see your wife?" Dove asks.

Ray touches Toby's tail, which flicks in annoyance. "Yes," he says.

"You should tell her about what happened." Dove trails her fingers along the glass of Paloma's tank. "I bet she'd be happy."

"You know, you're probably right," he says, sounding almost surprised.

Dove isn't sure if she should hug him, so instead she balls her hands up into fists and shoves them in her pockets. Ray turns to leave, but suddenly she doesn't want him to go. "Do you think . . ." she calls out. "Do you think Pebble will like it in Cincinnati?"

"They have an excellent facility," he says, facing her again. "I'm sure she'll be very happy there." He goes quiet, and Dove knows he's trying to imagine it: Pebble in a different tank, in a different aquarium. Pebble being gawked at by crowds of people. Pebble swimming with other manatees. It's the last part that Dove is unsure about—will Pebble be happy to discover she's not alone in the world? Or will she be annoyed at the sudden intrusion into her solitude? Dove wants to believe she'll be happy, but she also knows that's just her human heart projecting a story onto Pebble's animal one.

"Either way, I guess it's better than the alternative," Dove says.

Glancing back at the door, Ray nods. "You know, a long time ago, I promised someone I'd make sure that Pebble would never have to leave her home. But I guess sometimes you have to break a promise to actually keep it." He shifts his weight, and Toby climbs further up his arm. "I just wish she could see the Florida sky, once, before she leaves it forever."

"I know, me too." That's what feels wrong about this, she realizes. "What if we did it?" she asks suddenly. "What if we took the tent down? I mean, if they're moving her anyway."

Ray considers this. "There are some tools and a ladder in the storage room," he says.

Dove follows Ray through the door into the manatee enclosure. The room feels as familiar to her now as her own bedroom back in Lennox Heights—the greenish light, the earthy smell, the hum of the filters. It's so easy, under this tent, to get caught up in the magic or mystery of this lonely, forgotten pier with the fairy-tale creature trapped inside an old pirate ship. It's easy to forget that, most times, things don't get wrapped up in a neat little bow.

She can't believe it was only two days ago that she was begging Ray to let her swim with Pebble. How scared she was, and how silly that seems now, compared to all the really scary things that have happened in the past forty-eight hours. Like seeing her mother almost drown. And having to stand up in front of a huge crowd of people and speak.

And finding out her grandmother is dead.

"Hey," she says as Ray hauls open the storage room door. "I found out where Nana is."

Ray stops, his hand on the door handle. "Me too."

"I'm glad I'm not the only one who didn't know. I'm sorry if that sounds weird." She gazes past him, unable to meet his eyes. It's just so embarrassing she didn't know. And now that she does, all the clues were so obviously there. It's like every single moment she missed is playing inside her head, a montage that just keeps repeating itself.

"Dove." Ray searches out her eyes until she looks at him. "Your grandmother was very good at keeping the different parts of her life separate. Especially the parts that were most important to her."

Dove flicks the edge of her fingernail. "She told me she was going on a grand adventure."

Ray smiles sadly. "That sounds like something she would say."

Dove's eyes fill with tears. She throws her arms around him, and he pulls her tighter into him, stroking her hair as her tears fall. It almost—almost—feels as if it could be Nana holding her.

"Can we go see Pebble? In Cincinnati?" she whispers into his shoulder.

"Of course," he whispers back.

It doesn't take them long to open it up. The tent is rusted into place in some spots, but they manage to unhook enough of the canvas to separate it from the poles. As they pull it back, inch by inch, Pebble circles faster and faster, her tail paddling feverishly, her front flippers pushing off the walls as she ricochets around the tank. Dove imagines it must seem as though they are peeling back the sky. When they're finished, the tent now just a mound of canvas on the viewing platform, Pebble pokes her snout out of the water and huffs along the surface for a long time before rolling over onto her back, her front flippers resting on her belly. Dove doesn't know what it means—whether Pebble even notices what's above her, or whether all this has actually just been for them. She hopes she notices, though. She hopes she knows that someone showed her the sky.

Ray

We're coming close to the end, Rayna, and I feel as though with the end of this story will come the end of everything. It makes me want to stretch out the telling, make it go on forever, but I know that's not the way things work.

One day, several years after meeting Imogen, I entered the manatee enclosure to find her asleep on the viewing platform. There were some candy wrappers scattered around her, an empty wine bottle; her hair was wet, and her shoulders were covered in an old blanket we used for darkening the tanks. I debated letting her sleep, but the pool vacuum would have woken her up anyway, so I touched her shoulder and shook her gently awake.

"Ray," she said, rubbing her eyes. "Is that you?"

"Imogen, why are you here?"

She pushed her hair back from her face and sat up. "I fell asleep." My confusion must have shown on my face, because she reached into her pocket and pulled out a key, very similar to mine. "Don't worry, I didn't break in."

"Are you working here now?" I asked.

She laughed. "Ray, I own this place."

"You do?"

"Yes." She spread her arms wide. "All this is mine." Then she laughed again, for what seemed like a few seconds too long. "I could really use a coffee. Do you have any coffee?"

All there was in the staff room was instant, but she didn't seem to mind. We sat at the rickety table where I did my monthly inventory and drank the terrible coffee in silence. I had no idea what to say to her, Rayna. All this time, I had imagined the aquarium was owned by some government body or some num- bered corporation, and here was Imogen, telling me that Tom Sharples had lost the aquarium to her in a poker game in 2009.

"To be honest, I avoided it for a few months," she said. "When Tom first signed it over to me, I couldn't wait to come here. But then I had to work, and I kept making excuses. It just seemed like too much. Then I started getting notices that the operating budget was running out." She took a sip of coffee. "I was going to try to sell it. But then I met you."

"Me?"

"You just loved that manatee so much." She swirled the remaining coffee in her mug, peering down into the whirlpool as if in a trance. "Do you have any children, Ray?"

"No," I said.

"I have a daughter. Lauren. She doesn't talk to me. She won't even let me see my granddaughter. I don't know what I did wrong." She paused. "Well, actually, I do. It was everything. I did everything wrong."

I put down my coffee mug, taken aback. In all the years I'd known Imogen, she had never mentioned having a family, and I realized then how little I actually knew about her. At the time, the stories she'd told me about her work had made me feel as though she was revealing herself to me, when all along she had been hiding behind the camera lens, the same way I had been hiding within the walls of this ship.

"I get . . . too obsessed with things," Imogen continued. "Once I get an idea in my head, I can't let it go." The coffee in her mug swirled and swirled. Then she stopped abruptly, as though snapping back into the present, and took another sip. "The last time I remember things being good between me and my daughter was over twenty years ago. We were canoeing in the Intracoastal, and we saw a manatee. I tried to take a picture, but the light was too bright. And of course, because it's me, I couldn't let it go. I still can't. With this place, I thought it was my chance. But here's the thing, Ray. I *got* the shot. I got dozens of them. And still, for some reason, I keep coming back here."

"Maybe it's not the shot you really wanted," I said. "Maybe you just wanted that moment back."

Imogen smiled. "That's what photography *is*, Ray. Or, at least, the closest thing you can get to it."

I closed my eyes, watching the lights dance across the backs of my eyelids. Phosphenes, someone once told me they were called. It was probably you, Rayna.

"We tried for years to have a baby. It broke my marriage." I had never said the words out loud before. "My wife, she just wanted it so badly, I don't think she ever really accepted that it wasn't going to happen. It hurt to see her in so much pain. I felt helpless."

Imogen studied me. "What about you? Didn't you want it as badly as she did?"

No one had ever asked me that before. Still, I had thought I knew the answer, so I was surprised to hear myself say, "Yes. I did."

Instantly, grief flooded me. I'm sure you could count on one hand the number of times you saw me cry, so you might be shocked to learn that I cried then. "I've never told anyone that," I said, wiping my eyes.

Imogen patted my hand. "Maybe I'm not the one you should tell."

You asked me for a story, Rayna. And I'm beginning to understand that this was the one you were hoping I would tell, after all my fumbles and false starts. The story I owe you. I wanted a child. I wanted *our* child. I wanted to spend the rest of my life loving a person who was the best parts of us both, who would amaze and confound me every single day I had left on this earth. From the second I first set eyes on you, that was what I wanted. And when it became clear that wasn't going to happen, I grieved as deeply as you did. But I couldn't tell you the truth. Instead, I set you off, alone, on a little raft in the middle of a vast ocean, and forced you to try to steer your way back to shore. When you couldn't make it on your own, I blamed you. But I didn't take responsibility for leaving you adrift in the first place.

Imogen was right; I should have shared my grief with you, Rayna. We should have mourned together. But I was too stubborn. And no matter how I made you feel in the past, me shutting you out was what destroyed us.

I never saw Imogen again. But a few months later, I walked into the manatee enclosure one morning and saw a girl so like her it made my heart stop.

"You're Ray, aren't you?" she said to me, looking up at me with sleepy eyes, the same way Imogen had looked up at me several months earlier. And I knew, then, that I had to tell you. I had to tell you everything. If Imogen's granddaughter had somehow managed to bridge the distance between herself and her grandmother, I could at least attempt to bridge the distance between you and me.

I am so sorry, Rayna. I'm sorry for all of it.

For so long, I thought that ship was my life, but that's not true. You, Rayna, have been my life. I regret not realizing it sooner, and not being right here by your side, where I should have been all along. Soon, you and Pebble will both be gone, a thought that has always terrified me. But today, Dove reminded me that there is still so much life left for me to live, and maybe, somewhere, a new story awaits.

And no matter where I go, I promise you will still be with me. You will always be with me.

Imogen

2018

Imogen has always hated Christmas. It's still a month away and already Swaying Palms is festooned with lights and wreaths, lawn ornaments of penguins and polar bears and snowmen that wouldn't survive ten minutes in the Florida heat. At shuffleboard last night, Barb tried to cajole them all into wearing reindeer antlers. "Come on, it'll be cute!" she said. "We'll take a picture for our Christmas card." In the end, reason won out, although Barb still made them take a picture, the five of them standing in front of the court holding their sticks like they were posing for their rookie cards. Moments like that remind Imogen of why she doesn't play shuffleboard with them very often. But as she walked back to her trailer through the glowing streets of the park, she felt a gentle pulse of affection for these women, her friends, so unapologetically themselves.

Tonight, thankfully, she is alone. She's used to it, these days. When she was still working, the only time she was really alone was in her darkroom. Even when she was back home in Chicago, there was always something going on, some gallery or party to attend, a lecture to give, a man to warm her bed. The thought of being alone terrified her back then. It wasn't that she desperately wanted to be around other people, so much as she desperately *didn't* want to be alone with herself. But now, solitude feels like a balm. Often, she'll read, but other times she finds herself just staring into space, her hand wrapped around a glass of scotch, listening to the cicadas, not thinking about anything.

She is working now, though, sorting through hundreds of photos of the aquarium taken over the past several years and developed in a darkroom she'd rented under a fake name in a plaza on the north side of the Tamiami. She has to choose thirty to send to Fionnuala Meagher, the curator of the Kinghorn, a small but prestigious art gallery in Chicago known for having one of the largest photography collections in the Midwest. For the past few months, Fionnuala has been bugging Imogen to do a retrospective, the New and Collected Works of Imogen Starr. She has borrowed some of Imogen's more famous pieces from the Art Institute of Chicago, where Imogen donated her entire archive after she retired, but she also wants to include some that have never been seen before.

"You don't want them," Imogen told her the first time she called. "They're of a manatee."

"Hold please, darling," Fionnuala said, and Imogen could tell over the phone that she was googling *manatee*. "You don't have any of, I don't know, people?" she asked when she returned. "Or maybe some interesting architecture?"

"I don't do architecture," Imogen replied.

"Well, I wouldn't have thought you did giant sea creatures either, but here we are."

"It's these or nothing. And I mean *nothing*. No new *or* collected."

As she flips through the photos now, carefully sorting them into "no" and "maybe" piles, she's worried she's made a mistake. These feel like the most intimate photos she has ever taken, as though her own soul is completely exposed. All she can see when she looks at them are her own failings, all the emotions she's kept tethered close to her heart, unable to let them go. When her own window of vulnerability opened up, all she could see was loneliness and fear. Surely everyone else will be able to see it too.

But the show will bring in money, potentially a lot of it. And she owes it to Lauren and Dove to leave them something. Her will is a mess: just one more thing she has to deal with, and soon. She didn't intentionally cut them out, it just sort of happened. Along with donating her archives when she retired, she diverted most of her future royalties to various foundations, and of course all her liquid assets had been poured, quite literally, into the aquarium. But this was before she began writing to Dove, before that tiny crack in the door let the light in. Before what she had imagined to be impossible suddenly became possible.

So, she will push through and send the work to Fionnuala. The best photos, though, she's already kept for herself, hidden behind her newspaper clippings in the bathroom. She hopes that when they tear this trailer to the ground, the photos will go with it, along with everything else that her mother hoarded away. She hopes the next people who move here, with their slick new modular home, can feel her ghost rising up from the earth beneath them.

Across the carport, she can hear the faint sound of Carol playing "Feliz Navidad." Because, of course, Carol knows how much Imogen hates Christmas. *This is the problem with going from friends to enemies*, she thinks—the person who knows all your secrets can now use them against you. She misses Carol deeply, but too much ugliness has passed between them. They could never go back to being friends, after seeing what the other is capable of.

To drown out the racket, Imogen presses play on the CD player, and the opening chords of "I Only Have Eyes for You" unexpectedly fill the trailer. The song wallops her, sending her hurtling back through time, and she stops what she is doing and rests her hands on the table, her eyes filling with tears. Somehow, without even realizing it, she has become a maudlin old lady, sitting alone in her house among her treasures, haunted by the once long-forgotten past.

"David," she whispers. She closes her eyes and feels his hand on the back of her neck, the smooth, young skin pressing against her. What happens to young love when it's over? she wonders. Where does it go in the body, to lie dormant, waiting to blindside you in a moment of weakness?

Imogen refills her glass with scotch. Then she picks up the phone and dials Joy's number.

"I'm in the middle of dinner," Joy says when she answers.

"It's 10 p.m.," Imogen replies.

"For someone who travelled as much as you did, you don't seem to have a very good grasp on time zones."

"Oh, fuck." She forgot Joy is no longer in Lennox Heights. It's been so long since Imogen's been back there that it's fixed in her memory as it was ten years ago—Lauren on one side of town, Joy on the other, her little house on the corner, her wild backyard.

"What do you want, Imo?" Joy asked. "My curry's getting cold."

"I used to have this necklace, on a leather cord, that Lauren made for me." She doesn't know she's going to ask for it until the words come out. She meant to ask after the watch David gave her. But the moment she heard Joy's voice, the memory of David morphed into the memory of Lauren standing in Joy's backyard in her shorts and bare feet, her arms outstretched.

"You told me to donate all your things, remember? When I moved, I asked what you wanted me to do with those boxes in the basement, and you said 'get rid of them.'"

"I did?"

"I knew this was going to happen. You always do this—make snap decisions and then regret them later." On the other end of the phone, Imogen hears water running, then a clatter—Joy rinsing off her plate and depositing it in the sink. "Remember Jackie? Your rag doll? You told Mom she could give her away, then you cried for a week when you couldn't find her."

"Of course I don't. That was a million years ago." But she does, vaguely. Or rather, she remembers how easily her mother gave away their things, while never getting rid of anything of her own.

Joy sighs. "I did save a few things. I'll have a look through when I get back." She doesn't ask why Imogen suddenly wants the necklace. She doesn't have to. Imogen knows her sister, too, is hit with these flashes when the past seems as vivid as if you've travelled back through time. With anyone else, these lapses into sentimentality would be embarrassing. But with Joy, nothing is embarrassing anymore.

Imogen hasn't told anyone she's been to a doctor, let alone the diagnosis he gave her. She doesn't know when the end will come, but she can feel it in her body, on a cellular level, like stagehands striking a set—the show's over, the lights are on, the audience has gone home. All that's left is the sweeping up. Soon everything will be packed away, and the lights will go out again, this time for good. She's done her part. Cut ties with Dove, which was hard. Let everyone go from the aquarium, which was harder. The only person she's kept on is Ray. He will take care of it, keep it running until the next owner comes along. And he won't let anything happen to Pebble.

The only loose end is Lauren. But maybe that's the way it's supposed to be. Maybe she doesn't deserve to tie that one up. She could never love Lauren the way Lauren wanted her to. She never knew how. But maybe, during her last days here on earth, she can give her something else. She can give her the gift of not begging for Lauren's forgiveness, not forcing a reconciliation, not playing the dying card. She can give her the gift of letting her go.

Or maybe that's just a cop-out. Maybe her last days here on earth are meant to be spent becoming the woman Lauren needed her to be. She doesn't know the answer—what would be best for Lauren. But there's still time, however slight. She doesn't have to figure it out tonight.

"Goodnight, Joy," Imogen says. She swirls the ice cubes in her scotch glass. "I love you," she adds.

"I love you too, Imo," Joy says. "I'll call you tomorrow."

When the song is over, Imogen cues it up again, and closes her eyes.

Lauren

On the way back to Swaying Palms, Lauren and Dove stop at the beach. Tonight, like every night, the sun sets over Flamingo Key spectacularly, cinematically, and the shoreline is scattered with people standing in little groups to watch the show. Lauren and Dove sit by the lifeguard station—only a few feet from where they set up the other day—on a blanket they stole from the aquarium. A flock of seagulls roam along the water's edge, weaving between the crowds, and Lauren wonders if they recognize them, and if they're going to come back for another chunk of Dove's hair. She has a sudden, sharp pluck of affection for this place, its surreal beauty jabbing her like a finger in the ribs. *This is how it happens*, she thinks. *One minute you're cursing the cicadas and the sirens, the next you're letting them lull you to sleep.*

Jason took Dr. Harvey back to Swaying Palms and is probably on his way to the airport at this very moment. Lauren and Jason have agreed that she and Dove will head back in a day or two. "Then we'll talk, I promise," she said. She wants to spend a little more time suspended in the strange, liminal space of Florida, before reality sets back in. There are so many questions still unresolved: about her marriage, Dove's school, Imogen's estate, Gordon Lake. But all of that can wait. Right now, she just wants to sit here on the beach with her daughter, watching the sun set over the Gulf of Mexico. It doesn't feel like a very low-rise pump thing to do, and she's sure Dr. Lightfoot would not approve. But she can live with that.

As the sun sinks lower in the sky, Dove turns to her. "So, um . . . is Nana . . . I don't know, buried somewhere?" she asks.

Lauren winces. It hasn't once crossed her mind to find out. "I'm not sure, babes. But I'll ask Joy. She'll know."

"I'd like to visit her."

"Of course." Lauren stares out at the water. "You were emailing with her for a while, huh?"

"A couple of years." Dove pulls her knees up and rests her chin on them. "I'm sorry I didn't tell you."

"Well, I'm sorry I didn't tell you she was dead." She means it to come out sincerely, but she knows it sounds sarcastic, or too flippant. Honest conversations have never been her strength. "You know, there were so many things I wanted to ask her that I never did, and now I can't. That's the strangest part. She's gone, and so are all the things that she never told me." She pauses. "So if there's anything you want to ask me, you shouldn't wait."

Dove laughs uneasily. "You're not dying, are you?"

"No. But I could. We all could." Dove's eyes widen. "Oh god, sorry. That's not a very cool thing for a mom to say to her kid."

"You're not a very cool mom," Dove says. But Lauren can tell she's still uncomfortable, her fingers worrying the fringe on the blanket.

"Well, hey," Lauren says. "I had a terrible mother who had no idea what was appropriate to talk to a kid about, and I turned out okay." She watches a leggy egret pick its way between the gulls, delicately probing the sand with its beak. A young girl runs toward it, but instead of flying away, it opens its wings and squawks at her, chasing her off. *These Florida birds*, Lauren thinks. *They're really not scared of anything.*

"But you're not okay, are you?" Dove says suddenly, her voice tight. She turns to face Lauren, and when their eyes meet, Lauren is surprised to find Dove's are angry, accusing.

"Oh, babes, I'm fine."

"No, you're not!" Dove balls up her hands and presses them into the sides of her legs. "I live with you, Mom. I'm your daughter. Do you think I'm completely blind? That I can't see how fucking *not fine* you are?"

Her words hit Lauren like a meteor, punching a crater into the core of her. "You're right," she says finally. "I'm not fine. Things are really messed up right now." But Dove just kicks her feet in the sand, her cheeks flushed, her lips pressed in a thin line. "Do you ever feel . . . as though all the bad feelings you have are following you around? That even when they're not inside you, they're out there floating around in a metal ball or something, and you can't get rid of them?"

Dove stops kicking her feet. "I guess so," she says. "I mean, yeah. I do."

"It sucks."

"Yeah."

Lauren takes a deep breath. "I made a mistake, keeping you and Mom apart." She blinks back the tears that have suddenly sprung to her eyes. "So is there anything that you want to ask?"

Dove tilts her head to look at Lauren. "Do you ever wish you never had me?"

"Of course not. Not for one second."

"You guys always tell these stories . . . I don't know. It just seems like you and Dad were so happy before, and then I came along and ruined everything."

For the first time, Lauren understands the way things must appear to Dove. All those warm, fuzzy memories of her and Jason being young and in love, all those stories she's told, thinking Dove would find them romantic. Contrast this with what she's seen when they're together—the fights, the tension, the tedium. Of course all she can see are the differences between how things were then and how they are now. "Oh babes, no," Lauren says. "You *are* everything." Then she wraps her arms around Dove, who tenses briefly before she begins to cry.

Ahead of them, the sun finally dips below the horizon, to a spattering of applause from the crowd. Lauren keeps holding Dove until the last blush of red vanishes from the sky.

As they walk slowly across the darkened beach on the way back to the car, Dove asks, "So what are you going to do with the trailer?"

"I'm not sure yet, babes. I think maybe I'll come back down in a couple of months and try to figure it out. I might hire Cal to do some work on it in the meantime. At the very least, he can deal with the rat." She trusts Cal will take good care of Imogen's place. And even though she knows the answer to the question of where Imogen's money went, she has a feeling he can answer other questions for her, ones that she hasn't even thought to ask yet. So can Frank, and Barb, and all the shuffleboard women. Carol, too, of course. And Ray, who promised he would keep in touch. All these people who hold different pieces of the puzzle of who Imogen was and the life she led here. Maybe, with their help, Lauren can start to see a clearer picture.

And then there's Pebble, and Dove. The bridge between the Imogen who Lauren knew, and the one who existed here. Pebble can't divulge her secrets, but Dove can. One day, when they're ready, Dove will tell her what she knows, and Lauren will do the same.

"I do have another question for you," Dove says, as they reach the parking lot. "Do you know why I wanted to be called Dove?"

"No, babes. Why?"

"No, I mean do you actually *know*? Because I don't."

Lauren laughs. "Really?"

"Seriously. I can't remember."

Lauren thinks back. Dove was not yet three, her voice still as new to her as the teeth pushing through her baby-soft gums, when she stopped responding to her given name. Every time Lauren or Jason would call her Maya, she would simply say "Dove."

"Maybe you were trying to say 'love,' but you didn't know how to make an *L* sound yet."

"Oh my god, Mom, that's so corny." But she's smiling, and she bumps her shoulder against Lauren's.

In a few years, when Dove is off at college, Lauren imagines she'll tell the story of her name, late at night across her dorm room to her roommate, or sitting in the library with some other kids from her class, or around a table at the campus bar that she's finally figured out how to sneak into. Maybe she'll come up with her own story, a fusion of bits and pieces that she thinks might be true. Or maybe she'll make up something new, something completely different. After all, she was the one who took charge of her own story to begin with, and she can rewrite it as many times as she likes.

When Lauren and Dove get back to the trailer, they find the door ajar. Lauren tentatively pushes it open to discover several banker's boxes stacked just inside. The sides are labelled with dates, in what looks like her mother's handwriting. On one of them is written the word *Kinghorn*.

"What are those?" Dove asks.

Gently, Lauren picks up the box and puts it on the table. When she opens it, her breath catches. It's full of dozens of photos, of various sizes, all encased in plastic. "Look," she says, taking one out and showing it to Dove.

"It's Pebble," Dove whispers.

Pebble is facing the camera, her snout raised. There is no doubt that this is one of Imogen's photos. Something about the composition, the focal point always slightly off-centre. How the light seems to enter from all sides, then diffuse in the middle, at the heart of the subject, revealing it in a way that's both beautiful and unnerving. Drawing you in, and holding you there.

"They must be your grandmother's. Dr. Harvey said she had them."

Lauren and Dove go through the box, taking out each photo, one by one. They're almost at the back when Lauren sees it. At first, she doesn't understand what she's looking at. A young woman, her face partially hidden by hair. A crystal blue sky behind her. A slash of sunlight across the centre.

"Dove, it's you," she says, staring at the picture. Dove sitting in some kind of boat. Dove laughing, shielding her eyes from the sun. Dove somehow captured by Imogen's camera, then the photo developed and filed away in a box. It's impossible. But then again, yesterday Lauren would have said it was impossible that Dove even *knew* Imogen. Could time have somehow warped to allow Dove to be both here and there, with her and with Imogen?

"That's not me, Mom," Dove says, taking the photo from her. "It's you."

Lauren looks closer. It is her, at age fourteen. Sitting in the bow of the canoe, her oar raised and about to be plunged into the Intracoastal Waterway.

It all comes back to her in a rush: Imogen at her back, pointing out the gnarled root of a mangrove, a sandhill crane perched on a shoal, the gentle puff of a manatee's breath bubbling against the surface of the water. All of it, every last detail, clicking into place.

She touches her fingers to the photo. "I thought I had more time," she whispers. "I wanted more time." There's a burning feeling rising in her rib cage, a wildfire spreading across her chest, and she takes in a long, shuddering breath, trying to tamp it down.

"Mom?" Dove says.

"Yes, babes?"

"It's okay to be sad, you know."

Lauren doesn't say anything, but she reaches her hand out, stroking her index finger delicately along the contour of Dove's cheek. As her daughter stands in the glow of the streetlight coming through the window, Lauren is reminded of Dove as a little girl—her pudgy cheeks, her pale, unworried brow. So long ago, and yet there is so much still to come. So much still ahead, for both of them.

This time, she's not going to waste it.

Pebble

First the sky changed, and then the ocean.

Nothing had ever changed, so she didn't understand when there was suddenly a new space above her, the sky transforming from close to far away, cracking open with light. Nothing had ever changed, but now there was a glowing ball above her, and sometimes it seemed like it was right in front of her. She swam in circles, trying to catch it, the way she caught the round thing the humans threw at her, but every time, as soon as she reached it, it disappeared.

Nothing had ever changed, so she didn't understand when the edges of the ocean started coming closer and closer, until they touched the sides of her body, strange and stiff against her hide. Then the edges of the ocean lifted her up and the ocean was gone, and she writhed and thrashed in fear until a hand reached out to her, and soon after, everything went black.

When the light came back, the edges of the ocean floated away and there was a new ocean, but it was different. It was hazy and the edges were gone and she couldn't see the end of it—she couldn't see the sky, she couldn't see the ocean floor. As she hung suspended in the centre, she called out, the same way she had since as far back as she could remember. A sound she knew how to make but had never understood why; a sound that came from a place deep inside of her that she didn't know how to find. A sound that had carried to the edges of her old ocean and echoed back to her: her own voice reverberating in her ears, as though there were another her in the old ocean, even though she circled—she had circled and circled—and knew she was alone.

In this new ocean, she called out. The same way she had since as far back as she could remember. She called out. And waited for the echo.

And then, through the dark: not an echo. An answer.

Acknowledgments

Once again, I don't know how to even begin properly thanking my editor, the extraordinary Anita Chong. Working with Anita has been one of my life's greatest gifts, and I am full of gratitude for her brilliance, her clear-eyed vision, her kindness and generosity, and her unending patience and support.

I'm grateful to the exceptional team who made this book possible: my amazing agent, Chris Bucci; publicist extraordinaire Ruta Liormonas; the team at McClelland & Stewart and Penguin Random House Canada, including Stephanie Sinclair, Jared Bland, Sarah Howland, Tonia Addison, Kimberlee Kemp, Kim Kandravy, Jenna Cann, Erin Cooper, and Sofia Ramirez, as well as Gemma Wain and Eleanor Gasparik. Special thanks to the talented Kelly Hill for the gorgeous cover and interior design.

Huge thanks to all my people: Kirsti MacKenzie, Naben Ruthnum, Matthew J. Trafford, Kris Bertin, Kevin Hardcastle, Christine Miscione, Katie Boland, Peter and Natalie Smyk,

Jeff Nichols, Andrea Novoa, Taslim Alani-Verjee, Martha
Hunter, Laura Hanson, Tova Rosenberg, Sofia Leibovics and
Jamie Leibovics, Martha Sharpe, Rudrapriya Rathore, Dominik
Parisien, Jen Albert, Eden Boudreau, and Ed and Shelley Sullivan.
Thank you especially to my family: my parents, Richard Jones and
Shelagh Hagen, without whom I would never have met any mana-
tees at all, and my sister, Dr. Erin Jones, who taught me everything
I know about the human/non-human animal relationship (which
is only a drop in the ocean compared to how much *she* knows).

Thank you to the residents at South Winds Mobile Home
Association in Sarasota, Florida (including my late grandpar-
ents, Helen and R.H. Jones, and my uncles and aunts, Robert
and Marlyng Jones and Gordon and Sarah Jones), Randall
Buskirk and Penny Billings, Captain Misty and Ray at Crystal
River Adventure Center, the staff at the Siesta Key Oyster Bar,
and all the people of Florida fighting the good fight.

I also want to thank all my favourite manatees (although
really, they're all my favourites): Hugh and Buffet at the Mote
Marine Laboratory & Aquarium in Sarasota, Florida; Betsy
and Ariel at Homosassa Springs Wildlife State Park; and the
late Snooty at The Bishop Museum for Science and Nature in
Bradenton, Florida. I am also indebted to Craig Pittman and
his book *Manatee Insanity* (University Press of Florida, 2010),
Kristen Arnett and her essay "The Problem with Writing About
Florida" (LitHub, 2017), as well as the research and advocacy of
Save the Manatee Club. And a special shout-out to the guy at the
kayak rental place on Lido Key all those years ago who said, "Hey,
we just saw a manatee over there if you want to go check it out."

And, as always, thank you to my husband, Andrew, and Iggy,
my little landatee. You are the greatest loves of my life.

An unprecedented number of Florida manatees have died
in the past few years due to starvation caused by poor water

quality and algae blooms that have depleted seagrass beds in prime foraging areas. Under the federal Endangered Species Act, the U.S. Fish & Wildlife Service and the Florida Fish and Wildlife Conservation Commission currently list manatees as threatened. To learn more about how you can help, please visit savethemanatee.org.